PASSIONATE SURRENDER

Samantha's choked cry escaped, and she collapsed in Jack's arms. He caught her, then carried her across the room in two swift strides and set her upon the immense feather bed. He sat beside her and pulled her close. He touched her face, traced his fingers across her eyelids, her cheeks, her mouth. She turned her lips into his hand and kissed his palm, her hand cradling his, her eyes closed. Jack shivered at the feel of her mouth on his skin.

He brushed a soft curl from her cheek. The touch of her hair against his skin aroused Jack more than he could have dreamed. Soft. So soft. After denying himself so long, Jack submerged both h̲___ ̲__ ̲ Saman-tha's wealth of dark cu___ _____ finding and loosening _____ n to the floor. He lowe_ _____ Saman-tha's hair spill _____ t him, surrounding him

Abilene Gamble

Margaret Conlan

JOVE BOOKS, NEW YORK

ABILENE GAMBLE

A Jove Book / published by arrangement with
the author

PRINTING HISTORY
Jove edition / August 1995

ISBN: 0-515-11685-8

A JOVE BOOK®
Jove Books are published by The Berkley Publishing Group,
200 Madison Avenue, New York, New York 10016.
JOVE and the "J" design are trademarks
belonging to Jove Publications, Inc.

PRINTED IN THE UNITED STATES OF AMERICA

10 9 8 7 6 5 4 3 2 1

ACKNOWLEDGMENTS

This is my first novel, and there are some very special people I would like to thank.

My husband, Jorge, who has loved and believed in me all these years. I couldn't have done it without you.

My four daughters, Christine, Melissa, Serena, and Maria, who never doubted "Mom's Dream" and never failed to encourage me.

My mother, Benny, who always supported me no matter what. Thanks, Mom.

My critique group, the four most demanding ladies this side of the Mississippi. Jessie, Denee, Mary, and Barbara—you know what this means to me. You never accepted less than my best. Thank you from the bottom of my heart.

My agent, Laura Blake, whose unswerving support and belief in me means more than I can say.

My editor, Judith Stern, who turned my dream into reality.

And to Maggie Osborne, a wonderful writer and a very classy lady. Without her hard-hitting advice—and a well-aimed kick in the rear—this novel might never have been written.

Chapter

1

1871 Savannah

Samantha Winchester glared into William Eustice's leering, grizzled face. It was all she could do to keep from slapping the old moonshiner-turned-tax-collector. "Get off my front step, Eustice. My family owns this property until tomorrow." Standing her ground, Samantha searched behind her for the door handle. At least she would have the satisfaction of slamming the door in his ugly face.

Eustice's beefy arm shot out and blocked her retreat. A sinister light lit up his bloodshot eyes as he maneuvered Samantha between the brick and himself. "You ain't gonna slip away this time, missy." He grinned. "You and I both know that old Yankee blowhard ain't gonna meet your price. He's tighter'n a wad of Carolina chew. You're gonna come up short this time, for sure," he taunted, his cracked lips stretching into a yellow-toothed smile. "How you gonna pay that tax bill *then*?" His hand reached out to touch a lock of deep red-brown hair that curved beside her cheek. Samantha recoiled from the nearness of his fingers, and Eustice gave a low, scratchy laugh deep in his throat.

The stink of his stale whiskey breath nearly gagged her, but Samantha forced herself to stare into his hated face again. She'd be damned if she'd let him see he frightened her. William Eustice had swooped down on her family the day the very first carpetbagger crossed the Georgia state line, and he had not left them alone since. With the unerring sense of a predator, Eustice always knew the worst possible time to appear at the Winchester doorstep with a new tax assessment. Striving to stay one step ahead of him, Samantha had sold everything of value her family owned. Meanwhile, William Eustice watched and waited—waited for her to run out of things to sell. Samantha sensed that was when he would swoop down for her. She could see it in his eyes.

Samantha clenched both fists behind her, digging her nails into her palms. She'd like to scratch out his eyes that very minute, but she wasn't about to give Eustice the satisfaction. He'd haul her up before some little puppet of a Reconstruction magistrate, who'd probably side with Eustice and throw her into jail for assault. The thought of being locked in a cell where she couldn't get out, but Eustice could get in, made Samantha's blood run cold. "You'll get your money," she said at last. "Just like you always have."

Eustice leaned his face even closer, his arm blocking any move on her part. "Well, just in case you fall a little short, don't you worry none, hear? Ol' Eustice can be real accommodatin'. I'll find a way for you to work it off. A little at a time. So that family of yours won't go without, ya understand?"

Samantha felt his foul breath leave a film upon her cheek, and she flattened against the wall in disgust. "I understand perfectly, Eustice," she said between clenched teeth. "Now, leave what is still my doorstep this minute."

Eustice snickered in reply and pressed Samantha against

the brick, placing his hand beside her bosom. "Don't you worry none, missy. Ol' Eustice will take real good care of you," his whiskey voice taunted. "A whole lot better than that pasty-faced little pup of a husband ever did." His fingers insolently traced her cheek.

At the touch of William Eustice's hand, Samantha lost control. She slammed her foot down hard on his and shoved against his chest. "Get your hands *off* me!"

Eustice let out a yelp of pain and loosened his grip just long enough for Samantha to grab for the door handle. "Not so fast, you little hellcat! You're gonna give ol' Eustice a kiss!" he swore, his face flushed with the chase. One long arm reached out to snatch her back.

Samantha struggled in the restraint of his arms, trying to break free. She was about to dig her nails into his eyes at last when Eustice suddenly screwed up his face in pain and loosened his hold.

"Let her *go*! Let her *go*! You let my mother *go*!" a shrill, small voice screamed beside her skirts.

Samantha wrenched her arms free and looked down to see her son Davy kicking Eustice's shins.

Eustice let out a curse and snatched Davy by the back of his shirt, yanking him up off the ground. "Well, well . . . looky what we got here!" Eustice dangled the struggling little boy in the air. "Looks mighty like a little Johnny Reb to me."

Samantha flew at Eustice like a hawk, grabbing her wildly flailing nine-year-old son from his grasp. "Don't you touch him, William Eustice, or I'll scratch your eyes out!"

"I can't wait, missy!" Eustice cackled in reply, watching Samantha kneel beside her son and embrace him. Davy threw his small arms around his mother's neck and glared belligerently back at Eustice.

Samantha Winchester slowly stood and eyed her family's tormentor. Holding Davy close, she fixed William Eustice with a hard glare. "You'll get your money tomorrow, Eustice. Until then, get off my property. *Now!*"

Eustice gave a derisive snort, then spat onto the step. "Until tomorrow, then, missy. And not a day later," he warned, then turned and swaggered out the gate of Samantha's small front yard, slamming the wrought iron behind him.

She watched until he disappeared around the corner, the dark green spread of the magnolia trees obscuring his hulking figure. Eustice's stench overpowered even the heady perfume from the trees' waxy white blossoms. Her shoulders sagged with relief. She reached down and tousled Davy's light brown hair, so fine and soft, just like his father's. "Let's go inside and see if Mr. Turner has finished," she said, forcing the remnants of fear from her voice for her son's sake.

Samantha searched through the empty foyer for the plump figure of Joseph Turner, the appraiser. He was nowhere in sight. She grasped Davy's small, damp hand and led the way through the front hallway, heading for the kitchen and the one person who always knew where everybody was, or should be. Maysie. Before Samantha even got to the kitchen doorway, she was met by the elderly cook herself, broom in hand. Maysie's chocolate-colored face screwed up in aggravation while she fixed Samantha with a no-nonsense look.

"If that man opens my cupboards one more time, I'll swat him with this here broom. I swear I will!"

Samantha looked past her family's most devoted servant into the kitchen. There was rotund Mr. Turner measuring walls, scribbling on his notepad, unperturbed. She caught Maysie's eye and muttered, "I don't care if you have to swallow your tongue to do it, Maysie, but be nice. *Please!* If we don't get a fair offer, we won't have enough to buy train tickets."

Maysie screwed up her face in disgust and aimed a swat at an invisible behind with her broom. "Humph! Well, he'd better keep his tongue to hisself, then," she warned anew. "If he says 'peelin' paint' one more time ...!" Maysie glanced down at the small, quiet boy standing beside his mother. "And what's this I see?" She lifted Davy's little pointed chin in her worn, pink palm. "What's the matter with that eye, young man?"

Davy tried unsuccessfully to turn his face and the bluish eye away from Maysie's scrutiny. "It's ... nothing," he murmured.

Immediately Samantha sank to her knees beside him, an irrational flood of guilt sweeping through her. She hadn't even noticed Davy's eye, the confrontation with Eustice had distracted her so. What kind of mother was she? She made up for her previous inattention by consoling him profusely now. "Oh, Davy, what happened? Was it those Yankee boys again? Those Brewsters?"

"Yes'm. And Billy Richards, too." The small face nodded before bright blue eyes found hers. "But I got Johnny Brewster in the *nose* this time!"

"Davy! I've told you not to walk past their houses. They're nothing but troublemakers," Samantha chided as her heart gave a little squeeze. When her Savannah neighbors had lost their homes to the tax assessor, Davy had lost his playmates as well. Now Yankee opportunists and bullies surrounded the Winchesters' red brick home on Monterey Square. "I want you to stay out of trouble, do you hear? We'll be leaving soon, God willing. Would you do Mama a favor and stay away from those bullies, please?" she wheedled, watching a chastened Davy squirm uncomfortably in her grasp.

"But, Mama . . . I can't let 'em get away with saying things like that, can I?" He lifted pleading eyes to hers. "They called me a traitor . . . a dirty reb . . . and . . . and they said my daddy was a *coward*! He wasn't! You told me he died at Shiloh. I can't let 'em say something like that, can I?"

Samantha felt a little tug on her heart when she looked down into Davy's face, so like his father's. Paul had had those same huge, innocent, bewildered blue eyes. Much too innocent to be sent to war. Much too innocent to return. She straightened her spine and spoke evenly to her son. "Your father was a brave, brave soldier, Davy. He fought honorably for the Confederacy. He fell at Shiloh, protecting the men under his command. You should be very proud of him. I know *I* am."

She gazed deeply into her son's eyes, trying her best to imprint a memory of the father he would never know, deliberately ignoring her own twinge of regret. She'd barely begun to know her bridegroom herself when Paul had ridden so proudly off to war, new gray uniform much too large for his youthful frame. Childhood acquaintances for years. Newlyweds for days. And then he was gone. Leaving her only this tousle-haired gift as a memory.

Davy's worried brow lost its crease, and Samantha forced a smile. "Why don't you go and see if you can help Becky with supper? I'm sure she could use your help out back, peeling potatoes. I need to talk with Mr. Turner."

"Potatoes *again*?" Davy wrinkled up his slender face so that the tiny brown freckles sprinkled across his nose all squeezed together.

"That's enough out of you, young man," Maysie scolded. "You just be thankful we got that. And when you're finished peelin' potatoes, you can help me with the turnip greens.''

Davy's freckled mask screwed up again, but he replied, ''Yes'm,'' and marched stoically out the back door. Samantha felt her heart give another tug as she watched his too-short pants hitch up on his legs. She and Maysie could mend all the holes, but they surely couldn't stop Davy from growing. And there hadn't been money for new clothes in two years.

Samantha noticed Joseph Turner standing in the midst of their bare but immaculate kitchen, busily scribbling away in his notebook. ''Well, I'll find out if Mr. Turner and I are even close in our estimates. Keep your fingers crossed.'' She flashed a grim little smile at Maysie. ''The county says we owe seven thousand five hundred dollars, and this house is worth eight thousand without the furniture . . . what's left of it. Surely he'll admit to that,'' Samantha said, as much to herself as anyone.

''What happens if he don't?'' Maysie probed thoughtfully. ''Where in the world will you find money for tickets then?'' Her soft brown eyes clouded with obvious concern as she slowly wagged her head. ''Miz Sam, give up this foolishness 'bout goin' out West.'' Maysie's broom jerked in a westerly direction. ''Why don't we just head on up to Virginia with Mr. Winchester's family? Don't need no train to get there. We don't belong out West in some godforsaken place.''

Samantha stared down into those dark, compassionate eyes. Eyes that had watched and endured and suffered all the hardships her family had encountered since the war. She let out a deep sigh as she tried to explain what was in her heart. ''Maysie, I've told you. Paul's family is completely wiped out. They're struggling, living hand-to-mouth, just like we are. I cannot in all good conscience add to their

burden. There's nothing for us in Virginia. Only more dep-
rivation and want. The only place we have a chance to start
fresh is out West.'' Her hand gestured to the afternoon sky.
''Where we'll be free and we won't have to bend to *any*
man. Don't you see, Maysie? We won't be the vanquished
enemy out there. No more carpetbaggers pushing us off the
sidewalks. And no more bullies to taunt my son.'' Samantha's face took on an excited glow.

Maysie held her tongue and frowned. ''You got your
mind set already, I can tell. Well, all I can say is I'm glad
your mama ain't alive to see what you're doin'. Draggin'
what's left of this family into some heathen land. And
you . . . answerin' a public advertisement. For *wages*!''
Maysie's gray-curled head wagged again.

Samantha had to smile, even though she knew Maysie
was trying her best to scold her for her horrifying breach
of propriety. Working in an office for hire. Unthinkable.
But Samantha had long ago stopped caring what people
thought, whether they were relatives or members of the
dwindling population of old Savannah. She'd turned her
back on them when she started helping her father run his
shipping business during the war. ''Kansas may be rough
around the edges, Maysie, but I doubt that it's heathen,''
she said, smiling.

Maysie cocked a skeptical brow. ''You think this Jack
Barnett will be so rough around the edges he won't notice
you're a *woman*? What do you think he'll say to that?''

Samantha's smile disappeared. That same worry had
nagged her daily since the letter arrived two weeks ago
informing her she'd been hired for the position. What
would happen when this Barnett found out the truth? Would
he be as shocked as everyone in Savannah had been when
she'd asked for employment? Would he be furious at her
presumption? Or would he laugh in her face? Samantha

closed her eyes and chased away the disturbing thoughts. It was too late to think about it now. After tomorrow, her family wouldn't even have a roof over their heads. It would belong to Mr. Turner. The only future for them lay in Abilene. And Mr. Barnett, well . . . she'd *make* him want her. She'd convince him that she was the best bookkeeper he would ever find. She fixed Maysie with a determined gaze. "I'm going to rely on his sense of fairness. And if that fails, I'll throw myself on his mercy."

Maysie opened her mouth, ready to scold again, when Joseph Turner's high-pitched voice said loudly, "Mrs. Winchester, may I have a word with you?"

Samantha quickly turned to see Turner approach, a large notebook open in his hands. "Of course, Mr. Turner," she replied.

Joseph Turner pulled a large white handkerchief from the pocket of his swallowtail coat and mopped his forehead and receding hairline. "Goodness, I'd forgotten how humid these Georgia summers could be." He cleared his throat as he tucked the handkerchief away. "Well, Mrs. Winchester, I think that I've covered everything—unless you have any more furniture stored away somewhere. Frankly I was hoping to see more." His observant eyes scanned the nearly empty rooms.

Samantha gave a wan smile. She remembered when her father's Savannah town house had been bursting at the seams with furniture. Fine family heirlooms. Treasures from the Orient that his merchant fleet had brought home. All gone. "No, Mr. Turner. What you see is all we have left. We've had to sell practically everything just to keep up with the constantly rising taxes."

"Well, that's too bad, Mrs. Winchester," he tsked matter-of-factly. "I was surely hoping to see more. Of course, those few antiques of yours are fine pieces, indeed.'' His beady eyes shot over to her father's 150-year-old writing desk.

Samantha's gaze narrowed on the greedy little man, but her voice betrayed no sign of the contempt she felt at the thought of Turner possessing her father's pride and joy. ''Yes, they are, Mr. Turner. Now, sir, what is your total assessment, if I may ask?''

Turner stared down at the notebook he kept close to his chest. ''I'm afraid I couldn't go any higher than seven thousand three hundred dollars, Mrs. Winchester. Not with what I've seen. Paint peeling, walls cracked, almost empty of furniture.'' He pursed his lips.

Despite herself, Samantha couldn't keep her shocked reaction from showing. ''Mr. Turner!'' she cried, aghast. ''You cannot be serious! Why, this house is one of the most beautiful homes in Savannah. It's worth over eight thousand, and you know it.''

''Not to me, Mrs. Winchester,'' he replied with a raised brow. ''But perhaps you can find one of your old Savannah families willing to pay your price,'' he suggested with a sly smile.

Samantha's mouth tightened into a hard line. ''You know as well as I do, Mr. Turner, that the families left in this city can't even afford to keep their own homes, let alone buy others.'' Her voice was filled with an unladylike coldness. She, too, was glad her mother wasn't alive to hear her. ''Only outsiders like you have the money. You're forgetting, *we* are the conquered.''

''Yes, I realize these are difficult times, Mrs. Winchester. Difficult times, indeed. But business is business, after all. Then again, you're familiar with that, I imagine.'' He paged through his notebook. ''It says here that you disposed of your late father's shipping interests a few years ago, am I correct?''

"Yes, I did, Mr. Turner. As well as his warehouses before that and my mother's plantation before that. I've sold the furniture, the paintings on the walls, even the gowns in my closet. Just to keep riffraff like William Eustice from my family's doorstep."

Samantha scowled at the tight-fisted little appraiser for another moment before she turned away with a small sigh of resignation. She'd been through enough carpetbagger negotiations to know when to stop pushing. Turner's price was set. Now where in God's name was she going to find another two hundred dollars for the taxes? Let alone the money for train fare to Kansas? Samantha felt cold fear grab hold of her inside. Her dream of Abilene and a whole new life dissolved before her eyes. The image of her family being trapped in Savannah forever—at the mercy of William Eustice—brought a chill to Samantha's spine, freezing her Southern pride into submission.

"Mr. Turner," she said, her tone more conciliatory this time. "Perhaps you do not understand the dire situation of my family. If we do not raise the assessed bill of seven thousand five hundred dollars by tomorrow, Eustice will have us thrown into the streets. I cannot allow my elderly maiden aunts, my younger sister, my son, and my aged housekeeper to be subjected to such humiliation. I'm asking again, Mr. Turner. Please reconsider your offer," Samantha's soft voice pleaded.

Joseph Turner gazed into her eyes for a long moment. Samantha thought she saw a glimmer of compassion. But it was gone almost as suddenly as it appeared.

"Are you sure you've sold everything of value, Mrs. Winchester?" he pried.

"Everything, Mr. Turner."

"No . . . family heirlooms, perchance? Like jewelry?" His eyes settled on the brooch at Samantha's neck.

Her mother's brooch. And her mother's before that. Samantha felt every muscle in her body tense, rebelling at the thought of selling such a beloved and precious piece of her family to this avaricious little man. She could almost see his mouth watering. "This brooch has been in my family for generations, Mr. Turner. It's nearly two hundred years old. I couldn't possibly sell it," she protested quietly, her mind already accustoming itself to the painful decision.

"It's very handsome."

"Yes, it is, Mr. Turner."

"I'll give you two hundred dollars for it."

Samantha looked Turner straight in the eye. "It's easily worth five times that, and you know it."

Turner glanced aside with a sly smile. "Well, if you think you can find another buyer . . ."

Samantha folded her arms across her chest to keep the anger from spilling out. "Mr. Turner, I simply have to have more than two hundred dollars. You see, I'm not only settling my assessment, I'm also moving my entire family west. Out of Savannah forever. I must have the necessary funds to purchase train tickets."

Turner's beady little eyes blinked. "Out West! Now whatever would take you there, Mrs. Winchester? It's a hard, cruel life."

Samantha allowed a grim smile. "Not any crueler than here, Mr. Turner."

Joseph Turner stared into his book for a second before he spoke. "Well . . . I'm being foolish, but I'll go as high as two hundred thirty. Not a penny more."

Samantha met the appraiser's hard gaze. Thirty dollars wasn't enough for the six of them to get all the way to Kansas and start fresh. "Mr. Turner, I have to settle all six of us in Abilene, Kansas. Can you not relent?"

"Afraid not, Mrs. Winchester," he said, rocking back on

his heels, notebook clasped to his chest.

Samantha felt her anger boil inside at his greed . . . and her vulnerability. She turned away, ostensibly to ponder his offer, but actually to calm herself. Then, glancing down at her hands, Samantha saw the only thing of value she had left. She slowly slipped her diamond wedding band from her finger and held it out to Joseph Turner. "Here, Mr. Turner . . . this ring is easily worth five hundred dollars. I'm willing to sell it for one hundred if you'll agree to come with me now while I purchase the tickets and settle accounts with William Eustice at the same time. I would very much appreciate your presence when I visit his office."

Turner's eyes widened. "I'll say this much, Mrs. Winchester. You certainly are persistent," he observed with a wag of his head. "If you want to get to Abilene that badly, I'm not going to stand in your way. You've got yourself a deal." He extended his hand for the ring while Samantha slowly unpinned her mother's brooch.

Chapter

2

San Francisco

Jack Barnett observed the young man opposite him at the card table. No more than twenty, if he was a day, Jack decided with a weary sigh. And one of the worst poker players he'd ever seen. He could practically read the boy's hand on his face. Jack peered at his own cards and tossed two to the Frisco Star's felt-covered tabletop before he raised an eyebrow at the cigar-smoking silver-haired man beside him.

Thurgood Shafer transferred the cigar from one side of his mouth to the other without the aid of his hand and dealt two cards beside Jack's well-tailored coat sleeve. Glancing toward a hawk-faced balding man to Jack's left, Shafer grinned on either side of his cigar. "Okay, Westlake, what's it gonna be?" He removed the cigar long enough to toss down the small whiskey at his elbow.

Westlake tossed out a card, eyeing Shafer as he dealt another. Jack Barnett let his gaze settle on the earnest young man across from him, who was obviously sitting in on the first high-stakes poker game of his life. Watching the moisture cling to the young man's upper lip, Jack saw him mentally flounder. Draw? Hold? It was all Jack could do to keep from shaking his head in dismay.

"Okay, young fellow." Shafer grinned at the nervous young man, who was still clutching his cards so tightly Jack thought the spots would jump right off them. "What'll it be?"

The youngster observed each man at the table warily, then held out his cards. "F-f-four," he managed to say.

Jack closed his eyes. He didn't want to watch. Instead he inspected the two cards he'd just been dealt and discovered a third queen had joined the others.

An idea came to him suddenly. Jack almost kicked himself for entertaining it at first, but he couldn't resist. He'd watched both Shafer and Westlake systematically relieve the young man of most of his stake all evening. Perhaps a helping hand wasn't out of order. The boy was clearly in over his head and sinking fast. Jack reached to his tall stack of chips, threw two into the pot, and dropped his cards to the table. He leaned back with a satisfied smile and folded his arms across his expensive dress shirt.

Shafer eyed Jack with a pained expression. "I've seen that smug grin before, Barnett, and it's always cost me money," he observed, then glanced to his hand. Tossing them down with a curse, he muttered, "Not worth it."

Next, Jack turned his complacent smile on Westlake, whose eyes darted back and forth between his cards and Jack. "Well, Westlake, are you in or out?" he prodded, knowing full well Westlake's nervous movements were a dead giveaway of a mediocre hand. Westlake was only dangerous when he sat still.

Westlake peered once more at his hand, at the pile of chips on the table, and finally into Jack Barnett's slate-gray eyes, which revealed absolutely nothing. Only a trace of wry amusement could be seen. Westlake wrinkled his face into another scowl and dropped his hand. "I'm out."

Jack exulted inside. Next, he turned a slow, lazy smile on the boy, who tentatively added his two chips. Leaning forward, Jack caught the boy's nervous glance and said, "Son, I've got a real urge to see what you're holding, so I'll make it worth your while." He tossed two more chips onto the table.

The boy looked down at his dwindling pot for a moment, then jerked out two chips and threw them in, following Jack's lead without even thinking. That was the problem.

Keeping his smile friendly, Jack motioned for him to lay down his hand. With a hesitant little nod, the boy complied, spreading out what had to be one of the lousiest poker hands Jack had ever seen. It was all he could do to keep from flinching in pain at what he was about to say next. "Well, son, sad as this is to say . . . you've got me beat." Jack shoved his winning hand beneath Westlake's discards.

"WHAT!?" Shafer bellowed. "You let him beat you with a lousy pair of *fours*? Jesus H. Christ, man! What's gotten into you?" Cigar swiveling angrily from one side of his mouth to the other, Shafer glared at Jack in disgust. "I need a drink!" he declared, gathering his chips before he stalked off.

Jack shrugged with a sheepish smile and reached for the deck of cards. "I believe it's my deal," he announced sociably, watching the young man's astonished reaction at winning the pot. "Blackjack, gentlemen. Ante up," Jack declared. He waited for the whine of Westlake's voice. If it wasn't draw, it wasn't poker.

"God-a-mighty, Barnett! What've you been drinking?" Westlake curled a contemptuous lip at Jack. "I'm cashing in. Call me when you want to play *poker*!"

Jack concealed his triumphant grin while Westlake scraped back his chair and left. He let the cards ripple slowly in his hands, his long fingers shuffling from memory. "Where're you from, son?"

"Uh, St. Louis, sir . . . uh, I mean, Mr. Barnett," the youth stammered, his face flushed from his recent win. Spinning about in the chair, the boy waved excitedly behind him and pointed to his much larger pile of chips.

Curious, Jack peered through the open doorway, which led into the Frisco Star's grand foyer, and spied a petite young woman hovering outside the door, blond curls spilling from underneath her bonnet. The young woman's worried expression disappeared immediately at the sight of the tall stack of chips. This brief exchange only confirmed Jack's suspicions, and he resolved to get this pair out of the Star and away from the casino's smooth-talking and fast-playing clientele. Lambs to the slaughter, he thought, and dealt two cards facedown.

"Wonderful city, St. Louis," Jack observed with a friendly smile. "What brings you here? You and your ladyfriend, I mean." He gestured toward the doorway, where the young woman hovered closer.

The young man cleared his throat and checked his cards, tossing in two chips. "That's my wife, Polly. We got married last Christmas. My pa wanted us to take over his mercantile, but I . . . well, I always wanted something more than weighing sacks of flour and measuring cloth. I don't know . . . I guess I figured Polly and me, we could come out here and get a grubstake . . . maybe strike it rich. Like the papers are always saying. Gold! Just lying in the ground, waiting for you to find it." He stared off into space.

Jack held his tongue as he did every time he heard stories of broken dreams. Gold. Lying in the ground. Waiting to be found. When hell freezes over. More like standing in a creek till your back breaks, bending over a pan, sloshing and praying that a few gold flakes will settle to the bottom. In the six years since he'd arrived in California, Jack had heard more than his share of broken dreams. Creeks panned out, no gold waiting to be taken. Pipe dreams created by a feverish press. Greed sells papers.

He checked his two queens, dealt himself another card, then tossed in all three, facedown. "It's yours." Jack smiled lazily into the boy's shocked face "What's your name, son?"

"Uh, Adam . . . Adam Taylor, sir," he replied, face breaking into a huge grin as he pulled the chips into his mounting pile.

The soft brush of a hand on his shoulder caused Jack to turn. He grinned up at Marie Poirot's lovely, carefully made-up face and watched her settle in the chair at his side, her low-cut red silk gown rustling softly. Jack leaned back into his chair and shuffled the deck, in no hurry, letting Marie's hand rest comfortably on his arm. "I take it you didn't find any gold lying around on the ground, just waiting to be taken, right?" He dealt another four cards with a practiced hand.

"I sure didn't." Adam screwed up his boyish face in disgust. "It wasn't anything like I thought it would be." After scanning his hand, he tossed in five chips. "Neither one of us knew how hard it was gonna be . . . or how fast our money was gonna run out." Adam's youthful brow furrowed again. "Polly promised she'd stick it out with me as long as I wanted to stay."

"Sounds like she loves you, son," Jack observed, tossing in his five. "Enough to stand by you. Living on a grubstake is a far cry from being settled in St. Louis. Not many women would stick around." He dealt himself and Adam another card.

"And don't I *know* it!" Adam nodded vigorously, peering at his hand. "I promised her as soon as I could win train fare, we're headin' back to St. Louis. There's nothing here but sore backs and blisters. And dust. Oh, there's plenty of dust in those hills!"

Watching Adam stand pat, Jack eyed his ace and king and dealt himself another card, then shoved them all face-down onto the table. He felt a small squeeze on his arm and glanced at Marie's puzzled face. An ironic smile played on her lips. Jack winked in reply. Turning back to a delighted Adam, who was pulling in his winnings, Jack grinned across the table. "Now you're talking smart. From the looks of that little lady standing over by the door, you've already had your share of luck, son. If you two know what's good for you, you'll both skedaddle back to St. Louis, grab hold of that store, settle down, and raise a family."

Adam blinked up, apparently dazzled by the pile before him. "You bet I will! Oh, boy! Look at that!" He broke into a delighted grin and waved to Polly, who was looking considerably more relieved now.

"Have you got enough yet, son? To make it back to St. Louis, I mean?"

Adam immediately inspected his pile, his lips forming the numbers. "Uh, yessir . . . well, almost, sir. You see, I was kinda hoping to win enough so Polly and me could buy a house. So we don't have to live with my folks, I mean." He hesitated, fingering the pile.

Jack suppressed his smile. Talk about looking a gift horse in the mouth. With a wry glance to Marie, he carefully dealt another hand. "Well, son . . . I've got the uncanny feeling your luck is still holding. Shall we sweeten the pot and see?" Checking his cards, Jack pushed his lone stack of chips to the center.

Adam stared at the pile, obviously weighing his chances, and with the same perspicacity he'd shown all evening, quickly shoved in a pile of his own. "I'll take one card," he said, wetting his lips.

One's all you're gonna get, son, Jack thought as he dealt Adam's card along with his own. Spying the two kings taunting him, Jack stifled a groan and tossed them away. "Son, that little lady has brought you more luck than you deserve tonight. Now, you take my advice and rush straight over to that train station and don't move until the eastbound pulls in, you hear?" Jack leaned back into his chair and grinned at the bedazzled young man before him. From the corner of his eye, Jack saw Polly slowly draw into the room. He quickly rose to his feet and watched the blush of answered dreams color the young woman's face.

"Look, Polly . . . I . . . I *did* it!" Adam cried in exuberance. "We can go home now. We can even buy a *house*! Just like you always wanted." He jumped out of his chair and captured his wife in his arms, swinging Polly in a circle about him.

"Oh, Adam, I was so scared," Polly said with a gasp. "I mean . . . it was so risky and all. Gambling, I mean." She gazed up worshipfully at her newly rich husband. "Can we . . . can we leave now? For the station, I mean. I want to get home so bad I can taste it!"

Adam beamed down at his bride. "You can *bet* on it!"

Jack flinched at the reminder. Reaching out to shake Adam's hand, he looked the young man straight in the eye. "Let this be your last foray into the gambling life, son. There're more snakes in these casinos than you'll ever find in the California hills."

"Yessir!" Adam bobbed his head obediently. "You can bet on it." Watching Jack wince once again, Adam grinned sheepishly. "I mean, I sure won't, Mr. Barnett. Thanks for the advice." He scraped his huge pile of chips into Polly's little drawstring bag. The exuberant young couple practically skipped through the door.

Jack shook his head. Sometimes his own foolishness surprised him. At the light touch upon his shoulder, he turned to find Marie offering him a brandy, a knowing smile on her face.

"Ah, *chéri*, you amaze me sometimes," she said, her eyes alight. "Last night I watched you spend the entire evening relieving Freddy Chapman of his winnings, only to see you give it away to these two children tonight." She drew closer, her hand sliding playfully into his light brown hair before she placed a soft kiss upon his lips. "You are a puzzle, and a fascinating one, Jack Barnett," she whispered, her fingers lightly toying with his shirt buttons, a promise of delights to come.

Jack grinned down. "Perhaps you'll show me how fascinating you find me . . . later this evening." He caressed a tightly curled brown tendril beside her forehead while his arm slid about her waist in familiar fashion.

"You mean after you've spoken to your general?" Marie replied with a raised brow. "He arrived a few moments ago, *chéri*. Don't worry, I placed him in the front parlor, as always." Jack's lazy smile disappeared, and his arms left her, even though her hands still lingered on his chest.

He downed his brandy in a gulp. "This won't take long, Marie. I'll join you afterward." Jack took her arm in his and escorted her out into the foyer.

"For how long, *chéri*?" Marie murmured. "Every time your general appears, you disappear. Sometimes for months. I never know how long it will be."

Jack maneuvered her beside the ostentatious fountain in the Star's foyer. The posh casino's guests milled about, their voices adding to the palpable excitement that filled the air. Eyes were bright with the fire of anticipation, be it winning a high-stakes game, beating the roulette wheel, or meeting a new lover.

"You know I can't refuse him, Marie. He's the only man who stood by me years ago during the war. The *only* one." Jack's gray eyes burned with fierce memories of the war. "I'd walk through fire if Matthew Logan asked me!"

"I understand, *chéri*," Marie said with a sad smile.

Jack leaned over to leave a kiss upon her forehead. "I'll see you upstairs later, I promise." He started to pull away, anxious to see what adventure Matthew Logan had brought him.

Marie held on this time. "That was a pretty picture you painted a while ago for the boy," she teased, fondling Jack's silken cravat between her fingers. "Running off to St. Louis, a little store, a family . . . a pretty picture, *n'est-ce pas*?

Jack couldn't hide his smile as her tongue transformed St. Louis to its French namesake. "For the Adams and Pollys of the world, yes. But not for lone wolves like us." He captured her chin and kissed her lightly on the lips before he turned and strode into the Star's front parlor. Marie stared after him, holding his empty glass.

When he saw General Logan rise from a blue velvet armchair in the corner of the parlor, Jack felt a familiar rush of excitement flood his veins. He strode up to Logan, hand outstretched. "General, it's good to see you again!" he declared with a grin. "What brings you into this den of iniquity and vice?"

Matthew Logan grabbed Jack's hand in a hearty grip and clapped him on the shoulder. Piercing blue eyes, crowned by silvery eyebrows, lit up. "Why, you, Jack, of course! But you'd think I might find you in a more respectable setting. I keep hoping I'll see you settled down some day when I come to call. What do you say, Jack? Babies crawling over your knee, sweet little wife by your side? It's an awful pretty picture, don't you think?''

Jack shoved away any feelings that might have been aroused by the general's teasing. He remembered happier times before the war, before scandal and pain had separated him from his family forever. He smiled his laconic smile instead. "A family's not for me, General. I'm too restless to be tied down.''

"Well, thirty-two is a good age to start changing your ways, my boy. Don't wait too long, or no woman will want you." The general wagged a wrinkled finger.

Jack grinned at his former commanding officer. "Don't tell me you came all the way here to tell me to get married?''

Matthew Logan gave a hearty laugh, slapping his knee. "You're right, I didn't. Once again, Jack, I find the Government Investigations Office needs your very discreet and thorough services." His laughter disappeared. "I've put you in for commendations, Jack. You deserved it for your capture of those railroad grafters in Denver. Not to mention the payroll robbers outside Virginia City and the crooked land agents in the Dakotas," he said with admiration. "I don't know what the government, or I, would have done if you hadn't volunteered for those assignments.''

Jack gazed thoughtfully at the floor. He didn't want commendations. He was simply grateful to be given a chance to redeem himself in the government's eyes. And he had Logan to thank for that. Beneath the general's flattering words, Jack knew that Logan desperately wanted to give him an opportunity to erase the black mark that had lingered beside his family's name since the war.

Even now, after eight years, Jack felt the muscles in his gut tighten at the hateful memory. He could still feel the

burn of humiliation, still hear the sound of fabric ripping
as his captain's bars were stripped from his shoulder, still
feel the cold bite of the handcuffs as they snapped around
his wrists. And he could still see the emblem of his rank
lying at his feet, before Major Curtis Franklin's heel ground
it into the red Georgia clay. The fire of that remembered
rage and shame returned to flood Jack's veins once more,
searing through him. He forced his eyes up to Logan's
again, wondering how many assignments it would take to
reclaim his pride.

"Oh, I figure you would have found someone else to do
the job, General." He forced a self-deprecating smile.

"Bounty hunters or lily-livered Pinkertons, you mean,"
Logan snorted. "Can't trust 'em as far as you can throw
'em. We needed more than a hired gun, Jack. We needed
a *brain* behind it."

"General, all I've got to say is that this next assignment
must be something awful, considering how much you're
buttering me up right now."

Logan's wrinkled face broke into a smile. God, how he
wished his own son had turned out as fine a man as Jack
Barnett. There was no way in hell he'd ever believe that
story out of Georgia. If Jack had beaten some soldier the
way they said he had, then you could bet he had a reason!
Logan met Jack's gaze and let his smile fade. "This assignment may not be awful, but I think you'll find it re-
warding. The U.S. Army needs your skills this time, Jack.
That is, if you'll agree to help them out."

Jack felt his heart give a little leap. At last. The chance
he'd been waiting for. "You know I'd walk through hell
for you, General. All you have to do is ask," he said in a
quiet voice. "Fill me in."

Matthew Logan gave a large sigh and sank back into the
armchair. "Someone is robbing the army blind in Abilene.

The government started checking the army cattle agents they've got spread all over. Seems they turned up this one agent in Abilene, Kansas, who was paying two dollars a head more than anybody else! Well, I don't have to tell you, Jack, the army buys a lot of beef. So we're dealing with a considerable amount of money—and Abilene is one of the largest suppliers. The army got suspicious and contacted one of the cattlemen. Goodnight, I think. He drives one of the biggest herds into town each year. Anyway, this Goodnight told them what he got paid last year, and it was fully two dollars a head less! Well, I don't have to tell you the army investigators lit on that Abilene agent like fleas on a dog! Threw him into the stockade, then swooped down on his office and confiscated his records. Told him he'd rot in prison if he didn't tell them what he did with the money. They can't find any bank accounts to save their souls. Well . . . that agent swore up and down he didn't take any money. Said the cattleman was wrong, but he was shaking like a leaf when he testified.

"I tell you, Jack, he's either telling the truth or he's scared to death to say what he knows. Either way, the army is bound and determined to get to the bottom of this. They can't pour money into someone else's pocket. They're sure he's got an accomplice in Abilene or in Fort Riley, just outside. That's what they want *you* to find out. One of their own would be spotted for sure." Logan paused. "I'm hoping this assignment appeals to you, Jack. I know how much it could mean." His eyes softened on his companion.

Jack pursed his lips. His initial flush of excitement had drained away somewhat. His previous assignments had kept him constantly moving, stalking and outwitting lawbreakers, running them to ground, hauling them off to deserved punishment. Adventurous, sometimes dangerous, but always satisfying. They helped make up for the one criminal who got away during the war. The one Jack would never forget. Now, after all these years, the army was finally asking his help, and all they wanted him to do was sit in an office in Abilene and count cows! Jack grimaced. Still, he couldn't refuse Matthew Logan. He met Logan's piercing gaze. "When do you want me to leave, General?"

"Right away, Jack, if possible. Is your trading company profiting as handsomely as last year? Would your sudden absence cause any problems?"

Jack shook his head. "None whatsoever. I have my staff trained to take over whenever I leave town. I pay them well, and they respond with their loyalty. A fair exchange."

"Well, let's hope you think as much of your assistant on this job. We really tried to find the most competent one through advertisements, and we—"

"Assistant!" Jack interrupted with a frown. "General, you know I've always worked alone. I don't want anybody hanging over my shoulder, trying to tell me what to do. I'd probably wind up shooting him just to get him out of the way."

Matthew Logan chuckled. "Calm down, Jack. This man won't be underfoot. In fact, he'll be the one who's stuck in the agent's office, not you! We've hired a *bookkeeper*, that's all. Those army ledgers are confusing as hell if you don't know what you're looking for. Besides, we're not bringing you all the way from San Francisco to go over the books. That's his job. Yours will be to establish yourself as the new army agent, get familiar with the cattlemen, the local law, and the army. Find out who knows what. But then, I don't have to tell you your job, do I?"

Jack's smile returned. The general's description of the assignment made him feel better. *He* wouldn't be stuck in an office. The bookkeeper would be. "All right, General,

I'm convinced. Now, who is this clerk, and where will I meet him?''

Logan withdrew a small notebook from his vest pocket, perused a page, and said, ''His name's Samuel H. Winchester, and he should be arriving in Abilene sometime after June thirtieth, according to his letter. Forgive my presumption, Jack, but I've already written and told him to present himself to you at the army agent's office whenever he lands in town. I gambled you'd take this assignment.'' Glancing up, he gave a little smile. ''I really tried to choose the best applicant, but to be truthful, most of them sounded alike. Except this one—he had been chief bookkeeper for a shipping company. So I figured you two would have a lot in common.''

Jack lifted a skeptical brow. ''That was considerate of you, sir. But I hope I won't be in that office long enough to strike up a friendship.''

''I understand.'' Logan tore off the page and handed it over. ''Here's his name and qualifications. Oh, and before I forget, he specifically asked about living accommodations in Abilene. Wanted to know if they were provided. I wrote that they were, so I suppose you'll have to find the poor fellow a room.'' His eyes twinkled merrily.

Jack just gave a wry shake of his head while he watched the general laugh.

Chapter

3

The skinny little Abilene stationmaster mopped the sweat from his brow, his soiled white handkerchief already damp. If he didn't get into his office before the 12:10 pulled in, there'd be hell to pay. But how in blazes was he going to get past these two old biddies blocking his doorway? Ed Doyle pulled a pocket watch from his frayed vest pocket. Nearly noon. Doyle wiped again with his handkerchief, catching the trickle running down his forehead. He gazed beseechingly past the most formidable-looking bosoms he'd ever seen in his life until his eyes rested on two faces that surely would have dropped Medusa in her tracks. Doyle flinched. His voice whining in desperation, he pleaded again, "Ladies, *please*! I beg of you. I must be allowed into my office right away. The twelve-ten will be here any minute! Please, I—"

A dainty, white lace–gloved hand waved Doyle into silence once more. Mimi Herndon pulled up all five feet two inches of herself in imperial fashion, faded blue silk rustling despite its age, and gazed haughtily at the impertinent clerk. Mealymouthed little Yankee with his whiny voice. "Are you deaf, man?'' her magnolia voice chided. ''We have already told you your office will be returned as soon as our niece finishes rearranging her attire.'' Mimi couldn't think of a more delicate way to describe Samantha's hurried attempt to change into the only other suitable dress she owned.

The imposing woman next to Mimi folded her arms across her enormous bosom, which was encased in peach-colored silk, and lowered her scowling gaze to the cowering clerk. As generous of girth as Mimi was slight, Lily Herndon stared out over the fortress of herself and intoned, ''If this train is as punctual as the ones we've had the misfortune to experience so far, then you have nothing to fear.'' Her contralto dropped to the dusty station house floor.

''But . . . but . . . !'' was all Doyle could stammer in reply. The dour expressions on those two faces took his speech away. God-a-mighty! He sure hoped these old harpies were passing through. They had to be, for sure. They belonged in Abilene like a Baptist preacher at a saloon girl's wedding. Doyle licked his dry lips and swiped at his forehead again. He was just about to get on his knees and beg when he saw his office door open. Out stepped a tall, slender, and strikingly handsome woman with deep reddish brown hair. Doyle gaped despite himself.

Samantha smiled sweetly to her maiden aunts and approached Doyle. ''You have been ever so kind, sir, to allow me to use your office.'' She smiled warmly into his eyes, watching them liquefy. ''I do hope we have not inconvenienced you too terribly.'' She glanced toward Maysie, who was closing the office door behind her, Samantha's valise clutched in her hand.

''Uh . . . no, ma'am . . . not at all. . . . It was my pleasure . . . really,'' Doyle managed.

''You are too kind,'' Samantha said. ''If I might impose

on you for one more thing, sir, I would be most grateful.''

"Oh, yes! yes! Anything, ma'am. Anything at all,'' he babbled.

"Could you direct me to the office of the United States Army purchasing agent, please? Is it near?''

Doyle blinked. What on earth did this beautiful woman want with that new cattle agent who had just come into town? "Uh, yes, ma'am. You just go down to the corner and turn left on Texas Street, then head straight past the . . . uh . . . the Alamo Saloon, and you'll run right into it.'' Doyle deliberately dropped his voice as he mentioned the largest saloon in town.

Samantha gave him her warmest smile, which almost melted Doyle on the spot. Only a puddle would be there to greet the 12:10. "Thank you, sir. You have been ever so kind. Rest assured, I will not forget.'' She lifted her oft-mended navy blue silk skirt away from the dusty floor and approached a long wooden bench that was pushed against the station house wall. There sat her younger sister Becky, with Davy beside her. Davy looked as though he'd much rather be exploring every nook and cranny of this drafty old clapboard building, but Becky's arm was wrapped tightly around his shoulders, holding him in place and out of harm's way.

Smiling into Becky's worried blue eyes, Samantha paused before her for inspection. "Well, do I look suitable?''

Becky bit her lip. "You look beautiful, Samantha. If that Mr. Barnett doesn't hire you on the spot, he's blind as a bat.''

Samantha grinned. "I'm not supposed to look pretty, Becky. Merely competent.'' Her hand reached up to adjust Aunt Mimi's pearl-tipped hairpins once again. Trying to wind her mass of curls into a prim and proper bun beneath her little velvet hat had proved harder than she thought. Long tendrils and stray curls kept slipping out, dangling beside her face, spoiling the schoolmarmish look she'd strived to create.

Two small brown hands reached up to help her. "Shoo." Maysie swatted Samantha's hands away. "Let me do it. You can't see a thing. I don't want that Barnett fellow to think you're a washerwoman."

Samantha glanced to her sister's pale face, framed by strawberry blond curls, and her heart gave a little tug. Becky was trying hard to be brave. She knew exactly how Becky felt. They had been riding for days through barren stretches of land, treeless for miles at a time, clouds of dust billowing in the open train windows. It had been all Samantha could do to hold back her own tears as she watched her familiar and civilized South fade farther and farther behind them.

"Try to soothe Becky, will you, Maysie?" Samantha murmured. "She's so scared her freckles have disappeared."

"I'll see to it." Maysie gave the voluptuous bun a pat. "There, that ought to hold until you talk to the man. Now, as soon as you find out, you get back quick as a wink, you hear? I don't want this family havin' to sit with this heathen trash one minute longer than necessary!" Maysie cast her considerable frown about the empty station house. No trash to be seen yet, heathen or otherwise.

"Yes, ma'am." Samantha grinned. Turning, she caught Davy gazing wistfully out the window. She approached and knelt beside her son. "If you promise to hold Becky's hand real tight, she'll let you go outside and watch the train that's coming in, all right?" she said, forcing a cheerful tone.

Davy's face lit up, freckles and all. "Can I? Oh, boy!"

Samantha leaned forward, her heart filling with the sunshine of his smile. "Give Mama a kiss for good luck, sweetheart. She's going to need it."

Clyde Monroe pushed the brim of his weather-beaten hat back on his head. Tangled black curls, sprinkled with gray, straggled down his brow, falling into washed-out, faded blue eyes. A huge smile split Clyde's broad face as he stared at the tall, lean figure before him. "*Tarnation!* If you ain't a sight for sore eyes, Jack Barnett." His voice whistled and cracked. "What in hell brings you to this dusty ol' cow town? The last I seen, you was livin' high on the hog out in San Francisco."

Jack grinned. "Well, you know what they say, Clyde. Too much of that soft life spoils you. So I get away every chance I can. Keeps a man honest."

Clyde threw back his head and guffawed, his laughter bouncing off the rough pine board walls of the army agent's office, filling the small room with its raucous sound. "Whooooey! As God is my witness, I think both you and I got 'bout as honest as any man could get, back there in O–hi–o." Clyde shook his head wryly. "Sometimes I can still feel the grit on my hands, Jack. How 'bout you?"

Jack's smile vanished with the shared memory from years ago. Army prison. Swinging the hammer. Rocks splitting into smithereens—depending on whose face Jack pictured there. He straightened his spine imperceptibly. Sometimes he could still feel his shoulders ache. "Yeah, Clyde," he admitted softly. "I can, too."

"Well, whatever brings you here, I gotta say I'm mighty glad to see ya!" Clyde said, rubbing a hand across his stubbled chin. "More and more cattle drives will be headin' into town now, and things will start a-poppin'. We sure could use another steady hand to help settle down those cowpokes when they start bustin' loose." Clyde tucked his thumbs under his gun belt, which rode well below the generous belly above it.

Jack stared at his cowhide boots to conceal his smile. The thought that he'd ever see his big, bumbling, faint-hearted cell mate sporting a badge was incomprehensible. Clyde would turn tail at the first sign of trouble. Confrontation of any kind was against his nature. In fact, that's exactly what had landed him in the army's prison during the war—his decided aversion to confrontation, particularly when it had a bayonet on the other end of it. Jack looked into those faded eyes. "Clyde, what in hell are you doing wearing a badge? The last I saw of you, you were heading back to Kansas to hook up with your uncle."

"That's what I did, Jack. Ya see, my uncle was helpin' out the sheriff when I came to town. Then Uncle Lucas, he died . . . and, well, Marshal Smith asked me to stick around." Clyde gave a sheepish grin and scratched beneath his worn leather vest. "Heck, I didn't do much at all. The marshal, he did all the work. Until he got shot, that is." Clyde gave a little cough. "Anyway . . . the rest o' the deputies and me stayed on till Marshal Hickok came to town. We were kinda surprised when he asked us to stick around agin and help 'im out."

He gave a good-natured shrug and scratched his head, tilting the weather-beaten brim to the side. "It ain't that bad, Jack. Those cowboys get all rambunctious when they first ride into town, but they settle down soon as they get a few drinks and a pretty girl. Shucks, I purt near never have to draw my gun! And when I do, all I havta do is wave it around a few times. Those ol' cowpokes get so likkered up, they just about pour themselves into jail. So, whadaya say, Cap'n? Will you help us keep these boys in line, now that you're here?"

Jack felt a little pinprick hearing his rank once again. He

glanced over Clyde's shoulder and out the grimy army office front window. It was so dirty he could barely see the constant parade of grizzled, rough men troop past. Since the office was situated in the middle of town, Jack had already spied several faces peering through the window. "I'm afraid I can't help you out, Clyde. I'm here to do a job for the army, and I can't be rounding up drunken cowboys. Besides, I'm supposed to buy beef from them, so it stands to reason I can't be throwing their wranglers into jail."

Clyde's face fell. "That's a damn shame, Cap'n, 'cause I sure would like to work beside you agin—doin' somethin' besides splittin' rocks!"

"I'll take that as a compliment, Clyde." Jack grinned. "Oh, by the way, drop the 'Captain,' would you? I don't want anyone in Abilene to know I was in the army or the war. I don't want to answer a lot of questions, if you know what I mean."

Clyde nodded vigorously. "I sure do, Cap'n . . . uh, I mean Jack. Don't worry. I won't tell a soul. None of their business, anyway." He tugged the brim of his hat back down over his forehead and turned to leave. "Lissen, I've got to go talk to some folks, but I'll drop by and see you agin real soon." Clyde waved as he strode out the door.

Jack watched Clyde's bulky frame move past the window before he turned back to a scarred wooden desk where he'd already begun to search through drawers. The locked metal box that Logan had delivered to him before he left San Francisco contained two thick black ledgers. Now they sat on the only other desk in the barren office. There were no cabinets, no bookshelves, and no records. Nothing gave the appearance that a business of any kind had operated there. Jack thought the office had looked peculiar, but shrugged it off. The army had confiscated the books several months ago, Logan had said. Perhaps they had cleaned out the office as well.

He leaned over the old desk and peered into its cubby-holes. Absorbed in his search, Jack didn't notice the front door open or hear the faint ladylike cough. When the sound of a heavily accented Southern voice reached his ears, however, he jerked to attention.

"Mister Jack Barnett, I presume?" Samantha inquired politely.

Jack spun about and found himself staring in amazement at the woman who had just entered his office. He blinked. Whoever she was, she sure didn't belong in Abilene. There was too much intelligence in her face, as well as too much culture in that voice, for a town as rough as this. The sound of old Southern money mixed with magnolia in her drawl. Unmistakable. Jack let his eyes meet hers. He saw deep emerald pools of green that made him catch his breath. "Yes, I am, ma'am. May I help you?"

Samantha paused, ostensibly to clear her throat, but what she really needed was another moment to compose herself. Searching for this office through Abilene's saloon-filled dirt streets had been arduous indeed. She had never seen so much dust in her life, or so many loud, rough-looking, foul-talking, uncouth men in one place before. Even the hordes of Yankee invaders had looked better than most of the scruffy men she saw this morning—stumbling into saloons, jostling each other in the streets, jumping on and off horses, and making all kinds of improper suggestions as she walked hurriedly by. Samantha had breathed a prayer of thanks when she'd finally spied the army agent's office.

Now that she'd found the office at last, Samantha was astonished to discover the cat had stolen her tongue—the very moment she looked into Jack Barnett's slate-gray eyes. She swallowed and tried again. "Mr. Barnett, my name is

Samantha H. Winchester. Mrs. Paul Winchester. I . . . I am your new bookkeeper.''

Jack's mouth dropped open in astonishment. He stared at Samantha. Surely he had misunderstood her. ''Excuse me, ma'am. What did you say?''

Samantha cleared her throat and lifted her chin, meeting his astonished eyes straight on. ''I said that I am Samantha H. Winchester, and I am here as requested in General Matthew Logan's letter dated May fifteenth. He said to report to Jack Barnett at the army purchasing agent's office in Abilene, Kansas, as soon as I arrived in town.'' She paused. ''I am your new bookkeeper, Mr. Barnett. I answered the advertisement for employment General Logan placed in the St. Louis *Evening Dispatch.*''

Jack felt his mouth start to drop open again before he quickly snapped it shut. He glanced away from the lady's arresting gaze and stared at the scarred wooden desk across the room without seeing it, his mind racing.

What had gotten into Matthew Logan? Jack thought in amazement. A *woman*? In a place like Abilene? Good Christ! The general must be crazy. Having anybody underfoot would be bad enough . . . but a woman! God. Just having her in the office would bring every wrangler in town peering in the window, just to catch a glimpse of her. Christ. The general must be getting senile. Jack shook his head. There was no way in hell he could allow her to work on this assignment. The fact that she was a woman—and a beautiful one at that—would cause too much of a stir. Jack wasn't here to cause a stir. He was here to catch a crook.

Samantha used the opportunity of Jack's distraction to observe this tall, lean stranger who held her family's future in his hands. She had desperately searched for some sign of compassion in those gray eyes when she'd announced her arrival, but she couldn't see past the shock. Watching him absorb what she had just said, Samantha took in his features quickly, noticing how his light brown hair fell across his forehead, how the lines and crags of his face created depths and shadows. A nice face. Handsome, but not too much so, she found herself thinking before she realized it. Even though he was dressed plainly in a simple cotton shirt and denim pants, Samantha sensed that this was not a plain man. Something about him spoke of fine linen shirts and tailored suits. She couldn't put her finger on it exactly. Perhaps it was the way he held himself.

Jack took a deep breath, casting about for the right words to tell this lovely woman that there was no way in hell she could stay in Abilene and work for him. He turned and faced her once again. "Mrs. Winchester... I'm terribly sorry, but there's... well, there's been some mistake. You see, I assumed that Samuel Winchester was a man, and—"

"Oh, there has been no mistake, Mr. Barnett," Samantha interrupted, fear clutching her at the sound of rejection in his voice. "I deliberately misled you. By signing my name Sam H. Winchester, I knew that you would assume 'Sam' stood for Samuel. I profoundly apologize for my chicanery, sir. But the subterfuge was for a very good reason."

Curious that she would so readily admit her ruse, Jack prodded, "And that was . . . ?"

Samantha took a deep breath. "I believed that if I signed my real name to the letter of application, you would not have seen fit to hire *Samantha* Winchester, whereas *Samuel* Winchester might be more to your liking."

Jack felt a smile starting inside, but he pushed it away. The last thing he wanted to do was encourage this woman. Samuel Winchester might be more to his tastes as a book-keeper, but this version was proving entirely *too* much to his liking, despite what she'd just said. He forced a little frown. "Well, you're right, Mrs. Winchester. If General Logan had known you were a woman, he would never have offered you this position."

Samantha swallowed. "Even if Samantha is every bit as good a bookkeeper as the mythical Samuel?" she forced herself to challenge.

Jack held those accusing green eyes for a split second before he had to look elsewhere. He had expected her to sigh and turn meekly away when he refused her. Instead she was confronting him. Damn! What had happened to those simpering Southern ladies he'd heard tell of? There was nary a trace of a simper on *that* lovely face. He tried again. "Mrs. Winchester, I suspect I don't have to tell you why it would be a breach of propriety for the United States Army to hire . . . a female bookkeeper. Even in a more sophisticated city, such as St. Louis, it would cause a stir. Here, in a small town like Abilene, well . . . it just . . . it just wouldn't work out. People would—"

"Mr. Barnett," Samantha interrupted once more, feeling the heat of desperation rush through her veins. "I walked all the way from the train station through this town to find your office. It is my opinion that the local citizenry will not care if I'm employed in a public office. The people I saw were either falling into or out of numerous taverns, shouting at each other, or asleep in alleyways." She deliberately did not mention the sober few who had paid her a great deal of attention.

Jack's smile escaped, despite himself. He turned to stare out the window while he pictured this stunning woman striding down the rough-hewn plank walkways of Abilene, leaving dazzled cowboys and stupefied shopkeepers in her wake. If her lovely face and oh-so-feminine figure didn't stop them, that reddish brown hair surely would. Jack

couldn't remember when he'd seen hair exactly that shade
before. The shade of rich earth, copper and brown inter-
mingled. Lustrous, even pulled back on her neck. The few
times the lady's gaze left his, Jack found his eyes settling
there, drawn to the red-brown tresses. Several unruly
tendrils refused to stay restrained, and they curled beside
her face in entirely too charming a fashion. Keeping his
smile in check, Jack turned his attention back to her. "Mrs.
Winchester, you should never have walked through this
town unescorted. If I had known you were at the station, I
w—"

"Would *what*, Mr. Barnett?" she challenged. "I doubt
you would have escorted me to your office. You probably
would have tried to put me on the twelve-ten out of town."

This time Jack didn't even try to hide his smile. He
shook his head in wonderment. *Damn*, but she had a tart
tongue on her! If it wasn't for the drawl, he'd never have
known she was Southern. He couldn't help but notice that
Mrs. Winchester's no-nonsense attitude contrasted sharply
with the mouthful-of-molasses sound of her voice. It was a
darn shame he had such a weakness for women with ac-
cents. "Well, ma'am, you're right about that. I would have
done my best to get you on that train and out of Abilene.
St. Louis is much better suited to a woman of your obvious
taste and refinement." Perhaps a little flattery would pen-
etrate.

Not a bit. "I know no one in St. Louis, Mr. Barnett.
I have no family there, no home, no means of support,
no—"

"But you responded to the newspaper advertisement,"
Jack interrupted, taking his turn. If she was going to forget
her manners, so would he. "If you don't live in St. Louis,
how did you see the notice?"

Samantha caught her breath. The challenge in those probing gray eyes took her aback for a moment. "My mother's uncle left Savannah two years ago. He . . . he was trying to start again in St. Louis after being wiped out in the war." She glanced aside. "Unfortunately the strain of it all must have been too much for him. At least, that's what the doctor's note said. He was kind enough to mail me my uncle's possessions, all carefully wrapped in newspaper. We were the only family Uncle Winthrop had left. I saw your advertisement when I was unwrapping his belongings."

Jack's amusement had faded with the sound of one word. Savannah. The chilly breeze of memory swept through him, shivering his insides. "I'm sorry about your uncle, Mrs. Winchester," he started.

Samantha cut him off. "Mr. Barnett, I need this position," she pleaded. "I don't care if your local citizens approve of me or not. Would you please reconsider your refusal, sir?"

Shaken by the desperation he saw in her eyes, Jack hesitated. "Mrs. Winchester . . . where is your husband, your family? Why have they left you in a situation such as this?"

Pausing, Samantha let her solemn voice convey her emotion. "My husband is dead, Mr. Barnett. He fell at Shiloh with his regiment. The war has claimed most of my loved ones, either in battle or . . . or from the horror of it. My father, my mother, my only brother. All gone. Long ago."

Jack stared at the dust on his boots, anywhere but at the woman in front of him. A Confederate widow. Come back to haunt him. Memory's chill wind rattled through him again. He sent a prayer of thanks heavenward that he hadn't fought at Shiloh. Manassas, Antietam, Fredericksburg, yes. But not Shiloh. At least he hadn't killed her husband, whoever he was. Jack drew in a deep breath. "I'm terribly sorry about your loss, Mrs. Winchester. But . . ." He floundered, trying to find the right words.

Samantha jumped in. "Mr. Barnett, I'm an excellent bookkeeper. I really am! I'm sure I can help you here. My experience with my father's shipping business taught me a great deal. I promise you won't regret hiring me. I swear it!"

Eager to escape the painful subject of the war, Jack pounced on Samantha's admittedly intriguing background. "What sort of shipping business, Mrs. Winchester?" he asked. "I'm curious. You see, when I'm not . . . engaged in buying cattle, I oversee my own small trading fleet. Out West, in San Francisco."

Samantha's eyes widened in response to his words. Her heart gave a little skip. San Francisco. The destination of many of her father's clipper ships, so many years ago. She could still remember when those tall-masted vessels rode gracefully in the harbor, their acres of canvas folded like resting birds' wings, waiting. Waiting to fill with wind and lift off, sails stretched taut, leaning into the breeze, swiftly escaping their brief harbor perch. Impatient to ride the wind again. Samantha used to watch from her father's second-floor office window, watch them sail swiftly into the horizon, wishing she could escape as easily as they. Faraway places beckoned. But duty and family called louder.

She forced herself out of the past. "My father had a flourishing business before the war, Mr. Barnett," she said, not a little proudly. "Our clipper ships sailed to San Francisco around the Horn. We wanted to invest in the newer steamships, but the war started. After that we struggled to keep what we had afloat . . . for as long as we could. But finally everything was sold off. Piece by piece, ship by ship, warehouse by warehouse. Just to pay the outrageous taxes the Yankee carpetbaggers kept demanding." Samantha bit her tongue to stop the sound of bitterness escaping.

Jack watched her gaze off again, watched the sails reappear in her eyes, and felt a sympathetic twinge within. He'd worked long and hard to build up his own small fleet of steamships. How would it feel to lose it all? He stared at that lovely face, saddened by memory now, and let his gaze linger. It quickly found her wealth of earthen-rich hair, spilling voluptuously from the confining bun, and he felt himself respond despite himself.

He pushed the conflicting feelings aside. He could not hire this woman. To hell with propriety. It wasn't a fit job for a woman. Certainly not a woman like her. Why, he'd have to deal with cattlemen and cowboys and God knows what else. Jack meant to poke his nose into everybody's business until he found what he was looking for. In the process, he was bound to step on a lot of toes and create a few enemies. He always did. And he could not in good conscience expose a woman to what might become a dangerous assignment. Especially this woman. Samantha Winchester had obviously had more than her share of misfortune. Jack would be damned if he'd bring her any more. He cleared his throat, carefully choosing his words, before he dared look her in the face.

"Mrs. Winchester, I am sincerely sorry about your family's losses in the war. And while I agree the citizens of Abilene would probably adjust to your presence in this office, there is another reason I could not possibly employ you here." Jack watched Samantha's face lose its last bit of color, and he felt a little tug within. "This assignment has the very real potential for danger, Mrs. Winchester. I've been sent to investigate charges of fraud. And the army is reasonably certain the previous bookkeeper, whom they have in custody, had an accomplice. Probably here in Abilene. Now, that person will not be happy when I start sniffing too close to his trail. Consequently there is a real threat of retaliation on his part. There is no way I would *ever* put a woman in danger. I couldn't. I am sympathetic to your situation, believe me I am, and I will gladly pay your train fare back to Savannah. You will be much safer there, I assure you." He held Samantha's dark green eyes. The desperation there made his heart ache.

The ice-cold hand of panic clutched Samantha's heart, squeezing her chest so tightly she could barely breathe. She had failed. She had sold the last few precious mementos she treasured and gambled everything on her dream of a new life, dragged her little ragtag family over a thousand miles, bouncing and jostling on hard leather train seats to this barren wasteland to start fresh. And she had failed. There would be no new life. No fresh start. Jack Barnett had refused to hire her. She had brought her family all the way here so they could starve in the dust of Abilene, surrounded by drunken cowboys. What in God's name had she *done*?

Samantha pulled her gaze from the compassionate but firm one that held hers and sought to calm herself. She would not fall apart. She could not. Too much was at stake. Her family's very future. Perhaps their lives. She would not return to Savannah and William Eustice's clutches. Davy, Becky, and the rest of them deserved better than that. If they were going to starve, she'd rather have them starve holding their heads up in Abilene than beaten down under a tyrant's heel in Savannah.

She lifted her eyes to the kind face so carefully observing hers. Reaching down to the very depths of her soul, Samantha found the strength to swallow down her pride and do the one thing she swore she would never do in her life. Beg.

"Mr. Barnett, I understand your feelings," she began softly, finding her voice again. "But perhaps you do not understand my family's dire circumstances. We would most certainly not be safe in Savannah, for the truth of it is . . . we have nowhere to return to in Savannah. I have had to sell our last remaining property to pay the latest assessment that our Reconstruction government has assured me we owed. Our home in Savannah, complete with the last pieces of furniture we possessed, was sold last week to settle the bill. We barely had enough left for train fare, Mr. Barnett. We have no home in Savannah, not anymore. Neither do we have any family left to take us in, sir. What's left of our neighbors and friends . . . why, they can barely keep a roof over their own heads. They couldn't possibly take us in. And my late husband's family in Virginia was wiped out, except for a few distant cousins who are as devastated as we.''

Samantha glanced to the bare wall behind Jack Barnett's broad shoulders, her voice unable to disguise the last vestiges of resentment she harbored at the unfair and brutal treatment her countrymen had been subjected to since the war's end. The past six years had drained most of it out of her. Only a trickle remained. Another reason to escape the past and start fresh, somewhere new. Samantha had wearied of the taste of bitterness in her mouth.

"Uncle Winthrop was fond of saying that the South had been 'ground down about as thoroughly as any place since Carthage,' '' she said, a rueful smile playing with her mouth. "Dear Uncle Winthrop, he truly loved his history. Perhaps that's what broke his heart in St. Louis. He no longer had his books to console him.'' Samantha paused, reflecting for a moment before she lifted her eyes to Jack Barnett's stricken face.

"So, you see, Mr. Barnett . . . there is no home in Savannah for us to return to. No honorable one, at least.'' Her eyes narrowed, the memory of William Eustice looming in her mind. "One of our county's most avaricious tax collectors has made it abundantly clear that he is more than willing to take care of my family's needs, so long as I agree to . . . encourage his advances, shall we say? I don't think I need tell you what I thought of his offer, sir.''

Samantha watched Jack Barnett's jaw tighten as a deep flush colored his tanned skin. The fact that she had obviously touched some depth of emotion within him spurred her to an even greater honesty. ''And to be truthful, Mr. Barnett, even if we did have home and hearth waiting for us in Savannah, I still would not board that train.'' She waited until Jack Barnett's troubled dark gaze returned to hers before she continued. ''I refuse to live beneath the oppressor's heel any longer, sir. My young son deserves a better life than one with a rebel traitor's tag. He deserves much more, and I intend to give him that. I won't have my family return to a life filled with bullies and daily taunts and tax collector's threats. I would rather starve in the dust of Abilene than return to that.''

Watching Jack Barnett glance away again, Samantha let the emotion that flowed through her spill over into her voice, carrying her along on its ocean of feeling. ''Mr. Barnett, you said this assignment has the very real potential for danger. I have faced danger in one form or another for the past ten years. Invading soldiers during the war, rapacious carpetbaggers since then. I did not flinch, sir. I did not turn tail and run when I saw the Yankee soldiers spread out across our plantation fields, arm to arm, lighting their torches to burn our crops. I did not faint as my poor mother did when she saw BelleHaven go up in smoke, watching the wind carry the blaze to the barns . . . burning the livestock and everything within. And I did not turn away in horror when I watched my only brother, Jeffrey, rush toward the stables to save the horses . . . only to be consumed by flames himself.''

Samantha swallowed, forcing down the remembered horror from so long ago. The agonized screams of her young brother. The fear in her throat as she raced across the lawn, lifting her skirts to her knees so she could run faster. The terror and shock and revulsion that had swept through her when she reached him at last and found him writhing on the ground, despite the field hand's frantic attempts to quench the flames. The horrible feeling of helplessness that surrounded her, watching him die, unable to relieve his wretched suffering. Her mother sinking into a grief so overpowering she could not climb out.

Glancing at Jack Barnett now, Samantha saw his face turn ashen. His body went rigid, and to her surprise he suddenly turned his back and grasped the top rung of the chair behind him. Samantha lifted her chin and forced the ugly memories far away. She cared not if Mr. Barnett thought her brazen to parade her family's grim and grisly misfortunes before a stranger. There was no limit to how brazen she would be to provide for her loved ones.

"I'm sorry if these recollections have disturbed you, Mr. Barnett," she said softly. "Perhaps the war has calloused me to the sensibilities of polite conversation. Suffice it to say, I have had to deal with much that is unpleasant and a great deal that is dangerous. Consequently a disgruntled bookkeeper's accomplice does not frighten me in the least." Samantha let her gaze rest on Jack Barnett's broad back and waited. Waited for him to respond.

She would have to wait. Jack Barnett was too busy trying to control the tidal wave of nightmarish memories that engulfed him now to even attempt a response. It was the mention of her plantation's name, BelleHaven, that had riveted Jack to the floor. He could still see the graceful, carved letters on the signpost where it lay in the dust, trampled by his unit's men and horses after they had finished. Finished swarming across the fields in a wide swath, torches lit, setting everything in their path ablaze as they moved relentlessly along. The wind shifting, carrying the flames to the barns and stables. It was all seared into his memory. The smell of burning pitch, the acrid smoke of burning crops, burning wood, clouds of cinders swirling into his eyes, burning them, too, while he stood on a hillside and watched in silent horror.

Even now, Jack felt his stomach turn at the memory of such wanton destruction. So different from his early war years, when he'd marched into combat, fought brave men hand to hand. Saw the face of the enemy up close and looked into his eyes. Struggled and bled in the field, others dropping around him while he miraculously pushed on, leading the charge. Earning his captain's bars and a transfer out of the bloodbath in Virginia to Sherman's regiment near Vicksburg. A chance to rise even higher and faster, General Logan had said. Earn more praise for the colonel's son.

But when Sherman started his relentless march to the sea, Jack found he was no longer engaged in brutal but honest combat. Now he was the harbinger of destruction and devastation. While Jack's senior officer, Major Franklin, delighted in the role, Jack was repulsed by it. He could not find the enemy in weeping women's faces. The sounds of their anguished cries while they watched their family's only means of survival go up in smoke still echoed in his ears. Refusing to light one fire, Jack volunteered to ride perimeter and patrol for snipers, despite the derisive taunts of the major. Even so, Jack could never escape the guilt that swallowed him, watching the misery his unit brought upon these defenseless landowners. Women and children, mostly. Their men were dead or fighting elsewhere, leaving only the helpless behind.

And now, from out of his past, this woman had come—

not only stirring up disturbing feelings within himself, but also reawakening the one horrid memory Jack prayed he would someday forget. BelleHaven. Where Jack had reined in his horse on a nearby hillside, only to stare in horror at what he saw in the distance. Major Franklin pointing his men ahead, their torches still lit, aiming for the last of the fields, leaving behind a scene of terror. A man, engulfed in flames, screaming horribly, people racing from the mansion to help him. Jack's heart had caught in his throat at the sight. The screams. The horrible, horrible screams. The man writhing upon the ground. The women in the distance. The dying horses in the stables. The smell of charred wood and burning horseflesh filling the air, swirling into clouds around him, sickening him.

A searing, white-hot shame flooded Jack's body, engulfing him now just as the fire had swallowed this woman's brother years ago. He clutched the straight-backed chair so hard the wood trembled beneath his fingers. He had been present, had watched this woman's family destroyed, and been helpless to prevent it. Well, he may have been helpless then . . . but, by God, he wasn't helpless now!

Waiting until he felt reasonably sure his emotions would not betray themselves on his face, Jack turned to the widow Winchester at last. She observed him intently. Jack noticed her small reticule had been twisted into a misshapen mass in her hands. He forced his gaze to hers. "Mrs. Winchester, the position is yours." He watched the effect of his words play across that lovely face.

Samantha's heart nearly stopped. Her breath surely did. Her mouth dropped open in a most unladylike fashion. Almost unable to believe her ears, she stared at the somber face in front of her. "Oh . . . Mr. Barnett," she said when she could draw a breath. "You . . . you don't know how . . . how grateful I am."

"I think I do, ma'am," he replied, captivated despite himself by the transformation that had taken place before him. Samantha Winchester's smile lit up her face, chasing away the demeanor of the subdued widow. A smiling enchantress, emerald eyes alight, stood in her place. Jack had to grab hold of himself before he lost his balance. He could have sworn the floorboards beneath his feet had shifted suddenly.

"Mr. Barnett, I swear you will not regret your decision," Samantha declared. "I will work diligently, as many hours a day as you require, until I find what you're looking for. I promise you will not be disappointed in my effort, sir."

At this moment, Jack doubted he could find anything that was disappointing in Samantha Winchester. Forcing his gaze away from her unsettling one for his own sake, he distracted himself with action. "Mrs. Winchester, I believe you said you have your son with you. Where is he now, waiting for you outside?"

"Oh, no, sir. He . . . he and the rest of my family are waiting at the train station. I told them to wait for me there."

Jack walked to the door and grabbed his hat from a small wooden peg. "Well, I think it would be best if we get you and your family situated right away," he said, opening the door and holding it wide. "Exactly who else comprises this family of yours, Mrs. Winchester, if I may be so bold as to inquire?"

Samantha paused before answering. "Well, Mr. Barnett, perhaps it would be best if I let them introduce themselves." She smiled her most charming smile as she walked out the door.

Jack turned his face away and scratched his chin. He was desperately trying to obscure the grin that threatened to escape. He didn't dare turn around for fear of releasing the laughter that was teasing him inside. Laughing at himself and his own foolishness. Look what he had gotten himself into this time.

He peered out of the corner of his eye at Samantha Winchester's relatives again. A terrified girl who couldn't be more than nineteen. He couldn't tell for sure, she was so skinny. A button-nosed little boy whose huge blue eyes consumed his entire face. Such a thin little face. Much too thin. Even the elderly Negro mammy was toothpick thin. But at least she didn't look as if she'd flinch if he said "Boo!" as the younger ones did. Not that one. Her brown face was screwed up so tight, Jack expected her to snap his head off if he spoke to her.

And then . . . there were the aunts. "*Maiden* aunts," Samantha had whispered beside his ear before the ladies themselves flounced ceremoniously forward to inform Jack in no uncertain terms what they thought of this poor excuse for a town, the filthy condition of the railroads, the unkempt appearance of what few unfortunate citizens had crossed their path, and how distressed they were that their well-bred and educated niece had been forced by the Recent Unpleasantness to stoop to working for hire.

Jack had to plant both feet firmly to avoid being blown over by the force of their combined complaint. Thank God for Samantha's swift intervention and astute change of topic, otherwise, they would be haranguing him still. One thing for sure, Jack knew he couldn't parade Samantha's family all the way to the other side of Abilene and Mrs. Johnson's boardinghouse. One look at the rest of Abilene's citizens would throw those two old ladies into a spell of the vapors for sure. He'd have to get a wagon somewhere and bring them around the back.

Composing his face as best he could, Jack turned to address Samantha at last. "Do you have any more, Mrs. Winchester?" He arched a brow.

"More what, Mr. Barnett?" she asked innocently.

"*Relatives*, Mrs. Winchester."

Having seen the effort Jack Barnett had taken to keep a straight face while being lectured by her aunts, Samantha felt comfortable in letting her own smile escape. "Why, yes, I do, Mr. Barnett—but they're back in Virginia."

"For that I am most grateful, Mrs. Winchester. You may have brought more than Abilene can handle as it is," he said, unable to contain his amusement any longer. "The only suitable place for your family would be with Mrs. Lucy Johnson. She owns the house where I'm staying. It may be somewhat cramped with so many people, but at least it's on the far end of town. Abilene is a rough-and-ready place, ma'am, and I shudder to think what your aunts will make of it when they discover that."

"I'll see to it that they do not go out exploring, Mr. Barnett. Don't worry. I'm sure Mrs. Johnson's home will be quite suitable."

Jack watched the smile tease across her face for a moment before he addressed the eavesdropping stationmaster, who hovered nearby. "You, there . . ." At the sound of Jack's voice, the little man jerked to attention. "I'll need a wagon and horses on the double. These ladies have been in your station long enough."

"Uh, uh . . . yes, sir. Right away, sir." The stationmaster bobbed dutifully upon hearing the command.

Jack turned back to Samantha. "Now, Mrs. Winchester, let's see if we can get your family to that boardinghouse with your aunts seeing as little of Abilene as possible."

Chapter

4

Major Anthony Craig perched on the edge of his desk, absentmindedly slapping his short riding crop against his tight military breeches. A small, bent, brown-skinned man squatted at his feet, polishing the major's tall riding boots with a long cloth that slid expertly between his worn hands. Back and forth went the cloth, bringing a gloss to the black leather. Major Craig was oblivious to the amount of effort being expended below. His eyes were focused instead on the large, disheveled man standing in the center of his office. Dust coated the man's cowhide boots, as well as the rest of him. A holster bearing two Colt .45s rode low on the man's hips, just as the weathered black Stetson settled low over his eyes.

"You're sure there was no one else with him?" Craig probed.

"Nobody," Joe Taggert replied. "Word has it he came into town all by his lonesome and set up shop in the agent's office. Had to go buy all new supplies, I reckon. 'Cause me and Zeke didn't leave him much." A sly grin twisted Taggert's unshaven face.

Craig curled a contemptuous lip. "And brought me *nothing*!"

Taggert's dark hooded eyes settled on the immaculately attired major. Not a wrinkle or crease to be seen. Buttons so brightly polished, they could blind a man with their gleam. "I told you, Major, we brought everything that was there. The army must've got to it first—that's all I can figger. Those ledger books were nowhere to be seen."

As much as he hated to find himself in agreement with Taggert, Anthony Craig could not avoid the obvious. The army had swooped down on Jamison's office at the same time they were incarcerating that obsequious little clerk, before anyone was the wiser. Worse, they got there before Craig could cause the incriminating ledgers to conveniently disappear. His finely chiseled features settled into a dark scowl, etching two deep lines beside his mouth. The riding crop flicked impatiently against his muscled thigh.

There was no telling how long those army clerks had been combing the ledgers, Craig fumed. Who knew what they'd found? Jamison always swore up and down he'd hidden their tracks so well the army would never find them. And even if they happened to stumble close by accident, they'd still be unable to find the bank deposits without the account numbers. Without access to the St. Louis banks, the army could prove nothing. Craig swatted his thigh harder. He wished he shared Jamison's blithe trust in the army's stupidity.

Oh, they were stupid enough, the major thought bitterly. Too stupid to recognize real leadership when they saw it. Who had returned from the plains Indian raids with the most killed? Hundreds of savages dead! And yet he still watched his inferior fellow officers advanced before himself. *Their* shoulders adorned with braid and not his. *Their* duty assignments changed to the coveted East while he languished in this godforsaken backwater. Passed over time and time again. The knot of resentment in his gut had twisted tighter with each rejection. The ingratitude was more than he could stomach anymore. He would get his due from the army, with or without their cooperation.

"I'm forced to agree with you, Taggert," Craig said at last, his gaze drifting out the window to the dusty activities of Fort Riley. "They obviously slipped into that office and made off with the ledgers. We can assume the army is suspicious, but they haven't found any proof of wrongdoing yet. We can also assume that this new agent was sent here to snoop around while he's buying beef, hoping not to arouse our suspicions."

"What do we do now?" Taggert prodded.

Craig's small, cold eyes settled on him. "For now, I want you to keep track of that agent. Find out who he sees, where he goes, and make sure you check his office. Make it a point to walk past there every day so he won't think twice if he sees you. Who knows, you might find that office empty. If you do, take a look at any papers he had lying around. Got that?"

Taggert nodded. "Gotcha, Major. I'll get back to ya soon as I can."

Craig didn't notice him leave. He was too busy admiring the high gloss of his newly shined boots. Reaching inside his trim fitted uniform, he withdrew a quarter and tossed it beside the little man who still knelt on the floor. "It'll do, Pedro," was all he said.

Jack Barnett leaned over the desk, deliberately fixing his eyes on the open ledger pages and away from Samantha

Winchester's reddish brown hair, which spilled from its restraining bun in characteristic fashion. Loose tendrils and stray curls kept escaping their hairpins, falling about her face as she sat at the desk, head bent over the books in total concentration.

"I realize that the army's system must be entirely different from anything you ever saw in your father's business, Mrs. Winchester. Take your time. Don't try to figure it out in one sitting. Otherwise it'll make you want to tear your hair out, I'm sure," he said, then caught himself. Good Lord, why did he have to mention hair?

"You're right, Mr. Barnett," she agreed, scanning the columns. "It certainly is different. But I'm sure I'll find the similarities if I look hard enough. After all, bookkeeping *is* bookkeeping. Even the army can't change that." She gave Jack one of those smiles that caused the blood to pump through his veins a whole lot faster than normal. Jack was surprised how quickly he was growing accustomed to those smiles and the way they made her eyes light up.

"I hope you're right. The army manages to change everything it touches."

The sound of the office door opening made Jack turn. He saw Clyde Monroe standing in the doorway, gaping at Samantha.

"Well, don't just stand there, Deputy. Come on in and meet the army's new bookkeeper. Mrs. Winchester, let me introduce Clyde Monroe. He's one of the men in charge of law and order here in Abilene." Jack watched his shaggy old cell mate snap out of his stupor and slowly approach them both.

"P-pleased to meet you, ma'am." Clyde bowed his head respectfully after first snatching off his weather-beaten hat.

"Thank you, Deputy. I'm pleased to be here in this bustling new town of yours." Samantha beamed at him.

"Y-ya are?" Clyde stammered. He blinked at Jack in astonishment. "Has . . . has she *seen* Abilene yet, Jack?"

Jack laughed. "I'll have you know Mrs. Winchester walked all the way through town from the train station yesterday morning. I'd say she had a fair look."

"Jehoshaphat!" Clyde exclaimed, faded blue eyes bulging. "Ma'am, you shouldn't have done that! If you don't mind my sayin' so, a fine lady like yourself shouldn't be out a-walkin' in this rough ol' cow town by herself. Why, there're cowpokes ever' which way, and saloons, and, and . . . and all sorts of things that a lady like you shouldn't be seein'!"

Samantha kept her laughter in check while she watched this unkempt, shaggy-haired deputy with the hangdog face get as flustered as her two maiden aunts at the thought of impropriety. "You're very kind to be concerned, Deputy Monroe. But I managed quite well, thank you. While I cannot say I felt totally at ease on the streets of Abilene, I wasn't interfered with in any way. Actually, most of the citizens I observed were either imbibing at the time or suffering from the effects."

Clyde blinked, then turned to Jack. "Imbi—?" he beseeched.

"Drinking," Jack translated with a grin.

"Ohhhhhh, yes, ma'am." Clyde's shaggy head bobbed vigorously. "That *is* a fact. All the more reason you should let Jack or me here escort you whenever you want to go somewhere. Now, you promise me you won't go paradin' out about the streets of Abilene alone, all right? These cowpokes get all fired up at the slightest thing, and I wouldn't want you to put yerself in their way. There's gonna be a powerful lot more wranglers headin' into town from now on till fall. Abilene will be bustin' at the seams afore long.''

Touched more than she could say by this untidy and gentle man's concern for her welfare, Samantha smiled warmly. Clyde's eyes seemed to bulge even wider. ''I promise I shall not parade about unduly, Deputy. Thank you so much for your concern.'' It had been longer than she could remember since a public official had shown any concern for her at all. Abilene might be primitive, but it was beginning to reveal its charms.

Clyde blinked and turned once again to Jack, who merely clapped him on the back. Glancing at Samantha, Jack said, ''Mrs. Winchester, would you be so kind as to excuse me for a few moments? I've got to check on those cattle pens outside the train station and see if they're going to hold up to the herds that are heading this way. I'll return shortly.'' Grasping Clyde's arm, Jack continued, ''Clyde, why don't you walk with me?'' He forcibly escorted Clyde to the door.

''Pleased to meetcha, Miz Winchester.'' Clyde lifted his hat as Jack pushed him through the door. Once outside and safely out of earshot, Clyde turned to Jack with a huge grin. ''Whooooooooey! If *she's* workin' for the army, I just might join up agin!'' he cackled in glee.

Jack stepped over a raised board in the plank sidewalk. ''Between you and me, Clyde, I don't think they'd take you back.''

Clyde cackled again as they stepped down into the dirt that marked Abilene's main street. Small clouds rose up behind both men when they walked, while horses and wagons left miniature dust storms in their wakes.

''Jack, tell me true. What is a woman like Miz Winchester doin' here in Abilene? She don't belong here. God-a-mighty, but she don't!''

''Believe me, I tried to convince her of that when she

came for the job yesterday, but . . .'' Jack paused, moving out of the way of an approaching wagon. "Christ, Clyde! She and her family lost everything in the war back in Georgia. Soon as she told me that, well . . . I *had* to give her the position. I couldn't let her family starve.''

"Family?" Clyde cried, incredulous. "She's brought her family *here*? To Abilene? God-a-mighty!''

"Just her son," Jack teased. "And her sister . . . and her two maiden aunts . . . and her Negro housekeeper.''

Clyde stopped dead in the middle of the street, despite the fact that three men on horseback were heading straight for him. "Jehoshaphat, Jack! What in tarnation was she thinkin' of, bringin' all them women to Abilene?''

Jack grabbed Clyde's arm and yanked his startled friend out of the way of the approaching wranglers. "She couldn't leave them in Georgia to starve, Clyde.''

Clyde just wagged his head. "Well, I sure hope none of those women are as good lookin' as Miz Winchester, that's all I gotta say. Or we're gonna have cowboys beatin' down the door.''

Jack had to agree with Clyde. About Samantha, anyway. A fine-looking woman, she surely was. And he dared any cowboy to try knocking on her door while he was there. "Well, I don't think we'll have any trouble on account of her aunts. Those two ladies could drop a wrangler in his tracks just by looking at him. And her housekeeper looks mean enough to snap a stick in two if she were to bite it.'' He sidestepped a horse's hind end and swung himself up to the plank walkway leading into the Prairie Rose saloon. "But her younger sister sure is a pretty little thing, especially if we can fatten her up a bit. I told your aunt to go heavy on the beef for a while, and I'd pay her extra. I doubt the Winchester family has seen meat on the table for a long time. That little boy is skinnier than a range rabbit.'' Jack remembered the thin face with the huge blue eyes that had followed his every movement.

Clyde stopped dead in his tracks once again, even though Jack held the saloon door wide open. Loud voices could be heard from inside already, and it was only eleven o'clock in the morning. "You took all those women to Aunt Lucy's?" he cried.

"Well, where else would I take them? It's the only place in town that's suitable. Maybe a little cramped for sleeping space, but we're managing. Actually your Aunt Lucy was tickled pink to have all those extra ladies to talk to, if you ask me." Jack shouldered his way into the saloon.

Clyde didn't say a word. He simply shook his shaggy head and meekly followed Jack into the Prairie Rose.

Samantha cupped her chin in her hands as she hunched over the ledger. She squinted at the entries listed under purchases, matching them with the ones listed for the previous month, and the month before that. Thank God Mr. Barnett had told her to take her time, she thought with a sigh of relief. He was right about the army. These ledgers certainly were different from the neatly categorized ones she had once maintained in her father's shipping office. Who knew how long it would take her to learn her way around their system, let alone trace the missing money? Samantha sighed out loud this time, knowing she was alone. She didn't want to give Mr. Barnett any reason to reconsider his decision to hire her. She'd sit here all day and night if necessary to untangle the maze. Any man as kind and considerate as Jack Barnett had shown himself to be deserved nothing less than her very best effort. And he would get it, too, she vowed to herself. He'd gone out of his way to show kindness to her family, even at the train station. Hiring a wagon to take them to that nice Mrs. Johnson's boardinghouse. Giving Davy and her his own larger downstairs bedroom and taking the tiny room at the end of the hall for himself.

Samantha remembered the look on Jack Barnett's face when her son had seen the food spread out on Lucy Johnson's table. A small twinge of pride tried mightily to tweak, but Samantha wouldn't let it this time. She couldn't. She was too grateful. She was going to pretend she didn't overhear Mr. Barnett's whispered instructions to Lucy Johnson to "fatten them up." Even though her prideful heart rebelled at first, she didn't say a word. She knew how thin and bedraggled her family looked, especially to someone who had escaped the war's ravages. Someone like Jack Barnett. She'd swallowed her pride to get this job. She'd be damned if she'd let her pride take food out of her family's mouth. This man meant nothing but kindness. She could feel it as surely as she could feel the hot Abilene sun on her face that very morning.

Lost in thought, Samantha didn't notice the unshaven face that peered through the front window. Joe Taggert squinted through the grime in vain, trying to see who in thunder was sitting in the army agent's office. Looked mighty like a woman to him. That thought was enough to spur Taggert to check for certain, and he barged through the office door without so much as a knock.

"Well, well, well," he declared, a sly grin twisting his face when he saw Samantha jump in her chair. "Who do we have here, do you reckon? Don't tell me you're the army's new cattle agent?" He gave a short, derisive laugh.

Samantha sat very still in her chair. The look in the man's gleaming eyes made her blood run cold. She'd seen that look before, back in Georgia—every time William Eustice came to call. She forced the frightened feeling inside to calm, just as she had so many times before, and cleared her throat. "If you are looking for Mr. Barnett, I'm afraid you'll have to return later. He stepped out for a few minutes. He'll be returning shortly." She emphasized the last word, just in case.

Hot damn! Taggert thought. A little Southern gal! Way out here in Abilene. Didn't that beat all? And a looker, too. Damned if she wasn't! This job was gonna be a whole lot of fun! He swaggered across the office toward Samantha. "Well, maybe I'm lookin' for him and maybe I ain't," he said. "And maybe I'm just curious why the U.S. Army would send a woman to do a *man's* job. Buying beef, I mean." Taggert stood directly in front of Samantha's desk, staring at the large black ledger books with great interest.

Samantha immediately sensed that this man, whoever he was, had no business poking his nose in Jack Barnett's office. She forced herself to rise from her chair and step around the desk, deliberately blocking his view of the ledgers, even though that move also brought her unpleasantly close to this unwelcome visitor. The stale smell of whiskey and the pungent aroma of a body that had not seen soap and water for quite a while greeted her nostrils. She made herself stand there.

"Mr. Barnett is the army's purchasing agent. I am simply his bookkeeper. Now, if you'll kindly give me your name, sir, I will tell Mr. Barnett you came to see him."

Taggert grinned wider. Oh, my . . . would you just lissen to that sweet little mouth talk. Sweet as sugar, he'd bet. And full of spit, too. He could tell by the way she stood up to him right now. Sugar 'n spit. Hard for a man to resist. A familiar sensation started, down around his kneecaps, working its way north. Whether she was Barnett's bookkeeper or not, Taggert sure was glad little Miss Sugarmouth was in Abilene. Yes, indeedy! She'd make his work a whole lot more interesting.

"Well, ain't you the spunky one." His voice lowered, his eyes meeting hers suggestively. "What makes you think I dropped by to see Barnett? Maybe I came to see you, little Missy Rebel. Where're you from? I spent some time down Alabama way. You sure do sound a lot like them little gals."

Samantha forced herself to stand still. She'd faced men like this before. She'd learned to swallow down her fear and look them straight in the eye—and never blink. She tightened her mouth into a hard line and folded her arms, blocking his visual inspection of her bosom.

"Where I come from is none of your business, sir," she replied in the coldest voice she possessed. "State your name, and I'll tell Mr. Barnett you came. Then I want you to leave."

Taggert blinked at her rebuke and threw back his head with a laugh. Damn! Didn't she beat all? A whole lotta sugar and a bucket full o' spit! "Don't you worry none 'bout my name, little Missy Reb. If I want to see your Mr. Barnett, I will." He moved to the door and yanked it open, then glanced back and insolently let his eyes travel over her. "And you can bet I'll visit *you* again, Missy Reb." He gave a taunting laugh and swaggered out the door.

Samantha's shoulders sagged with relief. She knew he would be back. Men like him always came back.

Suddenly Jack Barnett's face appeared in Samantha's mind. She pictured herself telling him about the unwelcome visitor, his persistence, his obvious curiosity about what was going on, his obvious interest in her. Samantha paused for a moment, reconsidering. She would tell Barnett about the man and his visit and his obvious curiosity concerning the ledger, but she would say nothing about the equally obvious threat to herself. If she did, Jack Barnett might rethink his decision to keep her on. It would justify every concern he had raised. A woman in an office, working. What would people think?

It was obvious what that horrible man thought. She was there for the taking. Samantha pursed her lips in determination. She had handled men like that before, and she would again. Without help. She wasn't about to jeopardize her family's chance for a new start. She'd tell Jack Barnett nothing that would cause him concern for her sake. Nothing at all.

Major Anthony Craig looked up from stroking his stallion's soft nose and stared incredulously at Joe Taggert. "A woman? The army has a *woman* working with Barnett?" He whispered so his voice wouldn't carry to the surrounding soldiers, who were in the stable saddling their mounts.

"Yep. And a damn pretty one, too. Little rebel gal, from the sound of all that sugar in her mouth." He licked his lips as a lecherous grin spread across his face.

Craig's head came up again at that. He ran one hand through his light blond hair, brushing it out of his eyes, while his other hand lay patiently open. The grand chestnut stallion took his time nibbling the sugar in Craig's palm. "A *rebel*, you say?" His eyebrow rose with interest. "Whatever possessed this Barnett to hire a traitor as a clerk? I wonder if headquarters knows what he's done? I'm certain the United States Army would never hire a female clerk, and I'm positive they'd never consider hiring a former enemy!"

"Well, she's there all right, Major. And I'm mighty glad she is . . . if you know what I mean." He laughed. "It could make this job a *whole* lot more interesting."

Catching Taggert's eye, Craig also caught his message. Loud and clear. His own eyes lit up with a darker light. "Perhaps you're right, Taggert." He turned his attention back to his majestic horse and rubbed the stallion's soft nose gently. "I think perhaps I'll pay a visit to our little rebel. It might be fun, at that." The smile that curved the ends of Anthony Craig's thin lips contrasted sharply with the gentle movements of his hand as he caressed his horse.

Chapter

5

Jack paused just inside Lucy Johnson's darkened kitchen and stealthily closed the door. It clicked shut with a louder noise then he'd hoped. Many a year had passed since he'd tried to sneak into a house without disturbing its sleeping occupants. Grasping hold of his boot, Jack braced himself against the door while he yanked his stockinged foot free. First one, then the other. Reasonably certain he could now safely maneuver Lucy's creaky hallway without waking Samantha and Davy, Jack tiptoed across the kitchen, headed for his closet-turned-bedroom and a sound sleep. Now that he was relaxed.

Abilene might not have all of San Francisco's amenities, but it still possessed the essentials. Gambling, liquor, and women. Although Jack had sworn off the first for the duration of this assignment, he found the cow town's inescapable dust left him with a powerful need for the second—and Samantha Winchester's disturbing daily presence left him with an equally powerful need for the third.

As much as he tried not to, Jack had found himself observing her entirely too often these past two days. He would catch himself watching Samantha as she bent over the ledger books, her red-brown curls spilling about her face. Those curls taunted him from across the office, teasing him with their lustrous color, daring him to approach and see if they were as soft as they looked. It was enough to make Jack want to hide her hairpins.

He was grateful for the many duties that kept him out of the office—bargaining with cattlemen, inspecting the herds, gossiping with shopkeepers in the hope they might know something about the army agent with the sticky fingers. By now Jack felt he was on speaking terms with every cattleman in Abilene. It was a damn good thing that more arrived every day, because Jack needed every excuse he could find to escape the snare that his cramped little office had become.

Jack was not used to being distracted like this. He was quite accustomed to being attracted to beautiful women, and was equally accustomed to indulging himself. Frequently. But never while on assignment. He'd made a rule years ago, when Matthew Logan had first brought him into government investigations: no women while working. It was too risky. He never knew if an alluring face or laughing eyes hid secrets that might jeopardize his mission, perhaps his very life. Spying women might not be as common as spying men, but they existed. Jack had seen their work— or rather, the chilling aftereffects. Women could kill as easily as men. All you had to do was give them enough reason. He had decided early on that satisfying the momentary urge wasn't worth the risk. San Francisco's beauteous ladies would be ready and waiting and very, very willing when he returned.

Consequently Jack found himself totally unprepared for dealing with a potent and inescapable on-the-job distraction. He had violated his own cardinal rule. He'd brought a woman into his assignment. To be fair, he'd only halfway violated his rule. Samantha might be there, but he certainly wasn't dallying with her. He'd made sure his every action was gentlemanly to a fault. Jack could not enforce the same restrictions on his thoughts, however. And the thought of dallying with Samantha Winchester was occurring all too frequently of late.

Don't be a fool, he kept telling himself. *If there was ever a woman you could not have, it is Samantha Winchester. You've got no right to look at any Confederate widow. And that Confederate widow, most particularly. She'd probably shoot you herself if she knew what you'd done. Your men destroyed her home. Your men killed her brother. Don't be a fool, Barnett. Control yourself.*

But he couldn't. No completely. Jack could guide his every action to make sure he treated Samantha with the respect and kindness due a lady. But he could no more control his thoughts than he could control the clouds in that azure Kansas sky. And his thoughts, like those clouds, drifted more and more wantonly.

Jack tested Lucy Johnson's creaky hall floor, placing his weight a little at a time. A loud creak reverberated down the narrow hallway. Jack winced. Holding his boots in both hands, he crept past Samantha's doorway even more slowly, shifting his weight inch by inch. Just when he thought he'd passed without waking anyone, Jack heard Samantha's bedroom door creak open behind him. He winced again before he turned to face her.

He couldn't find her. Jack blinked, his eyes already accustomed to the dark, and nearly jumped out of his skin when he heard a small voice whisper below him.

"Mr. Barnett! What are *you* doing out here?"

Jack looked down and saw Davy Winchester standing in his nightshirt and bare feet, gazing up at him. Davy's huge eyes seemed to reflect what little moonlight shone into Lucy's kitchen. They stared up at Jack.

He swallowed. ''Uhhh . . . uh, I was, uh . . . I was just . . .'' Jack faltered, searching for a plausible reason for returning home this late, other than the real one. Something he could tell a nine-year-old boy.

''Were you thirsty, too? Boy, I sure am!'' Davy said, taking a careful glimpse backward before he quietly shut the bedroom door. ''Aunt Lucy made the best supper there ever was! We had ham and cornbread and beans and tomatoes she took from a jar and applesauce she made from dried apples she keeps in a big ol' urn underneath the house and, and, and biscuits, too!'' The whole time he whispered out the long menu, Davy was making his way surefootedly across the kitchen in the manner of an accomplished night prowler.

Jack just stared after him. Watching the small boy approach the water bucket, he quickly offered, ''Here, let me help you with that.'' He set his boots on the floor and made his way around the sturdy wooden table in the center of the room.

''Oh, *I* can do it,'' Davy chirped, flashing a smile that tugged at Jack's heart. The sound of boyish independence was unmistakable.

''Can you now? Okay, show me.'' Jack folded his arms and watched as Davy authoritatively trotted over to the cupboard and found Lucy Johnson's step stool. Dragging it across the floor, ignoring the low scraping noise, he pulled it against the dry sink, where the large metal water bucket sat. Jack held his breath as he watched Davy climb on top of the teetering stool and proudly flash him a victorious grin as he grasped the metal dipper.

''Don't you want some, Mr. Barnett?'' Davy held out the dipper when he had finished drinking.

"Why, thank you, son. Don't mind if I do." The dipper's cold metal shocked Jack's warm mouth as the sweet, cool water rushed down inside him, chasing away the taste of the Prairie Rose's whiskey.

"Where'd you eat supper, Mr. Barnett?" Davy's enormous eyes rested on Jack's face.

"Well, I, uh . . . I, um, decided to . . . to see some folks instead," he quickly lied.

"You didn't have *any* supper?" Davy cried, apparently incredulous at the thought of missing a meal. "Boy, you must be real hungry by now!" Without waiting for Jack to answer, he scrambled off the tottering stool and dashed to the cupboard again. Opening a lower cabinet door, Davy reached in and pulled out a metal pie plate, still a quarter full of pie. Flourishing it before Jack, he said temptingly, "It's Maysie's, and we got to eat it while it was still hot! She makes the best apple pie that ever was. Here, I'll get you a piece."

Jack was about to decline Davy's kind offer when his stomach decided otherwise. It growled. "That's real nice of you, son. It sure does smell good."

Davy hadn't bothered to wait for Jack's acceptance, but had scampered over to another cabinet and pulled a long butcher knife from the drawer. Jack flinched, hoping the boy didn't slice off a finger while he was trying to impress him. God! What would he tell Samantha?

Despite his misgivings, Jack managed to keep his mouth shut while Davy sliced through the flaky crust and carefully separated two large slices of pie. Even through the moonlit kitchen, Jack could see the juicy apple drippings run into the pan. He certainly could smell the spices. Cinnamon, cloves, allspice. His mouth started to water. He didn't even wait for Davy to invite him. He quickly pulled a chair to the table and held out his hand for the fork.

Davy presented him with one and placed the pie plate in the middle of the table between them both. "You're really gonna like this, I betcha!" he declared as he leaned over the table and shoved in a mouthful of pie.

"I bet you're right." Jack anxiously dug his fork into the tender crust.

Davy was right. Maysie's apple pie darn near melted in his mouth. Jack couldn't remember when he'd tasted pastry that flaky and light. The piecrust simply dissolved on his tongue. Apples, soft and sweet, greeted him next, spiced so deliciously he almost didn't want to swallow, lest he lose the flavor. He'd never tasted an apple pie that good before. Not in the finest restaurant in San Francisco. Or back East, either. Not even at home. A little tug of remembrance twinged inside him. His mother, God rest her soul, had never baked anything this good in her life.

"Ummm, good," Jack said after he'd swallowed at last. Winking at Davy, he shoved another piece into his mouth.

Davy quickly took the bait. "Ummmmmmm, good!" he pronounced loudly, then shoved in the rest of his slice, despite the fact that it was bigger than his mouth. Flaky bits of crust tumbled to the table while Davy manfully tried to maneuver this mouthful.

Not to be outdone, Jack looked Davy right in the eye. "Watch *this*," he challenged, and placed the remainder of his own slice in his mouth. It had been a very long time since Jack had been in an eating contest. He'd forgotten what fun they were. Closing his eyes, he emitted an exaggerated sigh of appreciation. "Ummmmmmmm-*mmmmmmm*!" His voice deliberately rose in emphasis.

"Ummmm, what?" Samantha's voice asked from the hall.

Jack nearly choked. His fork dropped onto the metal pie plate with a clank. He hastily pushed back his chair and scrambled to his feet, vainly trying to finish the enormous mouthful of pie. He had obviously won the contest. Now, if he could only swallow.

Grateful that Davy had raced toward his mother at the sound of her voice, Jack turned to see Samantha Winchester standing in the middle of the moonlit kitchen, barefoot, a shawl wrapped around her cotton nightgown, her magnificent mass of dark curls loose about her shoulders. Jack stopped chewing and stared. He couldn't help himself.

"Why, Mr Barnett, don't tell me Davy persuaded you to help him snitch some of Maysie's pie?" Samantha teased. "We told him he had to wait till morning."

Feeling a response of some kind was called for, Jack did his best, under the circumstances. "Umuhphawah!" he managed and released a dribble of pie juice down his chin.

Davy collapsed in a fit of laughter, which caused his mother to shush him quickly, finger to lips. "Shh! We don't want to wake up Mrs. Johnson!" she cautioned.

Jack took the opportunity of distraction to wipe his hand across his mouth, removing the incriminating juicy evidence as he swallowed the last of the pie. He stealthily cleaned his hand on the back of his pants. Lucy would probably wonder when she did his laundry.

"You're not supposed to talk with your mouth full, Mr. Barnett," Davy scolded with a giggle.

Glad for the darkened kitchen so Samantha couldn't see his embarrassment, Jack shoved his hands in his back pockets and gave them both a sheepish smile. "I'll remember that, Davy. The next time Maysie bakes a pie."

"And *you* mind your manners, young man!" Samantha gently reprimanded. "I have a sneaking suspicion that you were responsible for Mr. Barnett's midnight dessert. Now, give me a kiss and go back to bed."

"Yes, ma'am." Davy hugged his mother, then flashed

another smile at Jack. " 'Night, Mr. Barnett," he said and padded down the hallway, closing the bedroom door behind him.

Now that his mouth was no longer full and his accomplice had disappeared, Jack turned his attention toward Samantha. He was amazed how alluring a cotton nightgown could be on the right woman. He grinned. "You'll have to forgive us, Mrs. Winchester. We got a little carried away."

Samantha let the amusement she had hidden dance across her face. "There's nothing to forgive, Mr. Barnett. I haven't met anyone yet who could resist Maysie's pie. I snitched my fair share when I was a child." She came deeper into the kitchen, instinctively drawn closer to this man. When she had seen him play with her son a moment ago, her heart had given a little skip. Samantha smiled shyly up at Jack Barnett through the semidarkness now and felt her heart give more than a little skip.

Jack eagerly matched her shy advance and met Samantha in the middle of the kitchen. It was all he could do to keep his hands from the luxurious mass of hair surrounding her face. To distract himself, Jack smiled into her eyes and found distraction aplenty. "You have a fine boy there," he said.

"It's kind of you to notice, Mr. Barnett," she replied, holding his gaze for as long as she dared. She glanced away and paused, trying to find the right words to convey her feelings. "I cannot tell you how . . . how much I appreciate your many kindnesses to my family these past few days."

"It's been my pleasure, I assure you," Jack said, his attention drawn by that wealth of dark curls again.

At the sound of his low, soft voice, so very close, Samantha felt her heart give that strange little grateful skip she'd felt before. Yes . . . that was it. Gratitude. She glanced over her shoulder. "Well, I had best see if my son is really asleep. Good night, Mr. Barnett. I'll see you in the morning." She paused then, strangely reluctant to leave. "Perhaps tomorrow night you'd like to join us for supper. Mrs. Johnson is a wonderful cook, and I'm reasonably certain Maysie could be persuaded to bake another pie."

Jack hesitated a scant second. "That's a mighty tempting offer, Mrs. Winchester. I didn't know how hungry I was until I tasted that pie."

Stopping by her doorway, Samantha noticed Jack Barnett's boots beside the wall, which confirmed her earlier suspicions about his sudden midnight appearance in Lucy Johnson's kitchen. Samantha toyed with her reply for a moment, but couldn't resist. "I can imagine, Mr. Barnett. I rather doubt that the Prairie Rose serves supper," she observed lightly.

The faint sound of amusement tinging her voice caught Jack's attention right away. He decided he couldn't let that comment pass without a reply and closed the distance between them again. Just to see if she was smiling or not. She was. He folded his arms in front of him. "Mrs. Winchester, I'm curious. Considering the number of saloons in Abilene, how did you know I went to the Prairie Rose?"

Samantha leaned against her bedroom door. His sudden nearness caused her grateful heart to skip another beat. She glanced away. "Mrs. Johnson has been telling us all about Abilene. In great detail, I might add. Her descriptions of the local, uh . . . citizens were particularly fascinating."

"I can imagine. But frankly, Mrs. Winchester, I'm surprised that Lucy Johnson would discuss Abilene's local customs in front of your two maiden aunts or your younger sister. Hardly suitable dinner conversation, wouldn't you agree?"

Samantha's head came up at the sound of laughter in his voice. "Actually she told me while we were both washing dishes, alone. She said that the Prairie Rose was . . . how shall I say it . . . preferred by the few discerning gentlemen in town. And if I have learned anything about you in three days, Mr. Barnett, it is that you are most discerning indeed.''

Once again Jack was grateful for the darkness, for he felt a distinct flush creep up his neck. "I'll . . . take that as a compliment, Mrs. Winchester.''

Drawn by the light in those dark eyes, Samantha felt a peculiar warmth begin inside, as well as an unexplainable urge to banter again. "Actually, Mr. Barnett, there was something else that led me to that conclusion. Your companion's perfume still lingers. It's a much heavier fragrance than I use, therefore I couldn't help but notice.''

The tease in Samantha's voice and the laughter in her eyes caused Jack's pulse to race. That warning voice of conscience which stood ever ready to rein in his thoughts was swept away by the feelings spreading through him now. He savored the moment before he spoke. "Mrs. Winchester, with your acute powers of observation at our disposal, I expect we will have no difficulty whatsoever tracking down that embezzler.''

Samantha felt her face flush, partly from his praise, partly from the sound of his voice, so close. She turned to enter her bedroom at last, glad that the dark concealed her color. "Good night, Mr. Barnett.'' She smiled over her shoulder before she closed the door.

"Good night, Mrs. Winchester,'' Jack replied softly. With a deep sigh, he leaned down, grabbed his boots, and headed for his closet-bedroom. There would be no sound sleep tonight, Jack suspected, for he was far from relaxed now.

*   *   *

Jack settled back comfortably into Barney Peterson's barber chair, watching the plump little barber wring out a heated towel. "You're going to have to bring in somebody to help you, Mr. Peterson, if any more cowboys come into town. I imagine the first thing they all want is a chance to scrub off the months of trail dirt," he said when the barber held up the steaming towel.

"Call me Barney," Peterson replied with an engaging smile. He settled the hot towel over Jack's face, leaving him just enough room to breathe. "Actually the first thing most of them wranglers want is a drink." He chuckled. "*Then* they head over my way."

Jack reveled in the relaxing warmth, just as he'd enjoyed the soak he'd had in Peterson's huge metal washtub in the back. He'd taken care to lather more heavily than normal, making sure to wash away all traces of incriminating perfume. Jack smiled beneath the towel, remembering Samantha's lighthearted manner in the moonlit kitchen.

If he didn't know better, he'd think she was flirting with him last night. That was ridiculous, of course, he told himself. He was imagining things. Hoping, actually. Maybe there was a trace of a Southern belle in Samantha Winchester, after all. An old memory, perhaps, harking back to happier days. Jack refused to let his reawakened conscience interfere with his daydreaming. The warmth of the towel and last night's memories felt too good.

The sound of someone else entering Peterson's little shop startled Jack out of his pleasant reverie. Blinking as the towel disappeared, he looked up to see a tall, lanky young cowboy with a scruffy blond beard shift restlessly from one foot to another.

"Do you reckon I can be next, mister?" the cowboy asked the barber.

Peterson inspected the young man with a knowing eye

while he swirled shaving lather in a cup. "Reckon you can, cowpoke. Have a seat. I'll take you soon as I finish up here. You come in with Goodnight's herd this mornin'?"

The young man dropped his hat upon a nearby peg and settled into a straight-backed chair. "Yes sir," he answered politely, brushing his shaggy blond hair out of his eyes. "Just got in a while ago. Soon as we got those steers penned, I scooted over here. These whiskers have been itchin' me to death ever since we crossed over to the Indian Territory. I swore the first thing I'd do when I hit town was shave 'em off."

Jack noticed an infectious grin spread across the young man's face. "You sure it wasn't Cherokee rustlers who gave you that itch?" he asked between swirls of Peterson's brushful of lather.

"No, sir." The cowboy grinned wider. "Mr. Goodnight paid their trail fees right and proper, soon as we passed through. They didn't give us a speck o' trouble." He stretched his long legs in front of him, the spurs on his high-heeled boots scraping the worn pine floor.

"I figger your boss ought to be hankerin' to *get* some money from them cows, 'stead of payin' it," Peterson said, stropping his thin-edged razor on a nearby strap. "This time last year, Goodnight said he just about broke even. Told me he couldn't afford to run cattle outta Texas to keep wranglers in jobs and easterners in beef. He had to come out with somethin' for hisself."

Jack closed his eyes and arched his throat, relaxing into Peterson's capable hands, while his ears stayed carefully attuned. It was obvious he had found Abilene's chief source of gossip. When he felt the blade lift momentarily, he ventured, "Did you boys run all the meat off those cows?"

A lighthearted chuckle sounded. "No, *sir*! They're a mite skinny, but nothin' a good spell in the feed pen can't cure."

Peterson's expert blade swiped again. "You know who you're talkin' to, doncha, boy? This here's the new army agent. He's in town to buy your herd. So you'd best go down and tell Goodnight to fatten 'em up quick before Mr. Barnett here comes a lookin'!"

"Not the whole herd, son. Just the good ones," Jack said from beneath the shaving cream.

"Well, you can have 'em all, Mr. Barnett," the young cowboy decreed. "If I don't see another cow again, it'll be too soon."

"Aw, shucks, boy. That's what all the cowpokes say at the end of the trail," Peterson said as he wiped away the remnants of lather from Jack's face. "You're just tired of being in the saddle. Once you get a few drinks and a pretty girl or two, you'll start to get the wanderlust again. It's in yer blood."

"No, sir! It's not in *mine*," the cowboy replied with feeling. "I decided halfway through the drive this wasn't the life for me. I wanta make more of myself than just bein' a wrangler. Chasin' cows, eatin' dust, sleepin' on the ground. Nope. I'm gonna get me a better life than that." The infectious grin spread across his youthful face as he leaned his head back on his clasped hands.

"What are you planning on doing, son?" Jack asked when Peterson had raised him to a sitting position again. "Do you have any prospects?" Jack heard the sound of ambition in that voice. Something he didn't hear from too many wranglers.

The cowboy sat forward, his hands on his knees, and looked Jack in the eye. "No, sir, not yet. But I plan on getting some. I'm young. I'm strong. I'm not afraid of hard work. And I'm eager to learn a trade. I'll work at anything. Anything at all—just as long as it doesn't have four legs and a tail."

Jack grinned. He liked the cut of this young cowboy. There was an honesty to him that was refreshing. "Son, I have no doubt you will. You've got ambition. That'll take you pretty far in this life. What's your name, cowboy?"

"Cody, sir. Cody Barnes."

"Well, Cody Barnes, here's luck to you," Jack said, watching Peterson saturate his hands with shaving lotion. The heavy scent of bay rum wafted into the air. He caught Peterson's arm. "Go a little easy on that, Barney. I've got a lady in my office with a delicate sense of smell." Peterson chuckled and complied.

"Well, you can slather it on me as heavy as you want, sir." Cody rose from his chair when he saw Jack stand. "I want to attract as many ladies as I can. After I leave here, that is."

Jack dug into his pocket for a silver dollar, then caught Cody's eye with a devilish smile. "Then I'd recommend a trip to Peterson's back room, where he keeps the tubs, son. I've been downwind of you for a few minutes now, and to be honest, I haven't been attracted to you at all. So I doubt the ladies will be, either."

Cody threw back his shaggy blond head and laughed out loud, his face coloring. "I'm powerful sorry if I offended you, Mr. Barnett."

"You're just powerful, son. Use the tubs." Jack playfully tossed a towel Cody's way.

"Soap's in the dish," Peterson called out as Cody headed for the back room.

Jack handed the silver dollar to Peterson and fetched his hat, admiring his closely shaven jaw in the mirror. "I'll be back, Barney. You do a nice job."

"Thank you, Mr. Barnett." Peterson beamed, eyeing the silver dollar. "I haven't gotten one o' these since that army major stopped comin' in. Used to tip me real good. Long as I made a big fuss about him. But I accidentally nicked him once, and, well . . . he nearly flew off the handle, he was so mad! Damn, but he looked like he'd kill me soon as look at me! Tell the truth, I'm not so sorry he never came back. Never held with men who made too much o' theirselves, either. You know what I mean? Always lookin' in a mirror, prissylike. Anyway, I thank you kindly for the dollar. You come back anytime, Mr. Barnett.''

Jack paused and adjusted his Stetson, giving it the customary yank forward so it curved downward over his forehead. All the time he filed away Peterson's observations. ''What major would that be, Barney?'' he asked casually.

''Oh, one o' those over to the fort. You know, Fort Riley.''

''You remember his name? I'm supposed to say howdy to some of those fellows while I'm here.''

''Course I do. His name's Craig. Tall blond fella. Can't miss him. Never a speck o' dust on him. Said he's got some Mexican takin' care of his laundry, special-like. Don't that beat all?'' Peterson shook his head.

Jack smiled as he headed out the door. ''It sure does, Barney. It sure does.''

Samantha slowly moved her finger down the long column of figures that represented purchases, copying isolated numbers onto a sheet of paper, her mind instinctively comparing and cataloging as she went along, searching for items that had aroused her curiosity. She was only now beginning to decipher the army's peculiar way of categorizing revenues and expenses. Once she familiarized herself with the system, she was convinced she'd begin to find discrepancies. Right now, everything looked strange.

Bent over the ledgers in her customary fashion, more curls than usual falling about her face, Samantha was so wrapped up in her work she did not hear the office door open or the soft tread of someone entering. The commanding male voice that broke the silence caused her to jump straight up in her chair with a startled cry.

"Well, well, well . . . a *female* bookkeeper," Major Anthony Craig announced in a strident tone, quite pleased with the reaction he had just caused. Fear was an extremely useful reaction, he had found, especially when he was questioning someone. It made the subject ever so malleable. "I wonder if headquarters knows what this agent has done. Definitely not regulation army procedure." He strode into the office in imperial fashion.

Samantha swirled about in her chair and saw the impressive military presence coming toward her. The sight of that once-hated blue Union uniform caused an initial instinctive reaction. A brief wave of fear passed through her. There had been too many frightening encounters long ago. The feeling quickly passed, and Samantha was able to compose her features once more. "Mr. Barnett will be in shortly, sir. Perhaps you would like to come back later. Shall I tell him who called?"

Craig observed this little rebel clerk now that he was closer. Taggert had been right about two things. She was Southern, all right. That syrupy drawl of hers was a dead giveaway. A rebel through and through. What the devil was she doing in Abilene? And why had Barnett hired her?

His gaze narrowed appreciatively. Taggert had also been right about her looks. The major hadn't been close to a woman this striking since he'd spent his last leave in St. Louis, nearly twelve months ago. There had been nothing but coarse whores and ignorant peasants to slake his desires since then. Pearls before swine. But here . . . here was a face and form better suited to service his needs. His physical labors deserved better rewards than pockmarked, drunken bawds and frightened brown-skinned girls.

"You may say that Major Anthony Craig came calling, Miss . . . Miss . . ." he waved his immaculate white-gloved hand at her in patronizing fashion. "What *is* your name?" he demanded with a raised brow.

Samantha carefully folded her hands in her lap. Major Craig's disdainful manner had not gone unnoticed. Neither had the fact that he failed to remove his hat in her presence. She lifted her chin and looked the officious major straight in the eye. "My name is Mrs. Paul Winchester, and I am Mr. Barnett's bookkeeper. Now, sir, I repeat, if you have business with Mr. Barnett, I suggest you return later."

Craig flushed, taken aback by Samantha's high-handed manner and tone of voice. Who the devil did this little traitor think she was, talking to him like that? "You'd do well to mind your tongue, Mrs. Winchester. We don't take to sassy rebel gals around here. You're not in the South anymore," he warned, his voice dropping ominously.

Samantha used every ounce of backbone she possessed not to flinch under that gaze, although she saw much there to frighten her. Arrogance and cruelty shone out of his cold eyes, as well as a delight in wielding power. She let her own voice drop as low as possible as she met the major's stare. "Since you obviously have no business to conduct with Mr. Barnett, I suggest you take your petty taunts elsewhere, Major Craig. I have work to do." With that, Samantha calmly turned back to the ledgers.

The muscles in Anthony Craig's cheek twitched in fury as he glared down at her. How dare this little Southern clerk dismiss a United States Army major as if he were an annoying farm boy! His first impulse was to grab her by those dangling red-brown curls and shake her until she was blue in the face. However, the sight of the books on which Mrs.

Winchester was concentrating her attention swiftly chased that idea from his head.

The ledgers! They had to be! The army *did* take them. And now they'd given them to Barnett. Damn! Who knew how much this woman had uncovered? Craig's fingers ached to grab hold of those two large books and stride out of the office with them that very minute. Let Mrs. Winchester chase after him if she dared.

Anxious to take a closer look, Craig slowly approached Samantha's desk, forcing a more congenial tone into his voice. "How long have you been working here, Mrs. Winchester?" He craned his neck to try and read the page she held open.

The major's sudden nearness made Samantha's flesh crawl. She swiftly turned to face him and caught the direction of his gaze. Her sixth sense twinged an immediate warning.

Samantha rose from her chair and stepped in front of him, deliberately blocking his view of the ledgers. "I think you'd better leave now, Major."

Craig clenched his gloved hands at his sides, angered that she was thwarting his attempt to spy, and incensed that she had confronted him. Him! A major in the United States Army! He leaned forward menacingly. "Take care, little rebel. I hear you've brought your family with you. Kansas doesn't need any more traitorous trash. Better mind your manners, if you know what's good for you. *And yours.*"

Samantha felt an old and very cold fear grab hold of her heart. A fear she'd thought she wouldn't feel again. Despite the sinking feeling in her stomach right now, she managed to hold Craig's eyes. "The war's over, Major. And we're not in Georgia. Find someone else to threaten."

Craig had opened his mouth to respond when the loud slam of the office door startled him into silence.

"Who the hell are *you*?" Jack Barnett demanded, unable to control the anger he felt running through him at the moment. He'd glimpsed only a few seconds of Samantha's exchange with this man through the window, but it was long enough to see the look on her face and know something was wrong.

Jack took in the tall, blond army officer standing close to Samantha and observed the major's bars on his shoulder. A memory from long ago crept out of the past. Another major with the same cruel twist to his mouth, the same cold blue eyes. Jack forced the memory away. That was another time, another place.

He crossed the small room in two swift strides and stopped only inches from the haughty officer. "I'm Jack Barnett, cattle agent for the army. What can I do for you, Major?"

Anthony Craig took in those slate-gray eyes and decided they weren't shifty enough for a cattle agent. Jack Barnett didn't look like a man who haggled over the price of steers for a living. There was something else about him that aroused the major's curiosity. His voice. Jack Barnett's voice sounded like it was used to giving orders.

"I am Major Anthony Craig, assigned to Fort Riley, and I simply stopped in to acquaint myself with the army's new purchasing agent," he said in a tone that could pass for cordial.

"You've just met him," Jack replied evenly, not bothering to return Craig's small smile. The name rang a bell immediately. This was the man Peterson had spoken about only a few minutes ago. The one with the vile temper.

The major's smile twisted a bit. Barnett was obviously going to be an obstacle. Craig could see that right away. But he did not wish to arouse suspicion unnecessarily, so he forced himself to affect a more engaging manner. "Well, now, Mr. Barnett . . . what do you think of the herds you've seen so far? I've been told there will be more cattle heading for Abilene this year than ever before.''

Jack let his tone match the major's. ''Not bad. Skinny, as usual. I don't think they'll fetch as much as the cattlemen want, but the army will be fair.''

Samantha stared at the two men standing in front of her as they confronted each other, ready to engage antlers at the slightest provocation. She was fascinated by the change she'd just witnessed in Jack Barnett. Gone was his friendly, relaxed manner. A dangerous, coiled tension radiated from him now. She wondered at the transformation and held absolutely still.

Anthony Craig decided he'd get nothing from Barnett, and if he stayed any longer making idle conversation, he'd raise Barnett's suspicions for sure. Better to leave now and find a way to come back later for the ledgers.

''Mrs. Winchester, it has been a pleasure to find you here.'' Craig meant every word. He and Taggert would enjoy their work. He gave Jack a brief nod. ''Mr. Barnett, good day. If you have need of contacting army headquarters, do not hesitate to let me know. I'd be happy to assist you in any way I can.''

''Thanks, Major. I'll bear that in mind.'' Jack's gaze bored into Craig's until the major turned to leave. As soon as the door closed, Jack quickly approached Samantha, drawing even closer than he had last night in the moonlit kitchen. ''Are you all right, Mrs. Winchester? When I first came in, it looked as if Craig were threatening you. Your expression concerned me.''

Samantha found his worried, questioning eyes strangely disturbing. ''No . . . no, Mr. Barnett. He simply didn't appreciate my telling him he had to leave. But I didn't like the way he was leaning over the ledgers, as if he were trying to read them. The thought occurred to me that he may be the accomplice you mentioned.''

Jack probed her eyes for any sign of fear and found none. Only then did he relax. ''Yes, that thought occurred to me, too. Something about him doesn't ring true. He'll bear watching, I suspect.'' He glanced over Samantha's shoulders toward the desk and the object of Major Craig's apparent interest. ''I don't think we should leave the ledgers in the office overnight anymore. Something tells me they'll be a whole lot safer in Lucy Johnson's kitchen, on top of the cupboard.'' He let his face relax into his normal, easygoing smile.

Samantha felt herself respond. ''Might that be the same cupboard where Maysie keeps her pies, Mr. Barnett?'' she teased.

''One and the same, Mrs. Winchester.''

Chapter
6

"More potatoes, Mr. Barnett?" Lucy Johnson inquired solicitously. "Or perhaps you'd like more meat? Beans, maybe? I picked 'em fresh today."

Jack smiled up at the diminutive gray-haired lady standing beside his chair, a bowl in each hand. "No, thank you, Mrs. Johnson. I'm afraid I've disgraced myself at your table already. You ladies will have to forgive me. I'm not used to such delicious cooking." He watched Lucy's pale, creased cheek tinge pink with the compliment.

She turned away with a smile. "I declare, you've only had two servings. My Lucas used to have four. I'm not used to such light eaters."

Davy's high voice piped up, "Can I have some more of those mashed potatoes, Mrs. Johnson, please, ma'am?"

"Why, *sure* you can, boy!" Lucy beamed with pleasure as she hurried to the side of her crowded kitchen table, where she proceeded to mound a pile of potatoes on his plate that was almost as big as Davy's face. "I just love to see that boy eat! He'll start growin' like a weed any day now, you mark my words," she declared with a triumphant grin and set the nearly empty bowl near Clyde. "I oughtta know. All my boys were hearty eaters."

No slouch himself, her nephew eyed what was left in the bowl, then glanced at Davy's plate. Davy was halfway through the mountain already. Clyde sighed and scooped the remaining potatoes onto his plate, right beside the biscuits and tomatoes.

Lucy Johnson set the remaining bowl down and settled into her straight-backed chair. Glancing at the contented faces surrounding her, she sighed audibly. "Mercy sakes alive, I can't remember when I've had a tableful of such hearty appetites before. Surely does a body good to have someone to cook for." She nodded her head, agreeing with herself before anyone else got the chance.

"You're so very kind to put yourself out for us, Mrs. Johnson," Samantha said. "I'm afraid our family has invaded your home completely. You're very sweet to take us all in."

Lucy gave a dismissive wave of her hand. "Tut, tut, my dear. You're not putting me out at all. In fact, I'm pleased as punch to have you here. It gets pretty lonesome sometimes, since Lucas passed on. Only Clyde comes to visit nowadays." She turned and gave an affectionate pat to her nephew, who smiled behind his buttered biscuit.

"Don't the other ladies in town come to visit?" Becky spoke up in a soft voice.

Lucy Johnson's face screwed up in distaste. "Humph!" she snorted. "Until you and your family arrived, Becky, I was practically the only respectable woman left in Abilene. But there are plenty of the *other* kind in town. Too many, if you ask me." She gave an exasperated sigh. "At least they're not prowling the streets anymore, the way they did before the Devil's Addition got built to keep their wickedness away from the rest of us decent folk."

"Oh, my!" Aunt Mimi exclaimed, one hand fluttering at her breast. "You mean—"

"Yes, Mimi, she means *scarlet* women!" Miss Lily's contralto resonated across the table, setting the coffee cups to rattling. She turned toward the startled deputy. "Deputy Monroe, why don't you run those shameless hussies out of town? They'll corrupt the morals of the few upstanding citizens who remain."

Jack did his best to hide his amusement at Miss Lily's comment, especially when he noticed the flustered response of the ladies on his right. Samantha began to busily rearrange the serving bowls in the middle of the table, while a blushing Becky Herndon stared into her lap. He concluded by their actions that Miss Lily's lapses into embarrassing conversation were nothing new. Jack leaned back and stretched his long legs beneath the table, waiting to hear how Clyde would reply.

"Well, ma'am . . ." Clyde squirmed in his chair. "You see, we can't just run 'em out. I mean, the cowboys wouldn't take too kindly to that and—"

"*What*? You're letting a few unshaven men on horses tell you what to do?" She gazed at him with haughty incredulity.

Clyde swallowed. That face would stop a clock, all right. And it durn near took away his tongue, too. "Ma'am . . . I don't think you know how many cowboys are in Abilene right now. Why, this is the biggest cattle season we've ever had. We've seen purt close to a hunnert'n fifty thousand cows come through already, and it ain't even September yet! Why, I heard tell you can't see a thing from here to the Pecos. That's on account o' the dust from all them cattle headin' thisaway."

Miss Lily looked unimpressed with his excuse, but she made no reply. After a few seconds of thoughtful silence, however, Davy asked in a small voice, "Why'd those women turn red, Mama?"

Samantha blinked in surprise at her son, who was staring up in innocence. "What do you mean, darling? No one turned red."

"Miss Lily said they did. She said they turned *scarlet*."

Jack watched Samantha's cheeks flush almost as bright as the women in question. He was about to draw attention to himself with a loud cough and provide an opportunity for Samantha to handle her son's inquiry gracefully, when Maysie bustled to the table.

"You folks bettah eat that strawberry pie before it gits stone-cold," she announced in a voice that was used to being obeyed. "And *you* can help me serve it, young man." She grabbed the back of Davy's chair and yanked it away from the table, restoring order in one fell swoop. Davy reluctantly rose, his question still unanswered, and followed after Maysie while she cleared the table with more noise than usual.

Lucy Johnson turned a concerned eye toward Becky and Samantha. "You just make sure you never go walkin' around this town unescorted, Becky. It's not safe. And don't you go to that office alone, either, Samantha. Those cowboys won't bother an old lady like me, but they sure would head straight for pretty girls like you."

Becky lowered her head, blushing at the compliment. Jack noticed her strawberry blond curls tumbling about her shoulders and sincerely wished her older sister would follow suit, instead of trying to subdue her own unruly curls in a spinster's bun.

Not about to waste an opportunity to draw Samantha's attention, he said, "Mrs. Winchester promised me she wouldn't go walking around alone anymore, Mrs. Johnson. Otherwise, we'd have cowboys lined up outside the office, waiting to catch a glimpse of her through the window." He sent a lazy smile Samantha's way and was delighted to observe his comment brought a slight flush to her cheek.

"Oh, my!" Aunt Mimi fluttered again. "Please, Samantha, promise me you won't ever do that again! I just couldn't bear the thought of your being confronted by those . . . those . . . cowboys! Oh-my-oh-my-oh-my-oh-*my*! Thank goodness Becky is at home with us. Oh, dear, I don't know what I'd do if I had *two* of you to worry about!" She vigorously fanned her throat with a lacy white handkerchief, her pale blue eyes wide with distress.

"Calm yourself, Aunt Mimi. I'm quite safe in the office with Mr. Barnett, and Becky's safe at home," Samantha responded.

Her expression was dutiful, but Jack guessed that Samantha was as amused by Aunt Mimi's solicitude as he was. Amazing how he had learned to read her face in such a short time. He also noticed a distinct look of disappointment flash across Becky's pretty little face. The thought of being confined with her maiden aunts was obviously not an exciting one.

He noticed Maysie refilling his coffee cup yet again. Jack had obediently consumed every cup she'd served him that evening, and at this rate, he figured he wouldn't get to sleep until next week. But he wasn't about to say no, especially since her former scowl had changed to an attentive scrutiny. "Thank you, Maysie." He smiled up into her creased brown face.

Davy appeared by his side at that moment, holding a plate filled with the most delectable-looking slice of strawberry pie Jack had ever seen in his life. He gave Davy a wink and eagerly accepted the offering. His full stomach had miraculously made room at the sound of the word "pie." Davy grinned as if he'd read Jack's mind.

"Deputy Monroe," Miss Lily's voice intoned again, obviously oblivious to her nieces' previous discomfort. "I do not understand why the Abilene constabulary allows vice to run rampant. Why doesn't your chief of police drive those sin mongers out of town?" Every wrinkle in Lily Herndon's face creased ominously.

Clyde shuddered at the sight, then gazed beseechingly at Jack. Jack grinned. "*You're* the constabulary, Clyde. You and the marshal, that is."

Clyde blinked once, then stared at Miss Lily, aghast. "*Me*? Why, ma'am . . . I wouldn't stand a chance up against those cowboys!" he declared with a horrified expression.

"Confound it, man . . . your *marshal*, then!" she exclaimed.

Jack was about to come to his friend's rescue when Lucy Johnson beat him to it. "Miss Lily, our marshal's not about to run anybody out of town. He spends all his time in the saloon himself! Why . . . he's as bad as the lot of them, if you ask me!" She sniffed indignantly. "Cold-blooded murderer, that's what he is. Why, he's been heard to say he'd as soon shoot a man as a dog! The *idea*! That killer isn't fit to clean the boots of the man who went before him!"

Lucy's stern expression softened in sadness. "Tom Smith . . . now, *there* was a man. When Tom was here, we had law and order. None of this wild shootin' in the streets that goes on nowadays, no sir! Tom made a law. No firearms inside the town. He made it stick, too! Why, any cowboy who didn't go along got a whuppin'. Believe me, they came around." Her face darkened. "And to think he was killed by riffraff right outside town—over a trifle, yet. It was a cryin' shame, that's what it was."

Clyde gave a sigh of admiration. "Yep. Nobody could fight like Tom. Kept those cowboys in line without even drawin' his gun.'' He wagged his shaggy head sorrowfully.

"Who's your marshal now?" Samantha asked.

Lucy scowled. "To my way of thinking, we don't have a marshal. We have a hired gunslinger by the name of Wild Bill Hickok."

Jack slowly raised a dripping forkful of strawberry-filled pastry to his mouth and let his senses savor it while his thoughts went elsewhere. Anybody who roamed the borderlands knew the name of Wild Bill Hickok and the ruthless reputation that went with it. The fastest draw in the West combined with a heart of stone. Jack wasn't sure if a man like that would be a help or a hindrance in his investigation and decided the safest course would be to give Marshal Hickok a wide berth.

"Merciful heavens, I've never heard of such a thing!" Aunt Mimi exclaimed, both hands at her breast now. "Your marshal resides in a . . . a *tavern*?"

"How can he hope to influence the wicked if he is no better than they?" Miss Lily admonished.

"That's where you got it wrong, ma'am," Clyde spoke up. "Ya see, Marshal Hickok don't care nothin' about *influencin'* them cowpokes. He just shoots 'em. Dead. Believe me, the others come around real fast when they see their friends lyin' in the dust."

Miss Lily wrinkled her long nose in disgust. "Humph! It sounds as if the local citizenry is composed mostly of murderers, drunkards, and painted women. That's appalling!"

Davy quickly appeared at his mother's side and yanked her sleeve. "See, Mama, that's how those women got red. They *painted* themselves!" he declared into Samantha's startled face.

Jack coughed loudly and was about to ask for another piece of pie—in a very loud voice—when Maysie stepped in, her face screwed tight in aggravation.

"Young man, I *tol'* you not to pester the grown folks!" she scolded, hands balled into fists on her hips. "Now, if you don't wanna be sent to bed this minute, you'd bettah go fetch me some water so I can clean up these here dishes."

Davy turned from his flustered mother with a bewildered expression, but he dutifully grabbed the bucket and trudged out the door.

Jack folded his arms and leaned forward on the worn wooden table so he could deliberately catch Samantha's eye. When he did he gave her a reassuring smile and watched the pink tinge on her cheeks begin to fade. Now, if Maysie could only keep Davy's mouth shut, Samantha might recover her composure.

Lucy Johnson pushed back her chair with a scrape, glancing at Jack and Samantha as she did. "Goodness me, but I do need to move about for a spell or else my bones will freeze up," she said as she popped up from her straight-backed chair surprisingly fast. "You folks just sit still and enjoy your pie. Clyde . . . make sure you don't eat it all." She wagged a finger at her nephew. "Maysie, why don't I help you with those dishes?" Lucy immediately started bustling about the kitchen.

Jack Barnett toyed with his coffee cup, wishing dinner could go on for another hour or so, unwilling to lose the warmth around him. He hadn't known how lonely he was until tonight. Suddenly thrown into this jumble of maiden aunts, doting younger sister, bossy Negro cook, and a little boy who hung on his every word . . . well, it was more than any man could stand. Especially a man who had been alone for a long time. Sitting beside Samantha this evening, surrounded by loving family noise, had unleashed a torrent of need inside him. A hunger Jack never knew he had.

Lucy Johnson glanced toward him and said in an offhand way, "Feel free to stretch your legs outside a spell, Jack. I know a man needs to move around. Why, I expect you might want a breath of fresh air yourself, Samantha. What with bein' cooped up in that office all day, goin' blind over them ledger books."

Jack gazed at Lucy in astonishment and received a surreptitious shooing of her hand in reply. He didn't hesitate. Almost leaping to his feet, he pulled back Samantha's chair and gestured toward the door, careful to keep his smile in check.

"I think Mrs. Johnson wants to clear her kitchen, so we'd best cooperate." He ushered Samantha outside and glanced over his shoulder in time to spy Davy on their trail. The small boy had returned with the water bucket and was heading toward the doorway fast. Maysie reached out and grabbed his arm.

Delighted with the number of fellow conspirators he had suddenly acquired, Jack strolled to the edge of the front porch and motioned for Samantha to join him, eager to let the darkness envelop them both. Inhaling deeply of the soft, moist night air, he looked up into the star-filled black sky and saw diamonds scattered amongst the velvet. He felt Samantha's gaze settle on him while he continued to stare upward. "This is why I love the West, Mrs. Winchester," he said softly. "Where else can you see such a magnificent sight?"

Samantha's eyes lingered on Jack's darkened profile before she looked skyward. She took in her breath with an audible gasp. "How beautiful," she whispered.

Jack made use of Samantha's absorption and gazed at her in the darkness. Only an embrace away. His pulse raced at the thought. Jack couldn't remember when simply standing with a woman in the dark had been so arousing. He shifted a bit on the rough cottonwood boards, inching closer.

Partly to distract her, Jack pointed into the heavens. "Do you see the Big Dipper? Look over there...." Watching her nod in fascination, Jack visually rewarded himself. His eyes wandered over her face, which was illumined by moonlight, the round, smooth curve of her cheek, her lush, full mouth. Jack's blood rushed faster in his veins. It was all he could do to keep from closing the distance between them entirely—scoop her into his arms and let his hungry mouth taste hers, discover if it was as delicious as it looked. Only the warning voice of conscience held him at bay.

Watch yourself, Barnett! it rasped in his ear.

Almost as if she heard his immodest thoughts, Samantha turned to Jack and blinked at his unexpected closeness. She stepped back to a more acceptable distance, much to his disappointment.

Samantha folded her hands, unfolded them, straightened the pleats of her dark skirt, then entwined her fingers once more. She cleared her throat. "You'll be glad to know that I have made considerable progress in familiarizing myself with the ledgers, Mr. Barnett."

"That's good news." Jack watched several escaped tendrils brush against her cheek, and he shoved both hands into his pockets to keep his fingertips from itching.

"I'm sufficiently comfortable with the accounts now to begin a search for unusual entries." She straightened the folds of her skirt again.

Watching her fidget, Jack noticed Samantha's ringless hands, not for the first time. Partly to slow his racing pulse and partly out of curiosity, he asked, "Pardon my forwardness, Mrs. Winchester ... I can't help but notice the absence of your wedding ring. The white circle on your finger tells me its removal was recent. You strike me as a woman

who would treasure that symbol of marriage. What made
you part with it, if I might ask?''

Samantha held her entwined fingers before her and hesitated a moment before answering. ''I decided to trade
memories of the past for hope in the future, Mr. Barnett. I
sold my wedding ring for my family's train fare to Abilene.'' She faced him. ''Now you know how truly desperate
I was when I arrived in your office. I had just sold my
mother's two-hundred-year-old brooch to settle tax assess-
ments back in Savannah. We arrived here with nothing left
to sell.''

Jack glimpsed the pain that moment had caused her before she looked away, and he wondered at the price this
proud woman had paid to keep her family together since
the war. Standing up to carpetbaggers and tax collectors
alike, selling what few cherished heirlooms she possessed,
all to keep the jackals at bay. Not many women could have
survived a year of that existence. None that he knew, anyway. And then, to have the courage to gamble her very last
dime on the chance for a new life in a rough, raw cow
town. Most gentle ladies would have turned tail and run
the minute they spied Abilene . . . or fainted dead away.
Jack observed Samantha Winchester with a new admiration.
He'd known quite a few gamblers in his day, but none of
them had ever bet against such enormous odds as the lady
standing in front of him now.

Emboldened by her honesty, Jack decided to satisfy his
own curiosity. ''Tell me about your husband, Mrs. Winchester. Unless it still pains you to discuss it. How old was
he when he joined the Confederate cause?''

A small, sad smile crossed her face. ''I've had eight
years to heal, Mr. Barnett,'' she said. ''Paul and I were
childhood friends together . . . watched each other grow up,
in fact. We had always planned to wed. Our families were

very close, you see.'' Samantha sighed and gazed off. ''Paul was only twenty-one when he rode off to the war. Much more a boy than a man. I can still see him now, smiling and waving at me as he rode down BelleHaven's carriage road.''

The mention of that horrifying name from the past sent a sudden chill through Jack, shattering the night's intimacy. He stared down at the rough plank steps. ''A lot of good men were lost in that war, Mrs. Winchester. I'm sincerely sorry your young husband was one of them,'' he said in a tight voice.

Samantha turned and observed him quietly for a moment. ''It seems you didn't escape the ravages of that bitter conflict yourself, Mr. Barnett. Am I right?''

Every muscle in Jack's body tensed at her words. There it was, hanging in the air. The one question he'd dreaded hearing, yet could not escape. He knew she was bound to ask it sooner or later and had been practicing his answer for days—inventing lies, stumbling over the truth. The lies tasted bitter on his tongue, but the truth brought a wrench to his gut. Jack pictured the look of horror that would surely cross her beautiful face if he told Samantha the truth. Hate would erase the tantalizing light he'd begun to see in her eyes.

Jack turned to gaze into Samantha's upturned face, her expression one of genuine concern. His gut wrenched tighter. Even the night couldn't obscure the light of promise he glimpsed in those green eyes. Jack stared into them now and swallowed. He couldn't tell her the truth. He'd lose that light forever, and he'd be damned if he would do that. What he felt for Samantha Winchester reached too deep for him to give it up. If that meant telling half-truths, then by God he would do it!

''No, Mrs. Winchester, I didn't escape the war. I fought

with a Pennsylvania regiment . . . in Virginia,'' he said, carefully watching her. ''I served with Colonel Logan at Manassas and Second Bull Run . . . and that bloodbath in Fredericksburg.'' Jack saw Samantha's eyes widen and her cheeks pale, or maybe it was the moon's sudden brightness that blanched the color from her face. The sight made his heart pound against his ribs in fear, and his gut twisted painfully this time.

He leaned his face closer. ''But I wasn't anywhere near Shiloh,'' he swore desperately. ''Please believe that! I didn't kill your husband, Mrs. Winchester.'' Jack gazed into her face, praying he wouldn't see the hate he'd envisioned in his mind. He didn't. Shock darted across Samantha's lovely face instead.

Samantha stared into those slate-gray eyes that held her spellbound and saw the fierce desperation burning inside. She gazed back in confusion, unable to say a word. She couldn't. What she'd just heard had taken her breath away.

Jack Barnett had been a Yankee soldier. He hadn't escaped the war at all. He had been a part of it. He had been the enemy.

Samantha didn't know what to say. The tormented look on Jack Barnett's face told her she must say something. So did the plea in his dark eyes. She opened her mouth but found she was bereft of words. Jack's face tightened in pain.

She swallowed and tried again, but she never got the chance. The front porch was flooded with light as the door opened and her young son rushed from inside the house.

''Can I give you a hug before bed, Mama?'' Davy asked, glancing briefly to her before his gaze found the other person it sought.

A poignant tug pulled at Samantha's heart, and she

leaned down to embrace her son. "Of course you can, sweetheart."

The bright Kansas moonlight shone through Samantha's bedroom window, illuminating everything within as if it were day. This enormous moon was so unlike the hazy orb she had been accustomed to in Savannah. The brightness was startling and made it impossible for her to fall asleep. Samantha turned onto her back and stared at the ceiling. She closed her eyes, wishing she could shut out the confused thoughts that plagued her now. Above all, she wished she could erase the picture of the tormented face that would not leave her mind.

How could it be possible? she asked herself for the hundredth time that night. The Jack Barnett she had come to know in these past few days had shown himself to be a kind, caring man. Considerate of her and gentle with her son. A good man with a keen mind that his easygoing manner could not disguise. How could he be one of the hated enemy? It was impossible. It couldn't be true. And yet it was. The desperate look in Jack Barnett's eyes had told her it was true.

Samantha shifted restlessly, tugging the bedsheet from her legs, her emotional struggle tangling her body as well as her mind. She could not forget the dreadful torment she had seen on that strong face. Her heart had ached to find something to say, something to ease the obvious anguish Jack's confession had caused him. But she had not. Or could not. She knew not which. What *could* she say? This man had helped defeat her beloved homeland. How on earth could she want to comfort him when she and her family had suffered so much? She did not understand. Not herself, or her own feelings.

Kicking away the sheet's confining grasp, Samantha

squirmed on the uncomfortable feather bed, its feathers long since gathered into clumps. Whatever was the matter with her? she wondered. Had this man's many kindnesses to her family so charmed her that she could now forgive his past? He had been part of the destroying army, that hateful blue plague that had swept across her family's lands, leaving devastation and death in its wake. Samantha squeezed her eyes shut. Try as she might, she could not picture Jack Barnett among the many ugly faces that filled her memory. Was it gratitude that clouded her memory? Perhaps it was. Gratitude for his kindness. Yes. That was it.

Somehow Samantha found the thought strangely unsettling. An unfamiliar sensation deep inside told her gratitude was too mild a word to describe her feelings right now. Far too mild. Samantha threw her arm across her eyes and tried to block the relentless Kansas moonlight, as well as the confusing thoughts that tumbled through her mind. She must sleep.

Farther down the hallway, someone else stared wide-eyed into the moon's white face, not caring if sleep came or not. Jack Barnett lay naked beneath the thin cotton sheet, his head resting on his crossed arms, not moving a muscle despite the discomfort of his rude pallet on the floor. Sleep did not interest him. Too many thoughts plagued him to allow rest.

His confession had shaken Samantha, Jack could see that. A fool could have seen. And yet, the oft-feared expression of hate had not appeared on her lovely face. For that, Jack thanked God. But the confusion and shock that appeared in its place had given Jack no peace, and certainly no encouragement.

You're a fool, Barnett, you know that? the taunting whine of conscience jabbed. *What did you expect? You were the enemy. She knows that now. Whatever you imagined you saw in her eyes before is most assuredly gone now. Forever.*

The muscles in Jack's long, lean arms tightened as rockhard as when he had swung the hammer. Even half-truths had not saved him. Whatever made him think they would? Beneath his breath, Jack cursed himself for a fool. Why hadn't he lied? He gazed up into the moon's grinning face, searching for an answer. But he found none, only the fat Kansas moon laughing back at him.

Chapter
7

Jack glanced back through the open office door and caught Samantha Winchester staring at him. He quickly suppressed what pleasure her gaze brought. "I should return shortly, Mrs. Winchester. I've got to check on the new herd that came in this morning." Without waiting for her reply, Jack gave a polite nod and closed the door behind him.

He was about to head toward the stockyards when a voice called from behind. "You Jack Barnett?"

Jack wheeled quickly. Instincts born of years in battle still ruled every nerve. He spied a heavily bearded man ambling toward him, dressed in a worn denim shirt that contrasted sharply with the brand-spanking-new pair of red moroccon leather chaps. Two stitched black-leather crescent moons adorned each thigh. Jack made sure to hide his smile. He could smell the leather before the man. The Texans were in Abilene, all right. And their money was burning holes in their pockets.

"That I am, cowboy," Jack deliberately drawled. "What can I do for you?"

The fashionable cowboy shoved his tobacco wad to the other side of his cheek long enough to spit a brown stream onto the dirt street, holding down the dust. "Fer me, nuthin'." He grinned and revealed a large and handy gap between his front teeth. "It's George Littlefield who'd be a-wantin' you. Ya see, we just brought up the biggest herd that's ever been run outta Texas."

"Is that a fact?"

"Damn me for a liar if'n it ain't." The cowboy's sun-creased face broke into another grin. "The wranglers over to the stockyards said you'd be the army buyer. Mr. Little-field said to find you pretty quick, 'cause he wants to move these beeves *pronto*! You in the mind to be buyin'?"

Jack couldn't help but return the grin. "Not as much as you're selling, but I'll take a few off your hands. C'mon, take me to your boss." He turned toward the stockyards before the cowboy's voice pulled him back.

"We ain't gonna find him at the stockyards, mister. He's at the Bull's Head, wettin' down a powerful thirst. So, if'n you don't mind, let's step lively, 'cause I'm powerful thirsty m'self." The wrangler did an about-face and headed down the line of frame buildings that comprised Texas Street, Jack following in his path.

The diminutive form of a young woman suddenly appeared across the street. Although Becky's bonnet obscured most of her face, it couldn't hide the masses of strawberry blond curls clustered about her shoulders. Nor could the modest gingham dress hide the curves of her slight feminine body as she anxiously peeked around the corner of the general store.

Becky gasped at the sight of the crowded street in front of her. It teemed with all manner of dirty, unshaven, noisy, and terrifying-looking men, who were milling around, standing in raucous clusters, and striding about the rude plank sidewalk with their huge metal spurs jangling behind them. Becky flattened herself against the side of the clapboard building in terror.

Merciful heavens! She tried not to let the ice-cold panic freeze her completely. How would she ever find Mr. Barnett's office safely? She could have sworn Lucy Johnson said to turn right at Texas Street. Becky couldn't remember. She had been so excited to have the opportunity to see this wild cow town with her own eyes, to glimpse these cowboys at last. And now that she had, she was petrified.

She peered around the corner into the crowded street again. Her heart slowed slightly, watching the rowdy cluster closest to her disperse with loud, lewd farewells. The language brought a rosy flush to her cheek. Becky hesitated a minute longer, to see if any more men disappeared from the vicinity, before she inched around the corner and onto the rough wood walkway.

She took a deep breath and started walking as fast as she could, praying everyone would ignore her until she could find Jack Barnett's office. Her heart was in her throat as she watched a small group of cowboys laugh uproariously in the middle of the street. Thankful their laughter kept them from noticing her, Becky darted a quick glance at every window she passed.

If only Aunt Mimi hadn't taken such a bad fall, then maybe Lucy Johnson would have been able to help. But seeing Aunt Mimi lying pale and barely breathing had scared them all to death. And scared Mrs. Johnson into forgetting her earlier warning to Becky. Cowboys or no . . . Aunt Mimi needed a doctor.

Becky kept her head lowered, anxious to find Jack Barnett's office before one of those frightening men spied her. When she observed a group of men farther down the walkway, Becky started saying every prayer she'd ever learned, hoping the men would let her pass safely. Her heart pounded so hard it shook her slender body. When they caught sight of her, she hesitated just a bit. Not for long, but long enough for a nearby saloon door to open and a far more terrifying face to appear before her.

Joe Taggert stepped out of the saloon, took one look at Becky Herndon, and stopped in his tracks. His grizzled face broke into a lecherous grin as he swiftly stepped in front of her, blocking Becky's path completely. "Well, damn! What have we here?" he taunted. "You sure are a pretty little piece, if that's not a fact. C'mon out, Zeke! Looky what we got!"

A sunburned, red-bearded face appeared over the saloon door and lit up with a wicked grin. Dark eyes swept over Becky insolently. Zeke pushed through the swinging doors and stood right behind Becky, blocking any retreat. "Well, well . . . what have you found? Looks mighty juicy to me, Joe." He laughed.

"That new army agent must've brought in some young fresh ones. Ain't that thoughtful of him?" Taggert reached out and brushed his fingers across Becky's cheek.

Becky jerked away from his hand in panic. She opened her mouth to cry out, but her voice had vanished.

Zeke grabbed her about the waist from behind and drew her roughly against him. "Yes, indeed. A tender little piece, if I do say so." His free hand roamed across her breasts.

Becky found her voice and cried out, "Stop, please! Don't do that . . . let me go, *please*!"

Zeke laughed, his hand continuing to explore. Taggert stepped forward, grasped Becky's gingham bonnet, and yanked it off her head, throwing it to the ground. He sank his dirty hands into her wealth of strawberry blond curls. "Damn, but I love this pretty hair. You're gonna be a pure pleasure to ride, young one. Ain't she, Zeke?'' He snickered. Before Zeke could answer, however, a hard voice sounded from the open saloon door.

"Let her go, mister. Right now.'' Cody Barnes stepped out of the saloon.

Becky blinked through her paralyzing haze of terror and saw a tall, fair-haired young cowboy standing motionless before her. He glared at both her tormentors with a look that would have frozen a stone. Becky's eyes sought his in a desperate plea.

Taggert dismissed the young cowboy with a glance. "Go find yer own, boy. This one's taken.''

A long-barreled revolver appeared in Cody's hand in a split second. "I said let her go, mister. *Now!*'' He leveled the Colt at Zeke.

Zeke stared at the gun pointing toward his rib cage and released Becky, his hands up. "Hold on, there,'' he admonished as he stepped backward. Taggert looked over his shoulder, spied the revolver, and backed away with a curse.

"You okay, miss?'' Cody asked, looking at Becky with concern.

"You're mighty excitable there, aren't you, cowpoke?'' Taggert accused. "Me and Zeke, we were just havin' a little fun.''

Cody narrowed his eyes on Taggert. "It didn't look like the lady was havin' much fun, mister.'' He motioned toward Becky. "Why don't you step over here, miss?'' he suggested. "I expect you'd feel a mite safer.''

Becky obeyed, relieved to be away from her molesters and anxious to be closer to her handsome rescuer. She shyly glanced up into Cody's face, saw his concerned, blue-green eyes watching her, and felt her stomach quiver. "Thank you, sir, for coming to my aid,'' she said in a soft voice.

"My pleasure, miss.'' Cody nodded with a little smile.

Taggert eyed the couple and made a slight motion to Zeke at the same time. Zeke nodded and slowly drew his hand behind his back, where a knife was tucked into his belt. "You Texas boys sure do fly off the handle quick," Taggert said loudly. "We weren't planning to really hurt the little lady."

"It didn't sound like that to me, mister." Cody stared at him and away from Zeke.

On the other side of the street, Jack Barnett spied Zeke's stealthy movements. Jack had pushed his way out of the Bull's Head Saloon only moments before. Instead of heading toward the stockyards as he had planned, however, he found himself moving in the other direction for some inexplicable reason. Just an uneasy feeling he had. Jack had only gone a few yards before the uneasy feeling became a lump in his throat. There, around the corner, he saw Becky Herndon standing between two hulking cowboys.

Fearing the worst, Jack raced toward them as fast as he could, slowing only when he spied a familiar-looking young cowboy get the drop on the mangy two. Watching Becky step away from the others and toward the younger man told Jack what he wanted to know. The young wrangler had everything under control. That was when Jack spied the knife, tucked in the small of one cowboy's back, almost within reach of the hand stretching to grab it.

Jack crept up with the stealth the war had taught him and grabbed hold of Zeke's hand. He gave a painful wrench and twisted hard. Zeke let out an agonized yelp. "Looking for this, mister?" Jack taunted, brandishing the knife before Zeke's eyes.

Becky gasped, "Mr. Barnett!"

Cody Barnes blinked in surprise at his barbershop companion and quickly pointed his gun at a scowling Taggert.

Jack booted Zeke in the rear and sent him sprawling in

the dust at their feet. He slipped the long knife into his belt and glared at Taggert. "I'd better not see either of you two around this lady again, do you hear? Or Marshal Hickok won't get a chance to waste a bullet." Jack watched Taggert's scowl freeze on his face. "Now, go on . . . get out of here before I change my mind."

Taggert slowly backed into the murmuring crowd that had begun to form at the first sign of a fight. He helped Zeke to his feet and shot a hate-filled look at Jack Barnett before he stalked away. Zeke limped after him, nursing his arm.

Jack watched the pair shuffle off into the disappointed crowd, then turned to the two young people beside him. His glance ran over a considerably cleaner Cody Barnes, and Jack fixed him with a sly grin. "Well, well . . . Cody Barnes, if I recall correctly. I'm indebted to you, son. Had I known this young lady was roaming about Abilene, I would have been out here myself. Since I wasn't, I'm mighty glad you happened along when you did. Those two no-accounts have no business being around a lady."

Becky jumped at the opportunity to thank Cody Barnes again. "Ohh, yes . . . I cannot tell you how grateful I am, Mr. Barnes!" Her lilting Southern voice melted all over the words in excitement as she gazed worshipfully into his handsome face, causing her stomach to turn several flip-flops.

Cody's smile spread. "My pleasure, miss. Where I come from, we treat a lady with respect, and we sure don't cotton to the likes of those two varmints."

He grinned wider, and Becky's stomach flopped to her feet this time.

Watching this exchange with great interest, Jack did his best not to smile. In fact, he put on his sternest face instead. "Miss Herndon, I don't know what possessed you to disobey your aunt's advice and come to town, but I think you realize why she was concerned for your safety," he softly admonished. "Abilene has far more cowboys like those two and not enough like Cody Barnes. Now, I want you to promise me you won't be coming here again, all right?"

A chastened Becky nodded. "I promise, Mr. Barnett."

"Unless, of course, you have someone as capable as Mr. Barnes to escort you." Jack couldn't help but tease, watching Becky's delicate cheeks blush with obvious anticipation. "By the way, exactly why did you come here this morning . . . aside from curiosity?"

"*Oh!* Oh, my goodness! Aunt Mimi!" Becky gasped, clapping her hand to her mouth. "Aunt Mimi took a bad fall down the stairs this morning, and Mrs. Johnson was so worried she sent me for the doctor. She said you'd know where to find one, and I was looking for your office when . . . when . . ." She hesitated at the ugly memories.

Jack snapped to attention. "Don't you worry. I'll get him right away. Cody, would you escort Miss Herndon to my office? It's just down the street on the left. Her sister will want to know about this. Is your aunt conscious, Becky?"

"No, sir," she whispered, feeling incredibly guilty at the delay. What if Aunt Mimi died? Becky shuddered.

"Cody, I'd be much obliged if you would bring both ladies safely home."

"I'd be pleased to, Mr. Barnett," Cody replied with a nod.

Jack was about to walk away when a wonderful thought came to him. "Why don't you stay for dinner, Cody? I'm sure Becky's family will want to thank you in person." He caught the young cowboy's eye and winked.

Cody Barnes's face split wide in a grin. "That's real considerate of you, Mr. Barnett. I appreciate it." With that, he extended his arm to a blushing Becky Herndon.

Pleased with his matchmaking, Jack turned and made his way through the crowded street. First he would fetch the doctor. Then he needed some answers. And he knew just the person to ask. He glanced toward Barney Peterson's barbershop across the street. If anyone in Abilene knew the name of the two varmints who'd accosted Becky, it would be Peterson.

Anthony Craig sat tall and erect on his chestnut stallion, as if he could see for himself what a magnificent sight they made at the far end of the fort's drill yard. Two fairly straight lines of soldiers stood at attention in the yard, awaiting the drill sergeant's next command.

The major's heroic pose was spoiled, however, by the scowl twisting his features. "So . . . you let some cowboy keep you from taking the girl. Sounds like you're slipping, Taggert. You've never let one of those Texans get the better of you before."

Taggert slouched in his saddle, then spat over his shoulder, an irritated frown on his face. "He slipped up behind me, Major. Plain and simple. I was mighty distracted once I got ahold of that pretty little red-haired gal. He got the drop on me, that's all. And Zeke would've gotten him with the knife if Barnett hadn't come along when he did."

Craig watched the memory work its way across Taggert's face. Good, he thought to himself. Now Taggert would have a reason of his own to go after Jack Barnett. "It sounds like everybody in Abilene was slipping up on you," he taunted deliberately. "I'll wager Mrs. Winchester's maiden aunts could have sneaked up on you, too. You'd best look sharp, Taggert, or I'll look for your replacement."

A faint tinge of crimson crept up Taggert's neck as he sat up straighter on his horse. He squinted into the noonday glare and tugged on his Stetson, the black so coated with dust it looked gray. "Don't be so hasty, Major," he countered. "This was the first time—"

"*Not* the first," Craig interrupted harshly, leaning over the saddle to make his point. "You forgot about the ledgers, Taggert. I told you I wanted those ledgers out of that office."

Taggert cursed and spat again. "Hell, Major! Me and Zeke went that very night, but they were gone. Barnett and the little reb, they must've taken 'em clean away. There wasn't hide nor hair of them books in that office."

Craig peered scornfully down his aquiline nose at the demoralized Taggert. "They were gone because you *waited*, you fool! You should have watched until Barnett was gone, then arranged some sort of commotion in the street to distract that bookkeeper's attention and draw her out of the office long enough for you or that filthy Zeke to steal the books. It shouldn't have been too hard, what with a town full of half-drunk, carousing cowboys!" He snorted in disgust. "Do I have to do all your thinking for you, Taggert? What in God's name am I paying you for?"

Taggert flushed scarlet this time. "Just hold yer horses, Craig. We've got plenty of time to work on the little widow. Barnett leaves her alone in that office all the time. Zeke 'n' me will go pay her a visit in private." His mouth twisted into a leer. "That way, no nosy cowpokes will get in the way."

Craig nudged his chestnut stallion, and the enormous horse obeyed, turning toward the drill field, where the sergeant continued to bark orders. Fixing Taggert with a warning look as he came alongside, the major advised, "Don't wait long, Taggert. I don't want that rebel clerk to scrutinize those ledgers too closely. If the army hired her, she must be good. And that makes me uneasy. I want her out of town. It's your job to find a way to drive her out, understand? Whether you grab her or her sister, I don't care. Just make sure you show Mrs. Winchester how unpleasant life on the frontier can be.'' He caught Taggert's eye and smiled for the very first time. A cold smile. ''I want that little rebel to think the war is still going on . . . at least for her and her family. Do I make myself clear?''

''Clear as a bell,'' Taggert replied with a narrow smile.

Samantha pointed to the list of ledger entries she had copied onto a separate sheet of paper. ''These are the entries that aroused my curiosity, Mr. Barnett. They occur infrequently, which is why it took me a while to notice them. But now that I've familiarized myself with the normal monthly entries, I'm finally able to distinguish the unusual items.''

Jack leaned over Samantha's cluttered desk and focused on the long list of figures and away from her lustrous red-brown curls. With her head bent over in concentration, more curls than usual slipped through her pearl-tipped hairpins. Despite every intention not to, Jack glanced into the partially restrained abundance and noticed one hairpin about to wiggle free. His fingertips itched, aching to help it along. He jerked his gaze away from the tempting sight and stared at the confusing lists of numbers below for the second time. ''What have you found?'' he demanded, relieved that Samantha could make sense of those rows of figures.

Samantha leaned back in her chair, which placed her shoulder disturbingly close to the long-barreled revolver Jack Barnett now wore strapped to his thigh. The gun's polished metal drew her eye, and she felt a cold sensation within. She recognized the Colt army revolver that was standard issue for Union officers—had seen ones like it brandished at her family many times. Samantha shivered, then shook off the bad memories and responded to Jack's question. "At first glance, they don't appear any different from other disbursements and transfers following a purchase. Now that I've examined them more closely, however, I've noticed these transfers always match up with an unusual set of disbursements."

"Mrs. Winchester, I wouldn't recognize an unusual disbursement if it walked up and bit me." He frowned at the maze of figures.

Samantha found herself smiling all too easily into those intense gray eyes. "Stockyard fees, Mr. Barnett. For holding pens at the Devil's Addition, and for the cowboys to stand guard." She couldn't help but grin at the astonished expression the mention of Abilene's lewd and lively ladies' abode brought to Jack's face.

"What the . . . ?" Jack recovered with a laugh. "There *are* no stockyards at the Devil's Addition, Mrs. Winchester! The Addition is where the, uh . . ." He glanced away and pondered his choice of words.

Samantha helped him out. "I'm well aware of what is available at the Devil's Addition, Mr. Barnett," she said with a sly smile, enjoying his momentary embarrassment for some reason. "If you'll recall, Lucy Johnson made it perfectly clear who resides there . . . and it certainly isn't cattle."

"Perceptive as ever, Mrs. Winchester," he said with an admiring grin.

"That's what caused these entries to stand out when I examined them the last time. So the other night after dinner, I thought to ask Lucy Johnson. She assured me there were no stockyards at the Addition." Her expression sobered quickly. "This may be the clue we've been looking for, Mr. Barnett. I'm so sorry I neglected to mention my discovery earlier, but I completely forgot in yesterday's commotion over my aunt.'' She exhaled a deep sigh. ''Thank heavens Aunt Mimi only fainted when she fell down those stairs. She's fortunate she wasn't seriously injured.''

''I'm just grateful she's recovered,'' he said. ''And no apologies are necessary, Mrs. Winchester. Your astute discovery more than compensates for any delay.''

The sound of praise in Jack's voice brought a slight flush to Samantha's cheek. She caught him observing her with an intensity that caused her heart to skip a beat, and she studied the tip of her ink pen instead. ''I want to thank you for rescuing Becky yesterday. She confessed to me what happened . . . with those men, I mean.''

''I didn't do the rescuing. Cody Barnes did.''

''Becky told me what you did, Mr. Barnett. If it hadn't been for you, that nice Mr. Barnes might not be alive now.'' Samantha ventured another glance upward. Her heart skipped a whole measure this time.

''Abilene is not quite civilized yet,'' said Jack. And until it is, I'm not taking any chances with the safety of you and your family.''

Samantha gestured to the bullet-filled gun belt slung low on his hips. ''Is that why you are now armed, Mr. Barnett?''

''Yes, ma'am, it is. Furthermore, I've asked Cody if he would hire on to stand guard in the office, since I'm gone so much of the time. It would ease my mind considerably . . . where you are concerned, that is.''

Samantha was swept into that concerned and very warm gaze and held motionless for a long moment. ''Mr. Barnett . . . I do not need a nursemaid. I am a grown woman, not some hothouse flower,'' she managed to protest.

''I realize that, Mrs. Winchester, but—''

The sound of the office door scraping open stopped Jack

in midsentence. After a second, Clyde's shaggy head appeared around the door.

"I've got a message fer ya, Jack," Clyde announced in his scratchy voice. Lifting his weather-beaten hat briefly, he nodded to Samantha first. "Littlefield wants you over to the stockyards. Seems he's cut out some steers that'll be more to yer likin'. I'll take ya to him, since I gotta go talk to ol' man Mose, anyway."

"I'm not leaving Mrs. Winchester until Cody Barnes shows up, Clyde. Now, you go and tell Littlefield that I'll be over there as soon as I can. Meanwhile, he'll just have to wait," Jack ordered in a brisk voice and gestured out the door.

Clyde gave an obedient nod. "I'll tell him, Captain," he replied, then stiffened. He peered guiltily over his shoulder into Jack's angry face, then flushed and hurried out the door.

Samantha had not missed the swift and curious exchange between the two men, nor had she neglected to notice the coiled-spring tension that emanated from Jack Barnett now. The easygoing manner was gone—so too was the compelling dark gaze. In fact, Jack kept his face averted now as he walked across the room. Samantha observed him intently, wondering at the swift and profound change she'd witnessed, all occasioned by Clyde Monroe's all-too-obvious slip of the tongue.

She pondered Clyde's shamefaced embarrassment and Jack's angry reaction. Had they served together during the war? Obviously. How else to explain Clyde's obedient reply to Jack's command? But, if so . . . why did one act angry and the other ashamed?

Samantha watched Jack stand stiffly beside his desk and wished she could ease his apparent discomfort. "Mr. Barnett, I assure you I will be safe here until Cody Barnes arrives. You should not hesitate to fulfill your duties. Please . . . I feel guilty delaying you.''

Jack met her eyes at last and was relieved there were no questions on her face. He fervently hoped that Clyde's slip had gone unnoticed. ''No need. Littlefield's cows aren't going anywhere. Remember . . . he's the seller. *I'm* the buyer.''

The office door scraped open again, but this time a loud squeal of childish delight accompanied it. Samantha saw her son scamper into the office, Cody's wide-brimmed Stetson balancing on his head. Swallowing his head, to be exact. Davy lifted the huge hat with both hands and laughed in delight.

''Look, Mama! Cody let me wear his hat. I'm a *real* cowboy!''

Samantha laughed. ''Well, you certainly look the part,'' she observed. ''But now I think you should return Mr. Barnes's hat to him.''

''Thanks, Davy.'' Cody gave him a nod as he accepted his Stetson. ''And you can call me Cody, ma'am.''

''You were sweet to bring him, Cody.'' Glancing at her son, she said, ''But I'm afraid you'll have to go home, sweetheart. This is an army office, and Mr. Barnett and I have a lot of work to do.'' Davy's bright smile disappeared.

''Don't worry, Mrs. Winchester, I'll take him home,'' Jack said.

''But Mr. Littlefield is waiting . . . you shouldn't delay your business. I don't want to trouble you,'' Samantha protested.

''Believe me, it'll be no trouble. Littlefield can wait long enough for Davy to find a hat that fits.''

Davy bounced in excitement. ''Honest? A real cowboy hat?'' He whooped in delight.

Jack laughed. ''A real cowboy hat, son . . . that is, unless your mother objects.'' He slanted a look at Samantha.

Samantha knew when she was outnumbered and gave in with a nod. Davy let out a pint-size version of a rebel yell and raced toward the doorway, where his benefactor was waiting. Jack turned to give Samantha a smile before he closed the door.

Cody set his hat upon Jack's desk and settled himself into a cane-backed chair across the room. ''You go right on with what you're doin', ma'am. I'm not about to disturb you,'' he said.

Samantha nodded with a little smile before she concentrated on the ledgers once more. This time, however, the unusual entries didn't hold her attention at all. Instead, she pictured Jack Barnett holding Davy's hand while they went out the door . . . Jack Barnett buying her son a real cowboy hat . . . Jack Barnett rescuing her sister from vicious men . . . Jack Barnett fetching the doctor for her aunt.

Samantha squeezed her eyes shut as she bent over the books. Jack Barnett. Jack Barnett. Every time she turned around, he was doing something for her family. She felt a little tug somewhere inside her chest. Kindly could no longer adequately describe the way this man treated her family. It was far too mild a word for the consideration he had shown toward them all.

She glanced at Cody, seated across the room, cleaning his revolver. Merciful heavens, she thought to herself. Jack Barnett had even hired an armed cowboy to watch over her. Samantha cupped her chin in her hand and stared at the ledgers. She couldn't remember the last time someone other than her family had given a thought about her welfare. Before the war perhaps? She smiled to herself. This new situation would take some getting used to.

If only she could find the right words to convey her gratitude, Samantha thought as she toyed with her pen. She longed to tell Jack Barnett how much his care and concern meant to everyone—and to her. Especially her. But every time she tried, the words seemed to disappear the very moment she looked into his face. She tapped her pen, impatient with her sudden inability to express her thoughts. The feelings of immense gratitude spreading over her right now had made her tongue-tied.

Samantha gave a frustrated sigh and stared at the ledger once again. The maze of figures was soothing, familiar, understandable. But for some inexplicable reason, Samantha found that this time when she tried to focus on the rows and rows of numbers, those feelings of immense gratitude kept slipping into her thoughts and destroying her concentration entirely.

Chapter

8

"*Oh!*" Samantha exclaimed with a start. Another sharp rattle of gunfire punctuated the air, and she relaxed into her desk chair with an exasperated sigh. Would she ever grow accustomed to those sudden bursts of gunfire in Abilene's streets? she wondered.

"Startled you, ma'am?" Cody Barnes asked with a smile. "You'll have to forgive 'em, Mrs. Winchester. It's just those new wranglers that headed into town yesterday lettin' off a little steam."

Cody rose from his chair and ambled toward her desk with a lanky grace. Samantha observed the lean young cowboy and marveled that Cody's boyish manner could capture her younger sister's heart in such a short time. There was no missing the flush she'd seen on Becky's cheeks these past two days.

"Why can't those cowboys find a quieter way to let off steam?" she asked.

Cody laughed. "I don't think they know any other way, ma'am, to tell you the truth. In fact, some of them don't think at all. Especially when they've been drinkin'." He drew closer and peered into the open ledger books on her desk. "If you don't mind me asking, ma'am, exactly what is it you're lookin' for? I've been watchin' you study those books for two days now, over and over again. Are you finding mistakes or something?"

"No, Cody, I'm looking for anything that's different . . . or suspicious. Anything that can't be explained easily," she replied, pleasantly surprised at his interest.

"What're you writing on that sheet of paper?"

She observed Cody for a second. Jack Barnett was right. There was more to this young cowboy than met the eye. The intent look of curiosity on his face testified to that fact. "Those are the items I've found so far, and I'm not even finished." She opened the last pages of the ledger and withdrew several sheets of paper, all filled with neat columns of account names and numbers.

Cody's eyes widened at the pages. "You really have been working, ma'am." He shook his head in admiration. "I sure do wish there was a way I could help you. Not with the bookkeeping, of course, but maybe with the copy work. Besides, I'm gettin' plumb bored to death just sittin' here watching you work. I'd rather be doin' something."

His offer brought a smile to her face. She was about to politely decline when she had another thought. "Perhaps you can, Cody."

"Anything at all, Mrs. Winchester. It'll beat sittin', for sure." He pulled up a chair beside her desk.

Samantha spread out the second ledger in front of him. "I want you to start at the first page and copy down every one of the entries I've marked with a little 'x,' all right? There is paper and another pen in the drawer."

She scooted herself around the corner of the scarred wooden desk so Cody and his long legs would have plenty of room. Samantha watched him arrange the blank sheets of paper, dip his pen into the inkwell, and bend his head to his task without another word. Samantha went back to her own perusal, glancing toward her new assistant occasionally. Cody scanned the ledger pages with a carefulness that eased her mind considerably.

Convinced that Cody was proceeding with due diligence, Samantha returned to her own meticulous investigation . . . and the mysterious numbers she had discovered circled in the margins. She had noticed them only this morning when she spied three initials neatly lettered at the top of that same page. A careful examination revealed another set of letters and numbers circled on the first page of the next month's entries.

Samantha had assumed it was only meaningless jotting at first, perhaps something the former bookkeeper had used as a reminder. But when she noticed a different set of numbers and initials on October's first page, and November's, and on the first page of each month that followed, her suspicions were aroused.

Samantha chewed on the end of her pen, lost in thought, pondering what those numbers and letters could possibly mean. She was so preoccupied she didn't even notice the appearance of Joe Taggert's face outside the office window. He watched them for a moment with a scowl before he finally turned and moved away.

Samantha dipped her pen into the inkwell and bent over the page, copying May's different set of numbers and letters. Suddenly the sound of gunshot resounded outside in the street, so loud and startling that Samantha nearly knocked over the inkwell when she jumped straight up in her chair. "Good heavens, Cody! What was *that*?"

Cody Barnes was already on his feet, his Colt in his hand. "I don't know, ma'am, but I aim to find out." He headed for the door, only to see it open before he got there.

Samantha caught her breath, wondering if some outlaw or drunken cowboy was about to rush in upon them. The thought of easygoing, friendly Cody Barnes being shot before her eyes sent a chill through her bones. The shaggy head that appeared instead brought a sigh of relief.

"Sorry 'bout the shootin', Miz Winchester," Clyde apologized as he shuffled into the office. "Ol' Jim Shane down at the general store just took on one of them wranglers off'n the Ferguson drive." Clyde's face spread into a huge grin. "He got tired of listenin' to that wild shootin', so he grabbed his carbine and met that cowpoke in the street."

"Merciful heavens, Clyde! He didn't shoot him, did he?" Samantha cried.

"Shucks, no, ma'am." Clyde chuckled. "He just stood there in the middle of the street, a-watchin' that wrangler come ridin' and shootin' off his pistol. Then ol' Jim, he loaded up his gun and yelled, 'Halt, you villain, or I'll shoot you full of holes!' Liked to scare that cowpoke to death. He took one look at ol' Jim and headed outta town." Clyde laughed out loud now. "I tell you, it was some sight. Ol' Jim, standin' there on his wooden leg, aimin' his rifle. Whooooey! That was a sight! It surely was."

Samantha tried to conjure the picture of an invalid managing to chase a drunken cowboy out of town. She shook her head in wonder. "Whatever happened to that poor man to cause him to lose his limb? Was he in some horrible accident with the railroad?"

Clyde's laughter disappeared. "No, ma'am, it weren't no accident. Ol' Jim lost his right leg in the war. Can't remember which battle he said . . . somewhere down South." He lowered his eyes to the dusty floor.

"Lots of good men lost more than that," Cody observed, shoving his revolver back into its holster. "On both sides of the war."

Samantha sat quietly, realizing how many others had headed west to escape memories of that horrible conflict. Broken bodies needed mending, hearts and minds ached to heal and start again, just like hers. She watched Clyde grab the door handle, obviously anxious to go. This intrusion of the war's memory made him uncomfortable. Something told her it had to do with Clyde's slip of the tongue a few days ago.

"Clyde," she called out before he could escape. "May I ask you a question?"

"Yes, ma'am, sure you can." He turned to face Samantha.

"I couldn't help hearing you address Mr. Barnett as 'Captain' the other day. I was wondering . . . did the two of you serve together in the war?"

Clyde stared at the floor again. His shoulders hunched forward as he shifted from one foot to the other. "Well, ma'am . . . I, uh . . . I, uh . . ." he stammered.

Samantha watched his nervous hesitation in fascination. "It's all right, Clyde," she offered. "Mr. Barnett has already told me he fought for the Union."

Clyde's face came up in an instant, his faded blue eyes wide in astonishment. "He *did*!?"

"Yes, he did. So when I heard you address him as 'Captain,' I assumed you two had served together. Your friendship goes back a while. Anyone can tell that." She smiled warmly at him.

"Uh, yes, ma'am . . . we do go back a ways. That is a fact." Clyde held her eyes for a moment, then glanced away.

Samantha watched Clyde intently. His apparent discomfort piqued her curiosity even more. It was obvious Clyde Monroe knew more than he was willing to tell, especially about Jack Barnett. Something was holding him back. Whatever could it be?

She prodded again. "Mr. Barnett mentioned he fought at Manassas and Fredericksburg. Is that where you served, Clyde?"

Clyde's face betrayed his anxiety at her questioning, and once again the shifting began. "Uh, yes, ma'am . . . that was it. Fredericksburg. Terrible, too . . . I want to tell ya."

Cody Barnes leaned against the desk and said, "I lost an uncle at Fredericksburg. My mother's brother. It was terrible bloody from what I hear tell."

At that, Clyde wheeled about and jerked the office door open. "Uh, excuse me, but I gotta go see to some business. I'll . . . I'll see you folks at supper." He charged out the door with uncharacteristic haste, leaving Samantha and Cody gazing after him.

"More coffee, Miz Johnson?" Maysie asked, her ever-present coffeepot in hand.

"No, thanks, Maysie," Lucy said and leaned back into her chair. Then she playfully tugged Maysie's sleeve, beckoning her face closer. "And don't go offerin' any more to Mr. Barnett, either," she whispered tersely. "I don't want him having to race out yonder in the back! Mrs. Winchester needs some walkin'—mighty bad, if you ask me."

Maysie's smile broke free. "You are *bad*, Miz Johnson. You know that?" she scolded.

"Humph!" Lucy gave an exasperated snort. "I'll be blessed if I understand young men nowadays, Maysie. Here it is, a beautiful summer night, without a cloud in the sky, and that big, fat old moon just a-grinnin' down outside. A perfect night for sparkin', to my way of thinkin'. And what do I see?" She observed the three men at the end of her table, then glanced over her shoulder to where Samantha and Becky were drying and stacking the dinner dishes.

"I see two healthy young men sittin' in my kitchen talkin' about cows! What in heaven's name would make Jack and Cody sit here with Clyde for an hour when there are two pretty women waitin' to be walked in the moonlight? What a waste of a summer night." She wagged her head. "I'm glad my Lucas had more sense. He knew what a summer night was for, all right, and it wasn't to talk about cattle!" Her paper-thin cheeks colored.

Maysie's face wrinkled into another grin. "You knows the old saying, Miz Johnson . . . you can lead a horse to water, but you can't make 'im drink." Her dark eyes settled on Jack Barnett.

Lucy's face puckered into a frown. "Well, all I can say is, I've been seein' some mighty thirsty looks come this way," she whispered as Samantha approached. Maysie turned away with a wink.

"There now, all done," Samantha said, adjusting the long sleeves of her dress.

"Why, thank you, ladies. You're so much help. I declare, I'm gettin' spoiled with you here."

"It's the least we can do, Lucy." Samantha smoothed out her worn silk skirt, then reached up a hand to rescue an errant hairpin. Not fast enough, however. Several lustrous curls tumbled beside her face. Samantha dutifully captured them once more, oblivious to the thirsty gaze coming from the other end of the table.

Lucy Johnson watched Jack intently. After a moment, she leaned back with a smile and declared in a loud voice, "Well, Samantha . . . you certainly look like you could use a breath of fresh air. Staring at them books all day has made you right peaked lookin'. You take my advice and step outside for a spell."

Samantha blinked at Lucy in surprise. The three men at

the other end of the table stopped talking immediately. Lucy grinned. "In fact, all you folks look a little peaked to me. I think everybody should scoot outside. Catch your breath a spell." Eyeing her nephew, Lucy admonished, "Not you, Clyde. I want you to go out to the barn and fetch more wood for the stove."

"Now?" Clyde complained.

"Yes, Clyde, right now. While the others are stretching their legs, you can work off that extra serving of pie by bringin' me some wood, if you please."

"Yes'm," Clyde said in a dutiful voice and rose from the table. Jack rose as well, but very slowly.

Samantha hesitantly edged toward the door. Part of her was eager to escape into the summer night's welcoming embrace, to cool herself in the slight breeze. The other part, however, remembered the unsettling sensations she had experienced the last time she was alone in the dark with Jack Barnett. She still hadn't sorted through them all. They were much too confusing. Whenever she tried to examine those strange feelings—analyze them as she did the tangled numbers in the ledger books—Samantha felt that unfamiliar sensation creep inside, which destroyed her concentration completely. She had never encountered a maze of numbers that could not be untangled. This maze of new feelings was proving much more difficult to understand.

Lucy gave Samantha a little nudge toward the door. Becky and Cody were already halfway there. "Off you go, my dear," Lucy prodded.

Jack stared at Samantha for a moment—when she wasn't looking. Then suddenly he reached down and tousled Davy's blond hair. The boy had not strayed more than six inches from Jack's knee all evening. "How about we go help old Clyde with his chores; what do you say?" Jack asked.

"Sure!" Davy cried in delight. Jack swung the small boy onto his shoulders. Davy vigorously urged his mount on with imaginary spurs as all three went out the door.

Lucy placed both hands on her hips and swore in astonishment, "Well, if that don't beat all. I'll *never* understand men!" Lucy sighed, then patted the table, gesturing for Samantha to sit. They were alone in the kitchen now.

"Did you want Clyde for more chores?" Samantha asked innocently.

"No matter. I just don't think it takes two and a half men to bring in a load of firewood." She shook her head.

"Mr. Barnett seems to enjoy helping your nephew. Have they been friends for long?" Samantha asked carefully.

"Land's sakes, yes. Ever since the war." Lucy smoothed the few wrinkles from her gingham dress without looking up.

Samantha heard the opening she was waiting for. "Clyde mentioned that he had fought with Mr. Barnett at Fredericksburg," she said. "I know that was a bloody battle. I'm grateful they both survived unscathed."

Lucy's head came up immediately. She looked Samantha straight in the eye. "Whatever would make Clyde say something like that?"

"This afternoon I mentioned to Clyde that Mr. Barnett said he'd fought for the Union . . . at Manassas and Fredericksburg. Then I asked Clyde if he had served with Mr. Barnett there as well. Clyde admitted he had." Samantha watched the surprise on Lucy Johnson's face change to sadness.

Lucy leaned over and placed her worn hand on Samantha's arm. "Jack Barnett served at Fredericksburg, that he did. With honor, too, the way Clyde heard tell. But Clyde wasn't anywhere near that bloody battlefield, Samantha. He was already in an army prison camp, where he was sent after Bull Run.''

Samantha's mouth dropped open in astonishment. "Wh-whatever for?"

"For failing to stand and face the enemy," Lucy said softly. "You've probably noticed my nephew hasn't much backbone to speak of. Clyde's good-hearted as they come, he is, but he sure isn't one to stand up to danger. 'Specially when it's holdin' a rifle.''

Samantha stared past Lucy's shoulder, her mind racing with frantic thoughts. Prison! Did Jack Barnett meet Clyde in prison? Merciful heavens! Was that possible? Her heart beat so hard, Samantha felt her rib cage rattle.

Lucy leaned closer to Samantha. "Clyde met Jack Barnett in prison, yes, but don't you go thinkin' for a minute that cowardice was the reason Jack landed on an Ohio rock pile. No, sir!" She shook her head vehemently. "Exactly the opposite, if you ask me! Clyde said Jack was leadin' a team of scouts somewhere down South when one of those scouts slipped off on his own. Jack found him later, runnin' out of a farmhouse that was all ablaze, a woman and child screamin' inside, unable to escape. Seems this lowlife had set the place on fire after he'd pleasured himself with both of them. The little girl, too, mind you.''

Samantha drew back in horror.

"I know, it makes you sick to your stomach." Lucy nodded. "Well, that's what it did to Jack, too, only he hauled off and grabbed that devil and beat the livin' daylights out of him! Would've killed him, too, if some major hadn't come along just then. This major, mind you, claps the irons on Jack! Court-martials him for striking an enlisted man. The *idea*. And that devil gets off scot-free after rapin' and murderin' those poor innocents! I tell you, it made my blood boil, just to hear Clyde tell it.''

Lucy drew a deep breath, then patted Samantha's arm again. "It would shame Jack Barnett somethin' awful if he thought you knew he was in prison. Promise me you'll never let on that you know."

Samantha gazed into her lap while her heartbeat slowed to normal. Her thoughts took a little longer, however. Jack Barnett. Imprisoned. Sentenced because he avenged a wrong. Somehow she had no trouble believing Lucy Johnson's tale. It squared exactly with the man she had come to know. Samantha pictured Jack spending the remainder of the war in miserable forced labor. The image brought a sorrowful tightening to her chest.

Now she understood the reason behind the pain she had glimpsed so often in his dark eyes. The idea of Jack being unfairly imprisoned and humiliated was too horrible to think about. A man as honorable and brave and good and kind and . . . and gentle . . . and caring . . . as Jack. A swift surge of anger rushed through Samantha that reached all the way down to her toes.

And something else. Deep inside her, where the maze of confused feelings lay hidden, another feeling emerged. But this one was recognizable. A deeply protective instinct, as strong as it was illogical, swelled inside her breast. Samantha couldn't understand this feeling any more than she understood the others that disturbed her. All she knew was that the thought of Jack Barnett being in pain in any way distressed her deeply.

Samantha gazed into Lucy's sad eyes and swore, "I promise he will never know."

Chapter
9

Cody Barnes placed a restraining hand on Davy's shoulder and peered down at the miniature cowboy striding beside him. "You hold that bottle steady now," he advised. "Your mama wants that ink in the bottle, not on you." Davy immediately smoothed his bouncing gait along the plank walkway that passed for Abilene's main sidewalk.

Although he knew the little boy would have difficulty staying with him, Cody walked faster. The simple errand had kept him away from the office much longer than he had planned. With so many drovers filling the streets, a walk to the general store seemed to take forever. Cody lifted his red bandanna to wipe his eyes. Too many hooves and boots were stirring up the dust, an unpleasant reminder of those long, long days on the trail.

Cody looked around him and shook his head in wonder at the number of cowboys clogging Abilene's main street. Lord have mercy! He didn't see how the town could hold any more. The Drovers' Cottage had been full for over a week, and the wranglers still kept coming. And the herds. Jack Barnett spent every day bargaining with cattlemen.

Lord knew where they were gonna pen all those cows. The stockyards were overflowing already.

Three surly cowboys stood directly ahead in his path. They were a sour-looking bunch, if ever he'd seen one, Cody thought to himself. All three had probably drawn nighttime guard duty. A pretty frustrating job, too, especially at the end of the trail when most wranglers looked forward to Abilene's celebrated pleasures. Nursemaiding the herd within earshot of everybody else's good time was enough to sour any cowboy's mood.

He reached out to guide Davy past the dour group, nodding briefly as he pushed past. " 'Scuse us, gents. Comin' through—'' Cody's voice broke off as the heavy butt of a revolver crashed down on the back of his head. He groaned, then sprawled on the rough planks, unconscious.

Joe Taggert stepped from around the corner with a smirk. He spied Davy staring down at his fallen comrade and sprang forward. "C'mere, little reb." He grabbed Davy by the arm and yanked roughly.

"Let me go!" Davy yelled and aimed a swift kick at Taggert's leg, hitting him full in the shin.

"Damn you!" Taggert cuffed the boy across the face, bringing tears to Davy's eyes and sending his new hat flying. The ink bottle spilled into the street as well, the thirsty dust quickly drinking up its dark contents.

"Let me go! Let me go!" Davy squirmed in Taggert's grasp.

Taggert hoisted the struggling boy under one arm as he headed for the hitching rail and his horse. "Much obliged, fellas," he said to the sullen cowboys who had provided the distraction. "Pay 'em, Zeke." Zeke pushed away from the clapboard building and dug into his pockets. He approached the group of men and dropped a silver dollar into each outstretched hand.

The trio didn't move, but simply gaped at Taggert trying to climb onto his horse while Davy thrashed wildly. The tallest and ugliest spoke up. "That cowpoke stole your boy, did he?"

"Somethin' like that." Taggert grabbed for the saddle horn but couldn't mount with the squirming child. "Shut up, boy!" He boxed Davy's ears.

Davy let out a high-pitched yelp of pain. "I'm not your boy! Let me go!" he yelled. Twisting himself around, Davy sank his teeth into Taggert's hand.

Taggert cursed and dropped Davy to the ground. The boy scrambled to his feet and took off—right into Zeke's grasp. Zeke yanked him by the arm until tears poured from Davy's eyes.

"Where do you think yer goin', sprout?" Zeke snarled. "Better watch out or yer pappy's gonna give you a whuppin'!"

"What's the kid done, mister?" an approaching cowboy called out, peering down from his horse in curiosity, while he reined in his mount to watch.

Taggert licked at the blood on his hand and narrowed his eyes on the little boy, who was still struggling in Zeke's grasp. Davy's cheek flamed scarlet from the last two blows. "Give 'im here, Zeke. I gotta teach him to mind his manners."

Despite a slight murmured protest from the surrounding crowd, Zeke gave the little boy a shove that sent him spinning into Taggert's hands. Davy flinched and closed his eyes. Taggert's lips spread tight over his stained teeth as he drew back his hand. Only the unexpected sound of a woman's voice caused him to hesitate.

"Take your hands off my son!" Samantha Winchester cried, pushing herself through the crowd of men. The general murmuring grew louder as the circle of men expanded to admit her into their midst.

Samantha's heart pounded so loud it thundered in her ears, shaking her slender body as she confronted the man holding her son. She was livid, but her voice was cold as a stone. "Let him go." Samantha fixed Taggert with a murderous glare.

Taggert lowered his arm and grabbed Davy by the shoulders. He insolently ran his eyes over Samantha and leered. "He bit my hand, and now I'm gonna teach him a lesson."

Samantha lunged toward her son, but Zeke grabbed her arm and held her back with a laugh. She wheeled around and slammed her hand into his face, slapping him so hard he stumbled backward. A rousing cheer rose up from the younger wranglers in the crowd. Samantha scanned the surrounding men in a desperate search.

If she could just find a weapon. The nearest mounted cowboy was only a few feet away. Samantha spied a rifle in the case tied beside his saddle and grabbed it before the startled cowboy had a chance to protest. She quickly pumped the lever and aimed right at Taggert's ugly face.

More than a murmur of approval rose up from the crowd at the sight of Samantha Winchester drawing a bead on Joe Taggert. Zeke took one look at the enraged mother and backed away, along with the rest of the crowd.

"Let him go . . . *now*," she repeated in a low, dangerous voice, steadying her aim on Taggert's head. Her pulse pounded in her ears as the sweat trickled down her face. Samantha didn't notice.

Taggert narrowed his eyes on Samantha. "And what're you gonna do if I don't? Shoot me?" he said with a sneer. "Sure you are, Lady Reb."

The taunt sparked something inside Samantha's overheated brain. She braced both feet and peered down the long black barrel. "I got a lot of practice shooting Yankee scavengers during the war," she lied. "And they were a lot farther away than you are right now."

A low roar of approval sounded behind her as the cowboys nearest Taggert stepped farther away. Taggert's smirk vanished. His mouth twitched instead. Glancing toward the man whose rifle Samantha had stolen, Taggert called out, "That thing loaded, cowboy?"

The young man brushed aside a lock of light brown hair and grinned. "Yup. Sure is, mister. And I think the lady's got you dead in her sights, too."

Sweat began to bead Taggert's upper lip. The raucous cowboys surrounding him sent up a chorus of encouragement to Samantha.

"Go on, lady! Shoot 'im!"

"Blow his head off, ma'am!"

"*Damn!*"

"Pull the trigger. Wild Bill would *never* hang a woman!"

Taggert's eyes darted around the crowd. Finally he released Davy, giving the boy a vicious shove that sent him sprawling in the dust at his mother's feet.

Samantha felt the tension drain from her tight shoulders, and she lowered the rifle to kneel beside her son, who was bravely trying not to cry in front of all the cowboys. She gathered him to her side, keeping the rifle close. Taggert glared at mother and son before he gave a derisive snort. Samantha warily watched his movements, not noticing the man who stepped forward out of the crowd now.

The man's elongated shadow fell across Samantha and Davy as they knelt in the dusty street, and she looked up to see a tall figure outlined in the noonday sun. His face was cloaked in shadow so she could not see his features, but Samantha recognized his voice the moment she heard it.

"You're pretty brave against women and children, Taggert. Let's see what you can do against a man," Jack Barnett challenged.

The sight of so many yelling cowboys just a few yards from his office had been enough to pull Jack from a group of arguing cattlemen only a moment ago. Once he got close enough to see Samantha holding a rifle on Taggert, he closed the distance swiftly. One look at Davy's scarlet, swollen cheek set his blood to boiling. Now that Samantha had Davy safely by her side, Jack could make his move at last. Taggert was his.

Taggert turned to the side and started when he saw Jack Barnett. "Get outta my way, Barnett. My partner's waitin' on me," he snarled, and nodded toward Zeke, who was already mounted, holding Taggert's horse by the reins.

"Not till you've dealt with me," Jack said in a menacing voice. He watched Samantha and Davy rise to their feet. "Are you all right, Mrs. Winchester, you and the boy?"

Samantha nodded, startled by the fierce light in Jack's eyes. "We are now." She returned the borrowed rifle to its owner, who leaned down from his horse to retrieve it.

Jack stepped closer and stared down into Davy's upturned face. The mark of Taggert's hand flamed across the small cheek. The sight made his gut twist. Jack removed his hat and offered it to the boy.

"Hold my hat, son. This won't take long."

Davy grabbed it with an eager nod, as if he sensed what was about to take place.

Without another word, Jack spun around and crashed his fist into Taggert's jaw, knocking him into the circle of startled cowboys. Taggert struggled to regain his balance, then lunged at Jack. Jack was waiting and sank his fist deep into Taggert's belly. Taggert doubled over in pain. Loud shouts grew wilder as the cowboys clustered around the two men.

Taggert tried to land a punch, but Jack met him again and again, sending the big man stumbling. Each time Taggert climbed to his feet and charged, Jack stopped him with a vicious blow. Blood streamed down Taggert's face from his broken nose.

Samantha anxiously drew Davy to her side and wished she were not so gratified by the brutal beating Jack was inflicting on the man who had tormented her son. At that moment, however, all trace of charitable instincts had drained from Samantha Winchester. She winced as Jack landed another punishing blow to Taggert's bloody face— winced, but did not turn away.

After falling to the ground yet again, Taggert scrambled to one knee and paused to wipe his hand across his bleeding mouth, peering up at Jack Barnett in hatred. He sprang from his crouch with an enraged snarl and grabbed Jack by the legs, knocking him to the ground.

Samantha gasped. Taggert sprawled on top of Jack and swung wildly. The cowboy chorus grew in volume, roaring so loudly she wanted to cover her ears. Petrified that Taggert had subdued Jack at last, Samantha pushed aside the wrangler who crowded in front of her, blocking her view. To her astonishment, she saw Jack land a fierce backhand blow, then roll out from beneath Taggert.

Jack leaped to his feet and wiped the blood from his own face before he reached down to grab Taggert by the shirt. In a move so swift it made the larger man seem almost weightless, Jack pulled him off the ground and planted another solid punch to his jaw.

Taggert went reeling and collapsed at the feet of the shouting, cheering cowboys. Two bloody teeth landed in the dust nearby and were promptly ground beneath the tall-heeled boot of a young Texan. Cody Barnes blinked to clear his blurring vision as he forced himself into the crowd. This was one fight he didn't want to miss.

Jack watched Taggert unsuccessfully try to climb to his feet. Any trace of mercy in Jack's soul was locked away tight. Taggert deserved none. "Pick him up," he ordered the wranglers closest to Taggert.

"He's done fer, mister," one of the men said.

"Pick him up." Jack fixed the man with a glare. The man gulped and complied, nudging his companion for help. They hauled a groggy Taggert to his feet.

Jack paused only a moment before he drew back and sent his fist crashing into Taggert's jaw one last time. Taggert spun with the force of the blow and fell facedown in the dust of Abilene's street, unconscious at last.

A roar of approval rose up around Jack as he wiped the blood from his mouth with the back of his stinging hand. He glanced to his bruised and bleeding knuckles and gave his hand a shake. "Load that worthless scum on his horse and let his partner have him."

"His partner's plumb gone, mister," a grizzled old drover cackled. "He lit off the minute you landed the first punch."

"Then tie him on his horse and send him out of town. If I see his face again, I might get really angry."

He turned back to Samantha and Davy. The boy held out Jack's hat and grinned, and Jack gave him an exhausted smile.

Samantha's heart lurched as she stared at Jack—this man who seemed to magically appear whenever her family was in danger, rescuing them, protecting them, as if he could sense their distress. Caring for them as if they were his own. No one had ever cared for her family like that before.

She had been alone so long, with no one to depend upon
but herself. Standing up to taunts and facing down threats
with nothing but her own bravado, when in reality she was
so scared she trembled beneath her petticoats. Doing what
she needed to do. Protecting and caring for her family.
What would it feel like to be cared for? To have someone
stand up for *her*? Samantha couldn't even imagine. Until
now.

A slow warmth began to spread through her veins as she
stared into the face of her exhausted champion. The feeling
that swelled inside her heart now was not immediately recognizable, but Samantha knew what it was not. It was not
gratitude.

She deliberately caught and held Jack's gaze while she
spoke. ''Gentlemen . . . let us hope Mrs. Johnson has
enough bandages, because I promise the three of you shall
not want for nurses.''

Jack sat absolutely still with his eyes closed, not moving
a muscle. He didn't want to spoil the sensuous enjoyment
of Samantha's gentle touch as she carefully cleaned the cut
beside his right cheekbone. Jack could have sworn it was
only a scratch, but apparently Samantha thought otherwise,
for she had been tending it for over ten minutes. Jack let
his pleasure at her lingering touch spread through his insides with a slow warmth.

''There now . . . I've finally stopped the bleeding. Your
cheek will feel tender for a while, I imagine,'' she said
softly.

Jack didn't reply. That would have necessitated opening
his eyes, and he didn't want to do that just yet. If he did,
he would see how close Samantha was standing to him. He
didn't think he could maintain his outwardly calm pose
then. She was so close he could hear her breathing, so close

he could smell her. Jack quietly inhaled the lemon-sweet scent of her, filling his lungs.

"It's remarkable you have only a few cuts, Mr. Barnett," Samantha observed. "What with the ferocity of that man's attack, I'm amazed you were not severely injured."

He let the sound of her admiration send its own special warmth through his veins, then answered. "Not remarkable at all, Mrs. Winchester. Taggert is a bully, not a fighter. He relies on his size to intimidate people." Jack opened his eyes and saw her face right above his.

Samantha held his gaze for a moment, then looked away, glancing about Lucy Johnson's kitchen-turned-infirmary instead. Cody Barnes sat very still while Becky fussed about him. Miss Lily stood in close attendance, a bottle of witch hazel in her hand.

"Should I call Miss Lily to check my handiwork?" she asked with a little smile.

Jack furrowed his brow in mock agony. "Please, no," he begged, remembering his stoic attempt not to flinch while her aunt had swabbed his cut face earlier.

Jack heard a loud "Ouch!" from the middle of Lucy Johnson's kitchen. Davy was not bearing up as manfully beneath Miss Lily's ministrations. Jack sensed it would only be a moment before Davy shattered the intimacy he and Samantha shared.

He did not want to lose the feel of Samantha's hands on his skin quite yet. They were so gentle. It was hard to imagine that an hour ago those same gentle hands had held a rifle on a bully and forced him to back down.

Jack remembered the slight tremble of Samantha's hand when she had lowered the rifle at last. No one else had seen. But he had. Just as no one else could detect the remnants of fear on her face when she knelt beside her son, while her snarling opponent hovered nearby. Jack's heart raced even now at the memory of Samantha's raw courage, and a surge of admiration swept through him.

He tried to catch Samantha's eye, but her attention was focused on the soft cotton cloth in her hand instead. She slowly folded it several times. Jack vainly sought the words to express his feelings, but Samantha spoke up first in a soft voice.

"Thank you for what you did this afternoon," she murmured.

"I wanted to make sure Taggert never came near you or your family again," Jack said, his voice dropping lower. "And I also wanted to send a message to the man who hired him."

Samantha looked up in surprise. "What do you mean?"

"I think Taggert was hired by the embezzler's accomplice to try to scare you out of town before you could find the proof we're looking for . . . in those ledgers, I mean."

Samantha drew back in astonishment, her face suddenly pale. She dropped the cloth and clapped her hand to her mouth. "Oh, no!" she cried. "*The ledgers!* They're still in the office. I forgot! Oh, Jack, what if someone stole them?" Samantha wheeled about and would have fled to the door that instant if Jack had not reached out and grasped her hand.

He jumped to his feet. The sound of his name on her lips gave him more than enough energy to race back to the office. The way Jack felt right now, he could take on two Taggerts. He held Samantha's hand between both of his. "Don't worry, Samantha. I'm sure Clyde has kept an eye on the office."

"But, Jack, you don't understand. I've just begun to make sense of those strange letters and numbers I found. I'm convinced they are the secret accounts we're looking for! There's a pattern for all of them, and they match the transfers, too.'' Samantha caught her breath. ''But we'll never decipher the puzzle if that criminal steals the ledgers. This whole horrible thing with Davy may have been meant to take me away from the office!''

Jack grabbed his Stetson and put it on with one hand, making sure he had a tight hold on Samantha with the other. He wasn't about to let her go. ''Then we'd best hurry,'' he said and headed for the door.

Chapter
10

Anthony Craig's fingers fumbled with the breast button on his newly cleaned uniform. No wonder he couldn't secure it properly. It was loose. Craig frowned at the offending button, then yanked off the jacket with a furious curse—which sent the rest of the buttons flying across the room. He threw the jacket to the floor beside his quaking servant.

"Your slut of a daughter had better learn to sew properly," he snarled. "Make sure she does, Pedro, or I'll take the crop to *you*!"

The older man crouched on the floor and snatched the garment before the major could make good his threat. Crawling about on his hands and knees, Pedro sought to retrieve the scattered buttons, while Craig stalked to his wardrobe and threw open both mahogany doors.

He scowled at the neat rows of cleaned and pressed uniforms and tried to calm himself. Ever since that slovenly Zeke had rushed into the fort and told him of Taggert's fate, the major had found it difficult to keep his temper. The drill sergeant was the first to feel his wrath. Sloppy drills. No discipline. Now, Pedro.

Everywhere Anthony Craig looked, he saw incompetence. How could he not lose his temper? That impudent little Southern clerk was still in Abilene, still poring over those incriminating ledgers. How long would it be before she found something? He jerked aside one immaculate uniform after another, hoping to find an imperfection. Another vent for his seething anger. Not only had that wretch Taggert failed at every miserable assignment, he had succeeded in drawing Jack Barnett's attention—and his wrath.

Yanking another uniform jacket off its hanger, the major sullenly worked the buttons, striving to get a grip on his anger. He had to maintain control. No one suspected his involvement with Taggert, just as no one knew of his scheme with the army agent. All that obsequious agent needed to do was keep his mouth shut in prison, and both he and Craig could retire wealthy men.

The thought of leaving his fate in someone else's hands did not sit well with Anthony Craig. Staring at himself in the mirror for several long seconds, he tried to quiet the unease that had settled in his gut. He glanced at Pedro, who was still on the floor, still searching for scattered buttons. The major adjusted his waistband and glimpsed one of the shiny buttons not far from his foot.

Craig stepped to the side to admire himself in the mirror for a final time, deliberately placing his booted foot on top of the missing button. He inclined his head and examined his profile. "Make sure you find all those buttons, Pedro. You don't want me to be angry when you bring your daughter tonight." He didn't bother to hide his smirk.

Pedro hesitated for a moment, then bowed his head before his shaking hand reached below the dresser to continue its vain search.

*　　*　　*

"You see . . . those letters and numbers were circled for the month of April. And these for May. They weren't noticeable at first, because each ledger page has numbers along the side." Samantha's finger ran down the edge of the page, while Jack leaned closer to observe the ledgers.

"One month, BC 479; another month, SLN 352; then, CS 619; and here, FN 802," she continued. "That's what made me curious. So I decided to make a list for each set, then I recorded the questionable transfers month by month." She sat back in her chair so that Jack could peer over her meticulously compiled lists himself. Samantha felt his revolver press against her shoulder and shivered— whether from the memories the army weapon stirred or from Jack Barnett's body so close to hers, she didn't know. She leaned forward again, away from the Colt strapped to Jack's thigh.

"Do you think those letters and numbers could stand for bank accounts?" she asked. "If so, a sizable amount was embezzled."

Jack followed her pointing finger to the totals of each column. "That's even more than General Logan estimated," he observed.

Scrutinizing the column headings again, Jack pondered. BC, SLN, CS, FN. What in hell did those letters stand for? He frowned, ignoring his wounded forehead, which still stung. Those letters had to stand for something. Bank accounts, maybe? It made sense. Any thief this clever wasn't about to hide embezzled thousands under a rock in the desert. But which bank and where? Back East? Impossible. That would be too far to transport all that cash on a regular basis. No, it had to be someplace closer. Jack scowled at the page and racked his brain, trying to make those letters spark something in his mind.

Samantha studied Jack's profile, although she knew it by

heart already. She was grateful to have the opportunity to gaze at him undisturbed for several minutes, without his dark eyes probing hers. Sensing he was about to turn, Samantha swiftly settled back into her chair, despite the closeness of Jack Barnett's very warm thigh.

She took a deep breath in an attempt to slow her pulse as well as her thoughts. "You don't know how thankful I was to see the ledgers still here, Mr. Barnett. I was praying the whole time we ran to the office." She lifted her head to find him watching her intently. Samantha gazed into those slate-gray depths and almost fell in.

"No more 'Mr. Barnett,' Samantha. I like the sound of 'Jack' better. Much, much better." He gave her a lazy smile.

Samantha hastily focused her attention on her faded blue silk skirt, smoothing out an invisible wrinkle or two. "I . . . I was so afraid the embezzler had made off with the ledgers. Then we never would have solved the puzzle. He would have spirited those books right out of town, I imagine, and probably taken the first train that came through. Headed for St. Louis or Chicago or wherever he could lose himself quickly."

Despite the fact that Jack was enjoying what looked suspiciously like a blush on Samantha's cheek, his pleasure vanished the moment her words registered in his brain.

"Samantha, you may have just given me the clue I was looking for," Jack said and crouched over the neat columns once again.

"Jack, what is it? What have you found?" she asked, excited.

"St. Louis. That has to be it. It's the closest city to Abilene large enough to host several banks." Jack muttered unintelligibly to himself until his face broke out in a sly smile. "Look," he said, pointing. "BC could stand for

Bank of Commerce. SLN, St. Louis National. CS, Central Savings. FN, I'm not sure yet. The embezzler would have any number of banks to choose from in St. Louis."

Samantha pondered the new information, comparing. "You may be right, but it seems so tenuous a connection."

"It's the only connection we've got, Samantha," Jack said with a determined expression. "Now all we have to do is find a way to prove it."

Jack Barnett needed no prodding from Lucy Johnson tonight. He scraped his straight-backed chair away from the table and rose as soon as Samantha finished her coffee. "Samantha," he said, extending his hand. "We need to discuss those ledgers again, but we had best go outside. I certainly wouldn't want to bore your family with the army's bookkeeping."

Lucy Johnson looked up at him in surprise, and Jack gave her a wink. Lucy broke into a huge grin. "Don't you young folks mind about cleaning up," she announced gaily. "It's high time I took a turn cleanin' my own kitchen!" Lucy practically sprang from her chair and began to gather dishes. When she approached the sink, she sidled closer to Maysie and motioned over her shoulder. Cody and Becky were halfway to the door already. "Jack Barnett could take lessons from that boy," she whispered.

Davy headed for the door himself, until Lucy's voice stopped him in his tracks. "Davy, you can give Maysie and me a hand," she suggested.

"We'll be back before you have to go to bed, sweetheart," Samantha promised her disappointed son before she followed Jack outside.

Jack quickly closed the door behind them, eager to escape into the night alone with Samantha. Much to his surprise, however, he discovered they were not alone. There, seated comfortably at the end of Lucy's front porch, were Becky and Cody. Cody fixed Jack with a hopeful look.

"An awful nice night for a stroll," he hinted.

Jack shook his head in admiration at Cody's quickness in laying claim to the coveted front porch. "That sounds like a suggestion, son. Does that mean you two don't want to listen to us talk about bookkeeping?"

Cody grinned through the dark while Becky shyly stared into her lap. "You might say that, sir."

"I figured," Jack muttered in amusement. He kept Samantha's hand clasped tightly in his while he led her across Lucy Johnson's dirt yard and into the dark. An eerie screech shivered through the night sky—an owl on the wing, searching for its prey. Heat still hung in the air, an invisible blanket of moisture, waiting to rise again with the sun's first rays. Jack felt the heavy blanket wrap around them both, cloaking them in the darkness.

He paused near the fence post and gauged their distance from the house. Only when he was certain they were far enough away to ensure some privacy did Jack release her hand. He looked down into Samantha's moonlit face, and his pulse hastened to keep up with his thoughts.

"I wish Cody would stop calling me 'sir.' It makes me feel a hundred years old."

Samantha laughed. "Someone took the time to teach Cody proper manners. Even my aunts are impressed with him." She paused for a moment, running her fingers along the rough wood post. Several jagged slivers protruded along its edge. "I believe you mentioned the bookkeeping, Mr. Bar—uh, Jack," she said when she turned to him.

Jack saw her eyes light up, and he had to take a deep breath to slow his thoughts this time. "I'm convinced our suspicions about those accounts are true, Samantha. In fact, I'm so sure we're right, I plan to wire General Logan tomorrow and tell him our plans.''

"What plans? Whatever are you talking about, Jack?''

Samantha had drawn closer to him in the moonlit night, and Jack had to use all his self-restraint not to pull her into his arms that very moment—taste the mouth that teased him through the dark. First with smiles, next with laughing words. Jack took another very deep breath.

"I plan to wire each of those banks in St. Louis and arrange appointments. We'll start with St. Louis National because it's the largest. Once we secure permission to examine their deposits, we'll see if our theories are correct or not.''

Samantha's smile vanished. *"We?"*

"I'll need your keen eye to examine those deposits, Samantha. We must see if they match up with the transfers on our books. If they do, then we've got him. Major Craig, that is.''

This time Samantha's eyes opened wide. "Craig really is the accomplice!''

Jack nodded. "I became suspicious after Becky ran into Taggert that day, so I began asking questions. I learned that Taggert and his friend were seen with Major Craig several times in the past year. They're probably on his private payroll. Think about it, Samantha. Everything Taggert did was designed to scare you away so we wouldn't find those hidden accounts. Taggert's job was to drive you off before we found the link to Craig.''

Jack watched Samantha gaze toward Lucy Johnson's frame house, light from its windows illuminating the concern on her face. "Don't worry, Samantha. As soon as we return from St. Louis with the proof we need, I'll confront him. Craig will find himself arrested before he knows it.''

"Major Craig frightens me, Jack. I've only met him once, but I've met his kind far too many times.'' Her face became somber. "He's the sort who delights in wielding power and does so with cruelty whenever he can. I'm concerned about what he'll do now that you've driven Taggert off. What if he comes for my family while we're in St. Louis?"

Jack reached out and took her hand. "Samantha, you know I would never allow any harm to come to your family. Don't worry. Cody will stay here to protect them. Everyone will be safe, I promise."

"I hope so," she whispered as she glanced away.

He kept her soft hand imprisoned between his while he teased, "Meanwhile, you should prepare a list. I imagine we'll be expected to return from St. Louis with gifts for everyone in your family."

Samantha started to smile, then stopped. "Jack, what makes you so sure those banks will allow us access to their accounts? By what authority can we—"

"If the United States government, the U.S. Army, and General Matthew Logan aren't good enough, then I have influence in my own right," he reassured her. "Leave that to me, Samantha." Her eyes lit up once more, and Jack felt himself respond immediately. But this time he was much, much closer.

Lucy's front door opened, and a shaft of bright light suddenly penetrated the darkness where they stood. Davy's small outline could be seen for one brief moment before Maysie yanked him away and shut the door.

"I suppose we should go in." Samantha sighed, maternal duty echoing in her voice.

But Jack did not want to go in. Not yet. He was standing closer to Samantha than he had ever been before and found her nearness made him forget all constraints, all warnings of conscience, everything—except her soft mouth just inches from his.

Jack leaned down and kissed her gently, taking his time. Samantha held absolutely still. Encouraged, he caressed her mouth again and again, lingering so long his breath mingled with hers. Unable to resist, Jack ran the tip of his tongue over her lips, ever so lightly. More a tease than a touch. He felt Samantha take in her breath with a soundless gasp. Raising his mouth from hers, Jack gazed for a second into her upturned face before he tasted again. Tasted and found honey.

It took every ounce of willpower Jack Barnett possessed to lift his lips from Samantha Winchester's this time. He watched her gradually open her eyes and delighted in the disoriented expression he saw there. Jack grinned and brought her fingers to his lips before he slowly walked Samantha to Lucy Johnson's front door.

Samantha struggled and tugged at the bedsheet that had entwined itself around her legs. Exasperated, she kicked until the sheet gave way at last and slid from her bare body. Shoving it to the floor, she spied her sleeping son curled upon his pallet and was grateful her tossing and turning had not disturbed him. She was also grateful for his sound slumber. God forbid he should awaken and see his respectable, ladylike mother lying naked in her bed.

The nightgown had been thrown to the floor an hour earlier. The thought of any cloth covering her overheated body was more than Samantha could stand. This oppressive Kansas heat surely put Savannah to shame! How was she supposed to fall asleep? She restlessly crossed her arm over her face, even though the shadowed moon shone no light through her window tonight. Samantha closed her eyes tightly. Sleep was impossible.

How in God's name could she sleep when every inch of her was on fire with the memory of Jack Barnett's kiss?

Every time she closed her eyes she saw his face and felt the warmth of his mouth on hers. The memory rippled across Samantha's skin once more. She squirmed about in the lumpy feather bed, wishing the uncomfortable clumps could make her forget the unladylike thoughts coursing through her right now.

It was no use. Samantha didn't even feel the lumps. The sensations Jack Barnett's kiss had awakened spread through her like a prairie fire. They flooded her veins and singed every nerve. She could have been lying on a bed of nails and wouldn't have noticed. Samantha was sure of it.

Tonight she had felt alive as never before. Every inch of her cried out. God forgive her, but Samantha could not recall ever feeling like this with Paul. Never had the touch of a man's hand holding hers sent her heart racing as it did with Jack. Never had her dear husband's kiss inflamed her senses as they had been set on fire tonight with Jack.

Jack. Jack. Samantha squeezed her eyes shut and whispered his name softly into the heated night air. Never had she felt what she had when his lips touched hers tonight. Never. A hunger had been awakened that gnawed inside her still and roused a host of unfamiliar urgings she had never felt before. Never—before Jack.

The tide of remembered sensation flowed through her again, and she deliberately let herself float, drifting, while her mind wandered free. Free to picture herself in Jack's arms, feel him against her, his mouth not leaving her this time, his mouth all over her. . . .

Samantha sat bolt upright in her bed. Her heart beat so fast, she thought it would jump right out of her chest. She couldn't even catch her breath. Good Lord! How was she ever going to fall asleep when her mind was conjuring such scenes? It was impossible. She must rein in her thoughts.

Samantha collapsed back into the lumpy bed with an

exaggerated sigh. She had to find some measure of control and grab hold of herself. She had to. Otherwise she might throw her arms around Jack at breakfast.

That image brought a heated blush to Samantha's cheek—and a measure of control. Small, but something. She would not make a spectacle of herself. Neither would she flutter around Jack Barnett like some schoolgirl waiting to be kissed again. What would her family think? Her maiden aunts would be speechless, poor dears. And Becky . . . well, her younger sister needed a better example than that.

Samantha took a deep breath. She was a lady, not a coquette. And despite the insistent urgings that kept tugging within, she vowed to act like one.

With a deep sigh of frustration, Samantha tugged at the bedsheet and wrapped herself in it, despite the heat. Maybe the cotton would hold in all the feelings that surged within her long enough to allow her to fall asleep.

Jack Barnett wasn't about to fall asleep. He was enjoying himself entirely too much, lying there naked in the dark, reliving over and over again his precious moments alone with Samantha. The feel of her soft mouth beneath his, the delicate lemon scent of her, the taste of her. The memories surged through him for the hundredth time that night, bringing their hot flush of remembered sensation—and a grin. A very large grin.

They would leave for St. Louis tomorrow. Jack didn't think he could wait any longer. St. Louis would provide the opportunity he longed for—the chance to have Samantha all to himself, alone, out of the arms of her doting family and into his own at last.

That oft-envisioned image set Jack's pulse to racing, while he slowly savored each step of the elaborate scenario already forming in his mind. He had it all planned. He would proceed with deliberate restraint, despite his surging desire. Woo her senses slowly, exquisitely, then gradually win this genteel Southern lady's heart as he had gradually won her trust. Win her to himself. And then . . . then he would pour himself into her. Empty every lonely part of him that ached and fill it with her. Drink in Samantha Winchester until his parched soul thirsted no more.

Jack lay perfectly still, despite the fever that raged beneath his skin. Practicing. Exercising the control he knew was necessary to rein in his desire. The passionate images that filled his brain had already coated his bare skin with a thin sheen of sweat. Powerful and intense as they were, Jack deliberately let the images pour through his head in a torrent—while he practiced. Soon the sheet beneath his skin was soaked, but Jack didn't move a muscle.

He would not lose his control. He could not. If Samantha Winchester ever glimpsed how hungry he really was, he might lose her. And Jack wasn't about to lose her again. He'd almost lost her once, when he told her he had fought for the Union. Now, by some wondrous stroke of fortune, he had been given another chance. This time he would hold on to Samantha Winchester and never let go.

Chapter

11

Jack placed his Stetson on his knee and leaned back into Gerald Wainwright's burgundy velvet wing chair, listening. A cacophony of city sounds rose up from the streets outside St. Louis National's second-floor window and assaulted his ears. Abilene had accustomed him to gunshots and wild cowboy whoops. He had forgotten how noisy a large city could be, especially one as busy as St. Louis. Wagons clattered, drivers shouted, carriages and pushcarts rattled, and hammers rang out as the next building shot skyward. And the whistles . . . always the whistles, as the steamboats plied the fast-running Mississippi and nudged their way into St. Louis's crowded harbor.

The low, throaty blast from another impatient riverboat sounded through the air and pulled Jack's attention back to St. Louis National's vice president. He settled into the velvet's plush embrace so he could watch Wainwright read General Logan's telegraph. Read it and sweat.

Wainwright pulled an immaculate white handkerchief from his breast pocket and dabbed at the droplets of moisture that had appeared on his high forehead. His mouth twitched. "This is highly irregular, Mr. Barnett, U.S. Army or not," he complained as he looked Jack Barnett in the eye. "We do not allow clerks to peruse our records for *any* reason, and most certainly not for a wild goose chase. Supposed embezzlers notwithstanding."

Jack glanced at Samantha, who was sitting primly on his left, before he studied Wainwright with a look of exaggerated calm. "Will it be necessary for General Logan to wire you a second time?"

Wainwright mopped at the considerable amount of brow showing beneath his thinning gray hair. He stared at the paper in his hand. "No . . . uh, that won't be necessary, Mr. Barnett."

"I didn't think so. Now may we look at the books, if you would be so kind?"

"Now?" Wainwright huffed. "Why, that would be impossible! First the board of directors must approve and—"

Jack leaned forward and fixed the vice president with a steady gaze. "You've got all the approval you need, Wainwright. Right there in your hand. Mrs. Winchester and I have appointments with three other banks while we're here in St. Louis, so we do not have time to waste. If you would call your clerks and tell them to bring the records we require, the United States government would be most appreciative."

Gerald Wainwright sucked in his breath, his face flushed crimson at Jack's order. "Very well, Mr. Barnett," he said, releasing a gust of air. "If you and Mrs. Winchester will follow me, I will show you to our boardroom. The clerks will bring the records there." He wheeled about unceremoniously and stalked from the room.

* * *

Samantha held her ink pen poised over the carefully out-lined columns, comparing the numbers written on her sheet with the amounts recorded in St. Louis National's deposit books. They were identical. Samantha's heart began to pound in excitement. She was right. The amounts matched exactly. It could not be coincidence. They had found the embezzled thousands.

She glanced at the place where Jack Barnett had been sitting beside her at the smooth walnut table, only to find him leaning right next to her shoulder. She felt her cheeks flush, partly from excitement and partly as the result of Jack's closeness. Regardless of the turmoil she encountered whenever she looked into his eyes, Samantha could not help exulting.

"We were right," she announced, loud enough for the army of clerks arrayed along the other side of the conference table to hear. "Every transfer matches a deposit of the exact same amount on the following day. This cannot be coincidence."

Jack frowned at the figures. "I venture to say we have found the evidence the army needs to keep that embezzler behind bars for a good twenty years. And his accomplice." Jack spun around and addressed an incredulous Gerald Wainwright, who was hovering nearby and making no attempt to conceal his displeasure at the proceedings. "Mr. Wainwright, would you be so kind as to compare the names on this sheet of paper with the record of account holders, please?" He withdrew a paper from the breast pocket of his jacket and extended it toward St. Louis National's vice president.

Wainwright snatched the paper from Jack's hand and strode over to his clerks, all neatly lined up in a row and looking extremely nervous. One man had run his finger inside his high winged collar so often the button popped off. It lay beside his chair just out of reach. Wainwright waved his hand at a bent, balding man who obediently began to search through a small ledger book.

The clerk scanned one page after another, then scribbled on a sheet of paper and handed it to Wainwright, who was rocking back and forth on his heels, hands clasped behind his back. The vice president grabbed the paper from the clerk and lifted his nose disdainfully before he spoke.

"Now, Mr. Barnett . . . you will see what a wild goose chase you've been leading us on today, wasting this bank's time. The idea! You may rest assured I will have plenty to say to this General Logan after we've dispensed with your flamboyant claims." Wainwright smirked while he unfolded Jack's paper and held the two sheets side by side. He hastily cast his eyes over both. "You see, these names you have given me are—" Gerald Wainwright stopped short and stared at the papers in his hands. His face drained of all color, and his mouth dropped open in obvious astonishment.

"Why . . . why . . . they are *identical*!" he exclaimed.

Jack waited until Wainwright regained control of himself. "Thank you for your cooperation, Mr. Wainwright, reluctant though it was. I want those records put under lock and key until further notice. I'll wire General Logan immediately and inform him of our findings. You should await his instructions, for the army will want to examine these records right away. I fully expect Mrs. Winchester and I will find identical evidence of embezzled funds stashed in the remaining St. Louis banks."

Wainwright blinked once but said nothing. Jack finally turned his attention to Samantha, who was observing the startled Wainwright with carefully concealed amusement. Jack recognized it only because he had memorized most of

Samantha's expressions by now. He caught her eye and smiled.

"Meanwhile, you'll have to excuse us, Mr. Wainwright. Mrs. Winchester and I must be leaving. You see, I promised to show her St. Louis on this trip, and I cannot think of a better time to start."

Samantha gazed in awe at the sight. Never had she seen so many ships together in one place. Even before the war had closed Savannah's harbor, the port there had never been as crowded with shipping as this one. She had always heard that St. Louis was a busy commercial center, but she had not realized how busy until now.

Every inch of space along St. Louis's levee was packed with immense paddle wheel steamboats. They filled the Mississippi shoreline, moored side by side, rubbing against each other cheek by jowl, vying for space. Their graceful white-railed decks were stacked one upon the other, two and three levels high. Some were empty, some were teeming with eager passengers pacing the decks, anxious to be off down the fast-flowing river, eager for commerce and adventure. Two tall black smokestacks rose like slender turrets above each boat and belched billowing clouds of smoke into the air.

Along the entire levee—shoreline and landing—she saw muscled, black-skinned backs sweating as dockworkers hefted huge bales of cotton off the many steamboat decks and into the numerous wagons that jammed every available space. Bale after bale headed for the railway depot and the Northeast, where they would be transformed into cloth and travel down this very same river in another form, ready to clothe a family.

Everywhere Samantha looked, there were people. Milling about, laboring, steering wagons, driving carriages, lifting, talking, laughing, arguing, hurrying. Her brain could barely comprehend the activity in front of her. Even in its prime, Savannah had never bristled with the raw energy she witnessed here. It made her heart race just to stand and watch it sweep past her.

And the noise! Unbelievable noise roiled up from the riverfront, swallowing her in sound, enough to make her ears ring. Shouts of laborers, a chorus of squeaking wheels as wagons groaned beneath their loads, banging metal, all underscored by the throbbing basso cries of the steamboats. So low, Samantha felt her bones shake.

"Take a good, long look, Samantha, before it all disappears." Jack Barnett's voice came from beside her.

His strange comment startled her out of her absorption, and she turned to observe him staring at the levee. "Whatever do you mean, Jack?"

"In another few years, most of what you see loaded onto these riverboats will be loaded on rail cars. These paddle wheelers have had their day. They'll be gone soon. Not all at once, mind you. But eventually they'll be replaced by the railways."

Samantha gaped at the enormous amount of activity in front of her. "Surely that's not possible. There are only a few rail lines. How could they replace all these steamboats? Look at the amount of cargo each one holds! It's quite impressive." She gestured toward the river.

Jack smiled to himself. Spoken like a merchant shipper's daughter. He reached out and captured her hand, wrapping it around his arm as he turned them both away from the busy scene. "The railways are still new, Samantha. Still stretching west. Once they get their main artery tracks down, then the connecting lines will spring up, just as they have in the Northeast and Midwest."

He deliberately nestled her arm tightly beside him so he

could draw Samantha close. ''Give these new railways some time. They'll connect all over this country, even out West. And once they do, the paddle wheelers will die. Mark my words. They won't be able to compete with the railroad's speed.''

Samantha tried to concentrate on Jack's informative treatise on the future of American freight transport, but she found it much more enjoyable to watch his gray eyes shine with conviction. And enjoy the sensations that caused along her spine. She couldn't help but notice when another light flickered there as well and glowed with more than conviction.

She observed the scores of people bustling about them on the dirt street and noticed more than one lady's glance drift toward Jack Barnett and linger. Samantha deliberately nestled closer to her handsome companion, surprised at the proprietary manner in which she placed her other hand around Jack's arm. A feminine declaration of enraptured attentiveness—as well as ownership. An unmistakable signal to every other female in the vicinity.

They neared the carriage Jack had hired for the day, and he took Samantha's hand to help her inside. Once within, however, he neglected to release her, Samantha noticed. She welcomed the opportunity of enforced closeness, the warmth of him seated beside her.

''Well, fair lady, would you care to sample some of Parkinson's famous chocolates? Or would you prefer pralines?'' he tempted.

''Why not both?'' Samantha teased. The warmth of his hand holding hers slowly climbed her arm.

Jack laughed. ''Well, I don't want to spoil your appetite. We'll be dining at one of St. Louis's finest French restaurants. Louis Cafferata's Queen. That is . . . unless you'd prefer to dine on chocolates.'' He grinned and raised her white-gloved hand to his lips for a brief touch.

Even so, it was enough to send the warmth well past her elbow. Nearly to her neck, in fact. Samantha swallowed. "That sounds wonderful," she managed and let his smoky gray eyes warm the rest of her, which they did until Jack turned his attention to the window.

Samantha followed suit and felt her pulse slow while she watched the busy St. Louis streets. Fourth Street teemed with traffic—horse-drawn trolleys traveling in both directions, wagons, carriages, pushcarts. There were people everywhere.

Jack leaned out the carriage door and called instructions to the driver, and the carriage quickly pulled to a stop, much to Samantha's surprise.

"Before the chocolates, however, we have some shopping to do," Jack announced, as if he were hiding a secret.

"Oh, but I don't have the list with me," Samantha said, disappointed at her own forgetfulness.

"We'll go shopping for the family tomorrow. Today I'm under strict orders from General Logan." He pushed open the carriage door and would have stepped out if Samantha had not refused to release his hand.

"What orders?" she pried. The secret still danced in Jack's eyes.

He raised her gloved fingers to his lips again, all too briefly to suit Samantha. "General Logan was so overwhelmed by your swift unraveling of the embezzler's scheme that he decided you deserved a reward." Jack's grin broke free at last, and his face lit up with pleasure. "He ordered me to take you to the finest dressmaker in St. Louis and send the bill to him."

Her heart gave a little squeeze. "General Logan ordered you to take me shopping?" she asked, not bothering to conceal her skepticism. Samantha gazed at Jack for a moment, then leaned forward and brushed her lips gently against his, lingering only as long as she dared. Long enough to send her heart pounding. The laughter disappeared from Jack's face in an instant. ''You are a terrible liar, Jack Barnett,'' she whispered.

He hesitated in the doorway for several seconds before he stepped out of the carriage and helped Samantha alight. Not a moment too soon. The struggle she had just witnessed in his eyes took Samantha's breath away.

She barely had time to collect herself before Jack lifted her gloved hand to his mouth and pressed his lips into her palm, holding them there despite the curious stares of passersby. Samantha's knees nearly buckled. If not for the throngs hurrying along busy Washington Avenue, she would have torn the glove from her hand and pressed her bare skin to his lips. The feel of Jack Barnett's warm mouth, almost but not quite touching her hand, burned well past Samantha's arm and consumed her entire body.

Jack held her hand beside his mouth as he spoke softly. ''We had best take you shopping, Mrs. Winchester.''

He led her inside Madame Charpentier's shop without another word. Samantha grasped Jack's arm tightly, for her legs did not feel strong enough to hold her.

Chapter

12

Samantha turned at the unexpected sound of a knock on her hotel room door. Her heart skipped a beat. Jack must have decided not to wait in the lobby after all. She hastened across the spacious bedroom and swiftly pulled the door open, eager to display another of Madame Charpentier's creations, even more anxious to see Jack's eyes light up as they had at last night's supper.

When she stared into the hallway, Samantha's heart stopped its rapid pounding. Jack was nowhere to be seen. Instead she saw the Southern Hotel's liveried porter holding a large box in his hands. She attempted a pleasant smile, despite her disappointment.

"This just arrived for you, ma'am," the slender young man announced.

"Why, thank you," she said and took the package. The porter gave a brief nod and left. Samantha closed the door and hurried to the bed, intrigued by this gift. Her curious fingers worked even faster when she noticed Madame Charpentier's name on top of the box.

What could this be? she wondered. She was certain Jack

had not left any packages at Madame Charpentier's shop. Samantha's cheeks flushed even now, remembering yesterday's embarrassment when she saw the dress boxes stacked high in the carriage. There were so many the coachman had had to carry some on top. Samantha had lost track of all her purchases because Jack made sure Madame Charpentier whisked each one away to be wrapped as soon as Samantha made her selections.

At first she had tried to hold herself in check, but she soon found herself overwhelmed. The lush colors and fabrics filled Madame Charpentier's shop, blinding her with their vibrancy. Reds, yellows, blues, greens, and every shade and hue in between. And the fabrics. Silks, taffetas, crepe de chine. Not only gowns, but gloves, hats, slippers, capes . . . all of it surrounding her, swirling about her, until Samantha almost felt dizzy. It was more than any woman could bear—especially a woman who had not bought a new gown in eleven years.

She succumbed the moment she sank into Madame Charpentier's red velvet settee. When Jack settled beside her, whispering in her ear, encouraging her to indulge herself, she gave up any attempt at frugality or restraint. Only when the packages were loaded into the carriage did Samantha realize her extravagance. Jack, of course, was delighted.

Samantha lifted the top from the dress box and paused, wondering what Madame Charpentier had sent. Perhaps the fashionable French dressmaker had sent a token of her appreciation for yesterday's buying spree. When she caught the first glimpse of royal blue silk, however, Samantha knew this gift was not from Madame Charpentier.

Jack Barnett had chosen this gown. Samantha knew it as well as she knew her own name. She remembered the way his eyes kept drifting yesterday to the mannequin that was clothed in the silk's voluptuous drape. Samantha, too, had let her gaze linger covetously on the graceful if daring gown, with its scalloped bodice and bared shoulders, but had steeled herself against it. Too dressy, too expensive, and much too revealing. There was no place in her life for a gown like that. Once upon a time, yes . . . but no more.

Samantha carefully lifted the sumptuous gown from the box and held it up, lost in thought. Its blue depths shimmered, enticing her touch. She stared at the gown for a long minute, imagining, debating.

She placed the gown on the bed and quickly began to unhook the emerald green silk that moments ago she had been quite anxious to display. No more. Although its fashionable cut and rich fabric would surely have set Jack's eyes alight—just as the crimson gown had drawn his attention last night—Samantha wanted more. She wanted more than that admiring and attentive gaze, more than that delighted spark in his eyes. She wanted the look that took her breath away, the one hiding in the back of Jack Barnett's eyes, the one that burned through her whenever it touched.

Samantha quickly removed the thin cotton chemise beneath her corset and delighted in the sensuous feel of bare shoulders. She caressed the rich silk as it slid over her body, taking time with its little hooks. When she had the dress adjusted at last, Samantha gazed at herself in the mirror and almost blushed. Almost, but not quite. She was too enraptured by what she saw.

The lustrous royal blue silk draped beneath her shoulders and across her bosom, accentuating her fair skin to perfection. The daring neckline left ample pale skin to contrast with the silk's lush blue. Samantha let out a long sigh, enthralled. She did not recall ever looking—or feeling—so beautiful.

A warm flush slowly spread over her as she stood gazing into the mirror. But this time she did not see herself at all.

She imagined another face in the glass. A face she suddenly longed to see, looking back at her with deep gray eyes. Samantha stood for several minutes, mesmerized.

Samantha suddenly turned from the mirror and hurried to the door. If Jack wanted to see her in this dress, well, by God . . . he would see her. But here in her room, not in the midst of the Southern Hotel's cavernous lobby with its impossibly high ceilings and scores of people walking about. No. She wanted to watch Jack's eyes light up in private.

She opened the door and hastily scanned the corridor, hoping to spy a chambermaid. When she did, Samantha motioned her to the door. "Would you give a message to Mister Jack Barnett, please? He's waiting for me downstairs in the lobby. Please tell him it is urgent that he meet me here."

The young, blond chambermaid nodded and headed for the stairs. Samantha hastened to the vanity and seated herself, her hands already loosening hairpins. She watched the dark curls tumble free and reached for a hairbrush, slowly rearranging her hair so that several curls would trail down her neck in the fashion she preferred. Madame Charpentier's splendid creation deserved more than a spinster's bun.

Jack Barnett hurried down the hallway to Samantha's room. Whatever had provoked her into sending a message to him in the Southern's lobby? Had she taken ill suddenly? She had been in the peak of health that afternoon. Could it be something she ate?

His mind invented one dramatic scenario after another as he scanned the room numbers, all the time cursing himself for tempting Samantha Winchester with so much rich food. He had been feeding her ever since they arrived in St. Louis.

That's it, he mentally kicked himself. *God Almighty, Barnett! You should have known better. This woman was living on a Spartan diet, and you bring her here and drown her in French sauces. Not to mention the pastries yesterday. And the chocolates. God, the chocolates.* Jack shuddered at yesterday's memory. *You'd better stop feeding her if you want her to have any appetite left for you!*

His own stomach tied in knots by now, Jack paused before Samantha's door. He held his hand above the wood before he knocked. He would cancel their reservations at Louis's Queen. Enough. They would find some plain, old-fashioned, Lucy Johnson-type restaurant. Something simple. Or maybe he wouldn't feed her at all. That might not be a bad idea.

Still immersed in his quandary, Jack hastily adjusted his gray silk cravat and knocked on the door with authority— anxious authority. So anxious, in fact, he barely waited for Samantha to open the door before he charged inside.

"Samantha, what is it? Are you all right? Your message . . ."

The rest of Jack's words got lost in his throat. He simply stared at Samantha Winchester with his mouth open as she closed the door and stood before him, a vision in lustrous blue silk. His eyes swept over her. Jack could have sworn the floor shifted beneath his feet.

He had dreamed of her like this. Her shoulders pale and bare. Her creamy white throat curved delicately, awaiting the touch of his mouth. The voluptuous curve of her body beneath the silk. And her hair. Dark red-brown curls cascading down her neck, dangling beside her face, escaped from their imprisonment at last and waiting for his fingers to set them tumbling free. Jack gazed, unable to stop, unable to believe his eyes. Surely he must be dreaming.

The desire he had striven so hard to contain spread

through him now—consuming, burning everything in its path. All his plans, his careful scenarios, were singed beyond recognition. "My God, Samantha . . ." he whispered. "You are too beautiful to bear. . . ."

His words sent a shiver down Samantha's spine. She watched those desperate dark eyes rake over her, devouring her. The hunger she saw reached into her very soul and lit a fire within. It spread through Samantha languorously, claiming every inch of her as it went.

She deliberately stepped closer, so close she could swear she felt his heat. Samantha gazed into his tormented face and whispered, "I wanted to thank you in private." Then she stood on tiptoe and lightly brushed her lips across his.

That brief touch of her mouth undid him. Jack swept Samantha into his arms and clasped her tightly, while he claimed that soft mouth for his own.

He ravaged her honey-sweet mouth. Plundered her sweetness and searched for more. Pressing Samantha's voluptuous soft body against him, he drank deep. Jack wanted to drain her into him, quench his thirst at last. Samantha shivered in his arms.

At the feel of her response, a faint whisper stirred inside Jack's heated brain. He drew his lips from hers at last, while he valiantly fought for control. She had but touched him and unwittingly brought forth a deluge. Hovering over her mouth, he watched Samantha slowly open her eyes. "God help me, Samantha, but I love you," he swore softly.

Samantha gazed into Jack's smoldering dark eyes and saw the desperate struggle still waging within. She gently placed her hand against his cheek. Jack's passionate confession resonated inside her heart and mind and soul— reverberating with truth. All confusion had melted away.

"Oh, Jack . . . I love you so," she whispered, her fingertips caressing his face.

Jack stared at Samantha in disbelief, as if he hadn't heard her correctly. Meanwhile, his heart pounded so hard he thought it would burst. He gripped her tighter. "Are . . . are you sure, Samantha?" he asked in a ragged whisper, his dark eyes probing hers.

Her fingertips brushed his lips and stayed. "I'm sure."

Samantha's words swept through him with the force of a flood tide. Jack buried his lips in her soft, warm palm and closed his eyes, unable to say what was in his heart. He could not. Not yet. He did not have the words. He simply pressed her hand to his mouth while he searched inside for some shred of restraint, something he could use to hold himself back before this avalanche of feeling overwhelmed him and he ravished this gentle lady in her hotel room.

Jack struggled within for the strength to release Samantha. Now, before it was too late. Slowly—very slowly—he forced his arms to let her go. If he held her another minute, he wouldn't be able to release her at all. The sensation of Samantha's soft body against his was more than he could bear.

"I had best take you to supper, Samantha . . . while I still can," he whispered into her upturned face. Jack reached for Samantha's arm, planning to lead her out the door before he changed his mind and abandoned his careful plans entirely.

Samantha's hand reached out and grabbed hold of Jack's shirtfront. She tugged gently, pulling him back to her. She gazed into his surprised face and whispered, "No."

Supper was not what Samantha Winchester hungered for. She wanted Jack's arms around her again, wanted to feel that hard, lean body press against her, wanted the heat to burn through the very silk that covered her. And she wanted his mouth. Oh, God, Samantha wanted his mouth to return.

Return and take her once more. Take all of her this time . . . and leave nothing. Samantha wanted to be consumed by the fire that blazed within her—the same fire she felt searing through his clothes. She wanted Jack Barnett in her arms, wanted to feel his skin beneath her hands, and his mouth . . . she wanted his mouth all over her.

Samantha gently pulled Jack closer. Placing her hands on his very warm shirtfront, she gazed into his eyes. "I love you, Jack Barnett. Did you hear me? I love you . . . and I want you." She swiftly slid her arms around his neck, pulling his mouth down to hers.

She kissed him. But it was more than a kiss. It was a cry. From so far deep inside her, Samantha didn't know where it began, or where it ended. Down deep in her soul. Aching with longing and need. Oh, God, how she needed Jack Barnett! With a need so deep it could not be plumbed.

Samantha's kiss went through Jack like summer lightning. He grabbed hold and this time he didn't let go. Jack pulled her to him. Pressed her soft, warm, female body against him. Answered her longing, her need, with his. His mouth demanded and claimed Samantha as his own.

Samantha sank into Jack's embrace, holding on so tightly she could not breathe. She didn't need to breathe. She needed him, needed him more than air itself. Her mouth yielded to his, surrendering beneath his fevered onslaught, yielding over and over again. Yielding and searching and asking. He answered. Jack's mouth subdued hers until Samantha moaned softly in his arms. A shiver started in the ground beneath her feet and finished at her fingertips.

At the sound of Samantha's impassioned moan, Jack tore his mouth from hers. He gazed at her delicate pale throat for one brief second before his lips descended. He ravished that white throat, choking off Samantha's cry before it could escape. His lips drifted down to her shoulder. The taste and feel of her bare skin intoxicated him. His mouth gently explored the smooth rise of her breast, his tongue trailing across the delectable curve the silk could not hide.

Samantha's choked cry escaped, and she collapsed in Jack's arms. He caught her, then carried her across the room in two swift strides and set her upon the immense feather bed. He sat beside her and pulled her close. He touched her face, traced his fingers across her eyelids, her cheeks, her mouth. She turned her lips into his hand and kissed his palm, her hand cradling his, her eyes closed. Jack shivered at the feel of her mouth on his skin.

He brushed a soft brown curl from her cheek. The touch of her hair against his skin aroused Jack more than he could have dreamed. Soft. So soft. After denying himself so long, Jack submerged both hands into Samantha's wealth of dark curls, his fingers eagerly finding and loosening the few hairpins and tossing them to the floor. He lowered his face to her neck and let Samantha's hair spill loose in abandon, tumbling about him, while he lost himself in the luxurious mass. What thin thread of restraint he had left vanished completely. He wanted to run his hands through those reddish brown depths while Samantha lay beneath him and he lay inside her. He could not wait another moment.

His hand was at her breast in an instant, caressing one moment, undressing the next. The silk gave way to his insistent urging and slid from her body. The corset could not prevail against his expert fingers, either, and it soon lay upon the floor.

Samantha barely had time to catch her breath before Jack's hands were upon her, wandering, exploring, gently removing the few garments she had left. She fell back upon the pink satin bedspread and shivered in anticipation.

But even anticipation could not prepare her for the feel of Jack Barnett's mouth on her skin, lingering, teasing, trailing fire in its wake. Samantha thought she would cry out—and she did. But only for a second, when his mouth lifted from her skin. And then, just when she thought she could catch her breath, his tongue returned to drive her wild. Samantha sank into the feather bed and moaned softly beneath Jack's tormenting mouth.

Suddenly Jack was no longer beside her, and Samantha quickly opened her eyes. He stood but a few feet away, shedding his clothes with amazing speed. She watched his lean, hard body reveal itself to her and felt the blood rush to her head at the sight. A man stood before her now. Not a sweet, timid boy like Paul had been, but a man. The difference sent a shiver through Samantha that reached into the marrow of her bones.

Jack hovered above her. Samantha gazed into his eyes as they swept over her, gazed past the hunger to the longing that ached from within, and reached out with her own. She opened her arms and beckoned. "Oh, Jack . . . please," she whispered.

Jack came to her with a groan of desire. He took her swiftly, thrust into Samantha with the hunger of all those years. Ravenous. Reached into her with his starving soul, deeper and deeper. Searching. Penetrated her softness with himself . . . with his longing . . . and need. The ache of all those years. Emptied himself. Emptied himself and was filled.

Samantha cried soundlessly as she shook beneath Jack, her body engulfed in spasms of sensations she had never felt before, wildly out of control. As wild as the man she held in her arms, whose very first thrust had sent her body exploding. Samantha held onto Jack tightly. If he let her go, she might shatter into a thousand pieces.

Jack plunged his hands into the softness of her hair while he let out an agonized groan, his body shuddering inside hers in release. Samantha cried out beneath him, succumbing to her own inner ecstasy. Shattering at last.

Release brought its own calm, and Jack buried his face beside her neck with a sound that was half groan, half sigh. Samantha heard his voice beside her ear, felt his warm breath on her skin, and held him in her arms. She shivered in response. Jack snarled his fingers into her hair possessively, and Samantha responded in kind—by wrapping her arms tightly around the man who lay inside her.

Chapter

13

Samantha pressed her cheek to Jack's warm chest as they relaxed into the Southern Hotel's enormous feather pillows. She slowly drew in her breath, inhaling his closeness. A faint hint of lemon clung to his skin from their long night of lovemaking. She smiled. *Her* scent bathed Jack Barnett now, not some saloon girl's heavy perfume. She had covered him with the fragrance of herself. Samantha slid her hand through the soft brown hair on his chest, her fingers playing lightly there.

Dawn had found them nestled in each other's arms, exhausted by the night's passions. They awoke to the sun's first rays streaming through undraped windows. Their desire stirred even before they, awakened by the realization they were in each other's arms still. Early morning's frenzy put the night's to shame. And now, spent, they rested within one another's silent embrace.

She trailed her fingertips across his skin, which was no longer damp from their feverish loving. Jack pulled her closer and captured the exploring hand, brushing his lips across her fingers. She exhaled a soft sigh of approval and awaited the further touch of his mouth. Instead Jack released her hand, easily slipping from her embrace as he rose from the bed in one smooth movement.

"I'll order breakfast. That way you won't faint when I next ravish you," he said with a grin as he yanked the bedsheet free and draped it around himself. "Although it's nearly noon, I think I can persuade the staff to oblige."

Samantha simply stared after him as he sauntered to the door, sheet drooping indecently down his lean, muscled back like some debauched Roman fresh from the baths, toga awry.

Breakfast did not interest her. There was nothing the Southern Hotel could deliver to her door that would satisfy. Only the touch of the half-naked man in her bedroom would suffice.

She had never felt such a riptide of need. Her sheer hunger had overwhelmed Samantha the moment Jack stood before her last night, his lean, naked body filled with desire. She could not get enough of this man. Every cell in her body seemed to cry out for his touch. He had driven her nearly mad, teasing her passion-swollen body with his until she cried out over and over again. She was exhausted and exhilarated, and she wanted him again.

Jack peered through the partially opened door and leaned out into the hallway, exposing his firm buttocks to her view. "You there, boy!" he called. "You can earn a ten-dollar gold piece if you return here in five minutes with a trayful of breakfast."

Samantha didn't hear the bellboy's reply, but she assumed it was positive because Jack closed the door and strode back to the bed, toga dropping at his feet. Samantha stared in open admiration.

"Really, Mrs. Winchester," he said with a devilish smile. "What would your maiden aunts say if they saw your face right now? Hardly the expression of a genteel Southern lady.'' Jack knelt beside her on the bed.

Samantha ignored the teasing grin. All she saw was his bare skin so close to her once more, inviting her hands' caress. Her fingertips tingled. She reached out and let her hand trail down his chest, slowly traveling lower. Jack captured it once more.

''Not until after breakfast, my ravenous one. I need my strength, even if you don't.'' He laughed and kissed her palm.

''But I'm not hungry.''

''I should think not after last night . . . and this morning.'' He leaned over and kissed the tip of her nose.

Samantha moved forward into his kiss, hoping for more. When there wasn't, she opened her eyes and gave a loud, resigned, and very dramatic sigh while she watched him stretch languorously across the bed. ''Jack, you've been feeding me ever since we arrived in St. Louis. Surely we can miss one breakfast,'' she said, her tone deliberately suggestive. She let the sheet fall away on purpose and reclined against the pillows.

''Samantha Winchester, you are an irresistible temptress,'' he murmured. His hand reached out to touch what his eyes had already claimed.

Samantha exulted inside . . . until she heard the knock on their bedroom door.

Jack gave her an apologetic grin, then sprang off the bed. Samantha stifled her groan and sank back into the pillows, pulling the sheet beneath her chin in frustration. Jack reclaimed his toga and opened the door, accepting the tray from the eager young bellboy, who thanked Jack loudly and profusely upon receipt of the gold piece. Jack slammed the door shut and strode across the room, where he placed the heavy laden breakfast tray in the middle of their bed with a flourish.

"Breakfast, madame. The best the Southern has to offer."

He proceeded to uncover baskets of biscuits and rolls and muffins, round china pots nearly overflowing with jams and honey, and squat copper tubs filled to the rim with butter and sweet cream. Jack knelt in naked splendor on the edge of the bed and poured Samantha a steaming cup of strong black tea, presenting it to her with the equanimity of an English butler.

The seductive aroma of hot bread tickled Samantha's nostrils, tempting her despite her frustration. "Thank you . . . monsieur," she mimicked and accepted the cup, sipping slowly while Jack spread a large biscuit with butter and jam.

"Take a big bite, and no arguments. You'll need your strength to peruse those accounts at the Central Bank this afternoon." He held the delicious smelling biscuit under her nose.

Samantha obliged and acknowledged her enjoyment with a sigh of pleasure. The biscuit was so flaky it practically dissolved on her tongue as the thick strawberry jam filled her mouth with its sweetness. She took another bite.

Jack devoured his first jam-drenched biscuit and quickly prepared another, emitting various satisfied noises as he did. "Perhaps we'll have time to visit the First National's offices as well," he said, pouring himself a cup of coffee from the Southern's snow-white china pot. He took a large sip. "After all, the vice president must have wondered why we canceled our appointment this morning." Jack caught her eye with a wink.

"I do hope you don't plan to explain the exact cause of

our sudden cancellation." Samantha smiled provocatively over the top of her cup.

"I think not." He grinned, then finished off his second jam-laden biscuit. Several drops of jam skidded off the side of the top-heavy pastry and plopped to his bare chest. Jack retrieved them with a swipe of his thumb.

Samantha watched his enthusiastic dispatch of the Southern's breakfast with great interest as a wonderful idea presented itself to her. She drained her teacup and placed it on the tray, then spread a biscuit with jam from another pot. Instead of sampling the pastry, however, she swirled the jam on her fingertip and tasted. "This raspberry is simply delicious," she said, scooping up a fingerful of jam and extending it to Jack. "You must try it." Without waiting for a response, Samantha touched her sweet offering to his lips.

Jack captured her finger, raspberries and all. The touch of his greedy mouth reached all the way down to her toes. She leaned closer and teased her tongue across his chest, licking away the remnants of jam. He held very, very still. Her errant finger toyed across his lips while she placed a kiss in the hollow of his neck. Jack sucked in his breath. Samantha teased her tongue up his neck, aiming for his berry-sweet mouth—slowly, excruciatingly slow. She never got there.

In one swift movement Jack had pushed the Southern Hotel's breakfast tray off the bed and spread Samantha beneath him. The delicate china teapot crashed to the floor, spilling its contents across the Persian carpet. Pots of jam and butter and cream upended in reckless piles on both sides of the bed. Biscuits rolled beneath chairs and wardrobes, spinning giddily across the room. The honey pot came to rest beside the coffee server, its golden contents mixing with the coffee's dark brew as they merged into a tawny puddle beside the cedar chest.

The bedroom was a shambles. Clothes were still strewn about with abandon from last evening. Those few areas of carpet and polished walnut floors visible were now covered with food or broken crockery. Crumbs were everywhere.

Jack devoured Samantha's swan white neck while his hand slid between her thighs, separating them, holding her captive as his mouth explored lower and lower. Samantha's voice rose in an anxious cry of pleasure.

He would replace the crockery. He would replace the carpet. Hell, he would replace the whole damn room if he had to. Jack didn't care. Only the soft, demanding body beneath his mattered to him now.

"You be Major Craig?"

Anthony Craig jerked his attention from the papers on his desk. He hadn't even heard the office door open. Fort Riley's muffled drone of activity outside his window disguised smaller sounds like opening doors. He observed the tall, gaunt man who stood inside his office, hat pulled low, red bandanna bunched around his neck, dark clothes coated with dust as if he had ridden a long way in the late July heat.

"I'm Major Craig. Who the hell are you?"

The man squinted, and something that resembled a smile twitched his lips briefly. "My name's Salem Todd, Major, and I'm prepared to do you a favor. If the price is right, that is." He shifted his weight and hooked a thumb beneath his gun belt while he assessed Anthony Craig.

The major leaned back into his desk chair, a sneer twisting his lips. "Oh, really? And what favor could you possibly do for me, Mr. Todd?"

"I've got some information you might find interesting."

Craig snickered derisively. "Frankly, Mr. Todd, I doubt

you have learned anything in your entire life that I would find even remotely interesting. Now get out of my office before I call my orderly and have you thrown out.'' He gave an imperious wave of dismissal and bent to his paper-work again.

Salem Todd did not move. He simply narrowed his gaze on Craig, while his voice dropped lower. ''That's where you're wrong, Major. You see, we both know the same fellow. You do remember Isaac Jamison, don't you?

Craig held still at the name of the clever bookkeeper who had helped him rifle the army's purse. He reclined in his chair once again, his face an impassive mask while he studied the whip-lean stranger. ''Who are you?'' he demanded with more than a touch of menace in his tone.

''I told you, Major. My name's Salem Todd, and I shared an army cell with your good friend Isaac. Until a couple weeks ago, when I finished my time. I thought I'd drop by and give you Isaac's regards.''

Craig's pulse quickened. ''What do you want?''

A smile creased Todd's sunburned face. ''You ain't been listening, Major. I already told you what I want. I'm willing to tell you what I know for a price.''

''I don't think you know anything, Todd.''

Todd grinned wider, revealing jagged, tobacco-stained teeth. ''Don't be so sure, Major. I know all about your little scheme. How much you and Jamison stashed away before the army caught on. I even know where. And I know some other things, too.'' The crocodile grin spread. ''Some things you don't know, Major.''

The blue vein in Anthony Craig's temple throbbed as anger flooded through him. Jamison had talked. That bastard! He knew he shouldn't have trusted the groveling little clerk to keep his mouth shut. Who else did he confess to?

With great effort, he kept his emotions from showing on

his face. "So the sniveling little bastard talked, eh?"

"Not at first. But I finally persuaded him he'd live longer if he told me all he knew. I guessed he must know something pretty important. Why else would army officers be asking him all those questions after he was already in prison? I figured he hadn't told them everything."

Craig felt his anger die down to a simmer. Could he trust what this man was saying? Had Jamison revealed his part in the scheme to this man but not to the army? Who else had Jamison talked to? And what sort of questions did the army ask? How much did *they* know?

"What did the army want to know?" he demanded.

Todd's jagged smile claimed his face, taunting Craig. "Now that's what you'll have to pay for, Major."

Craig's glare turned lethal. "How much?"

Todd strolled to the desk. "I reckon a thousand dollars cash ought to get me to Mexico and set up in style. A man can live a whole lot cheaper across the Rio Grande. Little *casita* with a couple pretty *senoritas* . . . you know what I mean?"

Now that Todd was closer, Craig could see his bronzed face more clearly. One eye was covered by a black eye patch. There was also a trace of sunburned red skin visible around the edges of his coarsened brown neck. Newly burned skin.

Craig leaned forward, his voice a taut whisper. "First, I don't keep that much cash on hand. Second, how do I know you won't show up again, begging for another handout?"

Todd studied the major's tense features for a minute. "Don't worry, Major. I plan to stay in Mexico, where the only soldiers I'll see are *Federales*, and I got no quarrel with them. Now, if you're short of money, I guess you'd better borrow the rest from the army, like you and Isaac did before. I know they keep cash in those safes." He gestured behind Craig to the squat black iron safe in the corner. "I was in the army, and I remember how much money used to be stashed in these forts. So don't vex me, Major, or I might go visit the commander and tell him what I know." He angled one hip to the side, revealing a Colt .45 that hugged his leg.

A muscle in Anthony Craig's jaw twitched. This convict was dictating terms to *him*. A major in the United States Army. And he had to sit here helpless. Impotent. If he called the guard, the man would only spill everything he knew. There would be no time to escape. He gritted his teeth and shot a searing glare at Todd before he rose and went to the safe. Quickly spinning the dial through the familiar combination, Craig withdrew a brown leather portfolio from inside. He removed several bills and replaced the portfolio, slamming the safe closed.

"There. One thousand," he said, throwing the bills on the desk. "Now, what you have to say better be worth it."

Todd's one eye lit up. He scooped the money from the table and stuffed it inside his faded shirt while he fixed his benefactor with a smug look. "It's worth it, all right. Unless you don't mind giving the army the next twenty years of your life. You see, that little partner of yours won't be able to hold out until he finishes his term, Major. Now, I know that's what you two had planned, so the army wouldn't get suspicious and all. But it's not gonna happen. Jamison will never last. He hasn't sold you out yet, mind you. He wants that money too bad. Figured the only way he could get his share was to keep his mouth shut while he did his time."

"How come he told you?"

"I beat him pretty hard, Major. Believe me, he told me everything. The army had already figured out he had a partner in Abilene. Somebody who knew how the army did things. They even sent an agent out here to nose around. It seems the agent sent them a wire saying he was gettin' close. At least that's what this colonel told Isaac. He said the army wanted that other somebody mighty bad, and they'd be willing to make a deal.''

Craig's gut tightened. If what this man said was true, all of his meticulous plans had to be scrapped. He could no longer wait until his next tour of duty to resign his commission and unobtrusively retire. He didn't dare. He must plan his escape before Jamison implicated him. Slip away to St. Louis and gather his hidden thousands. Find a quick escape route to Mexico. But how? He couldn't simply disappear from the fort one day. There would be too many questions.

The muscle in his cheek twitched faster. This had to be carefully planned. First he had to find an excuse to be away from the fort for a couple of days. Catch the train to St. Louis and gather his funds before the army started sniffing around. Then he could return to the fort immediately. Do nothing to arouse suspicion. Then . . . slip away into the night.

He glared at Todd. ''What makes you so certain that spineless little worm will talk? He knows he'll lose the money if he does. What could the army possibly offer him to compare with that?''

Salem Todd fixed the major with a feral smile. ''Safety, Major. It seems ol' Isaac hadn't figured how bad prison life could be. You see, a couple of days before I got out, a bunch of the boys found Isaac alone in the laundry. The way I heard, they each took a turn with him. I don't think Isaac liked that too much.'' The smile turned to a leer. ''I hope you got a fast way outta town, Major. It wouldn't do for a fine-looking officer like yourself to land in an army prison. Fine-looking men are kind of special, you see. The boys get real excited when one comes along.''

A thin sheen of sweat broke out on Craig's brow, despite his attempt to maintain a belligerent pose. He forced his voice as low as possible. ''Believe me, Todd, I plan to be out of Abilene as soon as I tend to some unfinished business.'' He stared out the window, his mind seething with thoughts of revenge.

''Well, I'll be on my way. My business here is finished,'' Todd said with a smug smile as he turned to leave. ''Don't take too long, Major.''

''I won't need much time to settle accounts with that army agent,'' Craig swore between clenched teeth. ''Jack Barnett and his pretty little rebel will rue the day they interfered with me.''

Salem Todd paused at the door. He slowly turned around, all trace of the leer wiped from his face. ''What's that agent's name again?''

Craig's head lifted at the unmistakable sound of menace in Todd's voice. ''Jack Barnett. Why?''

''This Barnett wouldn't happen to be a tall, lean fellow with brown hair and gray eyes, would he?'' Todd approached the desk once again.

Craig studied the former convict. Tension radiated from the man's body now. ''Yes. How do you know him?''

Todd's one eye took on a fierce gleam. ''Let's just say we go back a ways . . . all the way to the war.'' He stared out the dusty window for a moment, Fort Riley's muted clamor punctuating the silence. Finally he perched on the edge of the desk. ''I'll take care of Jack Barnett for you, Major. For free. You see . . . I've got scores of my own to settle.''

''Why?'' Craig probed.

''See this patch?'' Todd pointed to his face. ''Jack Barnett did that to me, and he's gonna pay. Now, where will I find him?''

Craig leaned back into his chair, still surprised at this unusual turn of good fortune. He wouldn't have to delay his meticulous escape plans after all. ''You'll find him at the army agent's office on Texas Street, right past the Alamo Saloon.''

Chapter

14

Becky Herndon lifted the pale green gown from its box. "Ohhhh, Samantha . . . it's beautiful!" she cried, her face radiant with delight.

"I thought the color suited you perfectly," Samantha said with a smile. "It's not too big, is it? I had forgotten how tiny your waist is."

Becky sprang from her chair beside Lucy Johnson's kitchen table and held the gown against her. "Oh, no, it's perfect," she exclaimed and spun around in a circle, the gown swirling gracefully as she twirled.

Across the kitchen, Jack sipped his second cup of coffee slowly, enjoying the family noise that billowed around him. There were opened boxes and happy faces everywhere he looked.

They had brought presents for everyone. Davy, Becky, both maiden aunts, Maysie, Lucy, Clyde, even Cody. There were so many bundles when he and Samantha alighted from the afternoon train, that Jack had to rent the stationmaster's wagon to carry them all.

Jack watched Davy sprawl in the middle of the floor,

marching his wooden soldier into mock battle. Samantha reached down to tousle her son's light blond hair. Suddenly Jack remembered the touch of her hands on him. All over him, hungrily exploring, driving him mad. His body responded to the inflammatory memories, and Jack shifted his position against the wall.

Good God, he thought, sighing. How in the world could he begin a proper courtship—under the eyes of Samantha's two maiden aunts, yet—when all he could think of were those three days and nights of wild and reckless passion? It was impossible. There was no way he could endure a long, restrained courtship. He couldn't wait that long to feel Samantha's anxious, soft body beneath his again, demanding and yielding in turn.

Jack shifted against the wall. *Stop it, Barnett, or you're gonna go crazy. Get a hold of yourself. You'll have to find some way to speed things along without horrifying her aunts. You'll have to. You won't last like this. Think!*

He stifled another sigh and gulped down his coffee, thinking all the while. But all Jack could envision was having Samantha in San Francisco with him, standing at the harbor as they both watched his steamships sail for the Orient. Samantha and her family spilling from his Nob Hill home, its red-brick walls bursting, overflowing with people. Overflowing with family . . . and love.

Jack felt his heart give a familiar squeeze, the small tug he felt whenever he allowed himself to think of a family. A family for him. At first he was almost afraid to picture it. Afraid all of this had been a dream, and he would wake up alone once more. But each morning Jack awoke to find Samantha snuggled close beside him. This was no dream. It was real. She was real. He wasn't alone anymore. All those years of aching loneliness were over at last. He would take Samantha and her family to San Francisco and build a new life for them all, far, far away from the war's ugly memories. So far his past couldn't find him. The very thought sent Jack's heart pounding.

Samantha gradually moved away from her family's exuberant enjoyment of their various gifts and edged toward Jack. She gave him a smile only he could see. "Davy is delighted with the toy soldier. That was a stroke of genius on your part."

"Not really. My favorite childhood toy was a wooden soldier exactly like that one."

Samantha entwined her hands behind her back, as if she didn't trust them to stay by her side. "If you operate your shipping company with the same extravagance I witnessed in St. Louis, I shudder to think what your bookkeeper must say." She slanted a teasing look his way.

"Are you applying for the position, Mrs. Winchester? For if you are, I'm afraid I will have to refuse you. I have another position in mind."

Samantha glanced away, and a smile tweaked the corners of her mouth.

Jack pushed his advantage. "When can we tell them, Samantha? About us, I mean. May I propose to you tonight? Or must I wait until tomorrow?"

"Jack, hush," she whispered, her cheeks quickly staining pink. "You know it's too soon. My aunts would be scandalized if we announced our plans so quickly after the trip."

Jack glanced to the far side of the kitchen. Maysie and Lucy were drying dishes and observing Jack and Samantha at the same time. "Well, we haven't fooled either Maysie or Lucy. They've been eyeing us all evening. Why don't we let Lucy drop your aunts a hint?"

"I promise, Jack. I'll tell them in a few days. Things like this require a delicate touch."

Her choice of words sparked another image in his head, and Jack tried not to squirm. He leaned his face closer. "Don't take too long, Samantha. I won't be able to keep my hands off you for a lengthy courtship. If I become truly desperate, I might carry you off to Lucy Johnson's barn after supper one night. Just think what your maiden aunts would say to that."

He leaned back against the wall and grinned, while he watched Samantha suddenly scurry about the kitchen gathering empty boxes and paper—her cheeks flaming scarlet.

Jack sorted through the various piles of paper on his desk, hoping to find the misplaced purchase order. He had promised Littlefield he would meet him at the stockyards before supper. And Barton. And Hughes. And Goodnight. Jack gave a little groan. He wondered if he'd even get supper tonight.

Cattlemen had swarmed over Jack the moment he returned, prodding him for information. How many head would he buy? For how much? Jack hadn't had time to think about riding out to Fort Riley. Cattlemen wouldn't leave him alone long enough to think.

God only knew how many cows were penned in Abilene waiting to be sold, with more arriving every day. Every cattleman wanted to sell his beeves and pay off his wranglers before the price dropped. Jack had been to the pens so many times his eyes stung from the dust. Whenever he escaped back to the office to draw a clear breath, another cowman would barge in. Fort Riley and his confrontation with Major Craig would have to wait until these Texans gave him some peace.

He rubbed the back of his neck and sighed. "You don't have to wait for me, Samantha. I still have to haggle with Littlefield over some steers. And after him, there'll be others. Clyde can take you back to Lucy's. I'll be there for supper as soon as I finish."

Samantha looked up from the ledger she was studying. "I don't mind waiting, Jack. I've found a whole set of expenses that need to be recategorized. It could take hours." She arched her back in a feline stretch before she returned her attention to the thick book that lay on her desk.

Jack wondered how anyone could derive pleasure from recategorizing anything. "Very well, Mrs. Winchester. But don't complain later when you're hungry because those cattlemen have caused us to miss supper."

"I've learned to control my hunger these last few days," Samantha murmured before she glanced up again.

She sent such an incendiary gaze his way that Jack was astonished the paper in his hand didn't ignite. He tossed it aside and leaned over the scarred desk, both palms flat against the wood. "Don't tempt me, woman, or I'll chase you out to Lucy Johnson's barn and have *you* for supper. To hell with your maiden aunts' modesty and Littlefield's cows."

Samantha's cheeks tinged the delightful shade of pink he found so attractive as she quickly returned her attention to the ledger—without answering. Jack deliberately searched for the merest flicker of an eyelash that he could take as provocation, but he didn't see a thing.

He also didn't see the office door crack open or the tall, gaunt man who stood there watching. Only when the man's low, scratchy voice reached into the room did Jack come to attention.

"Well, now. Ain't that a pretty sight."

The sound of that voice raised hackles along Jack's spine. Even the hair on the back of his neck stood on end.

"It kinda makes up for having to hang around this cow town waiting for you to show your face, Barnett."

Jack wheeled around. There in the doorway stood Salem Todd, the one demon from his past he could never exorcise. Every rock he'd split in army prison had had Salem Todd's face on it. Jack's body went rigid with hate.

He stared into Todd's cruel, dark gaze while his hand hovered near his holster. "Salem Todd," he said, almost hissing the name. "Somehow I knew I'd get another chance to take you in."

"You're not taking me anywhere, Captain," Todd said with a sneer as he pushed the door wide.

Jack stiffened when he saw the gun in Todd's hand.

Todd's jagged teeth bared in a menacing grin. Killing Barnett was gonna be easier than he thought. Now that he had the drop on the bastard who had cost him his eye, he was gonna take his time. Make Barnett pay for what he'd done to him. Make him suffer. And Todd knew just the way to do it, too. He'd seen the look Barnett gave that little Southern gal sitting over there, staring at them both. She was a real looker, that one. And as Southern as the day was long, too. Couldn't miss it, soon as she opened her mouth. Wonder how much Barnett had told that pretty lady about the war. All the burning they'd done. Todd smiled at the memory. He could almost smell the pitch now. Damn, they'd burned those rebs out good! Nothing left but charred timbers and tree stumps. Wonder if the captain told the pretty lady about all that.

Jack poised, his hand over his holster, every muscle coiled tight, ready to spring at Todd's slightest movement. "What do you want, Todd?"

"I want *you*, Barnett. I'm here to make you pay for what you done to me in Georgia. You took my eye, and you're gonna pay." He kept his gaze on Jack while he turned his gun on Samantha.

Jack started forward, but the sound of Todd's cocked

revolver held him back. Samantha scrambled to her feet, knocking the desk chair to the floor. She stared at the two men, her face white.

"Keep her out of this, Todd. Your quarrel's with me," Jack snarled.

The sight of Todd's gun aimed at Samantha dissolved the hatred that had momentarily blinded Jack. Fear replaced it. His heart beat so hard his rib cage seemed to rattle. He knew Todd was twisted enough to shoot Samantha for spite.

"Don't worry, Captain. I ain't gonna shoot her unless you come at me. It's you I want. I just want to say my piece first and I want to make sure you stay put while I do." He shot Jack an evil grin. "I was watching you two through the window before I came in. Looks like you're kinda stuck on this lady, Barnett. I thought it was right funny you'd pick a Southern gal, though. Considering everything we did back there. You remember Georgia, don't you, Cap'n? All the burning, I mean. Burned them dirty rebs real good, didn't we? Nary a big house left after we passed through."

"Shut up, Todd," Jack rasped.

A malicious light danced in Todd's eyes now as he turned to Samantha's stricken face. "You mean the captain hasn't told you what he did during the war? Well, let me have the honor, ma'am. Our division didn't leave one big house standing. All the way to Savannah, we marched. Me and the boys, that is. The captain here rode his fancy horse. Yes, ma'am, we went straight to the sea, just like old man Sherman ordered. Spread out wide, torch tip to torch tip we were. Damn, it was a pretty sight! Flames licking up to the sky . . . dancing on those fields . . ." Todd stared off, as if remembering.

Jack watched Samantha grasp at the desk, as if to steady

herself. The expression on her face almost stopped his heart. He wanted to cry out, grab Todd, stop the lies, but he couldn't move. He was frozen to the floor. What could he say? Todd *wasn't* lying. Jack *had* been there. He had watched it all and been unable to stop even one fire.

His stomach twisted within him, bringing back the sick feeling of helpless rage he'd felt those long years ago. Watching the jaded, hard faces of the men in his unit as they threw torches into open windows. Lace curtains igniting like paper. Hungry flames licking up windowsills and walls, leaping across doorways to devour other rooms. Smoke billowing out of doors, whole houses ablaze. The splintering sound of glass as crystal chandeliers came crashing down from blackened ceilings. The frantic cries of women and children racing to escape the flames, risking their lives to save cherished heirlooms; frightened slaves scattering away, heading north toward freedom. And the screams . . . always the screams.

Jack could almost smell the acrid smoke, feel the cinders sting his eyes, hear the terrified screams. A shudder raced through him. He glanced at Samantha. She was holding onto the scarred desk as if unsure that her legs would support her, staring at Salem Todd, transfixed.

Todd studied Samantha's horrified expression and fixed Jack with a triumphant grin. Old scores were settled at last. Almost. Now, if he could only turn the screw a little tighter, he could force Barnett to move without thinking. That way he could get the drop on him. Then maybe he could enjoy that pretty reb lady before he skedaddled out of town. Take her out back where nobody could hear her scream. Slit her lily white throat before he rode off, too. No witnesses to leave behind.

"I don't wonder the captain never told you much," Todd said with an evil grin. "You see, he never got to finish the war like the rest of us. Major Franklin stripped his bars right there in the field. Dragged him off in irons for taking my eye. Barnett would have killed me, too, if the major hadn't pulled him off me.''

Jack clenched his hands into fists by his side. Rage and shame tore at his gut. He wanted to rip out Todd's throat, stop those hateful memories.

Todd sensed Jack's humiliation and searched for some wartime memory that was gruesome enough to attribute to Barnett in order to thoroughly disgust the lady. He didn't have to search far. One scene radiated in his mind.

"And all because I told the truth. Those stables wouldn't have caught fire if Barnett had minded the wind better. We lost a dozen horses we could have used just because he torched too quick." Todd's face took on an eerie light. "Burned up a boy right alongside the stables, too. He ran out to save the horses, I reckon. Poor reb bastard. All those women and darkies screaming around him. Couldn't do a thing." He glanced at Samantha, hoping for a shudder of disgust.

Samantha took in her breath with a sharp gasp. She wavered on her feet and turned a stricken face toward Jack.

Jack didn't see her turn. He didn't see the desperate questions in her eyes. All he could see was the vicious liar before him. He let out a strangled cry of rage and lunged.

Todd jumped back, caught off guard by Jack's sudden movement. He'd forgotten how quick the captain was. Unable to get a shot off in time, he slammed his revolver against the side of Jack's head with a vicious blow.

Jack staggered backward, struggling to find his balance. He sank to one knee and groped for his holster. Suddenly his instinct told him to drop.

A bullet whined right by his ear. Jack rolled to the side and cleared leather before Todd could get off another shot.

Panicked, Todd ducked out the door, firing blindly as he ran.

Jack's bullet splintered the door frame, narrowly missing its target. Only the sound of Samantha's scream kept him from firing again. He wheeled around. Samantha clutched at the table as if she were about to collapse.

Jack scrambled to his feet, holstering his gun as he rushed across the room. He grabbed Samantha by the arms, terrified that Todd's last shot had found its mark. "Samantha, are you hurt?"

Samantha shook her head, her face frighteningly white. She stared up at Jack with a dazed expression. "Th-there," she whispered and pointed to the desk.

Jack saw the second, unopened ledger, a singed black hole burned into the middle of the book. The bullet had buried itself within its pages, inches from her.

He caught her up into his arms. "Thank God you're safe," he swore softly above her ear. Samantha held very still, not moving in his embrace at all. Jack kissed her temple lightly before he released her.

Now that Samantha was safe, the desire for revenge flooded his body again, consuming his whole being. Todd. He had to find Salem Todd and bring him to justice once and for all. Frustration over Todd's vicious crimes going unpunished had gnawed at Jack ever since the war. Beating wasn't punishment enough for such a twisted killer. This time Todd would pay for his crimes. This time he would not slip away. He would hang.

Jack hurried to the window and peered into the street, his fingers busily reloading his revolver. Grabbing his hat from the wooden peg, he snatched a rifle from the corner as well as a nearby box of cartridges. He was already at the door before he turned back to Samantha.

She stared at him as if he were a stranger. Jack swallowed down the sudden need to explain, to counter Todd's ugly lies. Later. He would explain later. After Todd was captured. First . . . he had to find Todd before he got away. Jack couldn't risk losing him again. Even if he had to chase him all over Kansas.

"I've got to go after him, Samantha. He escaped once, and I'll be damned if I let him escape again. He burned a mother and daughter alive back in Georgia, and I can't rest until I've brought him to justice."

Watching her stare at him with the same stricken look, Jack felt his gut twist. He forced his face away and headed through the door. Only the unexpected sound of her voice brought him to a halt.

"Jack, is it true?"

Jack froze where he was. An icy hand reached into his chest and squeezed.

"Face me, Jack. Face me and tell me the truth. Was Salem Todd lying?"

Slowly Jack turned to Samantha. The stricken look was gone from her face. It was flushed now, her eyes hard and bright. Only because he knew her every move could Jack detect the slight tremor of her body. The icy hand inside Jack's chest squeezed tighter. He approached Samantha, his heart in his throat, and met her fierce stare.

"It . . . it wasn't like that, Samantha. Not like Todd said," he ventured. "I never set that blaze, I swear."

"But you were there, weren't you? At BelleHaven. You were there with the troops who burned my family's home."

Jack's very being recoiled from the searing intensity of her glare. "Yes," he whispered at last. "I was there. But I swear, Samantha, I never—"

She didn't let him finish. Her hand flew out in swift and sudden rage and struck him hard across the face. So hard, her own hand stung—and was as red as the imprint upon his cheek.

Samantha could barely breathe, she was so angry. He had lied to her. He had been there all those years ago, burning her home, destroying her family. Murdering her brother. He *was* the enemy after all. She glared at Jack in white-faced fury. Her jaw clenched so tightly she had to force out the words.

"Damn you, Jack Barnett," she swore. "You lied to me." Samantha shot him another furious glare, then turned and raced from the office.

Jack stared after her, unable to reply. He couldn't. The guilt he had carried all these years stabbed his heart, piercing him through. His past had finally caught up with him. He should have known he couldn't hide the truth forever. He'd been a fool to even try. He must have been insane to think Samantha would love someone who had brought her family so much pain.

He sank against the side of Samantha's desk, his mind flogging him. *You're a fool, Barnett. A blind, blind fool. What made you believe you could keep the truth hidden? How could you even think Samantha would love you if she found out? You were crazy to let yourself fall in love with her in the first place.*

The ache that had begun in his heart spread through the rest of Jack now, a saw-toothed pain that ripped at his insides. He couldn't have stopped himself from falling in love with Samantha even if he had tried. He'd been drawn to her from the moment she stepped into his office. Something inside her called out to him. He had needed her, needed her badly, and he hadn't known why.

Now he knew. She had filled him. Filled the emptiness that dwelt deep down. No other woman had ever reached that deep. Now that she was gone, the emptiness yawned inside Jack once more, waiting to swallow him whole.

Slowly Jack rose from the desk. He stared at Samantha's overturned chair for a moment, then reached into one of the side drawers and withdrew a sheet of paper. Dipping Samantha's pen in the inkwell, he bent over the desk and wrote. When he finished, he carefully folded the sheet in half, wrote her name on top, and placed the message beside the open ledger.

Grasping the rifle once again, Jack Barnett stuffed the box of cartridges into his pocket and purposefully strode out into the bright Abilene sunshine, without looking back.

Chapter
15

Samantha kicked the rock out of her path. The stone skittered across the summer-baked dirt of Abilene's outskirts. The back streets Samantha had paced for the last hour weren't subject to the same foot and hoof traffic that churned Texas Street into ankle-deep dust. These streets had few buildings and fewer people. Prairie bordered these streets. Sagebrush and scrub pine clung stubbornly to the harsh land, as if begrudging the slightest intrusion of man. Only the occasional bright splash of yellow broke the drab landscape. Golden sunflowers rose up tall and proud, boldly flaunting their vivid beauty for all to see.

Samantha halted long enough to watch the stone come to rest beside the nearest patch of flowers. Only then did she notice the sun dipping toward the horizon. Sunset's slanted rays colored the craggy rocks and boulders a fiery red. Even the crudest frame building seemed transformed, its angular shape and sharp corners accentuated by deep shadows.

She stared into the sunset and deliberately drew in a deep breath, trying to unwind the tightened coil within herself.

She had trod the backstreets of Abilene's perimeter twice—marching, not walking—while the cauldron of anger that boiled inside slowly died to a simmer. She could think at last.

Thought had been impossible at first; all she could do was feel. Fury at Jack's betrayal. And pain. He had lied to her. He had said he'd fought at Fredericksburg and Manassas. He'd never hinted he'd been to Georgia. *Liar.* He'd plundered her homeland like those other grinning blue devils. He had burned BelleHaven. Worse, he had set the fire that killed her brother. *Liar.* Murderous, plundering liar.

A wave of remembered fury washed over Samantha now, submerging her momentarily. Then it pulled back. Again. With each street she had trod in Abilene's late afternoon heat, she had felt her anger pull farther and farther back—like the tide, draining away, leaving her bruised and tender inside, as ravaged as any beach after a storm.

Jumbled and confused, her thoughts finally began to untangle themselves. Samantha sank down on the nearest boulder while reason began to hammer in her head.

What was she thinking? She knew what kind of man Jack Barnett was. She had watched him for weeks. Watched him playing with her son, fighting her battles, protecting her family, protecting *her.* She had fallen in love with this man. Held him in her arms. This man was no murderer. No brutal plunderer. He was no arrogant despoiler. How could she entertain such thoughts?

Samantha recalled her earlier angry accusations and winced. Was it her pride that had caused her to respond with such anger? She'd never allowed Jack to explain, let alone refute Todd's damnable tales. She had barely let him say a word in his defense before she stormed out of the office. Salem Todd was the enemy. He was the murderer, not Jack. And she had taken a murderer's word over that of the man she said she loved.

That thought caused more than a wince to travel through Samantha. She cringed this time. What in God's name was she thinking? Why had she let anger consume her so quickly, blinding her to reason? Had the bitterness from all those years of privation and humiliation been hiding inside her, waiting to explode? Waiting to strike out and hurt?

She held her face in her hands and sat motionless in the late July heat. Summer's dry cacophony of buzzing insects rose up in the still prairie air around her. The sun baked through Samantha's clothes. Baked through her skin, into her brain. She didn't move. Somehow the sun's dry, parched heat felt cleansing. She breathed in the hot, dry air and let it blow through her mind, blow away the last of her doubts and confusion.

Samantha rose from the rock and scanned the intersecting streets ahead. She quickly set off in what she hoped was the shortest way to Texas Street and Jack's office. Her stride was as brisk as it had been an hour ago, but it was no longer driven by anger. It was driven by need. It didn't matter what color uniform Jack Barnett had worn in the war. She loved him. He was no murderer. There must be some explanation for what happened in Georgia.

Samantha grasped her skirts and raced toward Texas Street, anxiety speeding her pace. She had to find Jack. Had to find him before he rode off after Salem Todd.

She was panting by the time she turned the corner of Walnut Street. Ignoring several dusty cowboys' startled looks, as well as their improper suggestions, Samantha sped past the Alamo Saloon toward the army office. By the time she pushed open the rough plank door, her heart was pounding as hard and as fast as her frenzied footsteps.

Samantha's racing heart skidded to a stop. Jack was nowhere in sight. The small office was empty. She was too late.

Guilt jabbed her with its bony finger. *See what you've done. You've lost him. It serves you right. You and your prideful tongue.*

Samantha slowly drew into the room, anxiety and guilt taking turns bedeviling her. Was Jack at the cattle pens with Littlefield, or had he already gone after Salem Todd? Surely he wouldn't have left without settling business with the cowman. Jack was so conscientious, so . . .

She spied the folded paper beside the ledger. Even before Samantha read her name, she knew the note was for her. Her heart sank to her knees. A farewell note. She opened the paper and read:

Dearest Samantha,

Forgive me for hiding the truth. I was afraid I would lose you, and I couldn't risk that. I loved you so much. I thought we could make a life for ourselves, far away from those terrible memories of war, but I was wrong. Truth, no matter how painful, has a way of revealing itself.

I know you may not believe me, but I swear I had nothing to do with the blaze that destroyed your home. I never set one fire in Georgia.

I have left money with Lucy Johnson so you and your family can travel to San Francisco and settle comfortably there. I've also left you a letter of introduction to one of the largest shipping firms in the city. I want you to build the new life you so richly deserve, Samantha. Please do not spurn my gift. It is the only thing I can give you now.

I have sent a wire to General Logan. The army can have the honor of arresting Major Craig. I intend to hunt Salem Todd to ground this time—bring him to justice or die trying.

Good-bye, Samantha. I pray you will find it in your heart to forgive me. I will love you always.

Yours eternally, Jack

Samantha stared at the letter. She pictured Jack writing this painful and poignant message, and unbidden tears gathered behind her eyelids, ready to fall. How like Jack. Even when saying good-bye, he was thinking of her. Doing the best for her family out of love.

With a hasty swipe of her hand, Samantha brushed the moisture from her eyes. This was no time for weeping. She folded the letter neatly and slipped it into her dress pocket, then grabbed her skirts and raced from the office. She had to find Jack—wherever he was.

"Samantha, you must be mad!" Lucy Johnson protested as she stood outside the barn.

Samantha didn't even turn to acknowledge Lucy's obvious concern. She kept on fastening the horses' bridles, yanking a strap tighter. When she finished, she climbed up into the seat of Lucy's farm wagon.

Lucy placed her hand on Samantha's arm. "Samantha, please listen to me. Don't go alone. Wait until Cody comes back . . . or Clyde. It'll be night before you get to Salina." Lucy shook her head, her whole face radiating worry.

Samantha pulled on a pair of black leather riding gloves and picked up the reins. She gazed down at Lucy with determination. "I cannot afford to wait for Cody or Clyde. I don't know how long Jack will stay in Salina. What if Salem Todd isn't there? Who knows which way Jack would ride then? Maybe he'll set off for Wichita. I can't afford to miss him, Lucy.''

''Samantha, you cannot go into those saloons looking for Jack. A woman alone . . . merciful heavens! I don't even want to think what might happen to you.'' Lucy shuddered and glanced away. ''It's all my fault. I should never have told you Jack headed for Salina.''

A smile briefly erased the tension that pinched Samantha's features. She reached down and patted Lucy's shoulder affectionately. ''You don't understand, Lucy. I would have gone out looking for Jack even if you hadn't said a word. You've simply given me the best chance to catch up with him. I've got some apologizing to do.''

''Why don't you wait? Stay here until Jack brings that scoundrel back for hanging. The circuit judge will be heading to Abilene any day now.''

Samantha's smile disappeared. ''I can't, Lucy. I can't risk losing him. Jack Barnett is the best man I'll ever find. Now I've got to search for him and tell him so. And I can't waste any more time.''

Lucy shook her head, a wry expression on her face. ''I told Maysie you two had the look of a couple of billing doves when you returned from St. Louis. I guess these old eyes are still pretty sharp.''

A bittersweet memory twinged through Samantha. ''You and Maysie were right. Now, you two mother hens take good care of all those chicks while I'm gone, all right?''

''Rest assured, we will. But I want you to promise me you'll be careful. Use this shawl to cover up with. No use lettin' every wrangler in Salina see what a pretty woman looks like.'' She unwrapped the woven black shawl from her shoulders and handed it to Samantha.

''Thank you, Lucy. I promise I'll use it.'' She placed it beside her on the wagon seat.

"I have something else that'll discourage those cowboys," Lucy announced, then hurried to the barn and disappeared inside.

Samantha watched in curiosity until Lucy reappeared with a rifle in her hand.

"That won't be necessary, Lucy. I borrowed one of Cody's revolvers from the holster he left in the kitchen." She reached into the deep pocket of her skirt and withdrew a long-barreled revolver for Lucy's inspection.

"I hope you borrowed some bullets, too." Lucy winked.

"Yes, ma'am, I did." She grinned and shoved the gun into her pocket. "Just in case Jack isn't in the first saloon I find."

Lucy laid the rifle across Samantha's lap. "Well, the way I figure, if those cowboys see you walk in carrying this, you'll never have to use the six-shooter." She patted the rifle. "I already checked. It's loaded. So you'd best be puttin' it away for now."

Samantha shoved the rifle behind her seat, then picked up the reins for the second time. "I'll be back as soon as I can, Lucy. And God willing, I'll be back with Jack."

"Be careful, Samantha. Please!"

Lucy lifted her hand in a wave as Samantha flicked the reins and headed the wagon west.

Chapter

16

Jack hunched his shoulders as he leaned over the bar and sipped his whiskey. The raw liquid seared his throat. It was all he could do not to grimace.

Aged all of two weeks, he decided grimly. What he wouldn't give for a fine Napoleon brandy right now. He took another swallow and steeled himself for the burn while he surveyed the Longhorn's customers.

The Salina saloon was full but not crowded. Jack could easily see each person from his place at the end of the bar. He had been stationed at this spot for the last twenty minutes, scrutinizing everyone who entered the saloon as well as every man who stood at the bar drinking. Each face was visible. Salem Todd's was not among them.

Jack shifted his gaze to the men who were seated around the saloon, even though he had surveyed them twice before. Several tables were crammed between the bar and the swinging entry doors. Each table had a poker game in progress, with anywhere from two to five men and several assorted saloon girls standing in attendance.

He studied the cardplayers from his vantage point. The only men he could not see directly were seated with their backs to him. One of those men was bald. The other had too broad a build to be mistaken for Todd. Jack slowly examined the other cardplayers. No sign of Salem Todd.

He gulped the rest of the cheap whiskey and scowled. Was it possible he had missed Todd? Had the varmint headed to Wichita? Jack was sure Todd would head for Salina first. It would be the perfect stopping point before making the long run to Mexico.

Jack squinted at the painting that hung behind the bar of a voluptuous nymph reclining upon a red settee. The nymph held two small fans that did an inadequate job of obscuring her lack of clothing. Jack stared, unseeing, trying to plan his next move.

There was no way he could have made it to Salina before Salem Todd. Todd had gotten a head start while Jack shared his plans with Lucy Johnson. If Todd was in Salina, where was he hiding? Jack had already searched two of the smaller saloons before coming to the Longhorn. No one had seen a man of Todd's description. Maybe he'd gone to one of the smaller saloons on the back streets.

Jack grimaced. Now he would have to search each and every one of those rat holes. Even if Todd slipped away before he got there, Jack was certain someone would remember seeing him. He was too distinctive looking for any bartender to forget. And if no one in Salina recalled him, then Jack would head to Wichita. If he rode all night, maybe he could be in town before daybreak. But first he had to be sure Todd wasn't holed up in Salina.

Jack motioned to the bartender. Information was worth another glass of this Kansas-by-way-of-Kentucky rotgut. ''Another whiskey,'' he growled.

The stocky bartender slapped his white towel across his shoulder and approached. He grabbed a bottle from beneath the bar and filled Jack's glass.

Jack pulled out several silver dollars from his pocket and plunked them on the bar. "One's for the whiskey. The rest's for information, if you can tell me what I want to know." He peered from beneath his hat brim and studied the bartender's florid face. Sampling the house's supply, no doubt, Jack thought.

The bartender's bushy gray eyebrows lifted in interest. "Just what do ya wanta know, mister?"

"I'm looking for a man who might've come in here tonight. He's tall. Real lean. Wears a black patch over his left eye. I guarantee you wouldn't forget him once you saw him. He would've come in just before sunset, or a little later." Jack tossed down half of the liquor. He didn't even notice the burn this time. His throat was numb.

The bartender squinted and stared off, his reddened cheeks wrinkling as he ostensibly pondered Jack's question. "Welll . . . now that you mention it, there was a fella in here right before I took off for supper. Had a couple of drinks over there." He pointed to a table that was now occupied by three sullen poker players. "Sat and drank all by his lonesome for 'bout half an hour. Stared at the door the whole time, as I recall."

Jack's nonchalant attitude swiftly disappeared. A bolt of energy ran up his spine. He leaned closer to the helpful bartender. "Listen, friend. You can earn yourself a ten-dollar gold piece if you know where that fellow is right now. Is he staying the night? You got rooms upstairs, don't you?"

The man's white towel flipped out and the silver dollars disappeared as if by magic. "We got rooms all right, mister, but they ain't fer sleepin' . . . if you know what I mean.'' He grinned for the first time and revealed a gold incisor wedged between tobacco-stained teeth.

''So where would a fella go . . . if he wanted to sleep, that is?'' Jack gave a sly grin.

''The Silver Star has got a couple of rooms to rent. Kinda drafty in the winter, I've heard tell, but this is July.'' He crossed his arms across his white shirtfront and stared at Jack expectantly.

Jack dug into his denim pocket for the promised gold piece. ''Much obliged to you, friend.'' He flipped it to the bartender, who caught it before the coin turned twice in the air.

A sudden swell of loud laughter drew Jack's attention then, and he turned to see a woman standing in the middle of the Longhorn Saloon, holding a rifle. Her head, face, and shoulders were wrapped in a black shawl and hidden from view. What was not hidden, however, had obviously caught the saloon customers' attention. An undeniably feminine form, every bit as voluptuous as the nymph's behind the bar, was very much visible beneath the shawl.

''What happened, little lady? Did ya lose yer man?'' an older wrangler called out as his companions at the poker table hooted.

''Maybe he went upstairs at Mort's one time too many,'' another cowboy cackled from the bar. ''Look out, girls. You're in trouble if them sodbusters' wives start comin' in here, lookin' fer their men.''

The woman's eyes darted nervously around the saloon in obvious search. Jack felt a prickle run up his spine as he watched the woman edge farther into the room. Something about her made him uneasy. He sensed she was completely out of place here. He shifted his position so he could have a better view, just in case one of these wranglers needed a lesson in manners.

A burly poker player seated near the woman reached out and snatched a dangling edge of scarf. "Here, let's take a look at ya. Maybe yer ol' man's got a reason to run fer cover." He yanked the scarf, and it fell away from the woman's head, revealing a mass of deep auburn curls too unruly for hairpins and a face that appeared more likely to attract than repel.

The hoots of laughter swiftly gave way to loud masculine shouts of approval. The woman wheeled about with a startled gasp, rifle drawn to her chest.

Jack took one look and dropped his whiskey glass. His stomach dropped even farther. Good Christ! Samantha. What in God's name was *she* doing here?

Before Jack could even form a sentence, two cowboys approached Samantha, their hands held high in mock surrender.

"You can shoot me if you want, darlin'. It won't hurt a bit. Mort's whiskey done killed me already," quoth one, with a tipsy grin.

"I jest wanta be first in line, ma'am," said the other, "when you start lookin' fer a replacement fer the man ya lost."

The laughter swelled louder, and Samantha jerked the rifle toward the men. The laughter grew even louder. The two men grinned at each other, then separated, one edging to Samantha's right, the other to her left.

Jack stepped forward, his gun already drawn. Salem Todd would have to be caught another day. Right now Samantha needed him. Her rifle could bring down only one drunken cowboy.

"That's as close as you're going to get, cowboy," Jack called out, aiming at the younger wrangler's chest.

Samantha wheeled about. "Jack!" she cried. Fear vanished from her face in an instant.

Jack deliberately did not look at her, his attention riveted on the surrounding men instead. "Now just back away from the lady nice and easy and you can live to drink Mort's whiskey another day," he warned. "You, too, cowpoke." He jerked his gun toward the older wrangler. "Step away. If you make one wrong move, I guarantee she'll get one of you and I'll get the other. And then everybody else will get another drink. Except for you two. You'll be dead. Think about it."

The cowboys apparently did, for they backed away from Samantha with alacrity. The roar of loud male voices fell to a low rumble. Jack kept his revolver drawn as he approached Samantha, just in case another cowboy had a sense of humor. He grasped her arm and drew her close. "Samantha, what in the name of God are you doing here?" he rasped into her face.

Samantha stared up at him, color flushing her cheeks. "I . . . I came to find you, Jack. I couldn't let you leave like that. We have to talk."

Jack gazed into her deep green eyes and felt his torn and ragged insides flinch with pain. He didn't want to talk. He couldn't. Every time he did, he only hurt himself more, reopening old wounds, probing. All the remembered pain came rushing back. God, would he never heal?

He forced himself to release her arm. The feel of her flesh through the fabric was more than Jack could stand right now. Glancing to the side, he eyed several eavesdropping cowboys sternly. It gave him an excuse to not face Samantha. She was too close. Close enough to smell her lemon verbena scent. He took a deep breath. "I don't want to talk about the past anymore, Samantha. I can't. You've heard enough. Go off to San Francisco with your family and start a new life. Do it for me, Samantha. Please.''

He clenched his jaw to stop talking, or he knew he would say too much. The ache in his gut had already started. *Damn*! Why did she have to come chasing after him? Asking him questions. Hurting him all over again.

Samantha studied Jack's tensed profile for a moment. ''I need to talk to you, Jack. There are things I need to say, things I need for you to hear. But I cannot say them in a saloon.'' Her voice dropped. ''Can't we go somewhere private and talk, please?''

Jack winced inside. He didn't think he could listen to Samantha's outpouring, for that was undoubtedly what her talk was meant to be. She wanted a quiet place so she could berate him without interruption, rail at him for his betrayal. After all, he deserved it. He had betrayed her by not telling her the truth about his past. He had seduced her affections under false pretenses, pretending to be an honorable suitor when in fact he was a cowardly liar.

The prospect of such a conversation made Jack's gut twist tighter. He might deserve it, but he sure as hell wasn't going to stand for it. He'd already flailed himself until he was raw inside. There was no way he would hand the lash to Samantha. She might finish him off. He needed something left to survive.

He turned to face her and tried not to allow her closeness to take his breath away. Her soft red mouth beckoned only inches below, her liquid emerald eyes beseeched his, and those glorious auburn curls were already loosened and falling about her shoulders. Jack swallowed down his rising desire. ''Samantha, I'm taking you back to Lucy's right now. You were foolish to follow me. I have nothing more to say. The war's over." He grabbed her arm and started to escort her toward the door.

Samantha jerked her arm from his grasp. "Yes, it was foolish to follow you. But I told you I needed to see you. Now, please . . . can we find someplace quiet to talk?"

Jack couldn't help but notice that the surrounding rumble of voices had grown softer and softer as their conversation proceeded. Several cowboys at the nearest poker table watched Jack and Samantha with more interest than they did the cards in their hands. He eyed Samantha sternly. He wasn't about to conduct his private business in the middle of a saloon filled with drunken cowboys. And he'd be damned if he'd let Samantha force him.

"I said, I'm taking you back to Lucy's," he proclaimed, his voice resonating with a low, no-nonsense tone. "Now . . . how did you come here, by horse or by wagon?"

Samantha's chin came up at the commanding sound of his voice. "Lucy Johnson was kind enough to lend me her wagon and horses."

Jack shook his head in disgust. "I thought Lucy Johnson had better sense. Letting you go off alone was a damn-fool thing to do. Come on, the sooner we return, the less Lucy will worry." He reached for her arm, but Samantha jerked out of the way again, stepping farther back into the saloon.

"No," she said in defiance. "I will not leave until we've talked."

This time every poker player in the room put down his cards and turned to observe the squabble in progress. Undisguised male snickering could be heard, as well as an outright guffaw or two. Jack heard it and set his jaw in aggravation. Damned exasperating woman.

He eyed her sternly. "You can talk all you like on the way back to Abilene. To yourself. I won't be able to hear because I'll be riding *behind* to make sure you get there."

He reached out and snatched the rifle from her grasp. "And I'll take this, too. Just in case you decide to aim it at me."

A loud wave of masculine approval welled up in the saloon following Jack's authoritative pronouncement. A chorus of "Atta boy!" and "That's tellin' her!" as well as an occasional "Good fer you, fella!" rang out. Samantha's face flushed with color.

Jack approached again, hoping she was thoroughly embarrassed by now and would come with him docilely. Much to his relief Samantha allowed him to take her by the arm. "Now you're being sensible," he said and started toward the door.

Suddenly Samantha drew to a halt, her features concerned. "Oh, the scarf!" she declared, glancing over her shoulder to where the black shawl lay on the floor. "Would you get it, please? It belongs to Lucy."

Jack went to retrieve the shawl from the wooden floor, which had been scuffed smooth. When he turned around, however, he dropped the shawl and stared at Samantha in amazement. She stood aiming a revolver straight at him. He blinked. Where in the devil did *that* come from?

The annoyance that had begun at Samantha's public recalcitrance swiftly turned to aggravation. Intense aggravation. Jack narrowed his gaze. "Samantha, what in hell do you think you're doing?"

"Whaddya think, fool? She's done got the drop on ya!" yelled a voice across the room. Raucous laughter followed the comment, as well as shouted encouragement from all corners.

A wheezy voice called out, "She must want to talk to ya mighty bad, young fella! I suggest you listen."

Jack's aggravation swiftly turned to anger as he felt his face flush. He didn't know what in thunder had come over ladylike Samantha Winchester, but he was going to put a stop to it. Right now.

"Put that thing away, Samantha, and come with me. We're going back to Lucy's." He deliberately forced his voice into the remembered tone of military command.

Samantha stood calmly, no longer flushed, apparently unperturbed by Jack's commands or by his discomfort. "Not until we have a chance to talk alone," she said. A chorus of suggestive sounds filled the air. Samantha didn't seem to notice. Instead she kept the gun aimed at Jack while she addressed the bartender. "You, sir. Are you the proprietor of this establishment?"

"Yes, ma'am, that I am," decreed Mort, face redder with amusement than whiskey now.

"Might you possibly have a quiet room where this gentleman and I could talk for a while?"

The chorus swelled with lewd noises now. Cries of "Hot damn!" "Go to it, ma'am!" and "*I'll* talk to ya! Ya won't have to force me at all!" ricocheted off the walls.

When the noise abated a bit, Mort replied, "We have rooms upstairs, ma'am. They're a dollar by the hour or five bucks a night. In case you wanta talk a long time." He gave Samantha a lewd grin, his gold tooth glinting.

Samantha looked Jack straight in the eye. "Would you give the man five dollars, Jack? And leave the rifle. We won't be needing it." Whistles, catcalls, and assorted lusty cheers greeted Samantha's request.

Jack couldn't believe his eyes or his ears. But he could trust his gut, and his gut told him he was crazy to stand here and let this spectacle continue. He handed the rifle across the bar to Mort, along with a look that froze the bartender's smile on his florid face. Jack folded his arms and faced Samantha with a glare that came from all the way inside. He made no move to comply with the rest of her request.

She studied him for a moment, then prodded, "Pay the man, Jack. We have a lot to talk about." A faint hint of a smile darted around her mouth, then was gone.

"Whoooooey! She must need to talk *real* bad!" the wheezy voice called again. Hoots and cackles filled the air in obvious agreement.

Jack whipped his head around and glared at the grizzled old geezer beside the stairs who had baited him. Instead of shriveling under Jack's fiery glare, however, the old man laughed himself into a wheezing fit. Jack turned his fire on Samantha, but she looked unfazed, which made him grit his teeth.

He let his voice drop to the floor. "The only place I'm going with you is back to Abilene. Now give me the gun."

Samantha observed him for another second, then nonchalantly reached up and loosened the remaining pins in her hair. The auburn curls cascaded about her shoulders to the accompaniment of various sounds of masculine approval. Then she looked Jack in the eye, aimed the revolver, and cocked it. The all-male chorus took in its collective breath.

She met Jack's steady but surprised gaze. "I really don't want to hurt anyone, Jack, but unless you go upstairs with me now, I'll be forced to start firing. And while I'm a fairly good shot, this saloon is awfully crowded. I might just hit someone. Accidentally, of course. And I'm sure you wouldn't want that to happen. So why don't we take our discussion upstairs. I have wearied of making a public spectacle of myself, haven't you?"

The men closest to Jack swiftly created space, moving away from him with a loud scrape of chairs. Jack heard the apprehensive murmur begin in the crowd and realized that

Samantha was right. This spectacle had gone on long enough. Swallowing down a gargantuan lump of pride, Jack turned without a word and headed for the stairs . . . until Mort's voice stopped him.

"That's five bucks in advance."

Jack gritted his teeth and dug into his pocket. He flipped the coins across the bar and marched toward the stairs, Samantha trailing behind—revolver still cocked and ready. The raucous chorus started up again, as if in relief that no blood was shed—especially theirs.

"Is that how you get all yer men, little lady?"

"Kin I be next? *Please*!"

"When you wear him out, I'm ready, darlin'! At yer service!"

"Whooooey! Taken at gunpoint, fancy that."

"My, oh, my, what a thrill!"

Jack clenched his jaw at every lewd comment. He'd ground his teeth so hard, he could swear he was down to the bone. He would talk to Samantha, all right. She'd get an earful when they were safely upstairs. Trying to ignore the catcalls, Jack strode to the stairs. Then that irritating wheezy voice pierced his armor of concentration.

"If she starts ridin' ya too hard, young fella, you jest holler. We'll come up and spell you till you get yer wind back." The old-timer cackled at Jack with what sounded like his last breath.

"Mebbe we'll take yer *place*!" guffawed a bewhiskered and shriveled old man next to him.

Jack ground past the jawbone with that. His face nearly purple with suppressed rage, he stomped up the steps. Samantha lifted her skirts daintily and followed, as if she were heading for afternoon tea.

"First door to the right at the top of the stairs," Mort called out.

Jack reached the landing and pushed the door open so hard it slammed against the wall. Samantha followed after, quickly crossing the room to adjust the kerosene lamp. The dimly lit room filled with a warm yellow light. She silently closed the door. They were alone at last.

Jack glanced around the small, sparsely furnished room. There was barely any floor space between the large brass bed, the nightstand, a wooden chair, and a rickety washstand in the corner. Even so, Jack strode as far from Samantha as he could without stubbing his toe on the furniture. He needed breathing room.

Samantha leaned back against the door, Cody's revolver resting on her breast. She watched Jack. The effort he was making to bring his anger under control was visible.

Jack forced himself to count to ten. Then twenty. Finally he gave up and stopped counting entirely. It hadn't worked. He was still mad.

"Is that why you came here, Samantha? To make a fool of me in front of a bunch of drunken cowboys?" he accused, his eyes boring into her.

"I'm sorry about what happened downstairs, Jack, but I wasn't about to let you take me back to Abilene until we had a chance to talk. That's why I came."

Jack exploded at last. "Goddammit, Samantha! I *told* you I don't want to talk about the war. Leave me alone." He stalked across the small bedroom and stood beside the partially open window, his back to her. A tattered lace curtain flapped lazily in the night's breeze.

"I don't want to leave you, Jack. I came to—"

"You came to *torment* me," he shot back.

"Jack, no, I—"

He wheeled on her suddenly, his face darkened by the awful memories that surged inside him now, welling up from their secret hiding places, waiting to swallow him once more. "All right, Samantha, I'll tell you about Georgia," he said in a fierce whisper, his eyes strangely bright. "I'll tell you what you came to hear. Then you'll leave me in peace."

Samantha caught her breath and drew back, but he held her in his gaze. "I thought I'd seen horrors enough in that bloodbath in Virginia, but I was wrong. Georgia was hell itself. Women and children, old men driven from their homes. Flames destroying everything our soldiers couldn't carry away. Fields, crops, houses, barns, horses, livestock . . . people. People whose faces were pinched with hunger, weeping as they watched the last of their provisions go up in flames."

Jack drew in a ragged breath. "I couldn't stomach it. I told my commanding officer I'd scout all the way to General Lee's camp if need be, but I wouldn't light one torch. I didn't care if he court-martialed me. But Major Franklin was afraid to charge a colonel's son, especially one who had just been decorated. I wish to God he had. Then I wouldn't have been there at BelleHaven."

He turned his face away, unable to look at Samantha. He grabbed hold of the shiny knob at the end of the bed rail as his voice died down to an anguished whisper. "I was out scouting and had just ridden up over a low rise overlooking your property when I saw the men torching the fields, the stable afire, and your brother . . ."

Jack closed his eyes, but it was no use. The scene still radiated inside his brain. Seared into it through the years. "Heading toward the flames, running . . . burning . . . the screams . . . the terrible, terrible screams—"

"Jack, stop . . . please," Samantha begged, her own face twisted with pain.

"No! It's what you came to hear, isn't it? I stood and watched your family destroyed and did nothing. I watched your brother die an agonizing and senseless death and could not prevent it. None of it. The senseless killing, the wanton destruction, the horror. God forgive me . . . the horror.'' His voice choked off hoarsely.

Samantha stepped away from the door, the revolver still clutched to her breast. When she approached Jack she gave a little start, as if remembering it, then placed the gun on the nightstand. Drawing closer, she reached out and touched his arm. ''No more, Jack,'' she said softly.

He jerked away, turning his back on her. The slight touch of her hand scalded him, right through his clothes. He couldn't bear it. ''Don't, Samantha!'' he rasped. ''It hurts too much. Leave me . . . leave me in peace.''

''No,'' she whispered. ''I won't leave you. Ever.'' She reached out and lightly touched his back.

Jack flinched, as if in pain. He stepped away again, even though he sensed she would follow. There was no escaping her in this tiny room. He felt her hands on him again, stroking his back, and winced.

She wasn't going to leave. She was going to stay there and torture him. Touching him gently, stroking him until he went mad probably. A shudder ran through him—sudden, involuntary, against his will, and complete. Jack's tensed muscles relaxed beneath Samantha's gently stroking hands. He surrendered with a ragged sigh. Death would be sweet torment.

''God, Samantha . . . don't do this to me. Leave me . . . please.''

As if in answer, Samantha encircled him with her arms, drawing herself close, pressing her face and body to his back.

Jack groaned out loud. The feel of her arms around him, her breasts pressing against him . . . sweet torment, indeed. He closed his eyes and swallowed down another groan.

Samantha shut her eyes, too. Shut her eyes and squeezed him tighter. "No, Jack. I won't leave you. I refuse to leave you alone to punish yourself. You've punished yourself enough, Jack Barnett. It's almost as if you're blaming yourself for the war. As if you were personally responsible for all the devastation and horror. Merciful God, Jack! What could you, one soldier, have done to stop whole armies? Don't you see? *You* are the one torturing yourself with these ghosts from the past. Punishing yourself over and over because you could not stop the ravages of war single-handedly."

Her words slowly penetrated the fog that had settled over his senses at the feel of her. Jack's thoughts groped through the sensual mist that enveloped them. He was so busy feeling, he could no longer think. What was she saying? War, ghosts, punishment, blame.

"The war is over, Jack. It's been over for six long years. For me it has been six years of mourning. Mourning for the past that could never be again, mourning for my family, my mother and father, mourning a brave young husband who was never cut out for war. Six years of loss and struggle. But all that's in the past, along with your fiendish memories. In the past with the rest of the war's ugliness and horror. It's time we buried the past, Jack. Both of us." She pressed her lips to his back and held him tightly.

Jack was almost afraid to believe what he had heard. Her voice was soft, muffled against his shirt. Perhaps he hadn't really heard what she'd said. Perhaps his ears had deceived him. Then . . . maybe not.

Maybe his ears could be deceived, but his heart could not. Jack felt her words inside him. Reaching inside—deep down to all the hurt. A surge of hope shot through his veins now, white hot. He clasped Samantha's hands and held them to his chest. He tried to speak but couldn't find the words.

Her voice came stronger now, no longer muffled. "I don't want to be enslaved by the past anymore, Jack. I want a future. I want to build a new life for my family . . . with you. That's why I came looking for you in Salina. I wanted to find you before you ran off after Salem Todd. I wanted to tell you that I love you, Jack Barnett. Jack Barnett—the man I met in Abilene, not some ghost from the past."

"Dear God, Samantha," Jack whispered, "I thought I'd lost you forever. When you ran out of the office, I—"

"I ran away because I was angry. Angry that you didn't tell me about Georgia. Angry about everything Todd had said. Angry about all those horrible things that had happened during the war. For that one moment I let all the hurt from the past rise up and cloud my judgment." She leaned her forehead against his broad back and sighed. "Forgive me for striking you. I didn't think. I just lashed out. It wasn't until I had paced Abilene's back streets that I could think clearly. And when I did I was ashamed. The Jack Barnett I fell in love with was no murderer. No ruthless destroyer. Salem Todd is a liar."

Samantha released her embrace, and Jack quickly turned to face her. He brought her hands to his mouth and pressed them to his lips. But she didn't let them stay.

She reached up and took Jack's face in her hands. Gently she touched her lips to his. "It's time to heal," she whispered. "The past is forgiven, Jack. Let us bury it now, so we can begin to build."

Her words were so soft Jack could barely hear them. The exultant pulse that pounded through his head nearly drowned out the breath against his cheek. He didn't wait to hear more. Not another word. There was no more need for words. Words were no longer enough. He needed more. Much, much more.

Jack caught Samantha in his arms and pressed her to him in a frenzied, desperate kiss. All his anguish, joy, pain, and hope poured forth. His heart had broken open at last and out flowed an ocean.

Samantha was nearly swept under. She grabbed hold of Jack and tore her mouth away, gasping for air. At the touch of his feverish mouth on her neck, Samantha groaned. It burned her skin wherever it touched. She had been so afraid she would not feel his mouth again.

A bolt of white-hot desire shot through Samantha. Sweet heaven! The feel of Jack against her. She could not stand it. She needed him right now, and she could not wait another minute.

Samantha reached up, placed a light kiss upon his lips, then quickly set about opening his shirt, her fingers nimbly working the buttons. Jack was unbuttoned before he knew it.

"Whoa," he said with a laugh. "Slow down. We have all night."

"Yes, and I intend to use it." She gave him a wicked smile. "I cannot wait another minute, Jack Barnett. So don't give me any argument or I'll take you at gunpoint, like the old-timer said." She yanked Jack's shirt out of his britches and pulled it over his shoulders and down his arms, leaving it to dangle inside out.

Since she had neglected to unbutton the sleeves, Jack found himself imprisoned by the cloth. Laughing at her impatience, he started to work the buttons himself, until her mouth touched his flesh. Jack caught his breath, his skin on fire.

Abandoning the buttons, Jack willingly gave in to his captor, let her wicked tongue and mouth molest him at will.

Each lingering kiss, each caress, sent his blood pulsing faster. Lazily her tongue traced a path from the hollow of his neck down the soft fur on his chest, down, down . . .

Jack jerked to attention. He fought his way out of the binding cotton while Samantha nonchalantly unfastened his belt, never losing her smile.

"You are an impatient wench, Mrs. Winchester," he declared as he sent the shirt flying across the room. "Perhaps I should take my time undressing you." He grinned while he slowly, methodically, worked the small pearl buttons on her dress.

"Jack Barnett, if you don't hurry up, I swear I'll yell for that old coot downstairs. Maybe he can tell you how to treat a hungry woman."

Jack laughingly obliged, unfastening Samantha's gown in record time. Petticoats and corset quickly followed, tossed hither and yon. He reached for Samantha, aching to feel her half-naked body against his, but she reached for him first. She playfully yanked at his pants.

"You've got some catching up to do," she teased and pushed away. Crawling on top of the brass bed, Samantha wiggled out of her chemise and pantalets, then deposited them daintily on the floor.

Jack stood and stared at the vision before him. God help him, he hadn't thought he'd ever see Samantha like that again except in his dreams. He still wasn't sure if he was awake or not. There was Samantha—his Samantha—in bed, waiting for him. Damn! If this was a dream, he didn't want to wake up.

Gun belt, boots, pants hastily dropped to the floor, and Jack was beside Samantha in less than a minute. He grabbed her. She threw her arms around his neck, and they both fell to the bed in an embrace.

Their kiss was long and deep and passionate, coming

from the very depths of their souls. Aching with need. Hands hungrily caressed, reawakening to each other's touch, each other's feel. Skin rubbed against skin, hard against soft, calloused against smooth, want against need.

Pent-up desire exploded inside them both. Jack pulled Samantha beneath him and inflicted his own kind of torture, delicious and slow. Samantha clutched at the faded cotton bedspread and moaned, her hair tangling about her face.

Holding his own desire in check, Jack devoured every inch of Samantha. His tongue and mouth teased her flesh until she begged him to stop. Breasts—kissed and caressed, all except the taut little centers that trembled for lack of touch. His tongue circled them again, teasingly close, and then withdrew.

Samantha writhed beneath him with a plaintive cry, but it was no use. He had caught her hands with his and held her captive while he molested her at will.

His mouth returned and kissed the lemon sweet valley between her breasts. Then slowly he dragged his tongue across one aching little center. Samantha cried out loud. Jack lazily suckled the trembling morsel of flesh, inflicting exquisite torment, until her cries turned to moans. Then he turned his attention to her other breast and started all over again. Samantha's cries caught in her throat.

"Jack . . . I can't bear it," she murmured.

He kissed the valley between her breasts again, then trailed his tongue down to her belly. "Oh, yes, you can, my sweet. All this and more." He released her hands so that his could roam free.

Samantha trembled beneath his touch, his fingers finding every sensitive spot. His hand settled between her legs, his fingers expertly teasing the hidden cleft. Samantha gasped. She grabbed hold of the brass rail behind her and held on as her body shuddered with pleasure, wave after wave taking her. She was no longer conscious of her cries, no longer cared.

Suddenly Jack's hand was gone, replaced by the light brush of his mouth. Samantha sank into the bed with a low moan. She shook beneath his mouth's exquisite torture, shattering, spasms racking through her, shaking so hard she thought she'd break.

Then all at once his mouth was gone, replaced by Jack himself. Samantha found her voice again, and she threw her arms around him with a joyful cry. Jack hovered above her at last. Her Jack. Returned to her once again.

Unable to hold back a moment longer, Jack thrust into her swiftly. His own desire at fever pitch, his senses tormented by their lovemaking, he let loose his control, set restraint free, and gave in to her joyous abandon.

He had Samantha beneath him again, her soft, willing body opening and receiving his. He sank deeper into her velvet, penetrated her soft flesh as far as he could go. No longer searching. Taking. Filling himself with her. Filling his emptiness. His need.

Samantha clasped Jack to her and cried softly as she whispered his name. She felt him shiver in her arms, then explode within her with a low moan, his voice beside her ear. Samantha shivered at his sound, exultant. Jack.

Slowly their bodies quieted, their breathing slowed, holding each other as one. Jack sank his face into her damp neck, his tongue tasting her heat. Samantha shivered.

"I'll never let you go. You realize that, don't you?" he murmured into the soft skin right below her ear.

She sighed in response.

"I also plan to announce our engagement the moment we cross Lucy Johnson's threshold. No more arguments, Samantha. I'd marry you tonight, right here in Salina, if I thought there was someone sober enough to perform the ceremony.''

Samantha's soft laughter tickled Jack's skin, and he lifted his face to gaze down into hers. Her eyes were the color of new spring grass. They smiled up at him.

"I do hope everyone downstairs was too intoxicated to overhear our . . . discussion,'' she teased.

Jack pulled away and stretched out beside her. "My dear, they probably heard us in Abilene,'' he taunted with a grin. "I'm afraid I'll have to build another story onto my home in San Francisco, to make sure your maiden aunts don't hear us and think you're crying for help some night. I'd hate to have them barge in and be thoroughly scandalized.''

Samantha gave him a playful push, but blushed anyway. "You are no gentleman, sir. To tease a lady so,'' she declared archly, her voice dripping magnolia blossoms.

"Just be thankful I won't tell your aunts you came to Salina and found me in the middle of a saloon. Forced me upstairs at gunpoint so you could have you wicked way with me. Imagine what your aunts would say to that.'' he remarked. "By the way, where is that gun?''

Samantha smiled slyly. "Right behind you.''

Jack turned and peered through the dimming light. The lamp's flickering gleam cast strange shadows across the walls and ceiling. He leaned forward and surveyed the room but didn't see the gun. "Where did you put it? I don't see it.''

Samantha didn't answer. She just kept smiling.

Jack peered at her, then sank back on the bed again. "All right, Samantha. Stop playing games. Where's the gun?''

"I told you, it's right behind you. Turn around and you'll see it.''

Exhaling an exasperated sigh, Jack did as she suggested—and found himself staring right down the barrel of

Cody's revolver. He shot straight up in the bed.

"Jesus God, Samantha!" he shouted. "Why didn't you tell me you put it on the nightstand? It's pointing straight at me!"

"Are you addressing that question to me or the deity? I believe you invoked us both." She returned his wicked grin from a moment ago.

Jack picked up the revolver, then leaned over the bed and shoved it safely beneath. "I think some lessons in the proper handling of firearms are in order," he said with a wry smile when he collapsed on the bed once again.

"You'll be the instructor, no doubt," she said, resting her hand on his chest. She ran her fingers through the soft brown fur there.

Jack folded his arms under his head and stretched out, gloriously naked, watching the dying lamp's flames cast their erratic shadows on the ceiling. The brush of her hand tingled on his skin. His body would have responded, but his mind was otherwise engaged—spinning daydreams into reality.

"There's so much I want to show you, Samantha. Once we get to San Francisco, I mean. The city's so alive, I swear you can feel its pulse on the street." His voice rose excitedly.

Samantha noticed and pulled her gaze from the pleasurable sight before her. Even in the darkened room, she could tell his face radiated excitement.

"You'll love the harbor . . . and the waterfront. Wait until you see the ships. There are ships from all over the world! Europe, the Orient, South America . . . you can barely count them all."

"Ummmm," she replied, her gaze no longer on his face. The gentle ministrations of her hands had yielded great results. Promising results.

Jack seemed oblivious to his body's response. His eyes were alight with visions of the future. "And the city. You'll love the city. Opera and concerts. Musicales and theater. Museums, too. San Francisco is no California backwater," he said proudly. "I think you'll be pleased when you see the quality of the collections there."

Samantha was already pleased, immensely so, by what she saw. She slowly let her eyes travel the length of Jack Barnett up to his face and smiled at his faraway expression. She resolved to bring him back to Kansas. Gently, of course.

She began by capturing his tone of voice. "Does your museum have an extensive Oriental collection?" Her hand trailed innocently across his arm.

"One of the finest in the country."

"How wonderful. I hope there's a varied selection of porcelain. My father used to import vases from all over Asia. I must confess I always enjoyed examining some of the more exotic specimens." She trailed light kisses down Jack's chest, down to the dark tangle of hair. "There were several very interesting scenes painted on a few of the vases. The figures seemed to be engaged in some rather intriguing pastimes." Her tongue slid down to his thigh, then lifted. "Ever since then I've been insatiably curious. Do you think we might visit the San Francisco collection?"

Jack didn't even hear her question. His senses were trying to adjust to the sudden jolt of sensation. Her mouth was traveling where it had never been before. All of San Francisco's glories vanished from his mind in an instant.

"Do you think we might?" she prompted, not hearing a response to her question. Her mouth hovered over his groin.

He blinked awake. "Might what?"

"Visit the museum when we're there."

"Where?"

"In San Francisco. Remember? You were telling me all about the glorious museum there." She hid her smile.

"Oh, yes . . . the museum. Yes, it's magnificent. It's . . . ahhhhhhh . . . yesssss . . ."

Her mouth had returned and trailed down his other thigh.

"Especially the collection of porcelain, correct? You do remember the porcelain, don't you?"

Jack most definitely remembered the porcelain. In fact, he doubted he'd ever forget the porcelain. Her tongue slid across his scrotum with excruciating slowness. He sucked in his breath in anticipation. Christ! She learned this by staring at Oriental vases? Impossible.

"God, Samantha . . ." He sighed eloquently. "I'll buy you a shipload of porcelain—just don't stop. *Please.*"

Alas, her tantalizing tongue did just that.

"Of course, studying the porcelain did leave many un- answered questions. But I was fortunate to find someone who proved to be a fount of knowledge. One of our cap- tains had a Jamaican wife who helped me sort through cargo. Evelina was an expert. On porcelain, that is." Her tongue traced the base of his shaft.

Jack stifled a groan. "Jesus, Samantha . . ."

"So you'll have to be patient. Translating art into reality is a delicate procedure. And I am experimenting, you real- ize."

"God, I hope so."

She nipped him on the softest part of his inner thigh. Jack yelped.

"That will be quite enough of your knavish humor," she reprimanded, then kissed the tender flesh.

"For God's sake, Samantha, stop talking," he croaked.

"You do not find my discussion of Oriental porcelain diverting?"

"God, no. I'm dying. Have pity, Samantha. I can't stand it anymore."

If Jack had had his eyes open, he would have seen Samantha's wicked grin. Since he did not, all he heard was the taunt in her voice as she repeated his earlier words to her.

"Oh, yes, you can, my sweet. All this and more." Her tongue flicked across the tip of his shaft for an instant, then was gone.

Jack didn't bother to stifle his groan this time. "Jesus God," he managed to whisper.

"Hush . . . it's too late for prayer." Her tongue darted again. And again.

Too late for prayer, indeed. In fact, Jack no longer knew if he was in heaven or in hell. Her tongue brought fiendish delight, and her mouth was divine torment.

That tongue slid along the entire length of his shaft this time . . . then left. He shivered. "You're going to kill me, Samantha," he accused softly.

"Not yet, darling." Her breath brushed against his member. "Not quite yet."

Suddenly all words stopped. Her mouth slid over him, taking him in to the hilt.

Jack let out a groan that could be heard in Abilene. He sank back into the lumpy feather bed. Her warm, wet mouth moved slowly, rhythmically, relentlessly. Jack plunged his hands into her hair and guided her, showed her how to pleasure him and how to drive him mad. To his infinite delight, Samantha mastered both quickly.

He felt his release build and was about to give in with a glorious shudder when suddenly . . . her mouth was gone. Jack fell back to earth. He stared through the moonlit room. The lamp had burned out long ago. Samantha hovered over him, ready to descend. Even through the dark, he could see the gleam in her eye.

"Wench," he cursed softly. "Wicked, wicked wen—"

He couldn't finish. Samantha had already settled over him, wet and warm, and he was caught in her frenzy. Swept up and taken away—far, far away, someplace he'd never been. Jack clasped Samantha tightly and held on as the storm raged through them both. Bodies and minds taken together.

At last they fell back, exhausted and spent. They lay in each other's arms for several minutes, sharing each other's breath, neither moving nor speaking. There was no need to. Jack pulled up the bedspread's edge until it covered them both, and they fell asleep.

Chapter

17

Jack blinked awake. What was it? What had awakened him? He strained to hear a sound in the darkness. Nothing. Had he heard something before, in his sleep? Some tiny sound that roused him? What was it?

Then he heard it again. The low creak of a door opening slowly.

Jack sat up in bed. Damn! He'd forgotten to lock the door. He glanced at Samantha nestled beside him and drew the bedspread over her. Peering through the darkened bedroom, he tried to distinguish the outline of the door. Had it moved?

It had. Ever so slowly. Even through the dark, Jack could detect the slight movement.

His heart pounded, chasing the last of the sleep from his veins. Who could be sneaking into their room? It was close to dawn. Surely none of those cowboys was still awake. Besides, any one of them would barge into a room, not sneak in like a thief.

Jack watched the door edge open a little more and instinctively reached for his holster. It wasn't there. Then he recalled it lay across the room on the floor with his clothes, dropped last night with reckless abandon. He normally hung it on the bedpost, especially in a place as rough as Salina. But last night had not been a normal night.

Then he remembered Cody's revolver. It was under the bed. Far under the bed, unless he was mistaken. Jack leaned over and reached beneath the bed, all the while staring at the door. He groped and found nothing. Silently cursing himself for not placing it closer, Jack grabbed the bed rail so he could lean farther.

His motion caused Samantha to stir. She blinked awake and raised to her elbows.

Jack quickly bent over her, finger to his lips. "Don't make a sound," he whispered into her ear. "Someone's at the door."

Samantha's eyes widened in fright.

Before Jack could reach over the bed again, the door flew open. Samantha sat bolt upright, grabbing the bedspread about herself as she huddled next to Jack.

The dark figure of a man stood in the doorway, enveloped in shadow, his face hidden. Samantha took in a soundless gasp. The man had something in his hand.

The hair on the back of Jack's neck stood on end. He didn't need to see the man's face. He already knew who was skulking in their doorway. He could smell the coal oil. The blood froze in Jack's veins.

Salem Todd's voice reached into the dark and grabbed them both. "Sorry to wake you two lovebirds, but I've got some unfinished business to take care of."

The sharp scrape of a match sounded, and a slight flame flickered, illuminating Todd's face in an eerie light. He touched the match to a cloth-wrapped stick in his hand, and the tiny flame whooshed into life.

Jack's heart caught in his throat. He could never reach

his gun before Todd threw the torch. "Take one step, Todd, and it'll be your last," he threatened.

Todd exhaled a dry cackle. His eyes glowed with a strange light as he grinned at Samantha and Jack. "No use lying, Barnett. I saw your gun over there on the floor. You got nothing to shoot me with, and you know it. This time I got the drop on you, with my torch. Believe me . . . I'm quicker with this than any gun."

Jack didn't doubt that for a minute. Sweat beaded on his forehead as he watched Todd edge into the room.

He couldn't risk lunging at Todd. That torch could land on Samantha. All it would take would be a few drops of that wretched coal oil clinging to her skin to draw the flames, and she would be engulfed. War's remembered horror came rushing into Jack's mind, and he shuddered.

"You'll never get away with it, Todd," Jack warned. "This time someone will see you. You're not in the Georgia countryside now. You're in the middle of town. You'll get caught."

"Not likely, Cap'n. Every cowboy in town is either dead drunk or dead asleep. The bartender's gone. Only the whores and their fellas are left. Along with you."

He gave them an evil smile. "I want to thank you for making such a ruckus tonight. Otherwise I never would have left the Bluebonnet to come over and see what was happening. Imagine my surprise when I saw you two heading up the stairs. Barkeep said you had a room for the whole night. I was glad to hear it. Gave me plenty of time to make my plans. I decided shooting wasn't good enough. I wanted to make you pay for what you done to me. You took my eye, and tonight you're gonna pay me back real good. I'm gonna watch you fry. You and your lady friend."

He waved the torch twice, back and forth in front of himself, fanning the flames higher. Samantha shrank against Jack, her nails digging into his flesh. Todd edged closer, apparently convinced his victims were at his mercy.

Jack watched Todd's gradual approach, and his gut twisted in fear. He hadn't been this scared since Fredericksburg. With every step that brought Salem Todd closer, Jack knew he had less time to react. Less time before that torch could land near Samantha. He needed something to throw that could block Todd's aim. Something heavy.

His gaze swept the room in a frantic search. Dawn's faint light outlined the room's sparse furnishings. Straight-backed chair, nightstand, kerosene lamp, washstand . . .

Jack quickly jerked his attention away from the night-stand as his heart skipped a beat. The lamp. It was heavy enough. But could he reach it without drawing Todd's attention?

"That's right, Captain. Look around all you want," Todd taunted. "There's no way out. I've got you good. You always kept away from the burnin' back in Georgia. But not tonight. Tonight you're gonna get real close." His dry laugh cackled, and he jabbed the torch at them, tormenting them.

Samantha clutched Jack tighter. He slipped his arm around her and pulled her against him. Using her obvious fear to obscure his movements, Jack moved closer to the edge of the bed—and the nightstand.

Salem Todd stepped farther into the room, the flames reflected in the maniacal light in his eyes. "You know I'm gonna burn her first, don't you, Barnett? So you can watch her die."

Todd was near enough now for Jack to see the madness. His fingers inched closer to the nightstand. No sudden moves. Nothing to alert the hunter. Let the madman rant. Jack's fingers touched the scarred nightstand's edge.

Please God, let my aim be true. Jack snatched up the

lamp and threw it at Todd's torch-bearing arm.

Jack's aim was on target. The lamp crashed into Salem Todd's arm and broke open, the last of the kerosene splattering his sleeve and coat. The torch wobbled in Todd's hand just long enough for the greedy flames to leap to his sleeve and then his coat. He was engulfed in an instant.

Todd shrieked in terror, beating at the flames with both hands. It was no use. Flames licked up his face and down his legs, dancing all over his body.

Samantha drew back and screamed at the hellish sight. Jack leaped from the bed and yanked the bedspread away to smother the flames. No one deserved to die like that.

It was too late. Consumed in flames, Todd let out a bloodcurdling scream and raced for the window. He crashed through the glass headfirst, sending shards flying as he fell.

A jagged shard grazed Jack's leg, and he quickly held up the bedspread to keep more shattered glass from slicing into them. Too much bare skin was exposed and vulnerable.

Suddenly voices could be heard down the hall, shouting. Jack hastily pulled on his pants, while Samantha sprang from the bed and wrapped the sheet around herself. They hurried to the window and gazed at the horrible scene below.

Salem Todd lay crumpled and lifeless in the dirt, his body still smoldering. Samantha shuddered at the sight and buried her face in Jack's bare shoulder. He embraced her tightly, thankful Todd's torch hadn't done its work.

Jack stared at Todd as an enormous wave of relief swept through him. Todd had been brought to justice, all right, and by a sterner taskmaster than himself. It was fitting that a fiend like Todd should receive a fiendish judgment. He had burned countless innocents without mercy, ignoring their frantic pleas. Truly, justice had been served. Jack felt some hidden muscle within himself relax at last.

"God Almighty! What's happenin' in here?" yelled a voice at the door.

Jack turned to see a frazzled saloon girl and her burly male companion rush into the room.

"Bessie said she saw some man falling from the window," the woman cried. She peered through the window, then drew back, her face paling beneath smeared rouge. "Lord have mercy! He's burnin' alive! We gotta do something."

"It's too late," Jack said. "He must have broken his neck from the fall. He threw himself out the window to escape the flames."

"Jehoshaphat!" the man proclaimed. "Ellie, you run for Doc Gaines. Meanwhile, I'll see how bad off he is. C'mon, mister, you can help me out." He motioned to Jack and moved away from the window.

Jack stayed where he was. "He doesn't need a doctor. He needs an undertaker. I told you, he's dead."

Both the woman and the man paused at the door. The man turned and eyed Jack suspiciously. "You sound pretty certain, mister. Could it be you helped him out that window?"

"What?" Jack cried, flabbergasted. "That man was a murderer. He sneaked in here to burn us *alive*!"

The man slowly approached Jack and Samantha. "That's your version," he replied in obvious skepticism as he folded his arms across his bare chest. Like Jack, he had apparently dressed in a hurry. "You got any witnesses, other than your lady friend here?"

Jack's jaw dropped in disbelief. He couldn't believe what he was hearing. This idiot thought he had murdered Salem Todd. "Witnesses? Here in the bedroom at the crack of dawn? Good God, man! I told you Salem Todd sneaked into our room. He came here to kill *me*!"

"Oh, really?" the man said, his brow creasing even more. "Now why do you suppose he would want to do that?"

Thoroughly aggravated by the man's refusal to take his word, Jack blurted without thinking, "He wanted to get even. He lost an eye when I beat him during the war. He came back for revenge."

"Jack, I think we should wait and explain to the sheriff," Samantha advised as she glanced at the tall, gray-haired man with the authoritative manner who stood beside them.

Jack fixed his interrogator with an emphatic stare. "She's right. I want to see the sheriff. I'll do my explaining to him."

The man's gray mustache twitched, either with amusement or an itch. He calmly returned Jack's cold stare. "You're lookin' at him, mister. Matthew Kirk's the name. Sheriff Matthew Kirk."

Jack's jaw dropped again—in shock this time. Holy God! The Salina sheriff thought he had killed Salem Todd in some fiery version of a grudge match. Good Lord, how did this happen?

Sheriff Kirk peered out the window again, then addressed the wide-eyed and bedraggled woman hovering next to him. "Looks like he's dead, all right, Ellie. Somebody else is already tendin' to him, so why don't you go find my deputy and tell him to throw one of those drunk cowboys out of a cell. I'm gonna bring this fellow in for questioning."

"Sheriff! You can't be serious," Samantha cried. "That man meant to kill us. Jack's telling the truth!"

Kirk stared with a wearied expression at the woman wrapped in a sheet. "Sorry, miss. I'm afraid I can't take your word for it." He peered at her closely. "Are you new here? I can't recall seeing you before."

"That *does* it!" Jack exploded. "Get your clothes on, Samantha—we're leaving. This man's blind as a bat. He can't tell a lady from a saloon girl." He snatched his shirt from the floor. Samantha stood where she was.

"Well, lah-di-dah! Ain't we grand?" Ellie snickered.

"Hold it right there, mister," Sheriff Kirk advised.

Jack turned and saw a long-barreled revolver aiming straight at him. His momentary flare of temper quickly died down. Jesus. He was being arrested. This was getting worse by the minute.

Trying another tactic, Jack slipped on his shirt and held his hands wide in a peaceful gesture. "Look, Sheriff . . . I know this could appear suspicious to someone who doesn't know the facts. Why don't you let me go back to Abilene and bring Deputy Monroe out here? He knows the whole story. He'll set you straight."

"I'll be sure to wire him first thing this morning. As soon as the telegraph office opens at nine, that is. I'll look forward to straightenin' all this out. Meanwhile . . . I'll feel a whole lot better if you're in my jail, rather than roamin' the streets of Salina." He motioned Jack forward with the gun. "Come along now. Walk in front of me so I can keep an eye on you. Ellie, girl . . . you grab his holster and gun and bring 'em along, okay? And you, miss . . . I think you'd best get your clothes on. If you want to visit your friend, that is."

Jack shook his head and let out a resigned sigh. He looked at Samantha and saw the worry creasing her face. "Don't worry, Samantha. As soon as Clyde gets here, it'll be all straightened out."

With that, Jack strode out the door, Sheriff Kirk following after. Ellie flounced away in their wake, Jack's gun and holster slung saucily over her shoulder. Samantha stared after them, speechless.

*   *   *

"You bring Samantha back right away, you hear?" Lucy ordered, grabbing the reins of Cody's horse. "I've lied to her aunts once, and I don't want to do it twice. Only Becky and Maysie know that Samantha's off searching Salina for Jack Barnett." She shook her head sorrowfully. "I should never have told her he went there. God help me, I shouldn't have. What if something's happened to her?"

Cody held his horse steady and looked down at Lucy as she stood outside her front gate. The first pale rays of dawn illuminated her concerned face. "Don't worry, Mrs. Johnson. I'll find her, I swear. And I'll bring her back, all safe and sound." He gave her a reassuring smile and turned his horse away from the hitching post.

He had started to ride off when all of a sudden Becky ran out of the house and down the path that led to the front gate. She hung on the gate, breathless for a moment, then pushed it open and raced to Cody. He leaned down in the saddle to greet her.

"Cody, be careful, please," Becky beseeched, reaching up to touch him, her face lifted for his kiss.

Lucy retired to a discreet distance.

Cody gave Becky his warmest grin and leaned closer, claiming a kiss—and a touch. Becky's arms were around his neck in a second, obviously wanting more. Cody obliged as well as he could, considering he was mounted. He encircled Becky's tiny waist and raised her on tiptoe, the better to reach her mouth.

Lucy went back into the house.

With a disappointed sigh, Cody finally released Becky and set her back on earth. Becky's arms slowly slid away from his neck. He captured her hands in his and held them for a moment. "Don't worry. I'll find your sister, Becky. I promise."

Cody gave her a good-bye wave and a bright smile, then turned his horse toward Salina.

Anthony Craig stared out the soot-smeared train window, not even noticing dawn's handiwork. Pale pinks and corals bathed the landscape outside his window, contrasting sharply with Missouri's deep forested green. Major Craig saw none of it. He was too angry. All he could see were the scenes that radiated in his mind. Scenes from yesterday. Scenes of humiliation and panic and fear and rage.

Craig's gut twisted with the memories: his humiliation when the bank officer had questioned his request to withdraw funds; his fear when the man left to consult with another, both men eyeing him suspiciously across their walnut-lined offices; his panic, which caused him to turn and flee the bank, terrified he would be confronted.

And finally, his rage. The searing hot rage that swept through Craig when he discovered the exact same scenario at each of the other three banks that held his sequestered funds. Thousands of dollars waiting for him, dollars that had been meticulously collected and hidden away, just out of reach. Now they were denied. Snatched from under his eyes.

There could be only one explanation. The army had uncovered the secret accounts and alerted the bank. The embezzled funds had been found.

Craig's gut twisted into a knot this time. All his plans for a new life had been snatched away as well. How could he start again with the few hundred he had in his possession? It was impossible. Even if he managed to escape to Mexico, he could buy only a small parcel of land. That wasn't the new life he had dreamed of, and he'd be damned if he'd give up his dreams!

After all these years of selfless devotion to the army,

Anthony Craig wanted the life of luxury he deserved—as a wealthy cattle baron south of the border. A *patròn*. That's what he would have his servants call him. He would be waited on, tended to, and obeyed. Oh, yes. He most certainly would be obeyed. He had been too long in the military to willingly lose the feeling of power over others. It was too heady and delicious. He would be obeyed, all right. Obeyed and feared.

His *hacienda* would stretch for miles. Cattle grazing free, tended by the meanest gang of *vaqueros* money could buy. They would drive the cattle to market. He would never need to show his face across the border again. He would be safe. Safe and rich. Wealthy beyond his wildest dreams. Rich enough to surround himself with fairer flowers than he'd been forced to sport with before. No more coarse sluts. No more drunken bawds. Ah, no. He would be the *patròn*. He would have the pick of the youngest and fairest women in his domain. And when he tired of one, he would choose another. Then another. And who would say no? He would be the *patròn*.

The scowl on Anthony Craig's face deepened as the fanciful images dissolved in his imagination. They were gone. Ruined. All of his careful plans had been destroyed by Jack Barnett and that meddling bookkeeper of his. Now, instead of luxuriating for several days in St. Louis in grand style and planning his triumphal entry into Mexico, he was forced to skulk around the railroad depot while he waited for the westbound train. He should be dining in St. Louis's finest restaurant, with a beautiful and willing wench by his side, not huddled in the rear seat of a train heading back to Abilene.

Damn Barnett and his little Southern clerk! If they hadn't started poking their noses into those ledgers, the army wouldn't have known where to start looking. Todd said

Jamison hadn't talked yet. And even if he had, he couldn't have pinpointed those hidden accounts without the ledgers. Oh, no. This was all Mrs. Winchester's doing. The army didn't have a clue before the little rebel widow started examining Jamison's books. She was the one who found the accounts. If she hadn't unraveled Jamison's codes so quickly, the army never would have become suspicious. He would have had time. Time to go to St. Louis and withdraw his sequestered funds with no one the wiser. It was all *her* fault. Damn her! Damn her to hell.

Major Craig's heated fuming formed a small circlet of steam on the dirty windowpane. What was he to do now? He could either flee to Mexico and live like an outlaw— and risk being taken by a bounty hunter—or he could return to Fort Riley and go on about his duties, then calmly await his arrest and court-martial, admitting his guilt.

The blue vein at Anthony Craig's temple throbbed at the thought of the indignity, the humiliation. Taken and handcuffed. Stripped of rank and marched away in chains before all the soldiers in the fort. Thrown into some dismal, filthy cell and locked away while he awaited trial. The hateful images radiated in his brain, searing through his mind, causing the vein to pulsate so hard it looked as if it would explode.

He clenched his jaw. He'd be damned if he let the army degrade him further. Strip him of rank and lock him away? He'd see hell freeze over first.

Craig hunched forward, elbows on his knees. He no longer made any pretense of gazing out the window. Not that he gave a damn what any of the few passengers on this early-morning train thought, anyway. He was too busy plotting. Plotting a way out of this miserable fate.

He could only hope those St. Louis clerks did not wire the army as soon as he left. Even if they did, the word should not reach Fort Riley that quickly. Not if the army moved at its usual laborious pace.

The major's tensed muscles began to relax at last. There was no need to panic. Not yet. It had been his experience that any message of importance usually traveled through layers of enlisted men before it reached the officers who knew what to do with it. He would have time to escape. The army's own inefficiency would allow him that.

He let out a slow, deliberate breath. No one at the fort knew he had gone to St. Louis. Everyone thought he was still in Abilene, talking to the cattlemen. No one had noticed when he boarded the eastbound train. And he would make sure no one noticed when he returned.

Craig stared, unseeing, at the worn, upholstered train seat across from him. There could be no mistakes if he wanted to slip off this hook. First he would ride back to the fort and unobtrusively grab the rest of his belongings. He would need everything of value when he got across the border. He'd also make sure he helped himself to whatever funds were in the safe. The damned army owed him that, at least!

It would be easy for him to justify another trip to town that evening. No one would question him. The cattlemen were begging for help. Abilene was almost in chaos. Cows surrounded the town. Tempers were strained. Abilene's dilemma would provide him with the perfect subterfuge for his escape.

A cold smile finally lit Anthony Craig's eyes. It was a perfectly plausible excuse to leave the fort. By the time the colonel or anyone else started asking questions, he would already be across the border.

Chapter
18

Jack reached through the bars of his cell and clasped Samantha's hand. It was cold. He gave her a wry smile, hoping to erase the concern that clouded her face. "Don't worry. Clyde will come as soon as he gets the telegraph. After he explains to the sheriff about Todd, everything will be all right. The sheriff will let me go."

"And what if he doesn't?" She glanced over her shoulder at the deputy, who was sound asleep in Sheriff Kirk's chair. She lowered her voice anyway. "What if the sheriff asks Clyde where you two met? As soon as Clyde tells him you were sent to prison for beating Salem Todd, the sheriff will be convinced you're a murderer!"

Jack paused to consider what she said. She was right. Everything he had told the sheriff so far sounded suspicious. If Kirk learned Jack's past history with Todd, he would be convinced of Jack's guilt.

A worried frown creased Jack's forehead now. He knew his old friend well. Clyde would spill everything he knew the moment Sheriff Kirk dropped Salem Todd's name. Clyde always talked first and thought second. God help him. His old friend could accidentally put a noose around Jack's neck.

A chill ran through him at that thought. God in heaven. He needed someone else to vouch for his character other than the well-meaning but loose-tongued Clyde. Someone whose reputation was unassailable, someone who—

Jack didn't have to think anymore. He knew whom to ask. He leaned closer to Samantha. "Samantha, you have to go to the telegraph office as soon as Sheriff Kirk returns. I want you to send a wire to General Logan in Washington, D.C. right away. Tell him it's urgent that he reply immediately. Tell him what happened and ask him to explain why I was sent here. Also . . . also have him check army prison records. I'm betting Todd got thrown into an army jail sometime during the war, or afterward. If not for arson, then theft. He was a criminal. I'm sure he slipped up sometime. There ought to be a record. Ask Logan to send any records the army has on Salem Todd."

He squeezed Samantha's hand tighter. "We need to show Sheriff Kirk just what kind of man Salem Todd was." Digging into his pants pocket, Jack withdrew several coins and offered them to Samantha.

Sheriff Kirk entered the jailhouse then, causing the dozing deputy to awake with a start. The sheriff scowled at him. "Goll darn it, Baker, I pay you to stay awake on the job! Now, what would you have done if those two slipped the key off the hook while you were sawin' wood?"

Baker glanced sheepishly toward Jack and Samantha. "Sorry, Matt. I just sort of . . . drifted off."

Kirk snorted and dropped his hat on the peg behind the door. "Well, see that it doesn't happen again. Mr. Barnett here might turn out to be a murderer." He eyed Jack sternly from beneath bushy gray eyebrows.

This time Jack refused to be baited. He realized he had

blundered badly when he blurted out his previous relationship with Todd. This time Jack simply wagged his head and said, "You've got it all wrong, Sheriff. Todd was the murderer, not me."

"That's your story." Kirk plopped himself behind the desk, in the chair Baker had quickly relinquished. "I just had a real interestin' talk with Mort, the bartender over at the Longhorn. Seems he remembers talkin' to you last night. Said you were real interested in findin' this fellow, this Salem Todd. Mort said you paid him ten dollars gold just to learn where he was. Said you also asked where this Todd might be spending the night. Wanted to know how to find the place and all." The sheriff leaned back in his chair and rested his dusty boots on the desk, all the while observing Jack with obvious interest.

Jack felt the sweat begin on the back of his neck, but he held Kirk's gaze without batting an eye—or demonstrating no anxiety whatsoever. He sensed Kirk was searching for some outward sign of guilt. Jack was damned sure not going to provide any.

"You're right, Sheriff. I *was* asking about Todd. That's because I was tracking him down to bring him to justice," he said in his calmest voice. "Todd raped a woman and her little girl back in Georgia, then set their house on fire and burned them alive."

This time it was Jack's turn to stare and wait for Kirk's reaction to his grisly statement. Kirk's skeptical expression disappeared and was replaced by a worried frown.

"You trying to tell me you're a lawman, Barnett?" he demanded.

"No, Sheriff. I'm just trying to tell you why I was searching for Todd. I was aiming to take him back to Georgia and see him hang for his crimes."

Kirk surveyed Jack for a long moment. "Maybe you got

impatient. Maybe you decided to hand out your own justice.''

Jack shook his head slowly, never losing eye contact with Kirk. He wasn't about to lose this staring contest. He'd be damned if he blinked. ''Nope. I tried that years ago, and I paid a terrible price.''

Kirk was about to say something else when the jailhouse door suddenly swung open. In strode a lean and lanky young cowboy.

Jack blinked this time. He watched Cody Barnes approach the sheriff without even looking toward them.

''You're the sheriff?'' Cody inquired.

''That I am. And what can I do for you?'' Kirk observed the young man.

''I'm looking for a woman, a lady by the name of Samantha Winchester. She headed here from Abilene yesterday, looking for a fellow named Jack Barnett. Her family's right concerned about her. I'd be real grateful for any help you might give me, Sheriff.''

Kirk's mustache twitched until a smile slowly pulled at the corners of his mouth. ''Well, young fella, you'd better be prepared to be plenty grateful, 'cause I've done all your work for you.'' He gestured toward the cells. ''There they are. Both of them.''

Cody spun around and gaped. ''Mrs. Winchester! Whwhat . . . ? Mr. Barnett, what are you doing in *jail*?''

''We've been wondering the same thing, Cody,'' Jack answered with a smile.

Samantha drew close to the startled young man. ''Is my family terribly worried, Cody? I know I acted rashly yesterday, racing after Jack, but I simply had to find him.''

Cody tipped his hat in a respectful manner before speaking. ''Mrs. Johnson didn't tell your aunts, Mrs. Winchester. Just Becky and Maysie. But they're powerful worried.''

The once-drowsy deputy perched on the edge of Matthew Kirk's cluttered desk, watching these exchanges with obvious interest. "I'm gettin' confused, Sheriff. Barnett came here lookin' to find Todd. Then this pretty lady came here lookin' to find Barnett. Now this cowboy's come here lookin' to find *her*!" He shook his shaggy blond head. "Seems like they're all lookin' fer each other. It don't make no sense."

Kirk rose from his chair and eased around to the front of his desk, where he perched beside his deputy. "Right now it doesn't, but we'll wait and see what turns up. Don't fret yourself, Baker."

Samantha turned to Jack and gave him an encouraging smile. "I'll be back as soon as I send the telegraph." She patted Cody's arm in a reassuring fashion, then hurried out the door.

"Who are you sending a telegraph to, Barnett? Your lawyer?" Kirk tweaked.

Jack fixed the sheriff with a wry smile. "No. I've asked General Matthew Logan to send you a wire explaining why I was sent to Abilene. I'm hoping he can vouch for my character, Sheriff. To your satisfaction, of course."

"He'll have to do a lot of vouching, Barnett."

Cody stared at the sheriff with apprehension, then slowly drew near Jack's cell. "Mr. Barnett, what happened?" he whispered as he leaned closer. "Why are you in jail? All Mrs. Johnson said was that Mrs. Winchester came looking for you."

Jack slumped into a more comfortable position against the thick iron bars. The metal's cold penetrated his cotton shirt. "This is a long story, Cody, so let me back up a little," he began. "The day before yesterday in Abilene, a man named Salem Todd burst into the office. He came to kill me."

Cody's blue eyes widened as Jack explained. "Todd was out for revenge. He was a soldier in my detail during the war. One day he went off scouting alone and found a young mother and her daughter. He raped them both, then set their house on fire and burned them alive. When I found out, I beat him senseless. It cost him an eye. That's why he came after me." He shifted against the bars and grasped the cold iron, preparing for the wave of painful memories that always swept over him whenever he ventured this far into the past.

They did not come. Instead of shame and humiliation searing through him, Jack felt a sharp twinge. As if he had jabbed a tender wound. A wound that had only now begun to heal. Still fresh.

"What Todd didn't know was that I had vowed to bring *him* to justice if I ever got the chance." Jack deliberately let his voice carry, just in case the skeptical sheriff might be listening. "The other night in Abilene, he missed me but almost killed Samantha before he ran off. That's when I took out after him. I figured he could get as far as Salina before dark."

Jack rested his elbows on the crosspiece and draped his arms through the bars. "Once I got here, I started to track him through the saloons. I found someone in the Longhorn who had spotted Todd. I was just about to leave and search him out when Samantha arrived on the scene." A grin tugged at his mouth now despite his attempt to suppress it. "Of course I offered her my protection. For the evening, that is."

For the first time since Jack's long tale had begun, Cody smiled—at first boyish, then knowingly. "Yes, sir. I understand."

Jack's smile disappeared. "Salem Todd came at us just before the crack of dawn. Slipped into the room with a torch in his hand, ready to burn us alive. I woke up, and there he was at the door. Swore he'd make me pay for his eye. Raving mad, he was. He kept waving the torch closer and closer, taunting us. I couldn't reach my gun in time, so I threw the lamp at him. It hit his arm and splattered kerosene all over him. That was all it took. The torch almost leaped on him . . . as if it had been waiting for the chance.'' He stared out into the office as the grisly vision danced inside his head once more. He could almost smell the coal oil. ''Todd threw himself out the window to escape the flames.''

Cody was silent for a long moment. ''But why'd the sheriff put you in jail?'' he asked with a puzzled expression.

Jack glanced toward Sheriff Kirk, who had remained remarkably still during Jack's entire explanation. ''I guess the sheriff thinks I pushed Salem Todd out the window; that's all I can figure.''

''*What*?'' Cody cried and turned to the sheriff in obvious astonishment. ''Sheriff, that's just plain crazy! Mr. Barnett is no murderer. He's a cattle buyer for the army. It sounds to me like he was chasing a pretty bad hombre and got the better of him, that's all. You can't jail a man for that.''

Matthew Kirk faced Cody with a patient expression. ''You can if you're not sure about the facts, son. Right now all we've got is Barnett's word that this Todd was out to kill him. I need more than that.'' He eased himself back into the creaky desk chair and observed Jack once more.

Jack wasn't sure, but he thought he detected a slight lessening of the skepticism that had clouded Kirk's gaze before. He waited until Cody turned to him before he lowered his voice. ''I sent Samantha to telegraph the army. Maybe the sheriff will be convinced once General Logan vouches for me.''

"Mr. Littlefield and some of the other cowmen would ride out and vouch for you, Mr. Barnett. I'm sure of it." A mischievous grin appeared. "In fact, they might bust you out of jail. Steers are pilin' up pretty bad in Abilene."

Jack winced just thinking about it. Herds were already spread out all over. And more still coming. He arched a brow toward the eavesdropping sheriff. "Well, maybe Littlefield and some of the other cowmen can send those extra cows over here to Salina. Along with the wranglers, too. Sheriff Kirk doesn't seem to have too much to do. Maybe a few ornery, tired, and drunk cowboys shooting up Salina would keep innocent men out of jail. What do you think, Sheriff?" He shot Kirk an engaging grin.

Kirk simply scowled in reply.

"Do you really want me to get Mr. Littlefield?" Cody asked.

"No, Cody. But I do want you to wait outside for Clyde. The sheriff sent him a wire this morning telling him to ride over and vouch for me."

Cody's face lit up. "Then you'll be out soon."

Jack turned his head so his lowered voice wouldn't carry. "There's one problem, Cody. Clyde knew about my past history with Salem Todd. The truth is . . ." Jack paused, almost surprised at what he was about to reveal, surprised it no longer felt shameful. "I spent the last two years of the war in army prison because of what I did to Todd. That's where I met Clyde." He watched Cody's eyes widen, but they did not darken with disdain. "If Kirk finds out I went to prison for beating Todd, he'll be convinced I killed him. It won't matter what General Logan or Little- field or anybody else says. That's why I want you to wait for Clyde. Tell him what I've told you. Otherwise, Clyde will spill everything he knows as soon as Kirk drops Salem

Todd's name. And that could drop a noose around my neck.''

Cody looked Jack straight in the eye. ''You can count on me, Mr. Barnett. I'll wait for Clyde right across the street. He won't get in here without talking to me first.''

''I appreciate that, Cody.'' Jack found a smile at last.

Anthony Craig stepped down onto the Abilene depot platform. He could feel the heat radiate up from the baked wooden walkway, right through his expensive English boots. He peered up at the searing Kansas sun. Damn! It was the heat of the afternoon. He was hot, he was thirsty, and he was tired from the suffocating train trip. There was no way he could endure that scorching, miserable trip to Fort Riley without sustenance and a drink. A very cold drink.

He shook the dust of passage from his once well-pressed suit, grabbed his valise, and strode off toward the livery stable. He would change into his uniform, dine, then— when it was cooler in the evening—he would head back to the fort. With a little luck he could gather his belongings, as well as any available funds, and get away without drawing attention. Picking up his pace, Craig strode around the corner toward Texas Street, aiming for the shady side of the street.

When he turned the corner, he was greeted by a cloud of eye-stinging dust, so thick it nearly choked him. He grasped a hitching post until he stopped coughing. The street was clogged with men on horseback. He brought out his once-white handkerchief to rub his watering eyes as he wove his way through the crowd. Maneuvering around men and horses, he continued down the street.

As he edged beside the large and noisy throng, he happened to see two army officers riding in the middle of the crowded street. Craig was about to lift his hand and call out in greeting when a voice inside his head told him not to. Instead he remained where he was and watched the two young officers work their way through the horde.

They looked to be Captain Connor and Lieutenant Evans, from his regiment. What in the devil were they doing here? No one else had signed out to visit the cowmen. Why were they in town? A furlough in the middle of this dust storm? Not likely. And as junior officers, they didn't have the authority to assign themselves *anywhere*. So who sent them to Abilene on this scorching July afternoon—and why?

He peered after the young officers until he could no longer keep them in view. Then he turned to approach the livery stable.

The dark and cavernous stable brought welcome relief from the heat outside. Dust from hay and hoof hung suspended in the still air. Slanted rays of sunlight slashed oblique patterns across the stalls. Craig wiped his soiled handkerchief across his face and let the valise drop at his feet. Miniature dust storms rose up to dance, captured in the scattered sunbeams.

The horse in a nearby stall snorted at the sudden sound and shook his oatmeal-colored mane. Farther down the row of stalls, two other horses whinnied in answer. This hot afternoon swallowed noise.

"Hawthorne? Are you there? It's Major Craig from Fort Riley. I've come for my horse."

No answer—except an excited whinny from the farthest stall.

Irritated that the stable owner wasn't there when he wanted him, Craig headed toward that familiar whinny. He'd be damned if he'd wait for Hawthorne to return from the saloon—or wherever he had disappeared to this hot, miserable July afternoon. He'd saddle his own horse and leave without paying. That ought to teach Hawthorne to—

Suddenly a sallow-faced young man popped out from an adjacent stall, a pitchfork in his hand. His light brown hair was askew and filled with bits of straw. "Major Craig?" he asked, rubbing his eyes.

"Yes, I am. Is Mr. Hawthorne around so I can pay him? I've come for my horse."

"No, sir. He ain't come back from noon supper yet. But I can saddle yer horse fer ya." The young man scampered in front of Craig and headed for the Major's enormous stallion. "He sure is a beauty, he is," he said in admiration.

Craig accepted the compliment and let the youth ready his stallion. He pulled open his shirt collar and loosened his cravat. The heat seemed to hum outside—or maybe that was the locusts. He yanked at his shirt collar now. He'd be damned if he'd ride back to Fort Riley before sundown. He would be roasted in the saddle.

He was about to inquire where the youth's employer had taken his noonday meal when the young man spoke with a question of his own.

"Did those two soldiers find you at the train station, Major?" he asked as he cinched the stallion's saddle tighter.

Anthony Craig held absolutely still. If he hadn't known better, he could have sworn a chilly breeze touched the back of his neck. His pulse quickened. Was the boy talking about Connor and Evans? Was that where they were headed, the train depot? Were they looking for *him*? How could they know to go to the depot? No one knew he had taken the train to St. Louis. Sweat formed on the back of his neck now. He could feel it trickle beneath the open collar.

"What soldiers are you talking about, boy?" he asked in a casual tone.

"Two soldiers come over from the fort late this morning, and they were askin' Mr. Hawthorne about you. They wanted to know how many days you'd left your horse here." He gently stroked the stallion's nose. The horse stood docilely under the boy's attentive hands. "They said they were gonna meet you at the train depot, but if they missed you by accident, Mr. Hawthorne was supposed to tell you to find 'em there."

Sweat popped out on Craig's brow. "Did . . . did they say what they wanted? Is there a problem at the fort?" he probed, hoping the boy had overheard more.

The young man carefully slipped the bridle into place, fastening it as he talked. "I don't recall them sayin' there was any problem, sir. Just that they wanted to talk to you soon's you got off the train, was all."

Anthony Craig began to pace beside the stall now, his mind spinning. There was only one explanation why Connor and Evans were waiting for him at the train station. Those blasted St. Louis banks had notified the army, and the army wired Fort Riley immediately. No inefficient delays this time. Dammit! The colonel must have sent those young pups to bring him in for questioning. His pacing became more agitated, stirring up dust motes to dance in the sunbeams.

What would he do now? He certainly couldn't go back to the fort and gather his possessions, let alone rifle the safe. It was too late for that. All his carefully laid plans had been thwarted once again. He was trapped.

"Are . . . are you all right, Major?"

Craig wheeled about, startled by the sudden sound of the boy's voice. He stared at the youth, who stood at the door of the stallion's stall, then looked right past him into the slanted sunbeams.

He had to find a way to elude Connor and Evans. If they saw him, he would be forced to go with them, or draw attention to himself by his refusal. No. Neither choice was acceptable. He needed to think of another plan. He needed to find a way to escape before they could catch him. He needed . . . time.

"What's your name, boy?" he demanded abruptly.

"Bobby, sir."

"How would you like to earn a silver dollar, Bobby?"

Bobby's eyes popped open wide. "I sure would, sir!"

"Good. I want you to run a few errands for me. First I want you to bring me something to eat and drink. After that, I want you to go to the supply store and bring me a plain shirt and some britches. I . . . I promised one of the cowmen I'd help him out with his herd before I went back to the fort, and I don't want to get my suit dirty." He dug into his pocket. "Hurry back with the food before you go for the clothes, all right? I'm starving."

Bobby eagerly snatched the offered coins, then glanced over his shoulder. "Uh, I'm not supposed to leave the stable, Major. Mr. Hawthorne will get awful mad if I do."

"Don't worry, Bobby. I'll explain to Hawthorne if he appears. The horses are safe with me. Now you get going if you want to earn that silver dollar."

Bobby didn't waver a second time. He scampered out of the stable in an instant. Meanwhile Anthony Craig took his valise to the back of an empty stall, slipped off his suit jacket, and tossed it to the straw below. It fell in a crumpled pile.

Craig didn't even notice. His mind was too busy conjuring escape strategies. He had to elude capture long enough to slip out of town and aim straight for Mexico. If he had a decent head start, he just might make the border before the army caught up with him.

He reached into his wallet and scowled as he counted the remaining dollars. Not enough to build his dream. Not even close. The muscle beside his jaw twitched with suppressed fury.

Damn that little rebel clerk. All of his dreams were ruined because of her. He would be forced into an outlaw's life in some Mexican hellhole, and it was all her fault.

Craig felt the fury work its way through his gut. If there was only some way he could make her pay for what she'd done to him. Some way he could make her—

He paused as a sinister smile snaked its way across his face. There *was* a way. It was so simple, and so right. Not only would Mrs. Winchester pay for what she'd done, but she would also provide him the safest possible escape from the army.

Chapter
19

Samantha leaned closer to the cell bars so that Sheriff Kirk couldn't overhear. The iron felt cool to her cheek as she murmured, "Do you think I should telegraph Washington again? Perhaps General Logan isn't there. Perhaps I should wire someone else?" Even though she tried, Samantha couldn't keep all the anxiety from her voice.

Jack was sitting across from her—on the other side of the iron bars—resting his chin in his hand. He looked up and gave her a reassuring smile. "If the general isn't there, his aide will surely act upon it. Major Seward is a fine officer, and he's well acquainted with my assignments. Don't worry."

Samantha felt another pang of guilt. Jack kept telling her not to worry, reassuring her, and he was the one in jail. She wanted to comfort him so badly, but her own fears kept getting in the way.

She was scared. Scared that Clyde would slip and say something that could jeopardize Jack. Scared that General Logan would not answer her wire. And scared that Sheriff Kirk would ignore everything and keep Jack in jail.

She reached through the bars for Jack's hand. She didn't know what else to do. There were no words of comfort. All she could offer was touch. The warmth of her touch. Her flesh against his. Merciful Father . . . when would she feel that again?

Jack clasped her hand tightly and smiled reassuringly at her once more. "It will be all right, Samantha."

She opened her mouth to respond but never got the chance. The jailhouse door flew open with a bang. Deputy Baker awoke from another nap with a jerk. Sheriff Kirk merely glanced toward the door to see who was there.

Clyde Monroe nearly filled the doorway as he stood, gaping at them. Samantha couldn't help but grin. Large and rumpled and dusty—Clyde had never looked so good as he did now, coming to their rescue.

Clyde's gaze swept the small room. When he spotted Jack and Samantha, his jaw dropped. "Jehoshaphat!" he swore, air leaving his lungs in a rush. "God-a-mighty, Sheriff! What in tarnation are you doing puttin' Jack Barnett in jail? Every cowman in Abilene's been lookin' fer him. We got beeves bedded down ever' which way outside town. They're 'bout ready to stampede down Texas Street. Cowmen can't move 'em until they sell 'em. We need Jack back there buyin' beef, pronto."

All the while he was making this strident proclamation, Clyde had drawn farther into the room. He started to approach Jack and Samantha, but Sheriff Kirk headed him off.

"You're Deputy Monroe from Abilene, I take it," Kirk said, observing Clyde carefully.

"I sure am, Sheriff. And I'm here to tell you you got something wrong. Now, I don't know what happened last night, but I do know one thing for sure. Jack Barnett is no murderer.'' Clyde's faded blue eyes stared intently at the sheriff.

"You're sure about that, are you?'' Kirk prodded.

"Sure as I know my own name.''

"Did you know the man who died? A man by the name of Salem Todd?''

Clyde's eyes widened even more. Samantha took a deep breath and waited.

"No, Sheriff. Don't believe I do.''

Kirk studied Clyde for a long moment. "Were you in the army during the war?''

Clyde swallowed. "Yes, sir. I was.''

"Did you serve with Barnett?''

"No, sir.''

"Did you know that Barnett beat this Salem Todd so bad during the war, Todd lost an eye?''

Clyde swallowed again. "All I can say is, that fella must have done something pretty awful, or Jack wouldn't have done what you say he did.''

Kirk observed Clyde for another moment, then turned to look at Jack. Samantha was afraid to breathe lest she make a sound. Jack simply stared back at the sheriff without a word.

"You'd be willing to swear to this Barnett's character, Deputy?'' Kirk asked.

Clyde's shaggy head bobbed vigorously. "You bet, Sheriff. I'll swear on a stack o' Bibles!''

Matthew Kirk's mustache twitched into another smile. "That won't be necessary, Deputy.''

Samantha was about to take a deep breath at last when the door flew open again. Into the office strode a wiry little man, nearly bald. His face was screwed up into a frown. A large red-and-white table napkin was tucked into his collar and hung across the front of his shirt. He stomped over to

Sheriff Kirk and placed both fists on his hips.

"I would appreciate it if I could finish my noon meal before any more telegraphs are sent. I've just watched my steak go cold while I took down this message." He reached beneath the napkin and withdrew a folded wad of papers. He thrust it into Kirk's hands. "Here. Now kindly wait until I've finished eating before you send a reply." The little man turned and stomped out of the office.

Samantha caught her breath. *Please, God, let it be the message from General Logan.* She reached through the bars again and squeezed Jack's arm. Just feeling the warmth of his skin beneath the shirt soothed her. He placed his large hand over hers as he leaned forward. Samantha could feel the tension in Jack's body radiating beneath her palm.

Sheriff Kirk slowly opened the papers and began to read. Samantha swore she could hear each person in the room breathing, it was so quiet. The stifling afternoon heat seemed to muffle all outside noise. Or perhaps everything outside was too hot to move.

Her heart gave a little racing skip whenever the sheriff let out a sigh. She was so sure he was about to say something. He had to say something sometime. He had been reading for five minutes. Three pages. And not a word. Samantha scrutinized the sheriff's pensive features. His furrowed brow, his shaggy gray eyebrows that moved so expressively when their owner scowled, his frowning face, half hidden by a drooping mustache. She saw nothing that revealed the slightest clue as to his thoughts.

Sheriff Kirk exhaled a long breath, as if he had refused to breathe while reading. He shoved one hand into his back pocket and made a fan with the papers, then he strolled toward Jack's cell.

Samantha held her breath, her heart pounding in her chest as she watched Kirk approach. There was still no clue on his face as to his thoughts. She felt Jack's muscles stiffen beneath her hand.

Kirk stood in front of the cell and stared at Jack for a long minute, fanning himself with what Samantha hoped was General Logan's glowing affirmation of Jack's character.

"It says here that you're some kind of army agent, sent to Abilene to find an embezzler. Is that right, Barnett?"

Samantha made a conscious effort not to show her surprise. Why would General Logan reveal confidential information to this sheriff? She glanced at Jack, but he was locked in eye contact with the sheriff.

"That's right, Sheriff. General Logan sent me there to find a crook. He also hired Mrs. Winchester to examine the army ledgers. That's how we caught him."

"Was Todd the crook?"

"No, sir, he wasn't. I'm not at liberty to reveal the identity of the thief. Not until I get back to Abilene and arrest him, that is." Jack gave a grim smile.

Kirk scratched beneath his chin with the edge of the papers, still observing Jack noncommittally. "How come you're buying cattle for the army, then?"

"General Logan thought it was the best way to disguise my investigation. No one would be suspicious when I started asking questions."

"This General Logan seems to think right highly of you, Barnett. You have any idea why? I'm not partial to you at all."

Only because Samantha knew Jack's every movement could she recognize the effort it took for him to keep a straight face at that moment. She began to wonder if Sheriff Kirk was really as belligerent as he tried to appear.

"I can't think of a single reason, Sheriff. It was my privilege to serve under the general in Virginia, and I never

found a finer commanding officer.'' His face darkened.
"I'd walk through hell if General Logan asked me to.''

Kirk studied Jack for a moment longer. "I reckon you
already have, Barnett. So I guess I won't ask you to do
anything more.'' He gestured to Deputy Baker. "Open it
up and let him go, Baker. I'm satisfied he didn't kill that
fella.''

Samantha nearly jumped in exultation. She grasped the
iron bars to hold herself down, otherwise she might have
floated all the way to the ceiling, she was so happy. Jack
stood waiting for the door to swing open, seemingly in no
hurry.

"You're a free man, Barnettt,'' Deputy Baker said with
a toothy grin.

"Thank you kindly, Deputy,'' Jack replied as he strode
out.

Samantha couldn't wait another moment, and she didn't
care about the other men surrounding her. She threw her
arms around Jack and hugged him close, burying her face
in his chest, breathing in his scent. He had been given back
to her. His arms were around her quickly, and she felt a
light kiss beside her temple. She didn't even hear the loud
clearing of masculine throats or gentlemanly coughs.

Jack gently released himself from her embrace and drew
her beside him. He looked at the deputy, who was grinning
broadly, then at the sheriff, who wasn't. Only Kirk's mustache twitched.

"It's about time,'' Clyde declared. He removed his hat
and wiped his forehead. "We gotta get you back to town,
Jack, before those cowmen set up camp in the Elkhorn.
Freight train's comin' in tomorrow, and it won't wait.''

"Can I have my gun, Deputy?'' Jack drew away from
Samantha and approached the sheriff, who stood by his
desk.

Deputy Baker reached into a desk drawer and withdrew Jack's holster, handing it over, revolver and all. Jack buckled the holster, tied the leather thong around his leg tightly, then checked his gun—all without a word. Finally he turned to face Sheriff Kirk. Jack folded his arms and leveled his gaze on Kirk.

"That was a mighty long message you received, Sheriff. It couldn't all be compliments. What else did the general have to say . . . if you don't mind my asking?"

Kirk's mustache twitched again. "Logan had a lot to say about Salem Todd. Seems he spent the last five years in an army prison for burning down some warehouse . . . and a few other things. Didn't sound like too nice a fella to me. Glad he's not staying in Salina."

Jack's mouth twisted into a wry smile. "He'll be staying a long time, Sheriff. If you plan to bury him, that is. Of course, you could always drag his carcass out to the desert and leave him to the buzzards."

Samantha grimaced in distaste and decided that they had best leave before Jack baited the sheriff again. She cleared her throat and drew near to Jack, encircling his arm with hers.

"That's positively gruesome. Even a heinous killer like Salem Todd deserves a decent burial," she declared in a deliberately prim voice. She tugged on Jack's arm, trying to persuade him to break eye contact with the sheriff. Another staring contest was taking place.

"Have a nice ride back to Abilene, folks," Sheriff Kirk said as he glanced away from Jack. "I'm pleased to have made your acquaintance, Mrs. Winchester." He gave her a small nod.

Samantha returned his pleasant smile. "Perhaps we'll meet again under more pleasant circumstances, Sheriff. Right now we had best be leaving. My family is quite anxious about my absence.'' She emphasized her statement with a not-too-subtle tug on Jack's arm. This time he cooperated and led Samantha to the doorway. Clyde held the door wide open, looking relieved.

''Miz Winchester, I asked Cody to bring your wagon up to the hitching post out front before he headed back,'' Clyde said as he ushered them both out into the late-afternoon heat.

''That was kind of him, Clyde. Where did he go?'' she asked, shading her eyes from the sun's glare.

''Oh, I told him Mr. Littlefield wanted him back in town pronto. They need every wrangler they can lay their hands on, just to keep those herds from strayin'. I reckon we won't be seein' much of Cody fer a while . . . leastways till we load up some of them beeves on the freight cars and move 'em outta town.''

Clyde strode over to a dappled gray and loosened the reins from the hitching post. ''You folks won't mind if I ride ahead of you, will ya? I told Aunt Lucy I'd be back by suppertime, and I've got to see Littlefield first. I promised to let him know about Jack.''

''You go on ahead, Clyde. And tell Littlefield I'll be at the cattle pens tomorrow morning, bright and early. There's no way we can get home before dusk, and I won't buy beef I can't see.'' Jack broke into a wide grin.

Samantha realized she hadn't seen him smile since yesterday evening when . . . She deliberately kept that memory pushed away. They were miles from Abilene. She watched Clyde mount his horse.

''Clyde, please reassure everyone that Jack and I will return by early evening, would you?'' she called out.

''Yes'm, I shore will,'' he said with a polite tip of his hat. ''See you folks later.'' Clyde urged his horse down Salina's main street.

Samantha turned to Jack and matched his grin. "I don't mind riding home on an empty stomach, especially when I know Maysie's pie is waiting for me when I get there."

"My sentiments exactly, Mrs. Winchester," Jack agreed. With that, he caught her up in his arms and set her upon the wagon seat in one swift movement.

"What on God's green earth is Jack Barnett doing in jail?" Lucy Johnson asked out loud for the fifteenth time that afternoon. She dried the dish in her hand a third time, then placed it on its proper shelf in the cupboard.

"Well, at least we know they're all right. Both of 'em," Maysie murmured. "And you'd bettah keep your voice down, Miz Johnson. We don't want to get the ladies all upset." She nodded toward the elderly sisters across the kitchen.

Aunt Mimi was seated in Lucy's maple rocker and had one of Clyde's mammoth socks in her lap, darning a hole in the toe ... or rather, what was left of the toe. She hummed as she rocked, every few minutes patting a lacy white handkerchief to her cheeks and brow. Despite the heat, she was gowned to the neck in silk.

"Would you like some lemonade, Mimi?" Lucy asked.

"Oh, my, that would be nice, dear. Thank you so much." Mimi stirred a small breeze with her lacy handkerchief.

Miss Lily looked up from the book she was reading. "Might I have a glass as well, please? This Kansas heat is blistering." She, like her sister, was buttoned to the neck.

"I'll fetch it for you, Miss Lily," Maysie said. She approached the dry sink where Becky was stirring the contents of a pitcher and staring out the window at the same time. Maysie gave Becky a playful nudge. "Sounds like that handsome cowboy of yours is gonna be sparkin' some cattle tonight instead of some pretty young girl I know."

Becky blushed beneath her freckles. She glanced at Maysie and sighed. "How many men do they need to stare at those cows, anyway?" she complained, her face puckered into a frown. "All they do is moo and stir up dust."

"Are you talkin' about the cattle or the cowboys?" Maysie teased.

A smile pulled at Becky's frown until it won out. "The cows."

Maysie poured the lemonade into a glass and fixed Becky with a wide grin. "From what Mr. Monroe's been sayin', they need more cowboys than they've got. And the reason why, missy, is because most of those aren't milk cows you see stomping in the dust out there. They're steers. And there's a big difference, in case you hadn't noticed." She winked.

Becky blushed and waved Maysie away, turning her gaze out the window again. The sun's late-afternoon rays slanted into the kitchen, catching the red-gold of Becky's hair and burnishing it into copper.

Davy's blond head popped around the edge of the front door. "I fed the chickens like you asked me to, Maysie. Can I come in and have some of that lemonade now?"

"I reckon," Maysie replied as she handed a glass to Miss Lily.

Davy scampered over to Becky, who poured him a large glass. Davy gulped so fast he nearly choked.

"Aunt Lucy, do you know this cowboy coming up the walk?" Becky asked.

Lucy left the dishes she was stacking and went to peer through the window. A tall, slender blond man approached. "I've never seen him before," she said, a puzzled frown wrinkling her face. An abrupt knock sounded, and Lucy hurried to open the door.

There on the doorstep stood Anthony Craig. He doffed his hat in polite fashion and smiled at Lucy Johnson. "Excuse me, ma'am, but I'm looking for a Jack Barnett. My boss, Mister Littlefield, wants to see him over at the cow pens. Is Barnett here by any chance?"

"Why, no, he isn't. But we're hoping he'll return before nightfall."

Craig's gaze swiftly swept over the room. He paused. "Do you think I might wait for Mister Barnett here? I surely don't want to miss him."

Lucy studied Anthony Craig for a moment. "I think it would be best if you waited back in town, mister. We'll tell Jack that Littlefield's looking for him." Her voice was noticeably cooler. She started to close the door.

Craig's arm shot out and pushed the door open. "I'll wait inside, thank you," he snapped and shouldered his way inside.

Lucy swiftly stepped back. The others in the kitchen stared in obvious surprise at the unannounced visitor's rude entry. Lucy fixed Anthony Craig with a scowl and declared, "I don't know where you learned your manners, young man, but I suggest you go back and learn 'em again. Now, get out of my house this minute." She pointed toward the door.

Craig ignored her imperious command. "I shall do no such thing, Mrs. Johnson," he declared. "I plan to stay right here until Barnett and Mrs. Winchester arrive. I have a little surprise planned."

"Have you no manners, sir?" a contralto voice boomed. "Kindly introduce yourself before you barge into someone's home." Miss Lily rose from her chair, a volume of Shakespeare tucked under her arm.

The major blinked at the commanding sound coming from across the room, then a sardonic smile captured his face. "Ah, yes. You must be one of Mrs. Winchester's formidable maiden aunts. Forgive me, madam. I am Major Anthony Craig, formerly attached to Colonel Henderson's staff at Fort Riley. At your service." He gave a mocking half bow.

"Remove your hat when speaking to a lady, sirrah!" Miss Lily reprimanded, hands on hips, silk arustle. "And where is your uniform if you are a soldier? Why are you dressed like some impoverished cowherder?"

Major Craig arched a brow. "For your information, madam, I am no longer under the army's command. We have parted company, so to speak. Now, enough of your inane questions." He dismissed her with a wave of his hand.

"Are you deaf as well as rude? Mrs. Johnson told you to leave this house immediately!" Lily's face was flushed and she fairly shook with seeming indignation. Her finger pointed the way. "Leave, sirrah. At once!"

Craig wheeled on her. "*Silence*, harpy! I shall leave when I'm ready."

At his outburst, Aunt Mimi clutched at her throat and gasped, her lace handkerchief trembling like a leaf in a breeze. "Gracious, Lily! What a wretched man. He simply must leave," she fluttered from the rocker. The half-darned sock fell to the floor by her side.

Major Craig dismissed the maiden aunts with a supercilious glance and turned to the other three women, who had clustered together in the middle of the room.

Becky's face was so pale that each individual freckle stood out plainly as she hovered behind Lucy. Lucy's scowl had changed into a worried frown. Maysie simply glared back at Craig.

"What do you want, Major?" Lucy asked quietly.

Craig strode to the kitchen table and lifted a biscuit from one of the covered platters. He sampled it without asking.

"I came to tell Mrs. Winchester and Mr. Barnett good-bye. I'm afraid I won't be here for the trial—"

The rest of his sentence was lost when the door burst open and a disheveled and dusty Clyde Monroe stepped inside. "Whoooooey!" he announced, wiping his face with his kerchief, not even glancing in Craig's direction. "I tell you, I like to burned up ridin' back from Salina. I shore hope you've got some of that lemonade left, Aunt Lucy."

"Clyde—" she began, reaching out a hand to him.

Major Craig stepped in front of her and drew his gun, pointing it directly at Clyde. Clyde's blue eyes popped wide.

"Nice of you to drop in, Deputy," the major taunted. "You can have all the lemonade you want. Just step right over there with the others, where I can keep an eye on you." He gestured with his long-barreled revolver.

Clyde did as he was told and stepped toward the cluster of ladies. Davy peeked out from behind Maysie's skirts, where she was obviously trying to conceal him, and reached for Clyde's hand. Clyde took the child's small hand in his.

"Oh-my-oh-my-oh-*my*!" Aunt Mimi's lace handkerchief fanned faster. Her face had gone chalk white beneath her powdered cheeks. "What's to become of us now? Does he mean to shoot us? Mercy sakes alive!"

"Hush, Mimi," Miss Lily scolded. "He means no such thing. Only a madman would shoot women and children. And he doesn't appear mad, only ill mannered." She peered down the considerable length of her nose.

Craig smirked. "You're quite right. I am most certainly not mad. I am here to ensure safe passage for myself to Mexico." He walked to the front of the kitchen and faced them, then holstered his gun.

"You see, the army and I are not parting on the very

best of terms. In fact, Colonel Henderson has two men searching for me now. They seem to think I diverted some funds to my own accounts, and I decided not to try to convince them otherwise. Hence, my planned trip across the border. I shall be safe from their questions there.''

He glanced at the faces staring back at him, some scared, some angry, some belligerent. ''But I must reach Mexico to be safe,'' he continued as he strolled beside the table, as if in front of an audience. ''And for that I will need someone to accompany me. A hostage, so to speak.'' He gave a cold smile that did not reach his eyes.

''I'll go with you, Major. Leave these ladies alone.'' Clyde stepped forward, hands upraised as in surrender.

''Ah, the faint-hearted deputy wishes to be a hero, is that it? Well, I'm afraid I'll have to disappoint you, Deputy Monroe. You see, I had a smaller, more manageable hostage in mind. One I can keep in the saddle with me. A single horse travels faster and is harder to track than two.'' His gaze landed on Davy.

''Ovah my dead body!'' Maysie declared, her face screwed into an angry mask. She grasped Davy's collar and yanked him behind her skirts again.

''You'll have to fight all of us to take that boy,'' Lucy dared, fists clenched by her side.

''Never!'' cried Becky, face flushed.

''Oh-dear-oh-dear-oh-dear-oh-*dear*!''

''If you think we would allow our nephew to be carried off by a foul villain like yourself, then you are as ignorant as you are rude!''

Craig surveyed the chorus of protest without batting an eye. Then he drew his gun again. ''I'm afraid you will have no choice, ladies. The boy will serve as a perfect hostage. I'll take reasonably good care of him and leave him with some kindhearted soul before I cross the border.''

"You're gonna have to shoot every one of us to get that boy," Lucy said in defiance.

"Oh, I won't have to shoot *everyone*. One or two will serve quite nicely as an example, I think." He moved his gun in a slow arc around the room, pointing at each of the women.

Clyde stepped forward then, moving between Anthony Craig and his aunt. His hand hovered near his holster. "You'd better start with me, Major. 'Cause I ain't lettin' you take that boy. No, sir."

The major stared at Clyde with an incredulous expression. "I knew you were cowardly, Deputy Monroe, but I had no idea you were dim-witted as well. Please notice that my gun is already drawn. You have absolutely no chance of beating me to the draw."

"I don't aim to beat you, Major. I just have to stop you. That's all." Clyde jutted out his jaw.

Craig observed him for a moment. "Nobody's stopping me, Deputy. Least of all you." He fired once.

Clyde let out a cry of pain and dropped to his knees, clutching at his thigh. Blood spattered his pants leg.

Anthony Craig ignored the women's shrieks and approached a doubled-over Clyde. He slammed the butt of his gun against Clyde's head in a savage blow. Clyde slumped to the floor and lay still.

"Villain! Foul, foul *villain*!" swore Miss Lily, her whole body shaking.

Lucy started forward toward Clyde, only to be brought to a halt by the waving of Craig's revolver. "Stay where you are, Mrs. Johnson," he warned. "Unless you want me to shoot you, too."

Trembling, Lucy obeyed.

"That's better. Now do as I say and no one else gets shot." He slipped free a coil of rope that hung from his

belt and tossed it at Maysie's feet. "You, there . . . darkie,"
he commanded. "Bring that boy over to this chair and tie
his hands and feet."

Maysie thrust out her pointed chin and glared. "I'll do
no such thing." She clasped Davy tightly behind her skirts.

Craig gave her a condescending smile. "Do you need
another reminder? Whom shall I shoot next? The sweet-
faced younger sister or the sharp-tongued medusa?" He
pointed his gun first at Becky, then to Miss Lily.

"Foul wretch. Your deeds will drag you down to perdi-
tion."

His smile vanished. "Maybe I'll just shoot the old harpy
now and be done with it. That way I won't have to listen
to her harangues anymore." He deliberately aimed the gun
at Miss Lily.

Lily Herndon did not flinch. Instead, she flung both arms
wide. "Fire away, rank villain! Fire if you dare."

Craig rolled his eyes and turned away, aiming his gun at
Becky instead. She gasped and cringed behind Lucy.

"Leave her alone!" Maysie leaped forward.

"Then do as I say. Bring the boy here and tie him up.
Now."

Maysie hesitated, her face agonized as she glanced from
Becky to Davy.

"I assure you I will not hesitate to fire. As a soldier I
know precisely where to aim to ensure a slow and painful
death. Do you want her death on your conscience or not?
The boy won't be harmed, but *she* will die."

Davy scurried from behind the bevy of women and ran
to Major Craig, his small face pinched and pale. "D-d-
don't shoot! I'll go with you. Just don't shoot my sister,
please!"

"Child, *no*!" screamed Maysie. She lunged for him, but
it was too late. Craig had already grabbed Davy by the arm.

"Now there's a smart lad," he said to the obviously frightened little boy. He nudged a chair away from the kitchen table with the toe of his highly polished boot and plopped Davy into it.

"Please take me instead, Major," Lucy pleaded. She stood between Becky and Maysie. "Leave the boy here, I beg of you."

"The boy is coming with me. I can tell from your reactions he'll make the perfect hostage. There won't be a soldier or lawman from Kansas to the Rio Grande who will risk harming the boy by firing on me." He pointed at Maysie. "You, there . . . tie his hands and feet as I told you before. *Now.*"

Maysie picked up the coil of rope and gradually approached. Davy sat very still in the chair, his blond hair tousled, his face white. With a sullen glare at Craig, she began to tie Davy's wrists in front of him.

Craig stepped back to observe. Apparently satisfied, he said after a moment, "That's good. When you're finished with the boy, I want you to tie up the two exasperating aunts, then Mrs. Johnson and the girl. In chairs, back to back, with their hands tied behind them to the rungs. Oh, and don't forget Deputy Monroe. Just in case he comes to before I'm ready to leave."

Maysie scowled at him before she wrapped the rope around the ankles of Davy's high-topped boots. After tying the rope, she suddenly rose and headed toward the other side of the kitchen.

"Hold on! Where do you think you're going?" he demanded, raising the gun level with her chest.

Maysie simply sniffed in annoyance and reached inside a cupboard drawer. She held up a butcher knife. "I need somethin' to cut the rope with."

Craig studied the knife in her hand. "Don't think you

can fool me into letting you walk around with a lethal weapon in your hand. No, no, no. Find a smaller knife to cut the rope.''

She hesitated for a second, then replaced that knife and reached inside the cupboard for another. She withdrew a paring knife. Sending Craig a sullen look, Maysie returned to Davy's chair and severed the rope.

"Very good," Craig said in a patronizing tone, then waved his gun. "Now, start with those two old harpies in the corner."

Chapter

20

Jack reined in the horses and pulled the wagon to a halt the moment he saw two army officers riding toward him. Twilight was deepening, so he had to strain to see the emblems of their rank, even after they approached his side of the wagon. "Good evening, Captain, Lieutenant. I don't believe I know your names," he said when they drew close.

Both officers touched their hat brims and nodded toward Samantha. The captain spoke as he reined in his horse. "Evening, ma'am, Mr. Barnett. I thought I recognized you, sir. I'm Captain Connor, and this is Lieutenant Evans. You probably don't remember me, Mr. Barnett, but I met you when you first came out to the fort in June."

Jack smiled at the two men. "What brings you into town, Captain? Did the cowmen recruit you boys to herd steers? Mrs. Winchester and I were trying to find Mulberry Street, but we can't because it's covered with cows."

"That's about the truth, Mr. Barnett," Captain Connor said. "Those cowmen have been missing you mighty bad. The eastbound freight pulls in tomorrow afternoon, and it needs to get loaded with beef you're supposed to be buying."

"Well, I sent word to Littlefield that I'd be at the pens early in the morning . . . when I can see what I'm buying." The two officers laughed along with him.

"Those cowmen were fit to be tied when you didn't show up the other day. Where did you go off to anyway?" Lieutenant Evans asked.

"I had a little business in Salina to tend to, that's all." He gave them both an engaging grin.

This time neither officer returned his smile. They exchanged a brief glance instead. "You didn't happen to run into Major Craig in Salina, did you?" Captain Connor asked.

Jack's smile disappeared, too. "You mean the tall blond fellow?" he asked, deliberately keeping his voice casual. "No. Why? Were you looking for him?"

"Yes, sir, we are," the captain replied. "We were sent here this morning to meet Major Craig at the train depot. The colonel heard that he'd been in St. Louis and would probably come back into town today. But we missed him. He must have gotten over to the livery stable where he'd left his horse without us even seeing him." He gave an exasperated sigh. "Anyway, the stable boy said the major paid him to buy food and clothes, then he took off this afternoon. Boy doesn't know where he was headed. He just slipped outta town."

Lieutenant Evans spoke up. "We were just wondering if maybe you'd seen the major in Salina or on the road. Colonel Henderson wants him mighty bad."

Jack felt Samantha's hand tighten on his arm. "Sounds pretty important. What's the major done?"

"We don't know, sir. All we know is it must be something important, because Colonel Henderson got two telegraph wires yesterday, and he's been madder'n a hornet ever since.'' He shook his head. ''I sure hate to tell Colonel Henderson we couldn't find the major.''

Jack exchanged a meaningful glance with Samantha before he turned back to the disappointed young officers. ''Well, boys, I'll sure keep my eyes open on the way back home. Maybe your missing major is hiding between some cows out there.'' He gestured to the prairie, which was black with cattle.

''Appreciate it, Mr. Barnett,'' Captain Connor replied, then tapped his fingers to his hat brim. ''Evening, Mrs. Winchester.''

The lieutenant simply tapped his brim as they both urged their horses away. Jack flicked the reins over the harnessed horses and eased the wagon forward.

''What do you think happened?'' Samantha wondered out loud. ''Did Craig go to St. Louis for his funds?''

''I think he did. And thanks to General Logan, the banks were ready and waiting for him.'' He edged the wagon around a corner, heading into the back street where Lucy Johnson lived.

''I was wondering why the general disclosed all that information to Sheriff Kirk. The army was already planning to arrest Craig.''

''Yes, but he escaped,'' Jack said with a scowl. ''Damn! After all that work, Craig slips away. It's my fault. I should never have gone after Salem Todd. I should have stayed and confronted Craig. *Dammit!*'' He urged the horses to a faster pace, and the wagon creaked as it swayed down the dirt road.

He pulled the wagon to a halt in front of Lucy's front gate, secured the reins, and climbed down from the seat. Samantha quickly came to his lifted arms, and he set her on the ground.

She placed both hands on Jack's chest and looked up at him. "Jack, you cannot blame yourself for Craig's escape. You had no way of knowing he would journey to St. Louis and discover the banks had set a trap for the embezzler. You went to Salina after another killer, and thank God you did."

She gazed intently into his face. "If you had not been there to outwit Salem Todd, he would have escaped to burn and murder again and again. Think about that, Jack. Todd was a vicious killer. It would have been a tragedy if he escaped. Major Craig is merely a thief. An embezzler. Yes, he stole several thousand dollars, but at least he didn't kill anyone. If he escapes, it will be unfortunate, but not tragic."

Jack met her intent gaze, and a smile slowly curved his mouth. "Mrs. Winchester, I am always astounded by your logic. I fear I shall never win an argument once we are married." He watched her return his smile, then leaned down to place a light kiss upon her mouth. Samantha held very still until his lips left hers.

Offering his arm, he guided her through the gate and down the dark path to Lucy's front porch. "Why don't we make our announcement after supper?" he suggested.

Samantha grinned as she climbed the steps. "I think that's a wonderful idea."

Glancing toward the windows, Jack noticed for the first time that Lucy's house appeared darker than normal for early evening. Usually the lamps would have been lit by now. "Maybe we won't be making an announcement after all," he observed as he stepped back to allow Samantha to enter the front door. "It looks as though no one is home."

Samantha pushed on the wooden door, and it gave way, opening to the dimly lit kitchen. "How strange," she said as she paused on the threshold. "Lucy would have all the lamps burning by twilight. Everyone *must* be gone. But where?'' She pushed the door wide and stepped into the room. ''Hello?'' she called. ''Where is everyone?''

She peered at the far side of the room and blinked. There sat her two aunts, back to back for some reason, gazing at her but not saying a word. Next to them sat Becky and Lucy, back to back as well, and as silent as the others.

Samantha stared at them, and a prickle of fear ran down her spine. Something was wrong. Something was terribly wrong. She could feel it in the air.

She stepped into the room, Jack following behind her. ''Becky, Lucy, what's wrong? Why didn't you answer me?'' she demanded anxiously.

Suddenly the dim room grew brighter, and a harsh and all too familiar voice came from the corner. ''They cannot answer you, Mrs. Winchester, as you can now see.''

Samantha's eyes had already adjusted to the brightness. She gazed at Becky and Lucy and her aunts. They were tied to their chairs and gagged. She spun around to face Major Anthony Craig—and let out a frightened cry.

Craig leaned against the wall, pointing a gun at her son's head. Davy was bound and gagged and seated in a chair, his captor's hand on his small shoulder.

''Oh, dear God . . . Davy!'' Samantha cried out. She started to rush forward, but Jack grabbed her arm and held her in place.

''What the hell do you think you're doing, Craig?'' Jack demanded as he stepped in front of Samantha.

''What does it look like, Barnett?'' Major Craig answered with a sneer. ''I plan to take the brat hostage so I will be ensured a safe trip to Mexico. No lawman will dare shoot if he thinks he would harm the boy. Thanks to you and your rebel clerk, my plans have been abruptly altered.

So I think it's only fitting that you and she help me escape."

"You'll never make it to the border, Craig. I'll stop you first."

Anthony Craig let out a derisive laugh and placed the revolver above Davy's left ear. "Oh, no, you won't, Barnett. You won't dare touch me, and neither will anyone else. Not the law and not the army. I'll see to it. I'll use the boy as a shield if necessary. Whatever it takes to get me to Mexico safely. Once there, no one can reach me."

Samantha pushed away from Jack's restraint and stepped forward, her hands outstretched. "Leave my son here, Major," she pleaded. "Take me instead. *Please*, I beg of you."

Craig insolently ran his eyes over Samantha, and his mouth twitched, as if savoring the idea. He gave her a taunting smile. "As attractive as the thought is, dear lady, I'm afraid I will have to refuse. You see, I need a more manageable hostage. One that can be easily slung over my saddle. Now, kindly step back with Barnett. Having either of you too close makes me anxious . . . and you wouldn't want that, would you?" He glanced down at Davy and patted him on the shoulder, gun still at his temple. "Oh, and kindly remove Barnett's gun and holster and bring them to me. We don't want Barnett to make any sudden moves around your son, now, do we?"

Samantha gazed at Jack with a stricken look and bent to do as she was told. Then she carefully approached Craig, holding the gun and holster in front of her. He snatched them from her hands and waved her away. She drew close to Jack once more.

He reached out and pulled her beside him. "Give it up, Craig. You'll never get to Mexico. You've got to eat and sleep sometime. And I'll be right behind you," he threatened in a low voice, his eyes locked on Craig's.

Major Craig's eyes narrowed on Jack. "I think not, Barnett. You won't be riding anywhere after I leave."

The menace in Craig's tone froze Samantha in place. Her son had a gun to his head and was about to be snatched away by a madman. And it was clear that Craig wasn't going to leave Jack alive to chase after him. Merciful God! What could she do? Craig must be stopped. But how?

Samantha glanced about the kitchen and for the first time spied the bulky outline of a body lying in the corner. "My God, is . . . is that Clyde?" she cried, pointing.

Jack wheeled around and stared at the body. "Goddamn you, Craig. You killed him!" he swore, his face darkening.

"I didn't kill him. I just shot him in the leg and knocked him unconscious. The idiot advanced on me after I had already drawn." Craig leveled his gaze on Jack. "I won't be so gentle with you, Barnett."

Samantha saw the tension tighten Jack's features, the strain of holding himself back. Frightened he might lunge at Craig, she placed a restraining hand on his arm. His muscles were hard beneath his skin. "Jack . . ." she whispered, her gaze pleading restraint. They could do nothing that might jeopardize Davy's safety. Her insides twisted into a knot at the thought.

Craig glanced toward Maysie, who was hovering behind Samantha and Jack. "You, there . . . take the rest of that rope and tie up these two. Barnett first. It's dark enough now to travel."

Samantha spun around and saw Maysie slowly approach, a coil of rope in her hands. She stared into Maysie's black eyes helplessly.

Jack shook off Samantha's hand and stepped forward. His face hardened, his eyes boring into Craig's. "I'm not going to let her tie me up, Craig, and you can't force me to. You won't shoot the boy, because he's your best chance to escape. You've said that yourself. Now, let him go. Maybe the army will be lenient if you do.''

Anthony Craig pushed away from the wall, anger flooding his face. "Leniency? What do you recommend, Barnett? I hand myself over to you and beg for mercy? You must be mad!" he spat. "I will not grovel before my inferiors. Oh, no. I plan to avenge myself from across the border, where the army can't touch me. Now shut up and sit down so the darkie can tie you." He gestured for Maysie to approach.

Jack folded his arms and glared in reply.

Samantha watched a muscle twitch along Craig's jaw and went cold all over. Jack was baiting a madman. To her surprise, Craig lifted the gun from Davy's temple and wagged it toward Jack. She caught her breath, her heart pounding in her chest. Dear God! Would she lose both of them?

"You've made a good point, Barnett," the major said, a malicious light shining from his eyes now. "I can't very well shoot my preferred hostage, can I? I suppose I will have to choose another victim. Or perhaps two."

At that, he aimed the gun toward Becky and Lucy, tied back to back. Becky's light blue eyes went wide with terror. Samantha sucked in her breath in a gasp, which brought a smile to Craig's lips.

He looked Jack in the eye. "I'm an excellent marksman, Barnett. I assure you I can kill both of them with one bullet. Being seated behind each other like that makes it ever so easy. Just one shot through both their throats. Even if I'm a trifle off center, it will be enough. It will still be a mortal wound."

His voice sounded calm, almost matter-of-fact, to Samantha. As if he were discussing military tactics. She stared at him. He was truly mad. How could they possibly fight a madman? She glanced at Becky and saw her sister's terror. The cold hand in her gut twisted tighter.

Samantha tried to swallow, but her mouth was so dry she couldn't. She reached out to Jack. "Jack, please. Do as he says."

She watched Jack struggle inside. Once he was tied to the chair, he would be helpless. For him, that would be unbearable. He looked into her eyes, and she saw the agonized decision.

Still glaring defiantly at Craig, Jack walked to the chair and sat down. Maysie approached him hesitantly.

"I hate to do this, Mistuh Barnett," she said with a mournful expression.

Jack didn't reply. He still had his gaze locked on a triumphant Major Craig. He put his wrists behind the chair. Maysie dropped to her knees and began to wrap the rope around his arms.

"Secure him well," Craig advised, the revolver pointed at Davy once more.

Maysie gave the knot a final yank, then glared up at Craig. She began to climb from her kneeling position, fumbling in her pocket with one hand and bracing herself on the chair with the other. As she rose, her hand settled briefly on Jack's open palm. Just a second, but long enough to press a small paring knife flat in his hand.

Jack blinked, breaking his staring contest with Craig. Meanwhile, his hand closed around the small knife.

Maysie stepped in front of Jack and approached Samantha, holding out the rope. "Miz Sam," she said in an apologetic voice, "you'd bettah sit down."

Samantha's gaze darted frantically from Maysie to her captive son. Holy Mother of God, how could she sit helplessly by while a madman ran off with her son?

"Please, Major . . . let me kiss my son good-bye. I beg of you," she beseeched, hands outstretched, her eyes imploring.

Anthony Craig hesitated for a moment, then acquiesced. "Very well. I shan't begrudge a mother's farewell. But beware . . . any attempt to grab the boy will cost another family member dearly." He edged away from Davy and turned his revolver toward Becky.

Samantha rushed forward and sank to her knees beside Davy's chair. Her fingers fumbled with the knotted kerchief wound about his face until it finally gave way.

"D-d-don't worry, Mama," Davy whispered, his little face drained of color. "He promised he wouldn't hurt me."

Samantha's heart cracked inside her chest. She threw her arms around her son and hugged him close. "Oh, Davy . . . I love you . . . I love you . . ." she crooned softly. She nestled her face into his soft hair, so scared she couldn't even cry.

She couldn't let Davy go. Craig would kill him. Or leave him to die in some godforsaken stretch of wilderness. Death had taken too many of her loved ones. No more. She would not give up her son. Not without a fight. Even if she had to fight the devil himself.

"That's long enough, Mrs. Winchester. The sooner we leave, the sooner I reach Mexico," Craig's voice prodded. "Come along, let him go."

Samantha slowly loosened her embrace and drew back. She brushed Davy's hair out of his face and kissed his wet cheek. "Be brave, Davy. I won't be far away, I promise. Watch for me." She gazed deeply into his eyes and repeated, "Watch me, Davy, all right?"

He peered out at her, perplexed, then gave a little nod. "All right, Mama," he whispered.

Samantha placed another kiss upon his cheek, then gradually rose to her feet. She deliberately wobbled for a second and grasped the back of Davy's chair for support.

"Have no fear, Mrs. Winchester. Your son will be released on this side of the border, safe and sound," Major Craig said, his voice unable to conceal its patronizing tone.

Samantha gazed into Anthony Craig's hard blue eyes and saw the truth hiding behind all the practiced lies. He would kill Davy as soon as he no longer needed him for protection.

Damned if she would allow it. She was looking at the devil himself, and he would not take her son. She had to stop him. But she had no weapon. Nothing but her bare hands . . . and her courage.

Samantha didn't stop to think. Didn't stop to see if Craig's gun was pointing at her or at Davy or at her sister. She shoved Davy's chair to the side and flew at Craig, her nails aiming for his eyes.

Craig jumped back, obviously startled by the suddenness of her attack. Samantha was on him in an instant, sinking her claws into his flesh like an enraged feline. He yelped in pain and shoved her away.

"Damn you, hellcat!" He brought his gun up to club her across the face just as someone else suddenly pushed Samantha to the floor.

Jack charged into Craig and knocked him sprawling. The severed edges of rope still dangling from his wrists, Jack wrestled Craig for the gun. Both men rolled on the floor, arms and legs flailing.

Samantha scrambled across the floor and out of the way. She headed to the corner where Maysie had already pulled Davy to safety. Samantha knelt beside her son, frantically trying to loosen his bonds as she watched the deadly struggle taking place in the middle of Lucy Johnson's kitchen.

Craig's fist jabbed, and his gun arm flailed wildly. Jack

grabbed for that waving arm and finally succeeded in capturing Craig's wrist. He slammed Craig's hand to the floor. Again and again. Finally the revolver spun across the wooden floor and landed against a table leg.

Maysie scurried over and retrieved it. She carried the gun to Samantha, while the two men continued to wrestle, violently thrashing across the floor.

Samantha jumped to her feet, gun in hand, ready to fire. But the two men were wrapped together as they grappled, fists and elbows each landing blows.

Craig backhanded Jack, and Jack pulled away as if shaken. Craig drew back his hand, ready to strike again, when Jack's fist crashed into his jaw. Anthony Craig crumpled to the floor.

Jack grabbed him by his shirt and slammed him hard to the floor. Craig cried out and writhed beneath Jack. Jack released him and rose to his feet, straddling his conquered foe.

Craig pulled himself up on one elbow and curled over like a child. "Damn you . . . you . . . broke . . . my . . . jaw," he swore, his words so garbled they were barely intelligible.

Jack stared down in contempt. "You're lucky I'm not holding the gun right now, Craig." He leaned down and hauled Major Craig off the floor and threw him into his own vacated chair.

Craig whimpered like a wounded puppy. He cradled his broken jaw, obviously in pain.

"Maysie, tie the major securely, would you?" Jack caught her eye and shared a conspiratorial smile. "And make sure you don't slip him the paring knife, like you did me."

Jack deliberately waited for the major to glance up so he could taunt him with a triumphant smile.

Samantha rushed to Jack's side and threw her arms around his waist. "Here," she said and offered him the revolver. "I don't want to see this gun pointing at anyone anymore."

Jack took it from her hand and bestowed a kiss on her damp forehead. Just then Samantha felt a bundle of energy charge between the two of them. She looked down to see Davy wrapping his arms around her legs. Samantha bent down and hugged her son close, pressing him to her bosom.

She didn't say a word. There were no words to express the relief she felt. Davy was safe. Jack was safe. Her family was safe. Craig couldn't hurt them anymore.

Jack reached down and tousled Davy's hair, then gave Samantha's shoulder a light squeeze. "I'll go find Connor and Evans so they can take this thief to jail."

Davy squirmed out of his mother's embrace and gazed pleadingly up at Jack. "Can I go with you, Mr. Barnett? Please!"

Jack didn't hesitate. "Sure you can, Davy. You can help me find them," he said with a grin. Glancing back at Samantha, he offered her the revolver once more. "This time you can point the gun at someone who deserves it. Keep an eye on him while Davy and I round up those officers. They can take Craig back to Fort Riley. I don't trust myself to deliver him in one piece."

He glared over his shoulder at the anguished major, who looked too forlorn to be a threat to anyone. Glancing toward Clyde, who was still lying unconscious in the corner, Jack said, "As soon as your aunts are freed, have one of them untie Clyde and see to his wounds. I'll bring the doctor as soon as I can." He retrieved his gun and holster and strode out the door, Davy racing alongside him.

Samantha stood across from Craig and pointed the gun at him, as if he were not tied up. Meanwhile, she observed

Maysie loosening Aunt Mimi's bonds. Already freed, Miss Lily was busily rearranging herself. "Are you two all right?" she asked with concern.

"Oh, yes, dear," chirped Aunt Mimi. "Now that the dastardly wretch has been subdued."

Samantha blinked. There wasn't the slightest bit of a quaver in her aunt's voice. She glanced at Miss Lily and held her tongue. Lily Herndon was glaring at Major Craig with a lethal scowl.

"Miss Lily, would you please untie Deputy Monroe and see to his wounds until the doctor arrives?" she asked, hoping to deflect her aunt's ill humor.

"In a moment, my dear," Miss Lily responded, her voice even lower than usual. "First I have to tend to someone else." She promptly marched to the kitchen cupboard and withdrew a large black iron frying pan.

"What . . . ?" Samantha started to ask but was unable to finish. She stared in astonishment as Miss Lily walked up to the wounded Major Craig and slammed the huge frying pan down on his head. The sound of the ringing metal completely obscured the major's shriek of pain as he lapsed into unconsciousness.

Chapter
21

Captain Connor tipped his hat to Samantha. "I'm awful sorry about the scare Major Craig put your family through, Mrs. Winchester. You won't have to worry about him bothering you again. Not after what Mister Barnett told me. He'll be in prison for a long, long while."

Samantha glanced at the front door, where Lieutenant Evans was seen leading a pitiful-looking Anthony Craig outside. "That will make me rest easier, Captain, I must admit." She encircled Jack's arm with hers. He responded by pulling her closer beside him.

"Much obliged to you boys for taking him off my hands," Jack said as Captain Connor turned to leave.

"Well, we wouldn't want you to lose sleep. You've got a lot of beef waiting for you tomorrow morning." Connor grinned, then disappeared out the door.

Samantha turned to Jack and looked up into his face. He was smiling back at her. She threw her arms around him and hugged him close, right in the middle of Lucy Johnson's kitchen, surrounded by her entire family. Let her maiden aunts be scandalized. Let everyone be shocked by her brazen display. She no longer cared. She loved this man, and she wanted everyone to know it.

Jack tightened his embrace. The surrounding hum of approving family voices grew louder as their embrace lengthened. Finally Miss Lily's contralto resonated throughout the room.

"Don't just stand there like a ninny, Jack Barnett! *Kiss* the woman!"

Samantha lifted her face from the warmth of Jack's chest and laughed, glancing around the beaming circle of family members. She gazed up at Jack, who was grinning broadly.

"Do you think we can have a separate train to carry my family to San Francisco? Otherwise, we may die of their smothering attention before we arrive," she said with a grimace.

Jack drew Samantha closer. "And I wouldn't miss one moment of it."

Then, without another word, Jack took Miss Lily's advice.

Dear Reader:

I hope you enjoyed reading *Abilene Gamble* as much as I enjoyed writing it. Samantha and Jack had a very special love story to tell. A story of hope and healing.

I like hearing from readers, and you may write to me at P.O. Box 1386, Fort Collins, Colorado 80522. A self-addressed stamped envelope would be appreciated.

Sincerely,
Margaret Conlan

Recipes from the heartland of America

THE HOMESPUN ❧ COOKBOOK ❧

Tamara Dubin Brown

Arranged by courses, this collection of wholesome family recipes includes tasty appetizers, sauces, and relishes, hearty main courses, and scrumptious desserts—all created from the popular *Homespun* series.

Features delicious easy-to-prepare dishes, such as:

Curried Crab and Shrimp en Casserole

1 large can crabmeat	1 pint milk
1 can shrimp	2 tablespoons butter
2 tablespoons flour	1 teaspoon curry powder
½ teaspoon salt	1 tablespoon chopped onion
1 tablespoon chopped green pepper	

Cream the butter and flour. Add milk. Cook over slow fire, stirring constantly until slightly thickened. Add salt and curry powder. Stir until smooth and remove from fire. Put onion and pepper into cream sauce and mix well. Shred crabmeat and clean the shrimp. Spread a layer of crabmeat in casserole and cover with a layer of cream sauce. Repeat with shrimp and cream sauce. Repeat this until all is in the casserole. Bake at 300 degrees for 30 minutes before serving.

A Berkley paperback coming February 1996